1

New York City April 11th, 1982

The glimmering urban lights appeared as tiny stars descending from the heavens. They shined bright and glowed while lighting in and around the high-rise buildings and on the sidewalks and roadways spread out in neat rows of avenues and streets in the Upper East Side of New York City. That illumination within the otherwise dismal darkness became a tribute to those who worked late into the night in the towering office edifices. Other lofty skyscrapers housed plush apartments for prominent individuals and families who enjoyed luxurious lifestyles and dramatic city views.

Just after 10 PM on Monday, April 11th, 1982, Doctor Robert Bryant stepped out of his private elevator and into his penthouse apartment, nestled in the womb of that maze of flickering city lights. He removed the light cashmere sports jacket he had chosen for that invigorating spring day in the great bustling metropolis, now mellow and humbled after sunset. Robert gently folded the plush fabric and laid it over the arm of one of the sitting chairs near the elevator doorway. The handsome man appeared well-dressed, even in casual clothes. His tapered shirt and slacks revealed a muscular build maintained since his high school football days. At six foot three inches tall and 190 pounds of muscle, Doctor Robert Bryant, or Bob as his friends called him, appeared much younger than the 45 years he had turned two months earlier. He never wore a hat, and standing in the entryway, he used both hands to brush back his full head of black, wavy hair, intensifying the stunning dark blue eyes of his chiseled face. A few gray hairs appeared above his ears on each side of his thick crop of hair, styled shorter on the sides and slightly longer in the back.

Robert took a whiff of a pleasant scent permeating the air around him within his home as he proceeded into the large area of his foyer and smiled ever so slightly. 'She remembered,' he thought. Robert didn't smile often and usually forced such contrived gestures of happiness to be sociable. But he wasn't always like that. Once, he was the life of the party, friendly and outgoing, and loved by all. However, a tragedy twenty years earlier permanently changed him and his personality. Now, he was naturally distinguished, charming, and kind but lacked the lust for life he once possessed. Anyone who knew him years ago could easily see the change.

However, after smelling the sweet fragrance, he realized that Martha, his head housekeeper, remembered his suggestion and changed the scent she usually maintained throughout his penthouse. A wealthy man, Robert still appreciated the simple things in life and those who blessed him with them. He would remember to thank Martha. Her thoughtful gesture touched him deeply, a testament to their special friendship. He admired her immensely and made the hint of another smile as he thought of her.

Martha Weber, a woman just past middle age and of average female height, was originally from Germany. Her family escaped the Hitler regime while she was still a child. Robert acquired her native tongue to remind her of home occasionally. He also used that language whenever he discussed personal matters with her. Martha had closely bonded with Robert since he was a baby, and a friend who reunited them recommended her for the head housekeeper position. She never married and devoted herself to her work with unwavering dedication. She was a true professional, in Robert's opinion.

Robert was a loving and generous man who owned living accommodations on a separate lower floor of the building for Martha and any staff member who chose to live there or stay occasionally. Martha supervised a complete team that kept the two-story penthouse in pristine condition. Though rarely used by its owner for personal socializing, the spacious home mainly

My Dream Lover
The Uncut Version

by David Navarria

This release is the complete and uncut version of the beloved story My Dream Lover, published for the first time. For fans of the original release, this edition doubles the story elements omitted from the 2022 publication. It features additional parables and characters, changing the storyline of some, while extending the original characters' depth. This version better defines the personalities readers have come to know and love while enhancing the framework of the original narrative. Although it follows the same basic storyline, some readers of the earlier book feel that this uncut edition reads like an entirely different novel. It is the recommended version to read in anticipation of the scheduled upcoming sequel, which also promises a unique storytelling experience.

My Dream Lover: The Uncut Version begins with a short introduction of a character who reflects on past life's misfortunes and a scheme already prepared to correct them. It then fades back to 1953 to tell the beginning of the story. A heartwarming coming-of-age tale, rich with nostalgia and warmth, gradually unfolds about two young girls living in the shadows of their older brothers, renowned sports figures at the local small-town high school.

The brother of one of the young girls, in particular, seems far too perfect, and readers will wonder how someone could accomplish such feats. Many other sub-mysteries and strange occurrences hide within that same character's family, and readers will eventually discover them as all questions and suspicions are revealed later in the story.

A shocking tragedy ignites an almost impossible journey of mystery, deceit, suspense, and revenge in a bold and adventurous quest to reunite with a lost love.

Is love meant to be, or are all our destinies sealed by fate? Only time will tell as readers uncover the answer in My Dream Lover: The Uncut Version. This mature mixed-genre novel, which includes a touch of well-developed science fiction based on actual physics theories, explores the human condition and presents a uniquely crafted storyline for fans of intricate literature. Far from the original publication of 2022, this is the complete and full-length story originally intended.

My Dream Lover
The Uncut Version
David Navarria

For Grazia

DISCLAIMER ————————————————————————————————

catered to business dinners and affairs.

Robert strolled into his Upper East Side penthouse's plush living room. It had enormous windows that offered a spectacular view of Central Park and the West Side of New York City in the distance. He always maintained his athletic build and shape by using weights and running, usually doing four laps around the reservoir in Central Park upon waking up before breakfast. That amounted to about seven miles. Moving further into the large room, Robert spotted a bottle of wine and a glass sitting atop a wet bar on the opposite wall. It was an opened bottle of 1961 Chateau Lafite Rothschild. He had asked Walther, his assistant, to leave it for him before he left for the day. Walter LeRoy was also Robert's business manager and addressed all financial and administrative duties of the house and Robert's personal affairs. Some of Walter's duties included scheduling appointments, travel particulars, and keeping track of important dates. On occasion, he even arranged the clothing for his busy boss. Walter lived in his private quarters in the building. In addition, Robert had a personal chef, Alfredo, who studied culinary in the Tuscan region of Italy. Robert had carefully screened his staff, including his doormen and custodians. They were insured and bonded, and they proved their loyalty in small and large ways on many occasions, which their employer greatly appreciated.

Robert's curse in life was that he was born a super genius. He was so intelligent that he completed his doctoral dissertation by age twenty-two and became a Ph.D. in physics. During his first year of college, when most students were struggling to get passing grades, Robert went straight to his master's degree endeavors. That required him to teach some classes in addition to his studies. He completed his thesis and received his MS degree in his second year. With an IQ that was the highest ever recorded, Robert had unique gifts: He quickly picked up languages and had an incredible memory, even of the personal specifics of friends and acquaintances. Robert also possessed advanced intuition and physical abilities far beyond average men, so much so that he bordered the realm of a super being, always keeping those unique attributes secret and never flaunting them.

The only place off-limits to the entire staff was the securely locked laboratory that Robert had professionally installed on the upper level. It was only open to outsiders for cleaning or deliveries when he was present. Afterward, he immediately locked and secured it with an alarm system. Gunther Schmidt, Robert's friend and assistant, was the only other person who knew how to gain access to the lab. The entrance had two doors, an outer one and an inner one close to the first. Both always remained locked. There was a key for the first door and an electronic finger button combination locking device on the second door that required a five-digit code.

Having had a long and tiring day, the exhausted man looked forward to enjoying the fine Bordeaux while resting, watching the glittering lights outside, and listening to music before retiring for the evening. "I think you're ready," he whispered to the bottle of wine, assuming that the wine had aired out sufficiently. Then, the good doctor poured himself a glass. Before taking a sip, Robert stepped behind the bar and flipped a switch to play open-reel recorded music. He opened the door of the small refrigerator behind the bar, removed a little ceramic dish of imported cheeses that Walter had also left for him, and then placed the cheeses and the glass of wine on a cocktail table near the bar, positioning himself on a plush leather recliner next to it. Putting his feet onto the pedestal of the recliner, he pushed back on the chair and admired the late evening view of the city as he reached for his glass of wine.

Having a cultured appreciation of all music, Robert had chosen a selection of casual recordings from the late 1950s and early 1960s. When the Everly Brothers' song, 'All I Have to Do Is Dream,' began, he smiled. This time, it was a genuine smile because that song rewarded him with a pleasurable memory. It reminded him of his youth in the Ohio River Valley of Columbiana County. Robert cherished those thoughts and the smile for just a moment as he sipped his wine. Then his smile faded, and a tear began to form in his left eye. He began to recall his past day to change the somber mood that the memories from the song caused.

Earlier that Monday, April 11th, 1982, the 45-year-old physicist began his day with his usual exercise and running regimen. Then he proceeded to two meetings, and after them, he had a speaking engagement scheduled at 3:30 PM. A dinner reception in his honor followed that. Robert had lectured in Room 308 of historic Havemeyer Hall, which was part of Columbia University's Morningside Heights campus. Students and colleagues loved the mysterious professor and applauded him with cheers and screams when he came to the podium of the crowded hall. There was standing room only, so people filled the back and the aisles. Cries from the hall's multiple levels and balconies gave the impression that a rock star was stepping on stage.

Doctor Bryant was a celebrity in his own right. As a relatively young, good-looking, well-accomplished professor, writer, and lecturer, many students, teachers, and peers held him in rock star status. Winner of the Nobel Prize for Physics in 1968, Robert made many television appearances, and the world's top journalists interviewed him. He was friends with politicians, talk show hosts, and movie stars. It seemed everyone wanted a piece of the man who spoke before them that day. What was even more fascinating about him, other than him being an extreme genius, was his topics. He was known as the man who would someday break the time barrier. His theories and experiments revolutionized how humankind perceived time and traveled through it. However, that lecture was to be his last. Robert had already announced he would travel, and that day would be his final engagement.

So, the eminent professor sat there at the end of his day, enjoying his fine wine and cheese, and reflected. He remembered one character in particular from the lecture. A blond-haired young woman sitting in the third row at the left side of the hall caught his attention. Her wide eyes, smile, and expressions were the reason he noticed her. Those distinctive and beautiful deep blue eyes reminded Robert of someone he once knew, a young woman who was the love of his life years before. The memory of her wounded his heart, and when he opened the lecture to questions, Robert selected her first.

She had boldly asked him with a smile so familiar from his past, "Doctor, did you ever travel through time?" It was a logical question as many suspected Doctor Bryant was on the verge of doing so, and others thought he might already have. Yet Robert was still recovering from speaking to the young woman who appeared as if she had stepped out of a different time, and he remained gazing into her marvelous eyes. Still smiling and looking directly into Robert's engaging eyes, she added to her question, "And if so, were there consequences?"

Robert finally snapped out of the trance the young lady inflicted upon him and answered with his unique wit and charm, "I have traveled through time, but when I did, I tapped my shoes and said, 'There's no place like home,' and came right back." The young blonde woman and everyone else in the entire auditorium broke out in laughter. Robert's delivery of the joke made it work, and that same style made him an icon not only as a scientist but as a person. Then Robert's expression became serious, and he looked directly into the deep blue eyes of the young student and explained, "There are consequences to time travel, and caution is essential when or if ever someone attempts to travel through time." He added, "However, time has a way of healing itself," he gave the young student a big smile.

After remembering the day and the blonde, blue-eyed young lady, an exhausted Robert decided to call it a night and go to bed. It was already midnight. He arose from his recliner and glanced outside one of the large windows. A thick, gloomy cloud had rolled over the island of Manhattan from the West Side and hovered over Central Park. It seemed eerie and evil, possibly an omen of what was arriving. But Robert couldn't know what was in store for him in that coming time past midnight. Within hours, his life would change as mysteriously as that dreary specter floated before him. His eyes stayed fixed, mesmerized by it for several seconds before he journeyed to his bedroom at the end of the same floor. Robert undressed, leaving his clothes on the floor where they fell, and slid into the satin sheets of his king-sized bed. As he lay there, Robert reflected on his life. All the popularity in the world could not help one simple and personal issue that haunted him: he felt alone in the world. His life should have been different. The so-called demi-god harbored a secret nobody in his current circle of friends, associates, and acquaintances knew. Only the folks in what he now called his hometown knew what happened to Robert Bryant, but he had not been back there in years. As he drifted off, he thought of his earlier life and remembered. Robert would be traveling later that new day, Tuesday, April 12th, 1982, 'I'm finally going back,' his thoughts concluded.

2

New York-Rue, Ohio 1941- 1953

William Bryant stepped out the backdoor entrance of his Tudor-styled mansion in a residential section of New York City and into the cool air of the early spring afternoon of 1953. Even in such a remote and exclusive neighborhood, distant sounds of honking cars and the clatter of heavy trucks were apparent; such was the city's norm. William pulled out a package of Camels from the inside breast pocket of his light wool sports jacket, tapped the butt end of the pack, and removed a smoke with his mouth. He pushed back the protruding cigarettes with his palm and returned the Camels from where he grabbed them. William then reached into his trouser pocket for his favorite zippo. That cheap metal lighter had been with him for ten years and accompanied him through many harrowing times. He quickly glanced at the Army division insignia on the side before sliding the lighter against the fabric of his jacket to flip open the lid. Then, he raised it to light the cigarette waiting between his lips. William had picked up the nasty habit during World War Two. Now, he only smoked outside to limit his intake.

A hardened and disciplined man, tall with the build of an athlete, William had played high school football in the days of hardened leather helmets. Born in 1907, he followed his father's footsteps and entered law practice. William graduated with honors from Harvard Law School in 1931. Eventually, he became a fourth-generation partner in his family's lucrative legal practice.

Though shielded in mystery, a safeguarded secret about their children had existed between William and his wife, Naomi. Using his intrinsic skills and personal finances, he had already discreetly redeemed his son and daughter from the looming flames of wickedness before they sprouted worldwide. That heroic, elaborate action exemplified William's unwavering duty and responsibility toward loved ones. Those distinctive qualities extended to his country when, to his parents' dismay and his wife's, William left the family law firm in 1941, just after the Pearl Harbor attack, to join the US Army. He felt compelled to serve the adopted country of his ancestors to protect his family from the global dangers that would happen if he didn't. Already 34 years old at the time and being a lawyer, the United States Army made him an officer and stationed him in Washington, DC, after his basic training. William left behind his wife and two children, Robert, who was four years old, and Emily, who was just a baby. Being wealthy, he knew his wife and family would be financially secure if he died in battle. A determined man, William Bryant finally received overseas duty in 1943 after many requests.

Standing outside in the open air was where William always went to try to cleanse himself of the despicable things he saw and did in those bloodied battlefields of that war. He recalled those demons of his past clearly as his eyes gazed into the distance, his mind recollecting all his past deeds. As if praying, William recalled his promotion to Captain, preparing troops for the Normandy Invasion and seeing action at Utah Beach on D-Day, 1944. In his solitude of the outdoors, he bore witness to those things that changed him in many ways. It had to be in that open space and away from his family, where Captain William Bryant sought refuge from those dastardly deeds of war. He had to relive those events of the invasion in the clean air so that not a trace of the memory or thoughts of them, nor the ungodly fog of evilness he brushed shoulders with during that time, would even remotely stain or come near to those he loved.

"Keep moving!" he could still hear his commands shouted at the beach on that day as mortars, machinegun blasts, and shells erupted and blew apart many of his men right before his eyes amidst the ear-shattering noise. "Don't stop! Keep running!

Take cover over there!" William's lips moved in near silence as he softly muttered those orders as he had shouted them on that dreadful day; tears streamed down his cheeks in his solitude of memories that not even the freshest air could purify. Bloody stumps pumping thick red and other hideous colors he had never seen purged from the bodies strewn on the sandy shore were as fresh in his mind as they were on that day. William's hand reached past his left breast as he recalled the heavy blow that impacted his shoulder and knocked him off his feet and onto the blood-stained sand. The tormented man remembered lying face-up as he gazed at the colorless sky for what seemed like a lifetime until those grey heavens slowly began to move as the medics carried him away.

"You're going to be okay, Captain," a stretcher bearer whispered as he watched William respond to the ammonia-like scent of the smelling salts as he and his partner placed Captain Bryant on a cot. "The salts bring them around if it's their will to come round," the soldier said. "Some give up, but this one has the will. You learn to see it." William lay still from shock at the time, listening in a daze, but he would never forget the words of that medic for the rest of his life.

From that temporary aid post, the Army sent William to an old mansion turned hospital in England for medical treatment for his shoulder. After his recovery, Captain Bryant skipped the rank of major and was promoted to Lieutenant colonel and battalion commander in the Third Army Corp of General George S. Patton. He again distinguished himself at the Battle of the Bulge. Wounded again, this time in the leg, William Bryant returned home to America as a decorated war hero. Like many of those who served in that war, his wounds ran deep, and nobody could see the hidden deepest scars as he readied to resume his duties as husband, father, and partner at a major law firm.

William returned to his family law practice after returning from his war duties and recovering from his injuries. The Bryant Law Firm LLC was a prestigious multi-million-dollar law firm in New York City. In addition to being a full partner of the firm and other investments and properties held within, William had privately invested early in different properties. He had amassed a fortune, making him one of New York City's youngest multi-millionaires. The war had changed him, and as a wiser man, he never flaunted his wealth and became a humble man grateful for God's blessings and the family he had. William became a philanthropist, donating enormous amounts of money to various charities. Being an infantryman during the war, or 'foot soldier' as the Army called them, strengthened his humanitarian characteristics. And he bred that attribute of generosity into his children. William renewed his Christian beliefs after seeing so many offenses against God and desecrations of humanity. Before his Lord, he pledged to bring up his children to obey the laws of God and his commandments. He vowed to make a world for them with barriers to shield them from the inherent corruption of mankind. No matter the cost or pain to him, they would live in a better place and not know the sins of their past or his.

Naomi opened the back door of their large estate and quietly called, "Bill, the kids will be here soon," she smiled, knowing what was in store that day and how much it bothered her husband.

"I'll be right in, hon," William smiled back at his wife. Everyone thought William was fearless because he often displayed those traits in law, business, and European battlefields. William knew better, but he loved his wife, son, and daughter, and those inhumane war experiences and more than three years of separation from them had intensified those emotions. However, on that chilly day in early spring, William had to explain some news to his two children, Robert and Emily, which aroused quite a bit of internal trepidation. He regretted the announcement he was going to make. Naomi knew about the plans for over a year since they first discussed and finalized them. But they both decided it would be better to wait until they had a completed plan before informing their children. William lifted the sleeve of his jacket and glanced at his wristwatch, "They'll be home from school in less than five minutes," he mumbled as he dropped his cigarette on the small patch of grass where he stood and then headed toward the door. He left his memories of war in that space of the open outdoors and entered his home.

Emily, 11 years old, arrived home first. The school bus had dropped her off directly in front of the family home's walkway, just a short walk to the front door. She was much shorter than average for her age and had a slender build. Emily Bryant maintained an upbeat personality and worked hard to act like a young lady instead of a child–a term she detested. Very bright, she was naturally inquisitive and had worn her mother out with questions ever since learning about the upcoming family meeting.

"Am I late?" she immediately asked as soon as her mother opened the front door for her. "Did I miss anything?" An appealing but somewhat demanding look appeared instantly on her face as she brushed back her dark blonde medium-length hair with her hands.

"No, dear. You're right on time," Naomi replied with a smile, thinking her little girl was growing up sooner than she wanted. "Daddy isn't here. And Robert's not home yet."

"Where is Daddy?" she inquired, putting her schoolbag and lunchbox on a chair by the front door and waiting.

"He's out in the backyard, dear," then quickly added, "But don't go out there," as soon as she saw her daughter immediately turn and walk in that direction. "Put your things away, and I'm sure he'll be in soon. Be patient."

Naomi knew her husband well and why he went outside to get fresh air–often awakened at night from William's dreadful nightmares since first returning from war. She also understood how much he dreaded this moment. They had spoken about it often recently. Now, the time had come. William appeared from the back door when Naomi's last words parted her lips. He walked toward where his wife and daughter stood in the foyer. Their son, Robert, entered from the front door a few seconds later. No one had heard his car pull up into the front driveway.

There, in the foyer, the Bryant family stood together. William bent over to kiss his daughter. He surmised it might be the last for a while. Knowing Emily, William realized she would be upset with the news. He also learned from experience that in such a mood, she would restrain herself from showing affection toward him as her punishment to him. "Hi, sweetheart," he said in a low voice as he kissed her cheek.

"Hi, Daddy!" she answered, "So what do you have to tell us? We're all here. I'm dying to know. Is it bad?"

"Patience, my love." William turned to his son and said, "Hi, Son. Did you break any hearts today at school?" He knew the girls had begun to notice his only son and joked with him often about it.

"That's terribly prejudiced, Father, and an exploitation of women," Emily answered for Robert. "Especially with a young girl–woman present," changing her wording mid-sentence.

William didn't respond immediately. He remained standing and thinking about how his beautiful little girl was becoming and learning new words and terms all the time now. Robert just smiled at the joke and his little sister's comment. He was also eagerly waiting but had formulated an opinion about the coming announcement. "I stand in error, young lady," William finally corrected himself. "And I apologize to the court."

Emily blushed but smiled at her victory. "Are you going to tell us now?" her deep blue eyes engaging those of her father.

"Yes, I am," William answered, "But why don't we all sit together in the living room? Come on, let's go." He took his wife by the hand and led the way.

William had prepared how to address the situation but decided to take a natural approach. He waited until everyone was seated. Naomi sat poised on a loveseat next to her husband. Robert casually sat in the corner of a couch, his left arm spread out, holding the back. Emily sat close to her brother and under his extended arm. Her hands were in her lap, and her legs crossed. The right one nervously kicked as if a doctor was checking her reflex. Emily always stayed close to her older brother. She developed a deep security with him during her early years while her father was away fighting in Europe. Robert remained Emily's protector ever since she first came home from the hospital as an infant after her delivery. As a self-ordained big brother, he had looked out for his kid sister ever since, as if sensing Emily's need for help with the anxieties that had inflicted her for as long back as he could remember. There was a strong bond between them. Robert always felt an inherent need to safeguard Emily, but on a subconscious level. It became part of his typical responsibilities, and he had always devoted time to his sister and routinely spoke with her on her level. Robert was born a genius with a tremendous intellect. However, he was never condescending to Emily. His discussions with her were always as a peer, and his patience demonstrated his love for her. He maintained the same subtle manner when he tutored her with schoolwork or even advised her about personal matters. Robert indulged his sister's juvenile curiosities and always endured her childlike behavior. As a patient and caring young man toward everyone, Robert's devotion to his sister was, however, more profound than with anyone else. Emily looked up to her big brother and thought he was 'cool.'

William lovingly observed his family before announcing what would lead to a transformation in their lives. William's delivery was eloquent and swift; he was a man who always got right to the point. His short speech was specific but compassionately expressed. The family was relocating to another state, and he conveyed that his children would come first and that he and their mother would do all they could to make the transition as easy as possible, especially for them. When he finished with the move's details, his children sat together with eyes gazing like deer at night, looking into a car's headlights. Naomi had bowed her head, facing her lap. She couldn't bear to see her children's faces but found reassurance in William's directness and tact.

After a minute of silence, Emily was the first to speak, "Oh, my God! My life is ruined!" she cried out. "My friends!" She was sobbing. Emily jumped off the couch and ran toward the stairs to get to her bedroom. That was her holy place, as it was to most little girls.

William arose and called his daughter's name. Emily ignored him and continued running up the stairs.

"Leave her for now, Bill," Naomi said. She expected nothing less from her daughter and knew it would be best to let her brew for a bit and approach her later. William complied with his wife's wishes and turned his attention toward his son.

"Dad. Really?" Robert said with a bewildered expression. Based on things he overheard, Robert thought their father would be leaving for an extended period, not that the family was moving. That fact was entirely unexpected for him. "What about my football?" those words were almost a plead as he looked at his father with a stunned expression. Then he thought about all of his friends. Robert was very popular in his circles because of his academic and sports achievements, which took a lot of effort. As a talented quarterback, he had just made varsity in his high school football team in his sophomore year, a feat that made him proud. He was also involved in a budding romance with Linda, one of the prettiest girls in his class.

"Robert, I promise you I will do everything to make this adjustment as easy as possible for you and Emily." William paused, now unassuming and concerned, "Your uncle already spoke to the high school principal and football team coach there." He hesitated again and swallowed. William now clearly appeared upset that he hurt his family's feelings but went on, "And I talked with your coach. He will call the coach at Rue High School and give him your records and his recommendation." He repeated the part of his speech that covered that this was necessary and that the location would be an excellent place for him and his sister to complete their school years before leaving for college. But now his words were softer, and his aura was of a meeker, more passive man. William stopped and waited for a response from his son.

Robert hated to see his father put into a subservient position. He loved and respected him and knew he was trying to do his best for his family, as he consistently demonstrated in many ways. Robert's tremendously advanced mind had the maturity to realize that and the futility of opposition to something already decided. He composed himself and replied calmly and respectfully, unlike his younger sister. "But I'll be playing in a hick town instead of the city," he replied passively as a light-hearted gesture that he bowed to his father's will. Robert smiled out of respect for his father and asked, "When do we leave?"

William walked over to where his son was standing and embraced him. "Thank you, Son," he said with sincerity. William stood back a pace and looked directly at Robert. His son was already taller than he was, handsome with the physical build of an athlete, respectful, and a fine young man–everything a father could want in a son. At that moment, he realized how much he loved and admired him. "I'm so proud of you, Robert."

"I'll speak to Emily, Dad," Robert said with another forced smile, "She'll come around."

In 1951, William's father, Charles, had called William into a private meeting in his office. Like William, Charles Bryant got right to the point regarding business matters, "The Bryant Law Firm has an opportunity to build an aviation plant," he assessed his son's reaction. That industry was booming in the years after the war.

"And?" William toyed with his father. Having a keen business sense, he knew his father well and sensed he was about to ask him to partake in this venture to some level.

Charles chuckled, "We know each other well, Son." Charles Bryant, the current head of the family law firm, felt that William should be the one to head this multi-million-dollar enterprise venture. "We need a lawyer who has a keen business sense and is tough," Charles was wooing his son, and William knew it. "William, you possess all three of those requirements."

"I was afraid you were going to say that, Dad. Flattery will get you nowhere," he chuckled back, knowing that he was getting sucked into this one way or another.

"Here's the bad part, Son–"

"I thought that was the bad part," William interrupted his father.

"No, William, there's more, I'm afraid, a lot more," Charles grimaced and continued, "This has to happen in steel country. The firm stands to make a fortune from this venture. Isaac, the CFO, has all the numbers and workups." Charles kept watching his son's reactions, "But you and your family would have to relocate."

"Wow! That was a fastball with no warning."

The father and son continued their meeting. Charles knew it would be a long one. Finally, Charles said, "Naomi's from that neck of the woods. She would probably be delighted to go back there. And her brother, Nick, knows his way around there. He can be a big help to us, which would be profitable for him."

"Naomi lived there a long time ago. You know where this is going, Dad. I'm not going to force her to do this. She'll have to be agreeable to the move."

"I wouldn't have it any other way, Son, but I know Naomi, and she'll agree that that area is a better place to bring up children than the city."

After considering his father's offer, William traveled to the Pittsburgh Tri-State Area, covering part of Pennsylvania, Ohio, and West Virginia. It wasn't a social visit; he went there to see his brother-in-law in 1951 to get a report about a potential property suitable for his firm's new business venture. As he stood together on a large piece of land in an unpopulated area with Naomi's older brother, Nick, William asked, "So, you think this is the best place?" As a favor and possible business opportunity for his brother-in-law, William had asked Nick to scout out an area outside Pittsburgh, PA, that could be suitable to house such a facility. The surrounding area of Pittsburgh was home to steel manufacturing in the US.

"Yep!" Nick replied, "We're standing just outside Midland, PA. This land is a little over a half hour from Pittsburgh." Nick pointed, "Remember we passed that steel mill? It's one of the largest mills in the area and sitting right over there." They glanced at the array of smokestacks spitting plumes of dark grey clouds. "Can't get any closer than that, Bill," Nick smiled.

"Price is right, too," William answered. "You did your job well, Nick. There's an opportunity for you here if I settle on it. I'll see to it, but I have to get the boss to go along," he smiled.

"If you mean my sister, then good luck," Nick chuckled. "Well, it's close to her old home. That should score some points for this location."

Charles and Nick proved to be correct. After considering all the facts and discussing them extensively, Naomi agreed that the area would be a better place for their children than the city. "We have to prepare them both, Bill; this will be a big change for them." Naomi gave her opinion to her husband.

"I know it will, but it will be better in the long run."

Naomi Stetson Bryant was born in a quiet town along the Ohio River, less than a half-hour car ride from the prospective property's location, just across the Pennsylvania border. Nicholas Stetson, or Nick, as family and friends called him, returned to his hometown of Wellsville, Ohio, after the war to resume working in his family's textile manufacturing company. He had married just before the war broke out and lived in the town. After returning from the Pacific Theatre of War, Nick built a house on one of the hills that overlooked his hometown. Nick was a bright businessman who knew properties in the area well. So, his recommendation sat well with William, who accepted the CEO position of the newly-formed aviation corporation after several discussions with his wife, Naomi.

In mid-1951, work began on Bryant Aviation, a division of Bryant Enterprises, with an expected completion date and operational by early 1953. That would give William's children time to finish their 1952 school year in New York City. The Bryant family would be moving to Rue, Ohio.

When the aviation plant was complete, it would consist of a monumental 100,000-square-foot building with a ceiling height of 40 feet for constructing the plane fuselages.

From Midland, PA, they planned to ship the airplane bodies by rail further downriver for final assembly at an even larger site under construction. Workers would fully assemble the planes in that much larger flattened area further south, adding the wings and internal components. Test pilots would be there to fly from a series of runways built around an even larger building structure. The Midland, PA plant would have a sizeable five-story office edifice constructed where William Bryant and his engineers and executives would work. Smaller warehouses and other buildings would also surround the fuselage building site. The Bryant Aviation Center in Midland alone would bring in hundreds of jobs that would please the residents in the surrounding areas.

In the spring of 1953, William and Naomi broke the news to their children, Robert and Emily, at the family meeting.

3

Rue, Ohio 1952-1953

Naomi and William Bryant stood together, looking down from a high cliff. The sun stood high, bold, and golden in the clear blue sky. It shined its magical blonde and straw colors upon the flawless blooming green trees surrounding Naomi and William on the grounds of a large three-story late-nineteenth-century Victorian-style mansion. Located on the higher grounds of Rue, Ohio, the front of the house displayed spectacular scenic views of the Ohio River Valley below. Dozens of double-sashed windows decorated the divided sectioned architecture of the home, adorned with several square and hexagon turrets of varying heights.

William explained the details to his wife, who, up to that time, fell in love with the house solely from its character, as she referred to it. "Believe it or not, it has 27 fireplaces throughout the three levels of this nine-chimney home," William proudly smiled as he spoke as if he had been the architect. "The third floor has several rooms with high ceilings, some with double-sashed bay windows. A wrought iron circular stairway at the front left room of that third floor leads to the peak of the house's largest and highest hexagon-shaped turret." He pointed up. "We can extend that room to make a stunning viewing area from the windows of that tower." Naomi had to shield her eyes from the bright, intense sun as she stretched her neck back and peered at the highest turret. William and Naomi stood within a rectangular eight-foot high stone walled barrier encompassing the five-acre property with a tall wrought iron gated entrance. A cobblestone driveway led to the large front door. To the right side of the doorway was a large porch extending halfway around the house. And on the left of that same doorway was an oriel window built at the base of the highest turret.

"We'll have to hire an Architect and engineers to evaluate the structure thoroughly," Naomi declared as her eyes glanced away from the turret and the gleaming sun. "They can draw up plans to restore and renovate any part of it needed to bring it back to its original unimpaired condition. That's how I want it," she smiled, her arms folded.

"I agree," William chuckled, "Boss," he added. Of all the towns they had explored, the couple chose Rue, Ohio, as the home for their family.

The City of East Liverpool, Ohio, is situated in the southeastern part of Columbiana County, Ohio. Nestled along the Ohio River, it borders Pennsylvania to the east, with West Virginia set to the south just across the river. It was known as the pottery capital of the United States in 1953. Just north and above the span of rock and boulder-covered hills of the western part of the city lay the quiet, residential town of Rue, Ohio. Established in 1820 as Hunters Ridge Village, it expanded and re-named after the American Civil War to honor a hero of a battle not far from it. Major George W. Rue of the 9th Kentucky Cavalry was one of the Union officers who captured Confederate Brigadier General John Hunt Morgan after he invaded the north in the summer of 1863 during that war. The major supposedly passed through the area's hills, now named after him. A statue of the major proudly stood in the town square of Rue, Ohio, which had a population of over 8,000 residents. It attracted a more prominent class of people during the industrial expansion of the river valley in the late 1800s and early 1900s. Owners of stores, factories, and businesses of Rue and East Liverpool and other distinguished and notable professionals and members of local society lived in Rue. Some had engaging scenic views of the valley below.

Naomi and William fell in love with the vision of living in a quaint, picturesque, historic town. Each block appeared like themes from a Norman Rockwell painting, from the town square to the pastel-painted rows of stores and the various and unique architecturally styled homes, all postcards of small-town America. Their efforts in the Victorian mansion resulted in a luxurious home; every inch of it was pristine, like when it was new, just as Naomi wanted. The plans remodeled all bathrooms throughout the house and bedrooms, even in the attic above the third floor. The blueprints included higher-wattage electrical wiring to accommodate other modern amenities like complete air conditioning throughout the home and kitchen appliances. Three elevators would top off the incredible achievement. Workers completed everything before the Bryant family moved in. They had utterly renovated the third floor. The architect removed one of the vast room's interior walls, where the wrought iron spiral stairway was so that visitors could enjoy an open lounge area. Then, they could ascend the circular stairs and glance through the six huge windows at the pinnacle of the largest and highest turret. From there, they could see breathtaking views of all sides of the house, including the valley below, or sit on a circular round couch and watch that view or the enchanting star-filled nights.

Carlo and Isabella Russo were married Italian immigrants who would act as a caretaker and a housekeeper, respectively. Naomi and William connected with them from the moment they first met and intuitively knew they were the right people, like family. They would live in a private house on the property. Naomi thought hiring individuals or companies for household tasks would be better than maintaining a complete in-house staff. Everything was in place for the Bryant family's arrival in late July 1953.

If Robert's patience with his overanxious younger sister, Emily, could ever have worn down, it would have been at the surprise birthday party her parents planned before they relocated to Ohio. It became an opportunity for Emily to see all her friends together in one place before the move.

Realizing Emily's juvenile age group of friends considered them 'squares,' William and Naomi approached their son for ideas about Emily's party. "Oh, Robert, dear, we need your help. Your father and I don't have a clue as to what we should do for your sister's party," a worried Naomi caught her son as he was getting ready to go out.

Trailing behind Naomi, William called out, "She's at that awkward age, you know, far too young for teenage fun but too old for a little kiddie party." They caught Robert entirely off guard at first. Then, a smile came to his face as he remembered the party his parents threw for him when he was 12. It was a disastrous kiddie party, an embarrassing memory for him, and a flop, but he never had the heart to tell them the truth. His friends still joked with him about it. As much as Robert didn't need a headache like supervising brats the way he imagined, he would never want to see Emily endure a repeat of the catastrophic party he had.

"I'll take care of everything. Mom, Dad, don't worry about anything."

"Oh, thank you, Son," William blurted out as a teary-eyed Naomi quickly embraced Robert.

"We knew you wouldn't let us down, Robert; we're just so lost," Naomi added, "We always knew we failed with your party, and we didn't want it to happen again." That came as a surprise to Robert. 'I guess I was the guinea pig,' he thought.

"Buy whatever you need, Son, whatever you think she'll like, whatever the cost," a relieved William smiled, "Oh, and Robert," William put his arm around his son and whispered, "I'll make this up to you. I really appreciate it."

Robert took charge magnificently. And he did it with the coolness and flair of a mature 16-year-old teenager. The diligent older brother wanted the event to be one his little sister would remember for the rest of her life, and he did his best to make it a spectacular event. Robert recruited a couple of his football buddies and their girlfriends to help him.

First, the party started outside. Four trucks arrived, each having mini amusement park rides. Kids wore candy necklaces as they went from truck to truck, enjoying the rides. An ice cream truck parked outside while clowns walked around dispensing cotton candy, popcorn, M&Ms, and Pixy Stix. Robert and his friends supervised everything. Naomi and William tried to help, but the kids seemed more comfortable with the teenagers.

Naomi had already had her precious furniture and decorations packed for the move. Workers removed all remaining things from the large living room to give the children more space for when the party came indoors. Boys and girls danced and hopped to a rented 45 rpm jukebox, automatically spouting songs and tunes they loved. Caterers supplied the food kids loved: Burgers, hot dogs, French fries, hot tamales, club sandwiches, and lots of desserts. Robert ordered a counter with stools and soda fountains brought into the room. A magician performance followed a clown show. There were several contests, including a sock hop. The Bazooka bubble gum competition to see who could make the biggest bubble combined with the loudest pop was a big hit. "Hey, look!" one of the little boys yelled, "They have cartoons now! I never saw that before! Wow! Bazooka Joe!"

Robert stood surrounded in the large living room, echoed by screams, laughs, and giggles from young girls and boys, averaging around 11 years old, dancing and tripping over each other–all fueled by the candy and other sweets provided. It seemed inflated balloons floated everywhere. The kids were of that adolescent time of life torn between the mischievousness of childhood and coming to that awkward age of prepuberty; those times when girls' dolls remained close, and interest in fashion was well in the distant future. Some girls tried to act like young ladies but failed miserably to the temptations of the alluring diversions and games. Robert held his cool as he and his new but soon-to-be parting girlfriend, Linda, and his football pals dished out activities, one after the other.

"Closer, no! To the right!" a group of girls screamed at the top of their lungs as another blindfolded young girl tried to pin the tail on the donkey. At the same time, Linda carefully guided her so the thumbtack didn't sting any of the other children.

"Give them more sugar." Robert's friend, Bill, chuckled, "That will put them all to sleep."

"You're so mean, Bill," though Linda couldn't help but smile.

"Okay, Kids!" Robert yelled. "It's time for the scavenger hunt! Everyone who's playing, line up!" That perked up some boys who rushed to the front of the forming line.

"Jump rope contest forming over here," Bill yelled to compete with Robert. The teens were having fun, too.

Robert announced the sock hop contest winner as two caterers rolled the triple-tiered birthday cake into the room. Most of the kids had exhausted themselves by the time their parents arrived to pick them up after Emily had finished opening all of her presents.

"Oh, thank you, Robert," Emily whispered at the end of the long day after everyone left. Her voice was hoarse from screaming and having fun as she tried to stay awake in Robert's arms as he carried her to her bedroom. Robert had spotted her asleep in a catlike position on a cushioned chair as Naomi directed the cleaning people as they cleared the mess left behind.

"You were great, Robert!" Emily's long eyelashes flickered as she strained to keep her eyes open from the sleep that began overwhelming her. "Everything was so swell! Thank you so much!" her groggy voice faded as she maintained her fight to stay awake, the fun and excitement of the day slowly beating any hope of that.

"You bet, Sis. I'm glad you liked everything," Robert whispered back as he placed her in bed. Emily still grinned as she succumbed to sleep, and her body, now secure and comfortable, moved into a fetal position. Robert covered her and kissed her forehead. "Sweet dreams, kiddo." He was pleased that he had accomplished his mission and given his sister a memory she would never forget.

"So... let's see... I think that's everything. Yep, it is," Robert smiled at his sister. "We got 'em all." He and Emily had been working closely together on a project to help her stay connected with all her friends in New York. "Mission accomplished." Robert assisted her in organizing a list of their phone numbers and addresses. Then he made mimeographed copies for her to keep in a safe place in case she lost any of her friends' contact information.

After Emily saw all her friends at the party and said her final farewell, she had come to terms with the reality of moving to a different state. Robert often talked to her about it at just the right moments. He helped her understand that she could still keep in touch and visit her friends occasionally. Robert focused on his sister's emotional needs to make her feel secure. He explained that the distance wasn't as great as it seemed and did other little things that made her feel more comfortable in ways that mattered to a young girl.

"I'll always be there for you in our new home, Sis," Robert told her. That was the most important thing he could have said and what she cherished most. Knowing that her big brother would be there for her made her feel safe and aware that Robert would always protect her in their new place. "Let's think about it as a journey," he told her as they packed for the move.

"An adventure!" She corrected him with a big smile, then kissed him on the cheek and hugged him around his waist while standing on her tiptoes. "Thanks, Robert," Emily said with a muffled voice as her head pressed against his chest. Whenever she was in her brother's embrace, she always enjoyed the combined scent of his cologne and his body chemistry; it triggered something in her memory that made her feel secure. "You always make me feel better."

Ever since Robert was a young boy, he sensed his younger sister's anxieties and helped her even in simple ways. After learning about the move, He realized that his father and mother were usually very busy at such a demanding time. And as much as they wanted, they sometimes could not address their children's personal needs. William and Naomi were grateful Robert substituted for them with Emily's crisis about moving. Her parents did, however, take personal time often to discuss the relocation to put her at ease. And they reinforced that she would always communicate with her friends in New York.

However, Robert had private reservations about the move that he kept from his little sister. He engaged in confidential discussions with his parents when Emily was asleep or not around. During those conversations, Robert demonstrated surprising maturity for a 16-year-old. Some of his concerns were typical for someone in his situation: worries about playing football, basketball, and baseball in a new place and the challenge of making friends. Nevertheless, he was confident he could handle these issues on his own, often using those discussions with his parents to express his thoughts aloud. He felt he wouldn't encounter challenges beyond his control regarding any of those matters.

Robert excelled in sports, was good-looking, and a pleasure to be around. However, the teens in Rue, Ohio, were different. He recalled it as almost a different culture when his family visited to see their relatives. Robert stood out, and he was aware of it. His main concern was fitting in. He had learned to do that with his schoolmates and friends in the city, but now he would have to achieve the same goal all over again, this time in a rural town.

Robert's parents always knew there was something special about their son when he walked, spoke his first words before he was eight months old, and began advanced reading before age three. By age four, Robert learned mathematics and taught himself Italian from a book his mother had in the house. Also born with remarkable coordination, he displayed his ability to learn to walk and run exceptionally well on his own.

"It's almost supernatural, Bill. We can't ignore this any longer," Naomi told William when she found out her son learned a foreign language by himself at four. She seemed genuinely upset and worried, displaying those emotions. "How could he be able to–"

"We will do something." William cut her off, "I'm working on it already," he said softly to be reassuring. However, Naomi detected that her husband's unworried demeanor meant he knew something she didn't. She suspected it was due to her son's time with his nanny, Martha Weber. "I have someone who has evaluated our son. He will begin instructing Robert for his special needs." William concluded. He always suspected a darker meaning to his son's exceptional abilities but never let on to his wife.

"Is it that same doctor who–"

"Yes, it is." William quickly replied to his wife's question. By her expression, he knew she understood.

Naomi felt a little easier when Doctor Friedrich Kruger, who specialized in gifted children, began teaching Robert. A previous doctor defined Robert as a genius before his grammar school years. A specialist tested his IQ, and Robert scored 200, abnormally high. They re-tested him again two weeks later, and he scored a 210. Robert's intelligence was increasing. William knew Doctor Friedrich Kruger, the professor who headed the school and taught their son a unique method he developed after years of studies. The doctor's philosophy included cultivating Robert's enhanced coordination, which some young geniuses also possessed but usually ignored. He devoted time to Robert's physiological abilities and not solely the unusually high intellectual facets of his advanced brain. That would allow him to enjoy bodily activities and create a fulfilled and pleasant personality. It would also avoid the frustrations and anxieties that many super-intelligent children often form. Physical and mental activities became welcomed and enjoyable to Robert. These attributes resulted from the professor's training that never forced any part of his cerebral or bodily education.

"I will now start the boy with basketball," the professor explained to the Bryants. William hired a trainer to show his son how to develop the advanced coordination he already possessed. Playing basketball improved Robert's advanced eye control, and, combined with his quick reflexes and instinctive agility, he established superhuman responsiveness to his opponent's body movements and reacted to them quickly.

When they felt their son was sufficiently prepared, his parents removed him from studying full-time under the professor. They put him in a regular public grammar school so he could enjoy a normal childhood like many parents of gifted children could understand and appreciate. On weekends, he attended Kruger's School for the Gifted, where he expanded his specialized learning. He attended regular school weekly and learned to blend in with his class. That strategy allowed Robert to make friends and not noticeably stand out among the other average students. To them, he became viewed as nothing more than an excellent student. When he was ready for high school, Robert Bryant was a unique and multifaceted young man.

"Which sport do you like the most, Son?" William proudly asked before school began.

"I like them all, Dad." Robert was thrilled to attend high school, where he could excel at all sports.

William laughed, "Well, you certainly are great in all of them." He was happy that his son was enjoying a normal life.

"Thanks, Dad."

Robert's adaptability was a key factor in his success. He excelled in sports and advanced studies, meeting his interests and increasing his appeal to others. He showed social adaptability by fitting in with other children and quickly making friends. When Robert was ten, his IQ score was an astounding 230. In the eighth grade, the school's guidance counselor discreetly suggested that he go straight to college, but Naomi and William disagreed. Nonetheless, the counselor believed that limiting him would hinder his potential.

Robert improved his incredible coordination and physical abilities under Professor Kruger and did remarkably well. By high school, Robert exhibited a multitasking ability that allowed him to learn his advanced studies independently while completing a regular high school curriculum. He continued to excel at sports in his first two years and appeared to be an intelligent young man who was exceptional in sports.

In his second year, with an IQ of 240, Robert was already a star varsity basketball player and had also been accepted onto the varsity football team as a quarterback. He threw 19 successful touchdown passes in just five games and was slated to be the starting quarterback in his junior year, as the current first-string was graduating. Then, Robert's father announced that they would be moving to Ohio.

As the date of the move approached, each member of the Bryant family grappled with their individual concerns: William worried about failing in his new business venture; Robert was anxious about fitting in at a new school; Emily struggled with the anxieties she had endured since birth; and Naomi felt the pressure of being the heart of a family adjusting to life in a new place. Nevertheless, they knew they had each other, and their love would help them overcome any unforeseen challenges. Robert sat next to Emily on what would be her first flight on one of Bryant Aviation's new private aircraft, a custom Douglas DC-7. His keen intuition sensed his sister's unease as she glanced out the window. "Everything's going to be okay, Sis," he whispered. Emily turned and smiled at her brother, knowing he would always be there for her.

4

Rue, Ohio 1953

A chilly breeze from the Ohio River flowed through the rocky hills, making for an unseasonably cool summer day in the small town of Rue, Ohio. Robert Bryant leaned against one of the wooden goalposts at the end of the football field, his duffle bag with clean clothes resting beside him. The scent of freshly cut grass filled the air as he stood in the bright sunlight. Standing well over six feet tall, his shorts and T-shirt highlighted his muscular build. He bent down momentarily to secure the laces of his Wilson high-top cleated football shoes and observed two plump mourning doves cooing and waddling together on the grass not far from the base of the wooden post opposite him. Out of the corner of his eye, Robert noticed several football team members had arrived early, standing no more than 15 feet away. They were chatting with a group of girls whom Robert assumed were there to watch practice. He cleared his throat with a soft cough–a nervous gesture, never realizing everyone had shown up an hour before practice to see him. His family's arrival had become the town's topic of conversation, attracting the players and girls eager to glimpse the new guy from New York. Yet, no one approached him, leaving him alone, standing against the sturdy wooden post that afternoon of August 3, 1953.

Rue High School had completed a new football stadium and attached gymnasium just one year before to replace the original ones built in the 1920s. The stadium was impressive and boasted elevated seating for well over 6,000 people, divided into visitors and home sides. It had a giant scoreboard and an array of several poled lights for night games. The gymnasium was equally imposing, with high-rowed seating and an enormous, varnished professional court and perimeter. Both complexes were compliments of William Bryant when he learned that his family was moving to Rue, Ohio. Permits and planning came swiftly, as did the construction. When William Bryant gave instructions, people complied. The Bryant family received no credit for the accomplishment in any way; William wanted it that way. It was a confidential charitable donation. People assumed that Rue taxpayers and the state had funded it, but only a few knew the truth. The town had graciously and secretly offered William a special box seating at each facility. Yet, William refused and paid for his, like all citizens who wanted such amenities. Frankly, he preferred to sit in the stands and only bought the box because his war injuries affected his leg and sitting position.

William also donated considerably to his family's new church in Rue, St. Michael's. That parish was in dire need of a new roof and more seating. William had his architects draw up plans for a substantial extension to the church building and a new paved parking lot. It was a considerable undertaking, done simultaneously with the school jobs. And, again, it was donated anonymously as a true Christian should.

Robert Bryant had thick black wavy hair, which enhanced his ancestral heritage's dark blue eyes. His long eyelashes contrasted the color of his eyes, making them appear even larger and more attractive. Robert was a good-looking young man, and the girls by his side succumbed to the handsome presence who stood near them. He heard giggles, cries, and whispers coming from what was now accumulating to a small crowd. Then Robert overheard comments about him. One girl with a squeaky voice insisted he looked like a young Cary Grant. That remark began a debate among the teenage girls.

"More like Tyrone Power," insisted another with a huskier voice. "Wow! Would I like to get my hands on him," she joked.

"I think He looks just like Robert Wagner," another insisted.

"Dean Martin!" yelled out another.

"You know you girls are speaking loud enough for him to hear you," reasoned one of the taller guys in the crowd. "It's not polite."

"You're just jealous, Roger," laughed another guy.

Robert assumed it was some type of initiation. He never realized just how attractive he had become, especially during the early part of the summer just before he arrived. His face had matured, revealing finely chiseled features. Though his mother and even Emily had commented about how handsome he was getting, Robert never gave much thought to it. Then, the conversations broke up just as the crowd spotted a figure entering the field from the school's back door. The girls and some boys immediately scattered to the stands, as only players were allowed on the field during practice. The remaining guys turned and began walking toward the same back door of the school to suit up for practice.

Coach Fred Wilson walked onto the field, took an unlit El Producto out of his mouth, blew his whistle, and replaced the thick cigar between his lips. He was a stout man of medium height and wore loose-fitting trousers, a pullover short-sleeve shirt, and low-cut white sneakers. "Roger, Bill, Jasper, and Stan," he shouted toward the departing guys, his cigar still in his mouth and rolling to his words. "I need you four out here for this. Get dressed, pronto!" he yelled.

"Yes, coach," they all quickly answered, almost in unison, as they began to run instead of walking to the locker room.

"Why'd he pick us to work with the city dude," asked Bill Patterson.

"He's supposed to be a pretty good quarterback over there," Stan Swarovski answered. "Or so my dad heard."

"Give him a chance, I say," yelled Jasper Wilcox. "If he's no good, he won't make the team. Simple as that!"

"Spoiled rich kid who wants to be quarterback, I think," added Roger LeBlanc. "Word has it his father has more money than God, I heard. We'll see if his arm can catch up to me." Roger LeBlanc had tied with Jasper Wilcox for the fastest sprinters on the team, and both were wide receivers.

Coach Fred Wilson turned and walked toward Robert Bryant, sizing him up as everyone waited. 'Good build and height,' he thought. "I'm Coach Wilson," he greeted Robert and extended his right hand for a shake.

Robert complied and said, "Nice to meet you, sir."

"Coach!" barked Fred Wilson. "We're not in the Army here, son." He made a poor attempt at a smile.

"Yes, sir, I mean, coach." Robert was a bit nervous, and it showed.

'Respectful too,' thought Fred. 'But can he play?' Coach Wilson explained to Robert that he had received his stats and recommendation from his former coach in New York. He went on to add that they might do things differently there and that Robert would have to comply with the ways of this school. Just as Robert agreed to that directive, another man appeared, holding a football, walking toward them on the field. He was a tall, thin man named Tom Hanlon, the team's assistant coach. Fred Wilson made the introductions while taking the ball from his assistant. Then Fred asked Robert if he played any basketball and baseball back home, and when Robert said yes, he invited him to try out for those teams as well. Coach Fred Wilson was also the boys' basketball, baseball, and track coach at Rue High School.

The four players returned with practice uniforms and gear. It was hard to tell their heights while they were running. Stan, the shorter of the four, had a heavier build but seemed quick on his feet. Jasper was taller and on the thin side, about six feet. Bill was about the same height as Jasper but had a more muscular build. Roger, one of the best players on the team, was about Robert's size and also with an athletic body. None of the four young men acknowledged Robert and looked directly at their coach. Fred Wilson threw the football to Robert and said, "Let's go." As soon as he spoke those words, a rainbow-colored haze descended low from the sky and slowly spread its vivid hues over the football field and stadium. As the kaleidoscopic colors hovered, a bright ray of light pierced through its center like a sword, and a gentle puff of wind blew over the stadium.

It seemed weird, but there was a familiarity to it that was warm and friendly, as if it were a compassionate embrace from the past offering a premonition. Then, the mystifying cloud dissipated as quickly as it came, leaving calm and tranquility in its wake. "What was that?" Fred Wilson asked Tom Hanlon, who just shrugged his shoulders in response, "Thought we might be having ourselves a twister."

First, Fred and Tom explained they would check out Robert's throws. Then, he would have to qualify in running speed, kicking the ball, and catching it. He would also have to display agility on the obstacle course some other players were already setting up across the field.

Robert demonstrated his throws many times at different distances. He passed the ball at a close distance to Stan at about 10 to 15 yards, then even closer at five yards. Fred Wilson made Stan pivot and try to fool Robert, which Stan did well, but Robert was on target every time. He threw and handed off the ball even closer at two to three yards. Bill repeated the same routine but at slightly greater distances. He went out from 15 to 40 yards, and Robert was accurate every time. Then, when Coach Wilson thought Robert's arm might be tired, he sent Roger and Jasper out longer. They crisscrossed the outer field. Robert still placed his throws fast and accurately at 70 and even 80 yards over and over. Coach sent his wide receivers all the way out to the end zone, and Robert was right on target.

"My God, the kid throws bullets," Fred whispered to Tom as he twirled his unlit cigar around in his mouth. "I've never seen anything like it! Not around here, anyway."

"He's good!" gasped Tom. "Real good!"

The guys and girls in the stands were in awe and speechless as Robert demonstrated his throwing skills on the field. He caught and kicked the ball as well as he had thrown it and gracefully passed right through the obstacle course. He sprinted fast enough to surpass Roger, tied for the fastest on the team. Then, someone stood up and clapped, which started a barrage of applause and whistling. Everyone in the stands was now on their feet to watch Robert.

Coach Fred Wilson walked toward the stands and signaled everyone to be silent. Then he strolled over to Robert and said, "You're our new starting quarterback. Congratulations, son." He smiled for real this time. "Go suit up for practice." Then he barked to another player, "Steve, get this man some gear!"

Roger, Stan, Jasper, and Bill jogged directly over to Robert. Roger was the first to introduce himself to Robert. "Nice throws, Robert. I'm Roger LeBlanc, wide receiver."

Jasper came alongside Roger. "Great throwing, Robert. I'm Jasper Wilcox, the better wide receiver," he laughed.

Stan was next and said, "Welcome to the team, Robert. Great work! I'm Stan Swarovski, tight end."

Then Bill told Robert, "I've never seen a better quarterback, and nicely done! I'm Bill Patterson, running back. Good to meet you."

Robert shook hands with all four of his new teammates as the other players jogged over to compliment him. With a big smile, he told everyone to call him Bob.

During practice, the crowd grew even bigger. People showed up unexpectedly. It was as if it was an actual game. Everyone couldn't restrain themselves when Robert threw the football. He even placed his bullets accurately when they set up offensive and defensive lines. Robert was as good even under pressure, further impressing Coach Fred Wilson. The Rue High School Football Team only won two games the last season. Their quarterback had graduated, and the team didn't miss him much. He was arrogant and didn't play his position well at all. Now that they had such a capable quarterback, everyone imagined a better year and was thrilled with the prospects. High school sports were important in the Midwest, even more so than in some cities.

An adoring herd of people surrounded Robert as he walked toward the locker room. Everyone welcomed him with compliments and praise while trying to get close to him. People of all ages, including parents, teachers, students, and even younger kids, showed up. Several girls giggled and tried to push through others to get a closer look at him.

Coach Wilson and Tom Hanlon finally came to Robert's rescue. "Okay, folks," Fred yelled. "Let's give the young man some privacy. You'll all see the team play on the 21st at our first game," he announced. Gradually, the coach and his assistant, aided by several teachers, dispersed the crowd. Robert was able to continue to the building with his teammates. Then, he noticed his sister, Emily, sitting on one of the lower seats of the stand, laughing and clapping. Robert turned and walked toward her. As he got closer, he noticed another young girl his sister's age sitting close to her. She looked like she could almost be her twin. She had blond-colored hair, but it was lighter, and her eyes were also blue but much darker and more profound than his sister's. Both the girls were thin and puny and appeared to be around the same shorter height for their age. They even dressed similarly. Both wore short pants, short-sleeved blouses, white anklet socks, and white sneakers. The only difference was the colors of their clothes: Emily's shirt was yellow with dark blue shorts, and the other girl wore a medium blue printed blouse with gray shorts.

Robert approached his sister and the other little girl with a big smile, but before he could speak, Emily screamed, "You were great, Robert!" She was laughing. "I mean, really great!"

Robert stepped up to her and kissed her on the cheek. "Thanks, Sis," he said. Then he turned to the young girl beside her and said, "Hi! How are you? I'm Robert."

The young girl blushed, but before she could say anything, Emily blurted out, "I'm sorry, this is my new friend, Coralie, but everyone calls her Coral. She's going to the Rue Grammar School with me." Emily appeared happy that she had met a new friend.

The young girl's eyes focused on Emily as she listened to her introduction, but then she rolled her big, dark blue eyes and looked directly into Robert's eyes. Coral said, "Hello," with a low, uneasy voice as she blushed again. "It's nice to meet you, Robert."

It was clear to Robert that she was nervous, so to make her feel more comfortable, he extended his arm for a handshake and said, "It's nice to meet you, Coral."

Coral put her tiny hand into his larger one and timidly said, "You're an excellent football player, Robert." Then she thought how stupid she sounded with her effort to be sophisticated.

Robert offered to drive them home after he showered and changed his clothes. Coral thanked him but said her brother was already taking her. Deep down, Coral was sorry that she couldn't take his offer. Robert said goodbye, gave the two girls one last smile, and then left to change his clothes.

"My God, your brother's so nice," declared Coral in a more comfortable tone. "My big brother torments me always," she complained enviously. "And he would never kiss me in public. Never! He only does it on holidays and other times when he absolutely has to." Coral was a little chatterbox with Emily when they were alone.

"No, Robert isn't like that to me. He's great, really good to me," Emily replied proudly. "I give him a hard time now and then. I know I do, but I can't help it sometimes, like when I get nervous; you know the feeling. But Robert has a lot of patience with me," she said fondly.

"Wow! You're lucky," Coral said in awe. "My brother has no patience with me at all. Your brother's very handsome, too," she giggled.

***

After about 15 minutes, Robert walked together, speaking with Roger LeBlanc. They had connected immediately. Both teens shared an intuitive and mutual likeness for one another from the onset and now headed back to where Emily sat with her friend. They both dressed casually in jeans, sneakers, and T-shirts.

"Hi, Roge," Coral spoke first to greet her brother.

"Hey," he responded to his sister.

"I didn't know your friend was Roger's sister, Em," Robert mused while he smiled at Coral.

"Unfortunately," joked Roger. Coral didn't verbally respond. She just gave Roger a stern look, squinting her dark blue eyes.

Then Robert introduced Roger to Emily. When Emily said, 'Hello,' Roger gave her the same casual 'hey' that his sister, Coral, had received in return.

As the brothers and sisters entered the student parking lot, a bright, brand-new 1953 Chevy Corvette stood out from the other automobiles. Some other cars were nice, but most were primarily older and beat up. Among the others, the pristine, white-colored Corvette sparkled like a beacon in the late afternoon sunlight. Roberts's parents gave him the brand-new car, which a Chevrolet representative delivered only a few days before. William Bryant had to pull some strings as they were in limited availability. The new sports car, recently introduced, had a planned production of only 300 Corvettes that year. Robert's father never spoiled his children and always taught them the value of money. But he wanted his son to adjust well in Ohio, and he appreciated how his son handled his sister's birthday party. William surprised Robert with news of the car a month earlier. All the young guys knew about the new model car's introduction, but no one in the town of Rue had ever seen one up close, only in magazines. So, a group of male teens stood around it with their girlfriends.

"Wow!" Roger exclaimed. "Whose car is that?" He turned and smiled at Robert. "It's yours, right?"

Robert's expression changed, and he felt utterly uncomfortable inside. Although Robert came from a wealthy family and received a generous allowance, he was never snobbish or arrogant. He didn't flaunt his possessions or try to stand out. From childhood, Robert developed a pleasant personality and was always generous with his friends. His specialized training played a role in this, but it was primarily William's influence. After witnessing the horrors of war and the resulting poverty, he wanted the best for his children while also encouraging them to share with others. Robert and Emily grew up to be kind and big-hearted toward their friends. "It is," Robert replied sheepishly to Roger's question. Then he added, "Hey, why don't you take it for a spin?"

"Really?" Roger was shocked.

"Yeah, and take your sister for a ride with you," he said as he took his keys out of his pocket.

Coral's eyes widened with excited anticipation. "Oh boy!" she couldn't hold it in.

"Never!" Blurted Roger as he caught the keys Robert threw at him. "I would never be seen with my kid sister in a car like this. It would draw too much attention."

Roger left to take the sports car around the block a few times. Robert turned to see an upset Coral–the beginning of a tear formed in her right deep blue eye. Emily went and put her arm around her new friend. Robert felt awful as he watched them standing there as Roger pulled out of the parking lot.

"You see what I mean," Coral whispered to Emily. "He's so mean to me."

Robert intervened, "Coral! Hey, listen! I'll take you for a ride another time."

Coral turned and looked at Robert, trying to maintain her ladylike demeanor while speaking to him. Then she said, "Thank you, Robert. I would like that."

"I promise! And we'll do it soon." Robert thought Coral was mature for her age. He moved closer to Coral, bent on one knee, and wiped away the tear that had formed in her right eye with his index finger. Then he gave her a big smile. Coral smiled back, and Robert noticed Coral had a mouthful of silver braces on her teeth.

Others who passed by commented about Robert's new car, saying things like "nice car, man" and "cool wheels," Bob. A girl around Robert's age said, "It's a beautiful car, Robert." She was pretty, with long dark brown hair and a pleasant smile. "My name is Denise Beck, by the way," she introduced herself.

"I guess you already know my name," replied Robert, smiling but feeling self-conscious that everyone knew his name already. "It's very nice to meet you. I guess we'll see each other at school?"

"I'm sure we will," Denise smiled, and her eyes widened. She smiled once more at Robert and left. Emily and Coral imitated Denise as soon as she parted. Both of them were jealous of her in the way many young girls are of older, prettier ones.

"I hate her," Coral whispered to Emily so Robert couldn't hear.

"So do I," and the two young girls giggled together.

"What's so funny?" Robert asked, smiling.

"Oh, nothing," the girls harmonized together, still giggling.

Roger returned, praising the car's handling and acceleration. He was incredibly impressed and repeatedly thanked Robert for letting him take it for a spin. Robert then told him he could drive it again. It was the beginning of a good friendship.

Emily said goodbye to Coral. They had already exchanged phone numbers and promised to call each other. They were also in a blossoming friendship. Then Roger and Coral left, waving as they did from Roger's souped-up maroon 1949 Ford two-door convertible.

Robert walked to the passenger side of his car and opened the door for his sister. "My lady!" He stood there gesturing her into the car.

"Service with a smile." Emily joked back as she climbed into the red bucket seat.

William Bryant retained Professor Kruger to continue Robert's nontraditional studies. He paid handsomely for Kruger's move to Rue and living accommodations. But, this way, their son could enjoy regular high school years and all the activities that went along with them, including Robert's gifted abilities in sports that he loved. He would maintain his advanced studies under the same professor who had already accomplished so much with him.

William was a kind and generous man. However, the average person never viewed his overwhelming humane qualities, only those of a business magnate. That unjust and insensitive reputation created by the local media is the one that followed him to his new hometown of Rue, Ohio. That's why their High School's Principal, Harry 'Hal' Morgan, and his guidance counselor, Annette Willis, were more than surprised when William extended his arms for a warm handshake to each of them, his face beaming with a broad smile and his demeanor humble and pleasant. "I really do appreciate you, Principal Morgan, and you, Mrs. Willis, taking time out from your busy day to see my wife and me," he said as his hands embraced each of theirs in succession.

The principal and his assistant were among those who knew of the Bryant family's generosity to the school and church and were shocked that such a powerful man would be so genuinely friendly and outgoing. "I know I speak for my assistant and myself when I say it is our sincerest pleasure to assist you and your wife. Please be seated, Mr. and Mrs. Bryant," he gestured with his hand for Naomi and William to sit before his desk in his office.

"Thank you," William pleasantly answered as he pulled back his wife's chair so she could sit first. "Please call me Bill."

"Okay, Bill." Principal Morgan blushed and answered, "Everyone calls me Hal. That is, except for the children." He chuckled, "I hope you will as well."

"That's a deal, Hal," William laughed back.

"So," Hal spread his arms apart, "How can we help you?"

William's expression shifted to concern: "I scheduled this meeting to talk about something very personal regarding my son, Robert."

Hal Morgan sensed that what he was about to hear was confidential and of great concern to the man who had already been such a gracious benefactor to his school. "Mr. Bryant," quickly altering his words, "Bill, you have our assurance that everything discussed in this meeting will stay here," Hal Morgan assured them.

"Thank you, Hal. I really appreciate that." William continued to explain Robert's overall situation concerning his mental capacity and the specialized college-level classes his son was attending.

Naomi filled in any facts her husband left out. She reiterated their shared desire for Robert to have a typical high school experience. "My husband and I appreciate that this information remains confidential," Naomi politely clarified, "to prevent the spread of gossip and hearsay."

"No student or teacher will know about anything discussed here," Mrs. Willis smiled as she repeated the principal's assurances. Naomi and William Bryant both expressed their appreciation. Robert would attend their typical curriculum and do his advanced college-level studies confidentially with Doctor Friedrich Kruger, the professor who trained him in his earlier years.

Naomi and William were relieved. Nobody would know that Robert was an exceptional genius. His sister knew he was very bright but not to such a level. He would appear to others just like he did in New York: an intelligent student highly talented in sports. The reasons for Robert's incredible brainpower, which allowed him to think quickly and be very agile, would remain hidden from others. Other facts, such as that he could assess much more than an average person and predetermine other people's moves and objectives, would also remain secretive. Those attributes and others taught to him by Professor Kruger made him the multifaceted young man he was. However, Dr. Kruger had not unveiled his truthful motive for continuing to tutor Robert. It seemed mysterious that such a prominent professor would move to such a rural town, even for the sum of money the Bryants paid him.

Already an upperclassman, Robert had no Freshman orientation as other newcomers to the school did. Principal Morgan asked Denise Beck, the girl Robert had met after his first football practice, to show him around the school. He wanted Robert to know his way around and become familiar with the normal operations of a student. Denise was thrilled to comply, and the two journeyed together throughout the school. She explained everything to the tall, handsome young man who accompanied her, very impressed with how much of a gentleman Robert was. He opened and closed doors for her and spoke and acted not as a typical high school junior but in a mature and cavalier manner. Handsome, charming, smart, and a gentleman, which was extremely rare, Denise thought, enjoying every minute of being with Robert.

The first day of school went well for Robert that Monday, August 17, 1953, already popular due to his demonstration of athletic skills. Robert became close friends with Roger LeBlanc, and they spent a lot of time together before the start of school. Roger introduced Robert to many of his closest friends during that time. Denise Beck, who usually met Robert after football practice, formally introduced him to many of her friends. Robert immediately liked Denise; his highly developed mental powers told of her kindness and purity. The guys admired him, and the girls adored him. He made other new male and female friends from the football team and his classes. Everyone enjoyed being around Robert's casual and pleasant aura. The town wasn't as bad as expected, and he didn't feel the least bit out of place in rural Ohio. Robert fit in well at Rue and was adjusting to being away from the home he once knew in New York. His high school class subjects were basic and simple to him, but Robert enjoyed physics among them. Even though Robert was already studying college-level physics, he liked seeing the primary form of it in the class he now took. For him, it was like an older boy picking up an old basic toy and being amazed at what might have attracted him to it when he was a baby.

The head cheerleader, Sue Peters, was in Robert's physics class and stood out among the other girls. She was a beautiful girl with long blonde hair and an hourglass figure, well-developed for her age. Most of the guys in school were attracted to her the most among the female teens, and Sue knew it and used it to her advantage. When Denise Beck saw how Sue eyed Robert, she thought she had lost any chances of having a closer relationship with him. However, having such an exceptionally advanced intuition, Robert saw through Sue's phony stage act. He also sensed the early stages of developing wickedness within her. Denise, in a state of shock, became the envy of every other high school girl, including a fuming Sue Peters, when Robert asked Denise to be his date for the homecoming dance after the school's football season opener game.

Emily also did fine on her first day of school. She and Coral became fast friends. The two girls had seen each other every day since that first football practice and spent much time speaking on the telephone. They went to each other's houses to play or listen to records.

"I love your home," Coral told Emily. "It reminds me of a castle," Coral giggled while romping through the large rooms as they played hide-and-seek one day at Emily's. In a split second, Coral's mind traveled to the far corridors of her imagination and envisioned being a princess while playing, having lords, dukes, and knights beneath her, and ruling with mercy and justice. "It feels like my castle," Coral giggled again.

"Your home is so charming, though, Coral." Emily's words snapped Coral back from her fantasy. "It's lovely. Really." However, in actuality, though it was a very nice but much smaller four-bedroom home, it didn't have the elegance of her friend Emily's family mansion. Also, Coral was always in awe of the luxurious surroundings, beautiful furniture, and things displayed around Emily's home. She particularly enjoyed Emily's extra-large bedroom, where they could hang around.

"I feel cramped in my bedroom," Coral said, "It's the smallest bedroom in our house. Yours is so large, and we have more room to play." At Emily's, she was also able to run into Robert often and always secretly enjoyed speaking with or just being around him.

"Your bedroom is cozy, and you have such a beautiful collection of dolls, so many nicer ones than mine."

"Do you really think so?"

"Yes, I do. They're all pretty, really beautiful and so unique. I love them all." Emily always went out of her way to make her new friend feel comfortable.

Emily met several of Coral's friends and fit nicely into their close-knit group. She, too, was adjusting to life in the rural town of Rue. So, when that first day of school came around, Emily had no anxiety whatsoever. She was among friends.

During the first week of school, Robert made good on his promise to give little Coral LeBlanc a ride in his car. The convertible top of his Corvette was down on a beautiful day in August. Coral had missed the school bus, and Robert noticed her small, thin figure walking home alone just a half block from her school. Robert swerved his Vette in front of her path. Coral hadn't seen him coming and was startled at first, then smiled when she realized who it was. Robert lifted his sunglasses and called jokingly, "Hey, baby, how about a ride?"

Coral laughed almost hysterically as she ran to the car. She opened the door excitedly and said, "Hi, Robert! Can I really come in?" Her mouthful of braces shined in the afternoon sunlight.

"Of course, my lady. I'm at your service," he answered, smiling at her, treating her like he did his sister. "C'mon in. We'll drive around on our way to your house."

Coral was so nervous; she was actually riding alone in a sportscar with Robert Bryant. Her only thoughts were of waiting until she told her girlfriends. Then her eyes widened and snapped into sharp focus as if she realized something. "Oh, Robert? Can you do me a big favor?"

"Sure. What?"

"Can you take me back to my school for just a second? I forgot to tell one of my friends something very important," she paused, "it would only take a second, I promise."

Coral looked worried, so Robert obliged her. It was only a

block back. "No problem, my lady. I remain at your service." He made an impressive U-turn with his high-performance car and drove her back to where there was a group of young girls waiting for rides home. Coral pointed to where Robert should stop within the center of the small crowd. Coral slowly stepped out of the sports car as it glistened in the afternoon sunlight, knowing all eyes were upon her. She stepped slowly and elegantly as if each stride was one upon the red carpet on Oscar night in Hollywood, turning her head and smiling at each of the shocked faces of her friends. Coral whispered something into the ear of one of the admiring girls standing in awe, envious of Coral's sudden status. All of the girls in the crowd smiled at Robert sitting in his super-charged sports car as Coral gracefully opened the door and sat melodramatically back in the car, leaning against Robert's side, her head raised and chin held high.

"Thank you so much, Robert."

Robert just smiled, shaking his head. He knew what had happened. The little actress, Coral, wanted the other girls to see her riding with him in his new sports car. He felt it was important to her, so he happily obliged without saying anything. Oddly, he was proud of her savvy cleverness. And it was the first time he realized a woman was developing in that child's body.

Shortly after, as Coral enjoyed her ride, she looked directly at Robert and blushed. Then she nervously asked, "Do you think I'll be pretty one day, Robert?"

"You already are!" He smiled at the diminutive figure beside him and said, "When you grow up, with that set of the most beautiful eyes I've ever seen, you're going to be a knockout!"

Coral smiled back at Robert; then they spoke about different things as they drove together around town before heading to her home. Robert coasted his car slowly because he enjoyed talking to Coral. They always instantly became involved in deep and engaging conversations. It was amusing and bewildering to Robert how Coral's mind could instantaneously metamorphose from one of a juvenile kid into the intellectual and philosophical one of a mature young woman. They arrived at

Coral's house before Robert wanted; he was enjoying himself.

Coral winked at Robert as if she was reading his mind and smiled before turning away, opening the door, and stepping out. As she leaned inside the car, her arms resting on the red padded door upholstery, her facial expression became serious as she said, "Thank you again, Robert, so much." Robert sensed that she appreciated him not making an issue about her plotted scheme, and she seemed touched. Looking into Coral's deep blue eyes, Robert wondered what it was he liked about her so much.

Then Robert waved to Coral's mother, who was waiting for her daughter outside the front door. She waved back and shouted out, "Thank you, Robert. I was a little worried when she didn't get off the bus."

Robert casually drove away, still awestruck about Roger's adorable kid sister's mature mind outgrowing her tiny body. But to Coral LeBlanc, it was the day she would never forget when she first fell in love with Robert Bryant.

Everyone was anticipating the big night, the Rue versus Toronto High School football game season opener. Tickets for the event sold out more than a week prior, the only known sellout in Rue's history. This year marked the first time Rue had such a competent quarterback, Robert Bryant. The fire departments from Rue and East Liverpool would be on hand to support the police with crowd control. As emotions ran high, there was a deep concern for out-of-control fans and potential fights between the rival teams. The police departments from both towns would be on duty with some support from the Highway Patrol. Most of the men in blue wanted to be there anyway to see the game.

"Remember, Robert, no matter the trail of how we acquire our talents and abilities, they are all gifts from God, whether directly or otherwise." William felt compelled to say that as he sat his son down for a talk before Robert left home for the game. He did so because he believed it to be the truth and because of a confidential and unrevealed reality about Robert's earlier years in case he found out about it before William knew. "Do the best you can, Robert. Win or lose, I don't expect any more than that. I'll be proud of you either way." Naomi was eavesdropping from the next room to hear the father and son talk. "Good luck, and you know I'll be rooting for you the most," William finally smiled.

"Thanks, Dad."

"Now get out there and kick butt!" William whispered.

"I will, Dad. Don't worry."

"Have a nice talk with your son, dear?" Naomi asked as she walked into the living room, and Robert was out of sight.

William cautiously glanced in each direction and gently slapped Naomi on the backside when no one was around. "I know you were listening, dear."

Naomi giggled, "I have no idea what you mean, darling."

"Oh, you two. Come here for a minute," William called to his daughter and Coral as he spotted them running past him. The Bryants were driving Coral to the game with Emily; Coral had spent the entire day at her castle with Emily before the big game.

William gazed down at the two small girls as they innocently looked up at him. "I invited the LeBlancs to sit with us in our box behind the sideline. I want you, Coralie, and you, Emily, to stay close," William addressed both girls. He tried his best to give them both a stern expression, but he could see the slight smile emerge on each of their faces and knew it didn't work.

"We'll try, Daddy," his daughter's smile widened, but Coral's expression remained solemn; her deep blue eyes widened.

"I know how you girls like to wander," William appealed, "But the stadium's going to be overcrowded because it's such a big game, and–"

"Oh, don't worry, Daddy, we'll stay close," Emily's facial mien was now as innocent as a saint, as was Coral's.

"We'll be very close, Mr. Bryant," Coral assured him, her face so serious he almost chuckled.

"See that you do. Large crowds bring in a different element." William bit his lip to avoid laughing at the girls' bemused expressions.

The Bryants and the LeBlancs sat in the reserved seating behind the Rue team's sideline. Naomi sat beside Louise, and William stayed close to Roger Sr. to discuss the game.

"Nice seats," Roger Sr. complimented William.

"Oh, you're welcome to use them all season," William smiled. "If you're like me, you'll be at every game."

"Yep! We will."

The families met right after the kids became friends. Louise invited the Bryants over for dinner first, and they had switched houses ever since. Louise introduced Naomi to the school's mothers' clubs and the local shopping spots, including the Italian delicatessen in town. They each shared their most secret and sacred recipes. Roger Sr. sponsored William as a member of the local lodge, the Rue golf course, and the country club just outside town. The families had become close ever since the Bryants' arrival.

Rue's team was buzzing with anticipation in its final meeting, just an hour before the season opener. Since Robert Bryant's tryout and first practice, he meticulously studied the Rue football team, identifying their strengths and weaknesses in offense and defense. He had suggested several plays to Coach Wilson and Tom Hanlon, which they had incorporated into their practices leading up to that first game. As the starting quarterback, Robert would have to make numerous split-second decisions, often deviating from the planned plays. However, Fred Wilson's guidance was clear–he wanted Robert to try and stay within the framework of the plays they had practiced.

The town of Rue had a spectacular presentation for that first game at home. The parade started at the far end of Main Street and marched along the lengthy distance to the town square, where the statue of Major Rue stood near the entrance to Rue

High School. A police car with an occasional whirl of its siren and continually turning red light atop it led the parade. An Army JROTC flag bearer holding the United States flag followed. Behind him, two other Junior Reserve Officer's Training Corps cadets marched. One carried the Ohio State Flag, and the other sported the Rue High School Flag. Behind them, the mayor of Rue sat in the backseat of the first convertible with his wife. Following the mayor, Principal Hal Morgan and his wife rode in a different convertible. A female uniformed majorette led three baton twirlers ahead of the 75-piece fully attired marching band. The head varsity cheerleader, Sue Peters, sat atop the backseat with four other cheerleaders in the next convertible, each holding pom-poms. There were three other cars with tops down to accommodate more cheerleaders swinging their pom-poms and letting out cheers from their bright, smiling faces. The Rue Fire Department had one of its finest firetrucks following them. It blasted its siren while firemen clung to rails and waved to the crowd of cheering townspeople lined up on both sides of the street. Many people joined the parade at the end, while others walked to their cars to drive to the school field.

As Coach Wilson went over last-minute details, the band music and cheering grew louder as it got closer. It sent a chill down the coach's spine, but he didn't exhibit any nervousness or fear in front of the players. Rue had won two games and lost eight the prior season, a record far from impressive. However, the team's morale soared this year due to one player, Robert Bryant, who was now team captain. He had managed to instill a sense of belief in the players, convincing them they could be winners. He did it through his performance and by assisting Coach Wilson with training. Witnessing Robert's advanced intuition, Fred Wilson gave Robert liberties not given to other players. He saw something in Robert. It was leadership, and Coach went with his instinct. Now, as the band came closer, he hoped he was right.

*

Before the game began, Emily and Coral worked their way under the stands, not abiding by a word Mr. Bryant had told them. At first, they had to crawl on their hands and knees. "C'mon, Emily, I heard there's plenty to find here." Coral smiled and turned to lead the way. As the headspace increased, the two girls could squat and eventually stand and walk under the higher seating.

Emily shouted, "Look, Coral, I found a whole quarter!"

"Oh, my God! I found a dollar bill! I told you!" Coral was ecstatic.

"Here's a dime and two nickels." Emily shoved the change into the right pocket of her shorts, then squatted, looking for more.

After a while, the girls took a break to add up what they had so far. "We'll divide everything when we're finished. 50-50 partners for life!" Coral smiled at Emily, "I have two dollars and 55 cents," her beam grew wider, "And a broken wristwatch and three marbles."

"I have one dollar and 86 cents, three Canadian pennies, a cracker jack box ring, and this wind-up toy," Emily announced.

"I only have more money because I found that whole dollar. And I have a lot of pennies!" Coral said to make her friend feel better.

"I have a lot of pennies too. My shorts are going to fall down pretty soon!" Emily laughed. "What are those things that look like stretched, deflated clear balloons?"

"I don't know," Coral answered, looking disgusted, "Don't touch them, though. They look gross!"

As the girls packed their findings into their short pants, they heard sounds. Coral grabbed hold of Emily, "What's that noise?"

"I don't know. Let's go see." Emily's anxiety surfaced.

"Be careful. There might be mice. Step quietly." Coral walked on her tiptoes, balancing herself as long as she could.

The two girls walked along the line of metal support beams of the stands, following the sounds. They became clearer and

seemed like cooing, moaning, and painful cries. They saw figures about ten feet away as they passed a beam and turned down
an aisle. The little girls looked on in horror, stunned, before
running the other way as fast as they could.

"Get out of here, you kids!" a yell rang out in the quiet se-
clusion of the underbelly of the stands. It sounded like an older
girl.

"What were they doing?" asked Emily. "I saw the backside
of, I think, a football player, but he wasn't wearing any pants
at all." Emily huffed and puffed from running. "I could see his
butt cheeks moving in and out," she giggled, still out of breath.
"Two different legs were sticking straight up right behind his
rear end!"

"Yuck! How horrible seeing a man's naked butt. Was it
hairy?" Coral's face grimaced in revulsion.

"How could I tell in the bad lighting."

"Those were Sue Peters' legs!" Coral whispered loudly.
"I'd recognize her legs anywhere. She's the head cheerleader!"
Coral huffed in harmony with her friend, "But what were they
doing?"

"I don't know," Emily was scared. "Do you think he was
hurting her? She was screaming."

"I heard stories about boys doing something to girls, and
then they have to go and stay with relatives for a long time–
months!" Coral looked worried, "C'mon, let's get out of here
before they get us!" She had vivid memories of her family visiting her aunt in Cincinnati. Coral didn't want to stay there for
months; she didn't like it there. Coral grabbed Emily's hand,
and the two girls ran together until they became lost under the
stands.

"I don't know where we are," Emily began to cry.

"Neither do I," Coral was already sobbing.

The small girls walked deeper into the gloomy stands, still
holding hands and not knowing where they were. They felt better when they came upon a grown man. As the light seeping
from above the stands filled the features of his face, they could

see he was an older man, and they both felt safe and secure.

"Hi, little girls, where are you going? Are you lost?" the seemingly kind man asked.

Standing about three yards away from him, Coral answered, "Yes, sir, we can't find our way outside. Can you point the way out?"

"Why, of course, I can. But first, I want to show you both something." Coral and Emily noticed that the man looked unkempt and unshaven, and his clothes were old and beat up as he slowly unzipped his fly and exposed himself. Emily's and Coral's eyes bulged in horror as they glanced at the ugliest thing they had ever seen unravel. Emily cried in horror, but Coral ran up to him and kicked the protruding, vile-looking thing as hard as she could. Then, she took Emily by her hand, and they both trotted away as the giant of a man fell to his knees, screaming in agony.

"What was that thing he let out?" Emily asked, crying again.

"I don't know," Coral began to shed tears also.

Suddenly, the girls could hear the sounds coming from the band leading everyone to the field, and they followed it to the bright light of the outside stadium. Both of them were out of breath as Coral took Emily by her shoulders and told her, "From now on, I'll always listen to whatever your dad tells us!"

Robert's strategy was a surprise to everyone, including the Toronto team. He didn't start with long passes, as everyone expected. Instead, he gained the first 30 yards in 9 plays by handing off to Bill Patterson, his running back, or by using short passes to his receivers. This unexpected move kept the Toronto team on their toes and gave his entire team the confidence it needed.

Toronto had an excellent team for the last several years. The prior year, they won eight and lost two. They were the winning favorite by a long shot, but Robert knew the Toronto coach would have done his homework. From practices and gossip, Robert had already gained a reputation. Chats in taverns along the river also passed on the name of Robert Bryant. Small-town news spread quickly in villages and towns of the Ohio River Valley.

When Robert threw an unexpected 70-yard pass from the 30-yard line to Roger LeBlanc, who was in the end zone for a first touchdown, the Rue fan crowd went wild. Mike Carlson, the kicker, scored the extra point from the three-yard line as the fans roared even louder. Sue Peters led the cheerleaders as the Rue offense proudly left the field.

The Rue High School football team's morale was high, and their defensive players also showed this. Toronto only gained 30 yards before kicking the ball back to Rue. Robert used his quick reflexes and agility throughout the first quarter to earn two more touchdowns. By the end of that quarter, Rue was leading 21-0.

Toronto's defense began to blitz Robert to stop him in the second quarter. Robert stood fast, analyzed quickly, and threw more successful touchdown passes. Despite the rushes, Robert used them to work against the other team. He used a play he introduced in practice. Roger LeBlanc didn't go out long. He pivoted and fooled the opposing cornerback. Then, Roger ran behind the line of scrimmage. As the Toronto players came in to rush Robert, he handed the ball to Roger, who took it and ran along the left side of the field. Robert swiftly found his way through an opening between the rush. He sprinted alongside Roger down the center of the grass turf. When Roger saw Robert was clear, he made a lateral pass to Robert, who ran the field to score another touchdown.

By halftime, Rue was leading 42-3. Toronto's kicker had managed a three-point field goal in the second quarter. Sue Peters and her cheerleaders and band members put on a short halftime show. Crowds of cheering people were trying to get to Robert Bryant as he was discussing plans with his coaches. Fred Wilson had to call in a few policemen to control the interruptions. Emily and Coral sneaked by the police guards and popped their smiling faces at Robert. Before Coach Wilson could grunt at them, Robert told him, "They're my sisters, Coach—and my good luck charms!"

"Well then, I guess you best rub their heads and kiss them hard so you don't lose your luck. You're doing real good out there, son."

"Thanks, Coach," Robert grabbed the two girls, who looked like twins, and held them tightly.

"We're so proud of you, Robert!" Emily and Coral harmonized quickly.

"Thanks, I love you both!" he kissed each of their foreheads. "Now, let me go win!" he smiled as he looked at them.

Emily giggled, but Coral's heart beat faster. Robert told me he loved me, she froze in deep thought. Emily almost had to drag her away. It was Sue Peters' dancing legs that sobered her up.

"Look at Sue Peters' legs now," Emily laughed. "Remember where they were just a little while ago?"

"Yeah, we might not see her for months," Coral had another flashback to her family visit in Cincinnati.

In the third quarter, Rue was playing like a winning team. They had utterly demoralized Toronto. Everyone on the Rue seating side stood and screamed, rallying their team. Nobody wanted to miss a play by Robert Bryant. It was the most exciting time ever in Rue sport's history. William ignored his bad leg and jumped up and down alongside Roger Sr. Louise and Naomi screamed cheers to their sons. In the third, Robert faked a handoff and ran the field again for another touchdown. By the fourth quarter, Robert threw long bullet passes to Jasper Wilcox or Roger LeBlanc, whoever was clear. Motivation made both wide receivers run faster than they thought capable. Roger caught one by the tips of his fingers, and the Rue side of the stands went crazy. As the clock ticked to end the game, the final score was 84-3. The gun blasted to end the game, and Rue High School fans were uncontrollable and rushed the field to get to Robert. Before they could grab hold of him, Robert threw a blazing pass with the game ball. It landed right between Emily and Coral as they obediently sat with their parents. Robert gave a big thumbs-up signal to his girls, as they each held on to the ball tightly, sitting in shock as everyone in the stadium watched them. It was a highlight in both their lives. A group put Robert on their shoulders and carried him to one of the convertibles that would drive him and the rest of the team in a victory parade back through the town.

The always humble Robert became like a celebrity after that game. But he took it in stride and never let it change his personality. That glamor rubbed off somewhat on Coral and Emily as mutual owners of the game ball. As with all things, Emily and Coral agreed to their motto, '50-50 partners for life,' and shared that game ball. It would proudly stand exhibited at Coral's home one month, the other at Emily's in a cycle of friendship that would never end.

5

Rue, Ohio 1953-1955

Nothing thrilled the fans in the Rue, Ohio, area more than witnessing the blazing speed of Robert Bryant on the basketball court. Watching him dribble the ball as he maneuvered across the court and outsmarted his defenders with quick decisions and moves was truly astonishing. His extraordinarily sharp mind made instant calculations. Hearts raced, and cheers erupted as Robert took daring shots from well beyond the three-point line, often nearing the half-court line, his powerful arms never missing. Cries from cheerleaders reverberated off the high walls of the breathtaking gymnasium as Sue Peter's legs leaped and stretched, leading the spirited girls in their harmonious rallies. Each game was action-packed as the young man who had gained local fame on the football field dribbled the ball, shot, or passed at astonishing speed. His deft movements while passing to his teammates were mesmerizing. Fans regarded Robert and Roger as the fastest and best players, collaborating seamlessly as they had on the football field. However, Robert appeared almost superhuman, nearly as quick as a bullet, and undoubtedly the fastest and best shooter by far. Everyone on the team recognized Emily and Coral due to the special treatment Robert showed them. They affectionately termed the girls 'the twins' or 'Robert's girls' after he tossed them the game ball following their first football season win. Eventually, the teams unanimously adopted Emily and Coral as official mascots. Their bony legs peeked out of the school's eagle costumes as they gleefully flapped their wings and donned feathered crowns, delighting the spectators. That first year, Robert led the football team to the regional finals. He maintained his fitness during football season by competing in cross country. Then he switched to indoor track to stay in shape for basketball, earning medals and trophies while breaking records in those sports, just as he did in his primary categories.

Sue Peters showed her darkest colors at the homecoming dance after the season opener football game when Rue beat Toronto. It was a horrible spectacle and a demonstration of her inner wickedness. Robert and Denise danced closely under the glittering light in the decorated gymnasium; balloons of their school's colors floated overhead. Sue brewed her revenge, and a plot unfolded to get Robert as her boyfriend. She would never allow Denise to embarrass her by taking Robert when Sue wanted him all to herself. She would take Robert and then dump him like with all the boys. Sue waited patiently for her moment, staying close to the punch bowl. A junior named Billy, who had succumbed to the feminine wiles of the young lady's advanced libido, became her accomplice. He rubbed up against Sue closely and told her, "It's all set."

"Hand me the glass," she didn't make eye contact with Billy as her body leaned against the decorative cloth-covered table supporting the punch bowl.

"Am I gonna get what I want?"

"Yeah, I'll give you more of what I gave you."

"A little longer this time?"

"Yeah, Billy, you'll get whatever you want," Sue licked her lips seductively. "It's your fault it didn't last longer, you pathetic, squirmy worm," Sue chuckled after humiliating Billy.

"You really know how to hurt a guy, Sue," Billy said. "But I'm taking a big chance. If Robert Bryant finds out I'm in on this, I'm a dead man."

"He ain't gonna find out," Sue smacked her lips, noisily chewing her gum. "Will the stuff work?"

"The guy in the lab who mixed it told me it's spiked with mooter, formaldehyde, phenmet-something, and–don't worry about nothing. He said he'd be all over you like a lion. All you gotta do is lose the other broad–get rid of her."

"Don't tell me what to do. Everything's planned. Don't worry."

"Sue, I'm only worried about getting what you owe me. So, remember our deal," Billy smiled. "Here's the glass," he passed the spiked punch to Sue.

The bottom corner of the tablecloth lifted, and out from under the punch table peeked the faces of Coral LeBlanc and Emily Bryant.

"What are we going to do," Emily asked Coral in a shaky voice.

"They're giving Robert something to drink." Coral's eyes widened with worry. "I don't understand what it's gonna do, though."

"What can we do?"

"We have to stop them!" Coral said, pulling herself from under the table. C'mon!" She helped Emily out.

"There's a phone call for you, Denise." Mrs. Williams, one of the chaperones, stepped between her and Robert, handing Denise a note.

"From who?" a surprised Denise asked.

"I don't know. A student from the upstairs office handed it to me."

"Oh, Robert, I better go upstairs and see what happened."

"Do you want me to come with you?"

"Oh, no, I'll be right back and let you know if it's anything important."

"I'll wait by the punch bowl."

As Robert reached the table, Sue reached out a glass and asked Robert, "Join me in a toast to a great game?"

"Sure."

Coral and Emily reached the opposite side of the gym, searching for Robert. Coral spotted him first. "Robert!" she yelled. "Robert, don't drink that!" Coral screamed as loud as she could. Her young, squeaky voice was too weak to travel over the crowded and noisy floor.

Emily caught up to Coral as they watched Robert swallow the punch in one gulp. "Oh, no! It's too late, Coral," Emily said as she stood beside her friend, both worrying.

Sue immediately spotted the young girls and whispered to a chaperone, "Those kids are crashing the dance. They're underage."

"C'mon, kids, let's go!" the burly man grabbed Coral and Emily by their shoulders, but they struggled to get loose. "You can't be inside here. Let's go!" He led them to the door. "Do you want me to call your parents?"

"No. We'll go," Emily said. Coral stuck her tongue at Sue Peters when she saw Sue smile while escorted out the door with Emily.

Robert's head began spinning. He looked white and appeared to be groggy. Sue intervened, "Robert, let me help you to your car. Come, you best rest for a while. You don't look too good." She grabbed Robert's hand and led him to his father's Cadillac parked in the lot. Sue pushed Robert inside the large back seating area and immediately got to work. Within seconds, Robert saw delusions of wickedness, and the eyes of the enchantress glowed bright red. He felt as if he was fighting a serpent as Sue's naked body slithered around him, doing licentious things to him. Sue laughed like a demon as she licked and touched Robert as if she owned him, a vessel of her desires. She was doing things to the unwilling young man he had only read about as her soft flesh worked magic on him. Robert always had a keen fascination for learning as much as possible about everything. Although love was a concept he couldn't comprehend, human sexuality captivated his intellect from a scientific perspective. He read books on the subject. The complexity of female sexuality was intriguing, causing him to study the many trigger points of feminine arousal. Robert practiced some of what he learned with Denise. Though never taking her virginity, he brought her to a level of pleasure she had never before even imagined, begging Robert for more. But now, in this corrupted delusionary state, he performed things far surpassing anything he did with Denise, pleasuring many more sensitive parts of this alluring creature seducing him. Robert fought back the unholy control, trying to restrain the stupor that besieged him. But Sue's nude, sweaty body slipped through each of his holds until he felt an ecstasy like never before, and he roared from that pleasure as Sue's evil laugh screamed to a higher pitch. Robert tried to escape the sorceress and opened the back door, his naked body falling at the feet of Denise Beck. Denise screamed in shock and horror and ran back toward the gym, seeing Robert's sister, Emily, and her friend, Coral, trotting toward her.

"No, girls, go back! There's nothing to see here!" Denise took the girls by their hands and led them away.

"Robert?" Coral softly asked as she maneuvered her small, thin body into Robert's room as he lay thinking.

Robert lifted his head and saw Coral standing at the doorway to his bedroom. One of the windows cast its tints of yellowish-orange afternoon light on Coral's face from her side, forming a diffused vision of the little girl. Under that pastel luminance, she looked older and appeared like a young woman speaking to him. "Not now, honey," Robert labored a smile. "I have some things on my mind."

"O, Robert, but I must speak to you." That face, which seemed wiser in the haze of the hallway's illumination, seemed upset. "It's very important that I do." For a split second, Robert wondered what Coral would look like when she became a young lady.

Robert could never resist Coral's demeanor whenever she asked him for something. He didn't understand why but knew it ran deep. "Okay, c'mon in."

Emily and Coral had been debating all morning about which one should tell Robert what they knew about the night before. They realized it had to be only one of them, as it would be more embarrassing for him if they spoke to Robert together. Emily and Coral even talked about going to his parents about it, but certain Robert wouldn't want that. Neither wanted to be the one who broke his heart, so they flipped a coin, and Coral lost. Tears shed from her eyes because Coral felt Robert would hate her for being the bearer of this news.

"Thank you, Robert." Coral stepped slowly, almost ceremoniously, into Robert's bedroom. Thoughts flooded her mind, some of them absurd. Coral recalled the dirty old man who had exposed that ugly thing and felt relieved that Denise had kept her and Emily from seeing Robert naked. She didn't want to know if he had something as hideous as that old guy under the stadium seats. Then, she quickly pushed that thought aside as she settled onto the edge of Robert's bed, wiggling closer to him. Coral took a moment to collect her thoughts and began to explain to Robert how she and Emily had been under the table where the punch bowl was. She recounted every word of what she and Emily had heard–every part of Sue Peters's scheme. She even remembered some of the names of the ingredients in the mixed brew but didn't pronounce them correctly.

Robert quickly grasped what Sue had given him in that punch drink, and now he fully comprehended what had happened. His face relaxed, and he smiled faintly as if a light had turned on in his mind.

Coral perked up, "You see, Robert. You're innocent," she smiled broadly. Then, watching Robert's expression change to one of despair, asked, "What, Robert? It's Sue's fault, not yours." Coral and Emily didn't understand what had happened in the car. They only knew Sue had caused it, and it wasn't good.

"Remember when I took you and Emily to the movie Abbott and Costello Meet Frankenstein?"

"Oh, yeah. I'll never forget it; It was so funny!" Coral smiled widely, remembering.

"Remember the nice guy who turned into the Wolfman? Even though it wasn't his fault he became a monster, everyone feared him, and he dived to his death, taking Dracula with him."

"That's not the same thing, Robert. Nobody fears you. When they find out what Sue did, they'll hate her!"

"They'll believe what they choose. My true friends, like you," Robert smiled at Coral, "won't believe Sue. The others will believe what they want. Why should I have to defend myself?" Robert spoke to Coral as if she was an adult like he always did, especially now with the window casting its colored tint, making the little girl look older.

"No! I hate Sue, and so does Emily. Even Roger does! He told Emily he wanted to strangle her. And so do I!" Coral's facial features contorted with anger.

Robert rolled over on his bed and slid to sit next to Coral. He wiped away two remaining tears from her big, deep blue eyes with his forefinger. Then he said, "Don't ever hate anyone, Coral. You're too beautiful for that." Robert smiled at her, looking directly into her big, beautiful, dark blue eyes. "Do you understand the difference?"

"No. I'm not beautiful. I'm just an ugly little girl," Coral glanced up and looked at Robert. "I know you tell me nice things to make me feel good, but I know what I am."

"Sue is the ugly one, sweetheart, not you. You only have to look to see that. You're the beautiful one."

Coral put her head on Robert's lap and spoke, her voice muffled. "I wish there were some way I could help you, Robert. I love you so much, but I don't know what to do."

"I know, honey, I love you too," Robert said, stroking her long, light blonde hair.

Sue Peters pretended she lost her virginity to Robert's demand and, by spreading such gossip, thus became the martyr in the homecoming dance scenario. She played the role well and manipulated the minds of students to believe Robert had taken advantage of her and that she was the violated victim. The truth was that most of the football team had been with Sue since she was still a freshman in high school. Sue made the rounds not only at Rue High School but also at rival schools.

However, the rumors Sue implanted into the students' minds in her manipulative way escalated and made Robert appear like a Cassanova, an unjust term he dreaded. It came to a boiling point when, after a basketball game in the locker room, a team member, Tim Robertson, kiddingly told Robert, "Hey Bob, save some of Sue for the rest of us. She's got plenty to go around." Robert's arm moved like lightning, and in the blink of an eye, his hand grasped Tim by his throat. Robert's eyes were bulging and reddened in anger. It was the first time anyone saw Robert's fury unfold; it was terrifying.

His best friend Roger intervened softly, "It's okay, Bob. It's okay." Roger gently put his hand on Robert's grip. Robert loosened his hold on Tim's neck and backed away. Tim stood gasping, trying to catch his breath.

"I'm sorry," Robert said embarrassed. "I don't know what happened to me. I'm so sorry, Tim. Are you all right?"

Tim coughed and finally caught his breath, "Yeah," his voice was hoarse, "I'm okay. No problem." Then he forced a chuckle and said, "If we ever get in a brawl with another team, I'm standing behind you, Bob." Tim looked up and smiled.

"Ah, Tim, I'm really sorry. I didn't mean it," Robert repeated. He had never lost his cool before, but the pressure of the situation had been building inside him.

"I should have kept my big mouth shut," Tim's voice was back to normal.

"No, it's my fault. The first five beers are on me!" Robert offered.

"I can go along with that," Tim said. "Can I get another five if I let you grab me again?"

Robert finally smiled. "No!" he chuckled.

"It's that Sue Peter's fault. Now she's got us fighting amongst ourselves!" roared Roger.

"Yeah to that!" bellowed Jasper.

"From now on, we all stay away from her, I say! Spread the word!" Bill yelled.

"You said it!" Stan hollered, "She's poison," and the rest of the team yelled in agreement.

*

Emily sat on a padded wooden armchair across from her brother at the round wooden planked table. A broad umbrella, propped in a hole at the center of the rustic outdoor table, shielded them from the sun, intense as it always is when it first begins to set. William and Naomi went to a friend's home for dinner that evening. Robert volunteered to take his sister out for a burger at Chuckwagon Burgers, a popular hamburger place in town. Emily was in her glory as that restaurant was a popular teen hotspot, and everyone would see her with her popular brother.

"So, Sis, how's everything going in school?" Robert smiled at Emily before a waitress came to take their orders.

"Good. I passed all my finals and think my report card average will be in the high 90s." Emily grinned.

"That's great! I'm so proud of you!"

"Oh! And my bowling team is going to be in the championships!"

"Wow!"

"It's really thanks to you, big bro," Emily grinned, "You know, from all that extra help you gave me."

"Oh, no! You earned that yourself. You've got the natural talent," Robert smiled. "I only showed you a couple of pointers." Emily loved to hear praises from her big brother, even more than from her parents. She felt all parents are obligated to do so, but not older brothers and sisters. Her friends seldom received compliments from their older siblings. Emily felt special because Robert always gave her attention and helped her. And especially that he was 'cool' and popular.

"Coral and I want to be cheerleaders when we're in high school, so we decided to begin practicing to be ready." Then she blushed, realizing the connection between cheerleading and Sue Peters. She didn't want to resurrect bad feelings for her brother.

Robert ignored the correlation and said, "You still have a little ways to go. You're just beginning junior high school in the fall."

"Well, we thought if we practice now, by that time, we'll be pros," Emily giggled.

A young waitress appeared on rollerskates. "Hi!" she said. Looking closely at Robert, she asked, "Are you Robert Bryant?"

Robert cringed, thinking it would be a comment about Sue Peters. "Yes," he answered.

The waitress blushed as she rolled a little forward. "I thought so, but I never get to see you up close. I usually have to sit high in the stands, and I'm a year behind you, so we don't have classes together. It's so nice to meet you."

"It's very nice to meet you," Robert greeted, and the young girl blushed a little more. "Next time before a game, run over to me, and I'll get you better seats," Robert told her, offering a wide grin.

"Oh, gosh, thanks!" she blushed an even brighter shade of red before taking their orders and skating away.

"You're quite the celebrity, Robert." Emily was a bit jealous but proud of her big brother's local fame.

"Is that right, co-owner of my first football win's game ball?"

The evening drifted on as Robert and Emily feasted on their fries, burgers, fried onion rings, and malted milks. Their brother-sister conversations were always deep and enjoyable for them both. Whenever Emily spoke intimately with her big brother, it resurrected good feelings from deep within her and her security with her brother since she could remember.

"Can you go for a sundae?" Robert asked as they chatted after finishing their meals.

"Oh, I'm so full!" Then, Emily looked devilish and asked, "Want to split one?"

"You got it, kiddo!"

They enjoyed the dessert of vanilla ice cream, rich chocolate syrup dripping down the sides, and covered with mixed-nut shavings and a cherry on top. They spoke about serious and trivial things as time stood still in those magic moments. Robert noticed Emily was of an age to use proper table manners but still young enough to sport a vanilla ice cream mustache. Robert loved his little sister and cherished the special time they shared.

"Robert?"

"Yes, my lady?" he smiled, addressing Emily nobly as he always humored her.

"Promise that everything will always stay the same between us," she revealed an expression of sincere maturity for such an adolescent girl. "And that we'll always do things like this together," her eyes widened and focused on those of her brother.

Emily's words moved Robert, and he responded with deep emotion. He spoke softly, answering slowly and affectionately, "I promise I'll always be there for you, no matter where we end up or what we do." Then, smiling at his little sister, he added, "Now, come on, I'm taking you to the penny arcade."

"Oh wow!" Emily hopped off her chair and was ready. That evening became a precious memory for the brother and sister, and one Emily would log in her diary. Going to junior high, the thought of Robert going away to college was a million miles away in Emily's mind that night.

"Hi, Dad."

"Robert," William turned in surprise, "Oh, you're home. I didn't see you when I came In."

"I was upstairs in the library reading. Did you have a good day?"

"Yeah," William said, waving his hand back and forth to indicate he'd had a decent day. "But I'm glad to be home," he added with a chuckle. "How was yours?"

"So-so," Robert answered. "You have time to talk, Dad?"

"Of course, Son," he looked around. "Let's go sit in the parlor," he motioned to Emily and Coral lying on the carpet watching the television, "it's quieter in there." Robert smiled and followed his dad. Robert always talked with his father and kept him abreast of everything going on in his life. He never wanted William to hear anything about him from a third party. Especially now, he wanted to be the one to tell his father about the Sue Peters incident, as embarrassing as it would be. Sitting in a cushioned chair, Robert dived into the story–the truth.

Not too many things surprised William after being a combat soldier. He had witnessed men as primal beings. He saw grown men often crying, soiling themselves, and soldiers shooting and stabbing themselves to get out of combat duty. He had seen fear in his men, and he also bore witness to their savagery with the inhumane atrocities they committed and their other violent sins against God. But, when he heard about his son's ordeal, William struggled with his emotions, forcing him to rise from where he was sitting.

Robert stood when he saw his father rise and begin to walk the few steps toward him. William embraced his son and softly said, "Sorry you had to go through this, Son. It isn't fair."

Robert quietly sobbed, "I just want you to know I'm telling you the truth, Dad. All the things everyone's spreading aren't true."

William slowly pushed his son back to arm's length. "Oh, Robert, of course, I believe you," he said. William bowed his head. "This is the real world, Robert, and I can't protect you from it." He knew his son was suffering from this injustice, just as he would be. "Son, the world can be beautiful," he paused, thinking, "or it can be a horrible place. But I'm so sorry you had to experience something like this at such a young age. This Sue Peters seems like a piece of work for her age." William shook his head in disgust.

"I just didn't want to date Sue. She's not a good person, and I liked Denise."

"Robert, I want you to know I'll help you with this in any way I can. We'll go through it together. You can talk to me whenever you want: at my office, at home, or even if I'm in a meeting. You tell my secretary to interrupt me to take your call.

"Dad, I would never–"

"I want you to! Tell me how you want to handle this and

if there's anything I can do right now." William forced a hint of a smile and said, "Robert, I'm proud of you for coming to me with this and for how maturely you've handled this so far. You're a tough young man."

"Well, Dad, I know Mom has to know, but I'd like her to know just what's necessary and that I didn't do anything wrong." Robert didn't mention anything about Emily and Coral's knowledge of the incident, as he promised he would, as long as they didn't do anything about it alone.

"Son, I'm sure your mother doesn't need any convincing regarding your credibility."

The war had exhausted William of any feelings of retaliation or vengeance; his heart no longer possessed such methods of reprisal. A man as powerful as William could have eradicated a person like Sue Peters from the face of the earth or had her sent to Alaska by a simple phone call. However, the war had relieved him of all hatred. What William mostly appreciated about his son's response and why he was so proud of him was that Robert never even possessed one speck of a feeling for revenge toward Sue. That's what gratified him the most. His son's only concern was that he and his mother believed him.

By sabotaging Robert's relationship with Denise Beck, Sue hoped he would give in to the pressure and start dating her. Sue didn't love Robert and was aware that he didn't even like her. What Robert told little Coral was true. Even in her innocent prepubescent state, Coral possessed the beauty of a woman within her. Yet, inside Sue, there was a darkness that wouldn't allow for love. Robert's acquired knowledge, combined with his physique and stamina, made him an incredible lover, almost like a machine. Sue craved that and longed to possess him. Her overwhelming desires needed him, and Robert's innocence or guilt meant nothing to her. Robert intentionally held onto that guilt because he found Sue to be a repugnant person, and he refused to engage with her on her level. He allowed Sue her victimhood but vowed never to find himself in a similar situation again. Robert decided to give up dating for the remainder of high school. Instead, he devoted his time to sports and excelled in baseball that spring.

Like football and basketball, baseball came naturally. Robert's sophisticated combination of timing and coordination allowed complete focus on the ball. It was all about the ball, and his predicted calculations allowed an incredible batting average in his first season. His pitching was just as impressive. It was rare to find a major league pitcher, let alone a high school player, who could pitch a perfect game. And yet, Robert had pitched two by midseason.

Robert Bryant's name still drew crowds for all sports in every season. People filled the stadium at Rue High School; coming from near and far, they wanted to see Robert play. Emily and Coral remained dedicated mascots, cheering for their brothers while wearing those funny costumes. They clapped and cheered enthusiastically, even out of that school-colored ensemble. Coral and Emily attended every game, as did their parents. The crowd continued to adore Robert, roaring for him whenever he played. The incident with Sue had faded into a distant memory.

Robert spotted Coral sitting alone in a stadium row after a game, wearing her mascot outfit, her skinny legs exposed, sticking straight, and stretched out from her seat. She looked upset, so Robert walked over to her. He noticed some younger boys nearby before he got close enough to say anything. When they saw Robert, they scattered, so Robert assumed they were teasing his little friend, and he had a curious reaction. They weren't precisely feelings of defensiveness that rushed through him, but more of a possessive nature. In that split second, he felt on the same level as those younger boys and as if they had insulted his girlfriend. Robert quickly snapped back to reality and walked closer.

"Hey, kiddo!" Coral jumped back a bit from surprise.

"Hi Robert," Coral forced a smile. She always did for her Robert.

"Why the monkeyface?" Then he noticed a few tears run down Coral's cheek. He sat down close to her and put his arm around her shoulder. He wiped her tears with one of his fingers.

Coral tilted her long neck to look at Robert and sarcastically asked, "Why did you call me a monkeyface? Is it because I'm ugly like those kids called me?"

"Oh, no, sweetheart, on the contrary. I didn't call you a monkeyface. I said it because even though you were sulking, you still looked as cute as a little monkeyface."

"But, Robert, I want to be beautiful for you," her eyes engaged his lovingly.

"I already said you are. You simply don't want to see it yet. Until you see how beautiful you are, can I call you monkeyface, only in private, to express my endearment to you?" Robert smiled broadly. Coral looked confused. One of the many things that attracted Coral to him was that Robert often spoke eloquently to her, almost like a poet, so Robert explained what a term of endearment was.

Coral snuggled close to Robert and told him, "Okay, it's a deal." She put her tiny hand in his large one, and they shook on it like when they always struck a deal.

"Okay. From now on, monkeyface will be my affectionate name for you, but only when we're alone.

Coral enjoyed hearing him say it to her because she interrupted endearment to mean Robert cherished her.

"By the way, those boys liked you. That's the way young boys act when they like a girl."

"Really?"

"Yep! Where's Emily?"

"She had a meeting with Mrs. Funk." As she explained, Robert saw his sister walking toward them, wearing that ridiculous outfit and holding her feathered headpiece in her arm.

The summer sun beat down fiercely on Robert as he broke the stillness of the pool. His athletic sculpted chest spread wide as he supported Coral and Emily on each of his shoulders. The two girls laughed and screamed, struggling against Robert's grip as he carried them to the deeper part of the cool water. He chuckled after releasing them as they doggie-paddled beside him, wiping their faces and eyes while enjoying the refreshing water with laughter.

"I'll pay five bucks to see that again!" yelled Roger LeBlanc Sr. as he lounged comfortably in a padded pool chair on the Bryant patio. The families often came together during the summer to enjoy the pool and the surrounding patio and terraces, which overlooked the descending levels of greenery behind the Bryant Mansion.

"Daddy!" Coral laughed uncontrollably, exposing her silver braces, glittering in the bright sun. "You're supposed to be on my side!" Coral now side-stroked, kicking her feet and wiping her soaked, light blonde hair away from her eyes and face with the fingers and palm of the hand of her other arm. Emily swam toward Coral, and they held hands while treading water together and staying afloat. As they did, Roger Jr. did a cannonball jump right next to them.

"Time to get out now, girls," Louise shouted. "Food's almost ready, and you have to wait a while before eating after being in the water." William worked the grill while Louise helped Naomi prepare the salads and other foods. Roger Sr. was the unofficial lifeguard and was in charge of watching the children.

Isabella stood up from her cushioned chair next to her husband to help organize everything. The Bryants included Carlo and Isabella Russo in most family gatherings, especially poolside barbecues with the LeBlancs. They regarded the Russos as family.

Emily and Coral sat wearing their fluffy, one-piece, colorful bathing suits, taking turns putting sun cream lotion on each other's backs. The two girls couldn't help but notice the bikini swimsuits that Robert and Roger wore that day. Their fathers didn't wear that style of swimsuit. Ever since that episode under the stands with the man who exposed himself before them, they became attentive to that curious area of men. They even rented art books from the library to learn about the anatomy of men. They didn't find additional information about that male organ, such as purpose or functionality. However, they learned some things from the girl's high school bathroom at the gymnasium after the football team raided it and left behind graphic drawings.

"Why do they have them, do you think?" a curious Emily asked her friend as they whispered at the poolside, discussing all the library pictures they had seen.

"I don't know. Maybe men pee more than women."

"I never saw Robert's. Did you ever see Roger's? Emily asked.

"See what?"

"You know," Emily glanced around to ensure no one overheard, "his thing. Like in the pictures."

"No!" Coral blushed. "How would I ever see it?" Coral thought and looked around before whispering, "But I felt Roberts," Coral blushed as red as a pimento. "When he picked me up once," she looked around again, "he was facing me." Coral giggled.

"You did?" Emily's eyes bulged. "What did it feel like?"

"I don't know," I guess like rubber." The two wide-eyed girls stared at each other until they laughed hysterically. Just then, Robert and Roger walked up to them, their bikinis fit tight from lying in the sun.

"What are you girls laughing at?" Roger asked. Emily's and Coral's faces were level with their brothers' waists as they sat directly before the two older boys. Both girls turned as red as beets.

"Both of you are getting sunburned. Better put cream on yourselves," Robert shook his head, thinking the blushing girls were red from sunburn. Robert was nearer to Coral, so he stepped closer to her to touch her reddened skin. Coral jumped back, terrified 'it' would touch her. "If it hurts, you better put cream on it, honey, right away." Emily had to hold her mouth to stop herself from screaming in laughter. Coral just glared at her.

There were several lakes Robert and Roger frequented in the summer, sometimes with their friends, other times alone to talk privately. Robert and Roger became closer during their high school years together. They both hung out with the guys at least a few times a week when the young ladies had other things to do. They would work on cars together in the afternoons and sometimes go fishing on small boats in lakes or along the Ohio River. Sometimes, they fished with the other guys in the early morning hours. During many summer evenings, they made small bonfires on the sandy shore of one of the larger lakes, and groups of girls and guys gathered there from different towns. They roasted their catches of fish and frog legs on the open fire. Local girls loved Robert for his sports celebrity status, his looks and build, and because he was a nice guy. Many of them constantly flirted with him, and he was always friendly and witty in return. He could be the life of the party often, but he wouldn't date any of them after what Sue did to him. Most of the high school girls knew what Sue did and how Robert acted because of it. That angered them, turning most of them against Sue Peters.

Skating was popular in the winter months. Usually, before dances or other school social activities, when in groups, the boys often talked about everyday things such as sports and cars and girls. But when the two buddies, Robert and Roger, spoke alone, they had serious discussions about their futures, apprehensions, and life challenges. Roger and Robert shared personal information and secrets and kept them confidential. The two young men had formed a deep friendship, would confide in each other, and knew they would always remain friends no matter where they went to college or what they did in life.

It was a typical bright summer day when Robert and Roger decided to take their sisters out for the afternoon. Some of Robert's kindness toward his kid sister, Emily, was rubbing off on Roger, as was his patience in dealing with the juvenile ways of the younger girl. It was that point, as in every young man's life, when the realization of leaving home sank in. Going away to college, meeting new people, and eventually marrying were just around the corner. Roger wanted to have some quality time with his sister, Coral.

Coral and Emily were absolutely thrilled to be seen with their older, popular brothers at Guilford Lake. In her imaginative mind, Coral pictured herself on a date with Robert.

As Roger sat up facing the water, he had difficulty concentrating on his sister with all the pretty girls dressed in bikinis along the crowded beach. Coral noticed her brother eyeing the girls and reminded him, "You are going steady with Lori Brown, Roge."

"Yep," Roger answered in a daze. Coral just sighed, knowing her brother's mind was miles away.

Emily and Coral sat, wearing cheap plastic sunglasses to shield them from the bright sun, pretending to be older and more sophisticated young ladies. Both girls thought how worldly they looked in shades. Roger faded off into one of those sleep-like trances being on any sunlit beach induces.

"Want to go in for a swim?" Emily asked Coral.

"No, I'm going to sit for a while," Coral answered as Emily trotted to the shoreline. Truthfully, Coral wanted to be alone with Robert.

"Want some lotion on your back?" Coral asked Robert as he lay on his stomach.

"Sounds good, monkeyface." And Coral got to work. She sat, her legs spread around the small of Robert's back as if riding a horse, just like she always did, her body stretched forward and back, rubbing cream onto his shoulders and upper back.

"Now, you're not going to get up quickly and trick me, are you, Robert?" Coral chuckled. Sometimes, Robert would abruptly rise when Coral sat like that, rubbing cream on him. He'd grab Coral's legs while holding them tightly and run around with her piggyback style, Coral laughing and screaming the whole time. He did the same thing to Emily, always when the girls least expected it.

"Not today. I promise. Oh, that feels good, monkeyface," Robert said as he felt Coral's dainty, little hands spread on the cool, refreshing cream and rubbed it in.

Coral giggled to Robert's sounds of pleasure as she labored, massaging the suntan cream on Robert's back. Then, for the first time, she noticed how hardened and firm Robert's muscled body was compared to Emily's. She always rubbed cream on Robert's back but never before noticed how different his body felt. Coral always knew Robert was strong because he was big and always picked her up and carried her and Emily together, but this was different. Coral's little hands worked the cream into Robert's flesh, kneading it, listening to Robert's soft cries of satisfaction, her lower body rubbing his to the motion. Suddenly, Coral realized she was enjoying touching Robert. It was weird and different from anything she had ever felt, and oddly, it exhilarated her. Coral moved her hands to Robert's well-built shoulders, rubbing the hardened muscles there, slowly reaching the upper part of his sturdy, solid arms down to his wrists. Coral's heart was racing, and she couldn't understand why. Her tiny hands feverishly rubbed the suntan lotion, feeling the same peculiar but euphoric reaction in her private fantasy.

"The cream is nice and refreshing, monkeyface, especially under the hot sun." Robert's voice startled Coral, snapping her out of her daydream. She slowed her movements, savoring the new sensation that touching him gave her for the first time, yet still unsure why.

Feeling Coral's hands now moving slowing and thinking her weak, skinny arms had done enough, Robert suddenly rolled over. Coral remained on top of him and almost screamed when she felt something unusual and realized what she was sitting on. Blushing, Coral quickly rolled off Robert as he said, "Let me put some on you before you get burned. Your face is already red from the sun."

Unable to find her voice, Coral finally chirped, "Okay." Her face now flushed even more from embarrassment.

Now, Coral lay on her stomach, feeling Robert's strong hands as if for the first time, still not comprehending why his touch now gave her such an odd but enjoyably stimulating feeling. Robert lowered her top slightly to rub cream thoroughly on her shoulders, Coral quivering with each stroke of Robert's hard but gentle hands. It felt like a lifetime to her. Robert's large hands completely encircled Coral's skinny leg from top to bottom, with plenty of room to spare. She moaned, "Oh, my God, that feels so good," Robert's hard hands on her soft flesh gave her an intoxicating sensation she had never before had. Coral was embarrassed that she complimented how she felt out loud. Anything that brought her this new kind of feeling wasn't normal. Coral thought she might be coming down with something or already be ill. Remembering having the flu and how her body had sensations came to mind. But they were terrible aches and completely different. These new sensations felt incredibly wonderful. Maybe she was delirious from a sun fever, which caused those funny feelings, and it wasn't from Robert's hands after all. That was it. How silly she had been. Coral felt her forehead and whispered, "I have sun fever. How stupid of me to think Robert had anything to do with how I felt."

Robert picked up Coral and held her in his arms. "C'mon, monkeyface. Let's go for a swim with Emily." He carried her to the shoreline and searched for his sister. "There she is!" Emily waved from the crowd in the lake, away from the beach. Robert set Coral down in the water next to Emily. Coral felt like a prima donna but knew she could never share the sensations her mind created with Emily, naively thinking it was sunstroke.

Robert walked along the marble floor of a quiet corridor in the old city hospital amid nurses and doctors administering to their patients, hushed sounds of sliding curtains, rolling food trays, and the gentle rattle of utensils surrounding him. A newer wing was still under construction, some parts already open and boasting the latest diagnostic, surgical, and other technological medical services. It was another charitable donation given anonymously by his father, William. However, Robert was looking for Susan Peters's room number in the damp, older, original hospital, which was now a drab and dreary site. He asked a counter nurse, "Can you tell me where Susan Peters's room is?"

The older nurse glanced at the young man over the half-framed eyeglasses placed midway down her long, thin nose; her white-peaked nurse's cap tilted slightly to the side atop her head's salt and pepper-colored hair. After sternly sizing up Robert from top to bottom, she grimly answered, "Just around the corner to your right," pointing one of her long, bony forefingers to direct him.

"Thank you, ma'am," Robert replied politely with a broad smile. As he neared the doorway to the room, he paused, filled with dread about what he was about to witness. He remembered his friends' stories about what had happened to Sue.

"Yeah, Sue was hanging around at Bosco's, you know, the place in East Liverpool where all the college crowd hangs out," Robert's friend, Stan, explained to him. Robert, Roger, and a handful of other friends were downriver at Jim's Tavern, their favorite bar, amongst a crowd of guys talking about Sue Peters.

"Is that the place at the diamond?" Roger asked.

"No. It's blocks past the diamond, down by the river," Jasper interjected.

"That's a wild bunch that hangs around there, isn't it?" Robert asked. "That's not a college crowd, is it?"

"Stan's got it wrong as usual," Bill laughed. "It's where those bikers and other riff-raff hang out–a bad crowd. Sue met her match, I guess," Bill said before swallowing the remaining beer in his glass and raising it to Charlie, one of the bartenders, signaling he wanted another.

"I guess Sue already did everyone in the local high schools," laughed Joey, a junior who just made varsity football. Robert glared at him, and Joey shut up and took a gulp of his beer. He had heard how Robert went off on Tim for talking about Sue.

"Not right what happened to her. Nobody deserves that," Jasper sympathized.

"What exactly happened to her?" Robert asked. He and Roger hadn't heard the news.

"Well, Sue was being herself. You know, flaunting herself to the men there. Making their girlfriends jealous."

"Hell, not the place for that, for sure. Even the women that hang out there are tough."

"And ugly, too!" Pete raised his glass of beer.

"So what happened?" Roger asked.

"Well, two gigantic guys were going to have sex with her! One held her down on the pool table. Sue laughed and egged the other big guy on until the women started beating on the men."

"To help Sue?"

"No! Because they were jealous."

"Wow!" Roger said as Robert stood listening.

"Then, the women began beating on Sue really badly."

"The women?"

"Yeah, for trying to take their men. The women broke up chairs and beat her with heavy wooden pieces, pool sticks, bar stools, and–"

"I heard one of the sweet ladies put the pool balls in a sack and beat Sue with them, over and over. Then, when the men tried to stop those big girls, a fight broke out between the women and men, but those big girls kept beating on poor Sue. They really messed her up. It became a free-for-all bar room brawl."

"Where were the police?" Robert asked.

"Police don't like to go to that place."

"Can you blame them?" Jasper asked.

"A lot of cops arrived amid all that chaos, but by the time they got there, Sue was unconscious, lying outside without any clothes. Those big women just tossed her out like trash."

"She's in really bad shape, Bob." Robert just stood in a daze. He couldn't believe what he was hearing.

"Let's go outside for some air, Bob," Roger led his best

friend outside.

The two friends stood alone. The river flowed below the train tracks across State Route 7, a small road that followed the river's bends, connecting towns. "Geeze, Roge, she didn't deserve that."

"I know, buddy, I know."

"She asked to see you, Bob," a short, small-framed girl named Betty told Robert. She met Robert at one of the pit-fire gatherings at the lake shortly after Robert heard the news about Sue Peters. Robert recognized Betty from school; she was one of Sue's last remaining friends.

"Why'd she ask for me?" Robert stood bewildered

"I don't know, Bob. I didn't talk to Sue. I honestly can't bear to bring myself to the hospital after hearing how badly she looks," Betty glanced down ashamedly. "Sue's mother called me and told me she keeps asking to see you," Betty looked into Robert's kind, dark blue eyes. "Will you go?"

Robert stood, wondering and shaking his head back and forth; curious and bizarre thoughts, some vengeful, clashed with rational ones as his intellect fought his emotions and reached his soul. He was already a victim. Was he stepping into another trap? The kindness of his very essence became the winner of that battle, and he answered, "Yeah, I'll go."

As Robert entered the room, a hospital bed was visible by the far window. A doctor and a nurse were changing a glass IV drip suspended from a high metal stand, and it obscured Sue's body. Robert waited for them to finish their work. As the two figures separated, Sue became visible. It was a horrid sight. Robert's body trembled from the shock of it. His legs shook, but he stood firm, tall, as he glanced at the mutilated face of the young lady who was once the envy of every female student at Rue High School. Sue's entire head had enlarged, and she had no face. Most of her hair was gone, shaven in spots, cut short, some pulled out from the beating. What remained in place of a face appeared as if a million bees stung her, each leaving a re-pulsive wound festering and accumulating to a hideous swollen batter of mutilated flesh. Only the center of one eye peeked out from under the repulsive mask; the other was gone, probably kicked out of its socket. Sue had no nose, but the stitches where her face had been, so many of them, made her appear ghoulish, like Frankenstein.

Robert crept slowly toward a pungent odor of rot, body waste, and medicine, which made the young man gag. Sue had a body cast encompassing her shoulders, arms, chest, and torso, and her legs hung suspended by pulleys, each in an entire cast. When Sue's remaining eye viewed Robert, a tear bled through that deformed eye socket.

Sue struggled to speak through her hidden lips; her voice strained from her throat due to her missing teeth and wired jaw. Her muffled, broken voice faintly whispered, "Ro... bert."

Robert tried to speak, but his throat choked. He nodded, and after a full minute, he whispered, "Hi, Sue."

Another small tear rolled from that vile eye socket, and Sue spoke slowly and softly, "I called you, Robert... because... I want to tell you... how sorry I am... for what I did... to you." Her words broke up as she mumbled. A nurse placed a glass of water close to Sue, then put a bent straw into the hole that was now Sue's mouth. Robert noticed a bloodied red-colored piece of flesh that was her tongue lick the fluid, and Sue gently swal-lowed and resumed speaking. "I know I might meet God soon... and want to ask... you to for... give me... please."

Robert fought to hold back his tears and stood motionless. "I forgive you, Sue," he answered, his voice unsteady.

"Thank... you, Robert. I wanted you... so badly be... cause... you're such a nice guy. I never dated ... anyone nice like you."

"I'll come back to see you. You rest now."

"No... Robert... I don't... want you... to see me like... this anymore... please understand."

Robert could see Sue straining to talk and nodded in agree-ment, "Okay, bye, Sue."

"Bye... Robert."

Among his friends, Robert only talked about the sickening experience he had with Sue at the hospital when he was alone with Roger during one of their buddy chats. He asked him to keep it confidential, and he knew Roger would. Robert waited before telling his father, needing time for his mind to process everything. William had noticed his son was unusually distressed and invited him to go fishing together.

"Now, here are your lunches," Naomi said, handing her husband a satchel. Inside are two thermoses: one for coffee and one for hot chocolate."

"Thanks, Mom," Robert bent down and kissed Naomi's cheek, then grabbed the fishing rods. William put his arms around his wife and kissed her goodbye.

Naomi whispered in William's ear, "I think it has to do with what we learned about Sue Peters, dear."

"I'll take care of everything, dear. Don't you worry." He gently poked the tip of Naomi's nose.

"I needed this, son," William said as he sat comfortably on his portable folding fishing chair at his and Robert's special fishing spot. "Fresh air, sunshine, it's worth a million dollars."

Robert smiled back, "Yeah, we haven't done this as often as I'd like to have. It's my fault with all the sports."

"Naw, you're only young once, Robert. Best to enjoy youth while you can."

"But, I enjoy this, too."

William smiled proudly at his son. Small talk turned to more serious themes, and finally, before William could even mention Sue as a possible root cause of his son's depression, Robert asked his father for a favor. "Dad, I want to ask you for some money–a large amount."

That surprised William. Robert never asked his father for anything. "Sure, can I ask what for?"

"I want to do something for someone," Robert glanced into

his father's eyes, "I want to do something for Sue Peters. I'd like her to get the best specialists to help her."

William was shocked and speechless for a few seconds. "Okay, Robert. I'll take care of it. I'll put someone right on it."

"I want it to be from me, Dad, and I want it to be anonymous, just like you taught me, from whatever I have in my trust fund."

William collected his thoughts and realized his son wanted to give from his heart. Robert knew everything William had would eventually go to him and his sister, but he wanted to be the one to give. "I see, son," William understood his son's sentiment from his own experiences. "You learned a lot," William said happily. "I'll put you in touch with my accountant, Isaac. You tell him whatever you need, and he can even set you up with the right people to get you the best doctors for the job. It will remain between you and Isaac. I won't inquire about anything."

"Thanks, Dad. I appreciate it."

"You don't have to thank me, Son. It's your money."

Robert just smiled as William leaned back, tilted back his old Army fatigue hat he now used for fishing, and rested under the tree where he sat with his son. He was never happier with Robert before that moment.

"Oh, Dad?"

"Yes, Son?"

"I was going through some old boxes in the attic," Robert paused as he cast his line far out into the river and then sat back in his chair. "And I came upon a weathered-beaten photograph of a young woman. The name Emily was scribbled on the back of it. From the date, she would now be around your age. Is there another Emily in our family?" William didn't answer, and from his peripheral vision, Robert could see his father's expression change, giving him the distinct feeling that he might have opened an old wound.

It was a couple of minutes before William answered. When he did, the aura of his bright, cheerful disposition changed. His voice sounded gloomy as he replied, "Yes, Son, Emily was my sister. She passed on years back."

Robert sensed it was a conversation his father didn't want to have then, and he replied, "Oh, sorry." He didn't bring up the subject again that day, nor did William.

In the early fall, before Robert began college, he spotted Coral standing on a street corner past the town square and the statue of Major Rue near the school with a small group of boys older than her. One of the boys was holding a basketball. Robert smiled at first, thinking they were all friends, but then some of those boys started to get physical with Coral. Robert could see that she was upset, and they were undoubtedly bullying her. Robert swerved his Corvette in front of the group, screeching brakes blared before he got out dressed in dungarees, sneakers, and a plaid pullover shirt and sported his varsity letterman. The jacket had the Rue school colors of blue and gold, a big gold R on the front left breast, and four badges for football, basketball, baseball, and track. The impressive, well-built, six-foot-three-inch tall figure didn't look happy as he approached the group. The six juvenile boys froze in their tracks. Robert told them to stay there as he walked closer. "What's going on here?" he demanded.

"Oh, Robert! Thank God!" Coral spoke while crying. All of the boys were too intimidated to speak. "They won't leave me alone," she sobbed. "He hit me!" She pointed to one of the boys, whose face quickly turned red. Coral looked cute standing there with her sailor-styled blouse and matching shorts that displayed her bony legs. One of the boys was still holding her light matching jacket but dropped it as he saw Robert glance at him. "I was waiting for Emily to go and play basketball at the school, and then these big kids came over and started teasing me and pulling my hair." She had to pause as she ran out of breath. "He pushed me, and I fell and scraped my knee." Coral lifted her long shorts to show Robert, "See?"

"We were just kidding, sir," one of the boys said formally,

referring to Robert. Everyone knew about Robert Bryant, and these kids were scared almost to death.

"You call this kidding?" Robert shouted at the boy. Coral was amazed. She never saw Robert get angry. "If this is kidding, then why is my friend crying?" He pointed to Coral. "I want all of you guys to get lost right now!" He shouted again. "And don't ever let me see any of you guys do anything like this again!"

"Robert called me his friend in front of everybody," Coral whispered as she stood there dreamy-eyed. Her big dark blue eyes stopped tearing as she watched Robert standing firm, tall, strong, and handsome. Coral's only thoughts were about Robert telling them she was his friend in public. She knew they were friends, but Robert only addressed her as one when they were alone. Now, he did it openly, even in front of strangers. It must have some hidden meaning. Then she remembered how Robert had told her he loved her before. Coral always thought it was a love between friends, not romantic love. Robert had told her more than once in private, and he told me I was beautiful. Why didn't I catch on? "Robert Bryant is my friend, but he loves me. My God, he does!" she mumbled in fascination. Coral felt like crying again but differently, touched by what he did for her and his comment that she interrupted as romantic, loving affection.

Robert waited for the kids to leave, which they quickly did and spread out in different directions while they ran. Then he walked toward Coral, squatted down, and looked directly into her eyes, "Are you okay, honey?" He brushed back her long blonde hair in a brotherly manner and dried her remaining tears with his index finger. "Let me see your knee again?" Coral was speechless as she gazed into Robert's eyes. Slowly, she lifted her shorts again to display her injury, her eyes still affixed to his. Robert removed a clean handkerchief from his back pocket while squatting. He patted it gently over her scrape and said, "It's going to be okay, sweetheart. The bleeding stopped." He gave her a big smile.

His eyes are so beautiful, Coral marveled–Robert's wonderful.

Just then, Emily came from around the corner. "What happened?" She shouted as she saw her brother attending to Coral's knee.

"Robert saved my life!" Coral shouted back. "He was amazing!" Then she explained the whole story of what happened in exaggerated detail. "He was wonderful, Em! You should have seen him!"

"I think I better take Coral home," Robert intervened. "I don't think she feels like playing basketball today. Come on. You can both squeeze together." Robert rolled up his letterman to fill the space between the two red bucket seats. Coral sat on the jacket close to Robert, partially on Robert's bucket seat. During the ride home, Coral leaned against Robert's body and gazed at him in awe.

Coral told her mother the whole story as soon as she arrived home. "He was wonderful, Mom; you wouldn't believe how much." She couldn't stop telling people, phoning all of her friends. And when she heard her father's car pull into the driveway, she ran outside and explained the entire episode to him.

That evening, Louise LeBlanc, Coral's mother, telephoned The Bryant's home. Naomi told Louise she heard the whole story from her daughter, Emily. They agreed just how terrible something like that could happen in their town. Naomi said that Robert recognized some of them from East Liverpool and thought they must have walked up the hill. After they finished their conversation, Louise asked to speak to Naomi's son, Robert.

Louise thanked Robert sincerely in their short conversation. Then she said, "I think you should prepare yourself, Robert. I think Coralie has a big crush on you. You know how little girls are."

"Yes, ma'am," Robert laughed, "I have a sister."

After dinner, Coral and Emily had a lengthy telephone conversation. Before they ended their call, Coral began to say something, then suddenly stopped.

"What is it, Coral?" Emily insisted. But Coral remained silent. "You know I'm going to get it out of you eventually, so you might as well just tell me now."

"Promise me you won't ever say anything to anyone?" Coral conceded.

"Yes, I'll keep it a secret. I promise. Now tell me what it is," Emily persisted.

"I'm in love with your brother. I have been for a while, but now I know he loves me back," she confessed.

Emily couldn't help from laughing. "You're still a little girl, Coral."

"Please don't laugh at me, Em. I know I'm in love with Robert. Maybe he doesn't realize it yet, but he loves me. He told me so, more than once."

Emily was silent for a minute. Then she said, "Okay, I won't say anything to anyone. But you'll get over it, you'll see."

"No, Em, I never will. I know it."

That night, Coral dreamed about Robert. She was a lady in distress, and Robert was a handsome knight, just like in the movies. He rescued her, and they fell in love and lived together in a castle exactly like the Bryant mansion. She woke up abruptly. "Oh, my God!" she whispered, "I'm in love with a knight in shining armor."

Robert continued speaking with Coral, realizing she had a puppy love crush on him. He knew she would outgrow it. Robert sometimes gave her rides and patiently pacified her when she asked him silly questions, just as he did with his sister.

One day, while driving in Robert's Corvette, having one of their deep, intense conversations, Coral raised a topic that caught Robert entirely off guard. "Robert," she smiled and looked directly into his eyes as he glanced toward her, "After we're married, what would you like to name our first child?" The braces on her teeth made her lisp slightly. Then she stopped and waited for his response.

Robert had no immediate reply but instinctively turned his head back to the road. From the corner of his eye, he noticed a red blur whiz by them, which startled him. "Did you see that?"

"Robert, you're deliberately trying to change the subject."

"No, a car just sped by us like lightning. Didn't you see it? It was red."

"I didn't see any car, Robert."

Still startled, Robert turned back to Coral. It was the first time he noticed that Coral had developed tiny breasts. They pressed ever so gently against the tight-fitting plaid button-down blouse she wore. His head immediately rolled back to face the road again as he realized his little friend was changing from a little girl. Robert knew Coral and his sister were late developers and felt sure that Coral and Emily didn't entirely understand the concept of 'the birds and the bees.' But he knew he had to think carefully before answering her question. He finally said, "Coral, honey, you'll be so beautiful when you get a little older that you'll have to fight off hundreds of fellows." He processed the words he had just said, then added, "You're not going to be even remotely interested in me by then."

"No, Robert, I will. We were meant to be together," she smiled as she spoke. "We always get along, and I love speaking with you."

"Alright, monkeyface. Let's wait 'til then. Okay?" Robert humored her.

Coral gave him a big smile and agreed to wait but added, "You'll see." They shook on it just as they did whenever they struck a deal. Then Robert wondered if his sister Emily's body had started to develop yet; he hadn't even thought to look.

"The beers are on, Bob!" shouted Jasper. Robert and Roger, along with Bill, Jasper, Stan, and a group of other teammates, were at Jim's tavern having some beers together and watching the pretty girl's skirts flying upward, dancing to the latest sounds of the jukebox, some wearing two-toned saddle shoes. When Elvis's song 'That's All Right' came on, a small horde of girls rushed to get to Robert first. He was the best dancer with the wildest moves, almost like the King himself. Then Big Joe

Turner's, 'Shake, Rattle, and Roll,' came on, and Robert obliged one more girl before retiring his dancing for the evening.

"Hey guys! Let's go fishing tomorrow!" Robert shouted over the music as he nursed a draft.

"Can't" yelled Stan over the loud sounds of rock and roll music. "Got to work on the car tomorrow."

"You working on that wreck again?" asked Roger.

"Yeah," Stan looked sheepish. "Bad clutch now."

"We'll help ya. Whatta ya say, Bob?"

"I'm in," Robert quickly answered, "And so are you, Jasper, and you other guys, too."

"Okay, okay, Captain," and the bunch of guys agreed one by one to their team captain's order, who just bought the last three rounds of beer.

Robert often saw little Coral at his house when she came over to see Emily and at her home whenever he went to see Roger. Coral and Robert continued enjoying interesting conversations when they were alone. Coral never ceased to amuse Robert and, at times, impressed him with her ladylike manners and intelligence. Aside from her premature mental maturity, there was something about Coral that Robert liked. However, he still couldn't put his finger on it. Robert knew he and Coral shared a unique bond. Coral became Robert's second little sister early on, and he treated her as such. Emily and Coral had been Robert's 'girls' since his first football game, and they wore those ridiculous mascot outfits for him. Coral always stayed focused and on her toes, quickly answering Robert's questions to impress him as she knew she did. Even though most people called him Bob or Bobby, Coral always spoke and referred to him as 'Robert.'

"Robert, why did you go see Sue Peters at the hospital," Coral asked him one day while he drove her home after he spotted her walking on Main Street just past the town square. Robert now understood news spread quickly in small towns, and

Rue was no different. "Kids are saying what she did to you was 'uncool' and 'square,' I heard." Coral used words she had just picked up from movies she had seen, which Robert thought was cute.

"Coral, honey, we all have to learn to forgive," Robert replied. "It would be a better world if we all did, don't you think?"

"That's what the priest at church always says. It must be hard for you though, Robert," she glanced up at Robert, "I mean after she hurt you like that." Coral displayed a consoling expression even though she still didn't understand what happened in Robert's father's Cadillac that night.

"She got hurt pretty badly, Coral." Robert didn't want Coral to know to what extent. "It's something I had to do."

"I know bad people beat her up, and I think it's wonderful you went. So do my parents," Coral hesitated, "And so do I. You're a good person, Robert." Then she thought to herself, That's one of the reasons I love you so much.

Robert could sense her thoughts, which were genuine affection, maybe even more. He hesitated, then said, "Thanks, monkeyface."

Naomi Bryant stood alone in the center of her son Robert's bedroom. She was there to arrange some things she felt he would need for college. Naomi slowly turned to take a panoramic view of her son's belongings displayed throughout the room. There were sports trophies and childhood photos of the family, some with just Robert, Roger, Emily, and Coral. Happy memories filled Naomi's mind. Robert had more recent pictures of his male and female friends mixed on walls or furniture pieces. She sat on the edge of his bed as her emotions forced her to do. Her eyes began tearing when the realization finally hit Naomi.

"The time went so fast," she whispered as solitude subdued her. "My baby boy is leaving." Robert was going away to college, and he wouldn't live at home anymore. She bowed her head toward her lap and sobbed, "They were such happy times we shared with our family. They all went so quickly," she remembered. Naomi was so proud of her son but wasn't ready to lose him. "No woman ever is," she softly muttered as she wiped away the tears dripping down her face. Naomi wouldn't show such emotions to Robert as she didn't want him in any way to feel remorse. It was a natural cycle for her son to become a man. She knew that. William would express his sentiments differently than Naomi did. Although her daughter, Emily, knew Robert was leaving, the reality of it hadn't hit her yet. But she also knew this was a new chapter in Robert's life, a step towards his independence and future success. This thought brought a bittersweet smile to Naomi's face.

Naomi knew Emily would take it very hard. Her children had closely bonded, and Emily had deep feelings for Robert and relied heavily on him; she always had her whole life. It was part of a secret history between brother and sister, shrouded in mystery, that only William and Naomi knew about. But, Doctor Kruger seemed to know more than he admitted; Naomi's woman's intuition told her that. However, William and Naomi never knew of the darker, more sinister side of that knowledge. Naomi only focused on her daughter being very emotional and dealing with anxiety, the root cause she never fully understood. It happened in her early years. "Her brother's departure will devastate her," she whispered.

But Emily would recover in time, her mother thought, just like everyone else. Change was inevitable; this was just another step in their family's journey. Then, the slender figure of the attractive woman in her mid-forties arose and exited the room, dreading that next week when she would be helping Robert pack.

Time seemed to move slowly for the Bryant family unit in the rural town during those past years. It flowed to the same tempo as the river that lay below them in the valley. The days crawled peacefully there, which was in deep contrast to the fast pace of the city from where they came. Memories of New York now rested in the far corners of the minds of each family member while they lived in the town of Rue. All of them had adapted well to the area's customs and enjoyed the fullness of life afforded them there. Rue had become their home, and even at such a leisurely beat, the years had passed before them.

Robert became a sports legend in the rural valley ever since his first win for Rue High School's football team. They went undefeated for two years during the regular season. Everyone wanted to see Robert Bryant play the game, so they packed the stadiums wherever he played. Robert helped Coach Wilson's football team make it to the regional finals in his junior year and the state finals in his senior year–quite an accomplishment for a small-town school in a rural area of Eastern Ohio. Robert spent time helping each player and giving them positive reinforcement. Robert motivated the team and inspired them to become champions. When they were up against a better team, Robert planted enthusiasm into each player. When he taught them to act like champions, they became champions.

Robert displayed a unique skill in all sports. His advanced speed, agility, and ability to calculate and make quick decisions allowed him to excel. He outmaneuvered his opponents and handled the ball as a natural. Robert Bryant made more three-point shots in basketball than any other player in his league. He pulled the Rue varsity basketball team together and built their morale as he did with football. While playing basketball for Rue, Robert scored 3780 points. He scored over 100 points in five games of his first season and over 100 points in six games of his Senior year. Rue went to the state finals two years in a row.

Robert's baseball record was equally impressive. His batting average was an astonishing 900 in his second season. As a pitcher, he incredibly completed seven perfect games; two were back-to-back. It was an incredible thing to witness. With his superior, record-breaking sports skills, Robert Bryant could receive a sports scholarship to any college he wished. However, he chose Harvard University, his father's alma mater, and had no plans to resume sports in college. That fact broke the hearts of many sports fans from every town who had followed Robert's years of high school wins.

Robert cherished his time with his parents and Emily and the many good times they had in Rue, Ohio. He also realized how many memories he had with Roger and those he had with his little friend, Coral, before leaving for college. After Robert began using that endearing term, monkeyface, with Coral often, it made him realize Coral held a special place in his heart, a love of a different type like the love he felt for his sister, Emily. Robert knew he would always fondly remember his little friend, Coral, and treasure the things they did together whenever he reflected on his time in the quiet town of Rue, Ohio.

When the time had come for Robert to leave his home in the town of Rue, Roger and his other friends prepared a special bon voyage party for him. Robert was the only one in the tight-knit group of guys going so far away to school. Roger LeBlanc, Jasper Wilcox, and Bill Patterson had accepted football scholarships. Roger was going to Youngstown University, Jasper and Bill to Ohio State. Roger would be able to travel home on weekends. A couple of the others would attend Franciscan University in Steubenville, Ohio, a daily commute through the small towns along State Route 7 that led to it. Stan Swarovski and others were going to go directly to work. Stan would help manage his father's butcher shop in East Liverpool. The others would seek employment in the many industries surrounding the region. Most of them would become steel workers, railroad employees, or work in the several potteries in the area. Several would begin to work at the Bryant Aviation Plant, where they obtained good-paying jobs arranged for them by Robert's father, William. So, the night before Robert's departure, all the friends and many other acquaintances packed into their favorite bar, Jim's Tavern, in a neighboring town downriver to bid farewell to their friend and local legend, Robert Bryant. That Autumn day would mark the last time they would all be together for a long time.

Roger was only one of the few who remained partially sober enough to drive some friends home late that night. Roger drove several guys but saved Robert for last. Roger couldn't see his friend off the next day because he had to go to Youngstown University to attend a school meeting. He accompanied his best friend, Robert, down the walkway of the Bryant home. There, they first shook hands, then embraced.

"Stay well. You'll always be my best friend," Roger held tightly to Robert.

"You too, Roge," replied Robert. "I can't believe I'm going away. I won't have anybody to talk to."

"Hey, I'm a phone call away, buddy." As they broke their embrace, Roger began to walk back to his car along the cobblestone path in front of the large stone circle in the courtyard. He turned back and hollered, "Hey, Bob! We'll probably see more of each other than we did before with you coming back as much as you will." Then, he laughed.

Robert laughed, "Yeah, we'll probably get sick and tired of each other!" Robert remained in the walkway and watched his best friend, Roger, drive away. Then, he went inside and directly to bed. The beer had gotten to him.

Robert's packing day for college was an emotional time. Finally, the reality of Robert leaving the family hit his sister, Emily. Before that day, she had put the idea into more of a linear perspective, relying on that strong, fearless young woman developing within her. But when she saw the packed bags, she lost control.

"What am I going to do without you?" she screamed as she ran into Robert's arms and cried incessantly. "What am I going to do?"

Her mother calmed her down as Emily realized her big brother was leaving and things would never be the same. Robert assured her he would be coming back to visit. He explained that she could call him anytime and travel to see him if he couldn't return. However, her parents realized it would take a while before Emily adjusted to Robert's departure.

On the day of his farewell, Emily remained in her room. A tearing Coral convinced her to come outside and say goodbye to her brother. "He's waiting for you, Em."

Coral led Emily as the two friends walked hand in hand, both crying. William was driving his son to the airport, and Robert stood leaning against the car when he saw the two of them walk toward them. Robert bent down on one knee to hug his sister. Emily just sobbed in his arms; she was incapable of speaking. After a long embrace, Emily could no longer control herself and ran back into the house and the safety of her room. Robert, still on one knee, turned toward Coral, and she fell into his embrace, crying uncontrollably. She remained there for a full minute sobbing before Robert spoke. "Take care, monkey-face," he softly told her, gently holding her face between his hands, massaging the sides of it. Seeing how upset Coral was, he tried to wipe away her tears with his forefingers, but it was futile as there were so many. Robert whispered, "I'm really going to miss you, sweetheart," as he kissed her cheek.

"I love you, Robert," she whispered in his ear. Then, gradually, Coral left Robert's arms and slowly walked back toward Emily's room. She glanced back before entering the mansion's doorway, the castle she loved so much, and watched as Robert kissed his mother again. Coral didn't open the door and remained poised as Robert opened the front passenger door, sat into the Cadillac, and saw it slowly drive along the cobblestone path to the open gated fence. As Naomi turned back to go inside, Coral left the front doorway and followed the car, whispering, "I love you, Robert," she spoke those words tenderly. Naomi smiled fondly at the cute little girl with a big crush on her son. After Coral watched the car with Robert pass through the entrance, she returned to her castle to comfort Emily, maintaining their friendship in good times and bad, '50-50 partners for life.'

One thing was certain: the name Robert Bryant would remain etched in the minds of everyone in the Rue, Ohio, area for a very long time.

6

Massachusetts, Rue, NYC, Youngstown 1955-1960

Unlike high school, Robert wanted to devote all his college time to learning. Cherishing those past years when he played sports, mixed in with other teenagers, and socialized, especially those he had spent in Rue, Ohio, Robert now yearned to exceed the boundaries he had learned by himself and those provided by Doctor Friedrich Kruger, his mentor since childhood. So, Robert put all his resources into his education at Harvard, his chosen college. However, those memories of Rue pained him more than expected. He shed tears whenever his mind shifted from linear studies to those emotional times, now almost emblazoned in his soul. Robert wondered if he did the right thing by leaving what he now referred to as his hometown.

In college, Robert held a reputation for being a super genius in academics. No longer wanting to hide his incredible brain power, he was ready to unleash upon the world his intellect that was beyond belief. His only respite was to take enough time off to date college girls who didn't want to maintain a steady relationship. Robert made sure of that as the memory of Sue Peters haunted him.

The first week after he left home, his sister, Emily, phoned him five times.

"Hi, Robert. I miss you terribly." Robert could hear the sniffles and pictured his sister crying, which upset him.

"I miss you too, Sis. I think about you all the time."

"When do you think you'll get back, Robert?"

Robert chuckled, "I just got here, Em. Don't worry, I'll be back. Remember, I'm only a phone call away."

That relieved his sister. "I know, Robert. It's just that I miss seeing you as often as I used to. I know I'm a nuisance by calling you so much."

"You're no nuisance, Em," Robert chuckled again, "I love it when you call me. You can phone as much as you want. Remember, I'm always here for you."

That was the medicine Emily needed; it made her feel strong. "Okay, I better go. I love you, Robert."

"I love you too, Emily. Bye for now."

"Bye," and she hung up the receiver.

The following calls included Coral, who also missed Robert and wanted to hear his voice.

"Hi, Robert. I-I–miss you." Coral stuttered as she didn't want to tell Robert she loved him in front of Emily.

"It's good to hear your voice. I miss you too, monkeyface. How are you doing in school?"

Emily and Coral each filled Robert in about trivial things, grabbing the phone away from each other at times to blurb something out but laughing and giggling the whole time as they did.

Robert always humored them when they telephoned him, but the girls' calls tapered off to once a week as time traveled further. As the years passed, Emily and Coral became high school students. They had to devote much more time to keeping up with the academics and activities that higher levels of education demanded.

Emily wrote letters to her big brother. At the end of each, she would mention how much she missed him and felt lost without him. She always added that Coral also missed him, which Robert assumed was under the personal direction of his second sister, as he referred to Coral. Greeting cards were Coral's choice of mail communication. Most adorned with hearts and cupids shooting arrows, Coral always wrote short, witty notes on the love-themed cards.

Doctor Kruger provided the university with documentation showing Robert's superior and advanced intellect. His extraordinary IQ alone spoke volumes, and they were happy to have him. So, in his first year at his university, an unrestrained Robert completed his Bachelor of Science in Physics degree. He unsurprisingly qualified for that degree while studying under the professor in his special school, even before he attended college. So, toward the end of his first year at the university, he began studying for his master's degree in physics.

Robert found time once to return home that first year. He did it at Christmas but couldn't stay long. The LeBlancs were out of town visiting relatives at the time, and Robert didn't get to see his friends Roger or Coral. That resulted in upsetting Coral much more than it did Roger. But Emily was in her glory while reuniting with her brother. Coral wanted to know all the details about Robert's visit as soon as she returned.

Robert casually attended law school at the university in his second year to please his father while simultaneously preparing his thesis for his master's degree in physics, which was another engaging and remarkable feat that, for Robert, was a breeze. He applied some of his time as a teacher of undergraduate physics while part of a research group, both cordially requested by the university. By the end of that second year at college, Robert had completed a well-received thesis and had acquired his MS degree. Robert didn't return home to Rue at all that whole year. He had absorbed all required law studies and books and passed the New York bar exam by the end of that year of college. He could eventually do an apprenticeship at his family's law firm if he ever decided to practice law.

Robert felt terrible that he couldn't return to see his sister for Christmas, so before Christmas 1957, he surprised Emily with plane tickets. Robert met Emily in New York City.

"Finally!" Emily hugged her brother at the airport. She didn't want to let him go.

"Wow, Sis!" Robert held his sister at arm's length, "Let me get a look at you." Robert gave Emily one of his broad smiles that ran a chill up her spine, "You look remarkable. You're not a little girl anymore; that's for sure." Robert realized how beautiful and grownup his kid sister had become at sixteen. She would be seventeen soon and had grown taller, and her figure had blossomed since he had last seen her.

"Why thank you, good sir," Emily gave a short but elegant curtsie.

The brother and sister 'did the town' together during her holiday recess. They shared a suite at the Waldorf Astoria on Park Avenue and visited all the major sights. Emily took pictures of everything with her Argus C-4 camera and flash, which Robert had bought as one of her Christmas gifts. Her brother patiently taught her how to use the camera setup in the hotel room. Emily shot black and white prints and used color slides for more brilliant and multicolored subjects. She looked so proud of herself in a practice photo that Robert took of her in the suite's foyer after he had processed a few rolls of film.

Emily was now a young lady and always tried to act accordingly as one when they dined together. That brought back fond memories of his dinner with his sister at Chuckwagon Burgers when she was still learning manners but couldn't help leaving an ice cream mustache on her lips. Robert smiled lovingly at the memory. Emily looked even older when she wore dress clothes, and Robert noticed glances from young male admirers.

Robert and Emily discussed their time together in Rue and everyone there. Robert asked about Coral and wanted to know how his little friend was doing. Emily went on to tell her brother about her adventures with her best friend, Coral. She ended the conversation with a bit of advice for her older brother. "You should call her sometime, Robert. She misses you tremendously, you know."

Robert felt terrible; with his busy schedule, he had overlooked an old friend. "I will," he promised. "In fact, why don't we phone her right now?" They did, but Coral's father told Emily that Coral was out shopping with her mother. "We'll call her again," Robert said to Emily, but with their time out all day and then arriving home late at night, they never got to call Coral back. "You know what? I'll call Coral after you leave." Robert assured Emily.

Emily and Robert skated together, holding hands at the rink of Rockefeller Center. The aroma of roasting chestnuts filled the air around them as they glided across the ice. Emily and Robert saw the twelve sculpted angels, each one standing eight feet tall along the Channel Gardens at the Center. That display, completed by the artist Valarie Clare about two years before, thrilled Emily the most because she had seen them on television and learned about them in one of her classes at school. Now, she could return and tell Coral and her other friends how beautiful they were before one's eyes.

Each night of the week after Emily spent so much time with Robert on her vacation, she returned exhausted. They filled each day with things the now young lady referred to as 'exciting.' Robert treated her as an adult, and she loved it when her big brother did. Once they arrived back later than expected. Robert had to carry his sister to bed while she moaned, "I'm not tired, Robert," in her sleep. It reminded Robert affectionately of Emily's surprise birthday party before the family left for Rue, which now seemed so long ago.

The brother-and-sister couple traveled by cab and shopped at Macy's, Lord and Taylor, and other stores, where Robert bought her several new outfits. They went to Broadway plays and dined at the finest restaurants. When their time together ended, Emily was sad and said, "The time passed so quickly." Emily didn't want to leave her brother. However, she had matured enough to compose herself properly and ladylike.

"I know, Em. We'll do it again over your summer recess if I can't make it back to Rue."

"Oh, Robert, please do come back," Emily's eyes widened with concern. "Everyone misses you so much. Roger, his parents, and all your old pals keep asking about you. And please remember to make that call to Coral. She'll be devastated if you don't."

"I will come back. Tell everyone I said that, and I promise I'll call Coral."

Emily hugged Robert tightly, kissed him, and said, "Thank

you, Robert. Thank you for everything."

"You must have thanked me at least a hundred times," Robert smiled. Emily did practically thank her brother a hundred times throughout their one-week vacation.

Robert took Emily to the airport by cab. "I hate to see you leave, Sis. I really enjoyed our time together."

Emily, on the verge of tears, composed herself. She stayed strong and stood on her tiptoes, putting her arms around Robert's waist as she had done her whole life, burying her head against his chest. "Bye, Robert," she muttered softly before turning away and walking toward the plane's entry. She glanced back once more and waved. Seeing Robert waving, she whispered again, "Bye, Robert," and passed through the open hatch to the airplane's seating.

Emily shed a few tears after the plane began to taxi along the runway.

"Who was that handsome young man you were with, young lady?" asked one of the smiling stewardesses as she helped Emily fasten her seatbelt. "I saw him before you boarded the plane." The hostess could see that Emily was upset.

"He's my older brother," she proudly smiled. From the sky, Emily glanced down and bid 'Bye' to her brother again.

Coral came over to Emily's house as soon as she returned from her Christmas trip, wanting to know everything they did, especially about Robert. Emily showed her all the photos Robert had printed for her before she left.

"I have color slides, too," she told Coral, explaining how Robert taught her to take pictures.

Coral sat silently, admiring Robert in the pictures as if she didn't hear Emily speak. "Robert looks well," she said finally, thinking he looked even more beautiful than the last time she saw him. Coral and Robert hadn't seen each other in a long time. He hadn't returned to Rue to see how beautiful Coralie LeBlanc was becoming.

"He asked all about you," Emily said to cheer up her friend, who she knew very well was love-sick over her older brother, Robert.

"He did?" Coral asked before she impatiently proceeded with a barrage of questions about Robert.

"We tried to telephone you while I was there."

"I know," Coral said unhappily. "I was out with my mom. My dad told me."

Emily and Coral continued to frequent dances and began to double date after Emily returned from her visit with Robert. Their parents were much stricter with their daughters than their sons. Emily brought that subject up with her parents, Naomi and William. Unlike a juvenile, she proposed her case like the lawyer she someday wanted to become. Notes in hand, she made her arguments, "Ladies and gentlemen of the jury..." Until she winded herself to her parents' amusement, especially William's.

"You've presented your case finely, counselor," William mused her. "However, this court judges that this case goes to postponement." Emily retried her case over and over to no avail. Going out with boys in High School didn't matter to Coral as much; she always had Robert on her mind then. That would change in college.

Some days lingered and passed at a slow, mellow pace; other times, they seemed to move as swiftly as the brisk winds that flowed between the hills, brimming with trees, in the unhurried river valley where the two girls grew up together and became young women in the rural town of Rue, Ohio. Eventually, the time had come for Emily and Coral to leave to go to college. Both girls were going to Youngstown University. They would board together in the same dorm room and travel home by car on weekends.

Emily's parents bought a new Ford Skyliner hard-top convertible for her graduation. Coral's parents surprised her with a brand-new light blue Chevy Impala convertible. Both sets of parents wanted their daughters to be safe on their weekly commutes. The girls loved taking the tops down on nice days, laughing and smiling at boys. They alternated their cars for their weekly trips to Youngstown as they usually drove together during their first year of college.

Once at college, Emily and Coral dated older male students; they were the ones who were of age to get them into nicer nightclubs and finer restaurants. Sometimes, they double-dated. They had fun as young college ladies, going out. They often ate together at diners, sometimes with male dates who couldn't afford better places. Though Emily had a much more generous monthly allowance from her parents than Coral had, she shared everything with her best friend as always, following the motto 50-50 partners for life, allowing them to do the town together, stag young women at times having fun. When the young ladies found time to go out in warmer weather, they took the convertible top down. They pulled into spots at diners that served customers at their cars, rollerskating to take their orders and skating back, holding a tray with their food. It always reminded Emily of Chuckwagon Burgers in Rue and the fond memory of having dinner with her big brother, bringing a tear to her eye every time.

Robert had fulfilled his promise to his sister to call Coral. He phoned Coral right after Emily had arrived home from her Christmas trip to New York City. At the time, Coral was ecstatic to hear from him, even more so because Robert wanted to know everything she was doing. He apologized for not calling her sooner and often enough but described how congested his curriculum was in college. He did miss his little friend and told her so, not realizing Coral was no longer a tiny, knobby-kneed little girl anymore, and young men were lining up to date her.

"I have fond memories of you, monkeyface," Robert told her. He sincerely did and missed her the same way he did Emily.

"I miss you too, Robert," and then she laughed. But hers was now a more mature-sounding laugh.

They talked for nearly an hour. Robert mentioned he would

call her again, and he actually did. He called Coral while she was in high school and occasionally chatted with her when he spoke to his sister in their college dorm. Since he hadn't seen her since she was a child, Robert noticed that Coral's voice was no longer high-pitched or squeaky; it had become smoother and more resonant, yet still soft. Her choice of words and speaking style had also matured, reflecting that of a young woman.

A few months after Robert's first call in early 1958, Coral heard the song 'All I Have to Do is Dream' by the Everly Brothers. She liked it so much that it became her favorite song and a personal way to think of Robert. Coral memorized that song, sang it softly, and even hummed it. It helped her remember him, sometimes bringing happy tears to her eyes as she relived those memories. While there were other songs Coral liked, 'All I Have to Do is Dream' remained her favorite, as the words had a deeper meaning for her. She hoped that Robert listened to it and thought of her when he did. Coral kept that notion hidden in the juvenile part of her inner self that most people have. On one occasion, when Robert called, he heard the Everly Brothers song playing in the background and commented that he liked it. "I like it too," Coral told him, lowering the volume as she felt silly explaining its hidden meaning for her, now no longer a child.

Time passed, and Coral and Emily danced at pubs and dance halls, deliberately twirling their skirts up high, exposing their now shapely legs, and laughing to the cheers and whistles from attracted young men. They were both ravishing young ladies now, and many guys came on to Emily and Coral, but they usually brushed them off as both girls wanted to play the field. Of the two young women, Coral was more attractive to young men. Though Emily was also beautiful, Coral was gorgeous. Young men found her irresistible, probably because of her carefree attitude and the daring way she dressed and acted. Emily wore more conservative clothes, whereas Coral's wardrobe was sexier, with lower-cut blouses, dresses, and shorter skirts and outfits. The way she wore her makeup also brought out her already exquisite facial features and made her look sexy and seductive, purposely to lure men to her. Coral unconsciously made herself a magnet to entice young men, no longer receiving the masculine attention that Robert had provided her since she was little. The intellectual level of her male peers was also lacking, and she missed the intense conversations she once had daily with Robert. Coral was going through puberty when Robert departed for college. That left her confused about her bodily desires at that time. Memories of that day on the lake when Robert's hands touched her flesh and she felt his hardened muscles with her dainty hands now plagued her mature body in a very different way. Coral was now a woman and had the natural carnal desires of one. Now, she felt eroticism whenever she reflected on that day when her body was only beginning to bud with sexual maturity. And Coral touched herself in the only way she found to relieve such sensual feelings.

Some young men were too forward and free with their hands when engaging Coral and Emily. "How dare you do that!" Emily shouted to one guy at a bar. Then she slapped his face as others in the crowded place watched.

"I can't believe you did that!" Coral told Emily as she walked toward her arm-in-arm with another young man.

"He had his arm around my shoulder, then he slowly slid it down and touched my breast. What was I supposed to do? Make love with him on the table?"

"Oops!" Coral covered her mouth and continued, "The old sliding hand routine. I know it well." Coral bent to whisper in Emily's ear, "You have to give them at least a decent feel, honey; just know when to make them stop." Coral smiled. "One time, I let a guy open my blouse and see my breast and feel my nipple. Oh, I moaned, you know, dramatizing," she giggled. "Then I quickly stopped him, watching his groin area shrink, enjoying his expression now succumbing to failure. I love being a tease and watching their things get excited." Coral and

Emily each privately remained infatuated with that male area of the body ever since that dirty old man exposed himself to them. When they later discovered what it was and its purpose, it became even more interesting, almost challenging for Coral. However, neither girl spoke about that time under the stadium stands nor admitted to touching one yet.

"I know you like being a tease. It's going to get you into trouble someday."

"It almost did," Coral spoke in a lower whisper, making sure the guy she was with couldn't hear, "I touched one!"

"You didn't!"

"I did. I wanted to know what it felt like," Coral giggled mischievously like when she was a child, "We were kissing passionately, and I saw his thing get bigger. I couldn't resist, and I began rubbing it," Coral's eyes widened, "before I knew it, he took it out, and it was in my hand."

"No! I don't want to hear anymore!"

"I had a hard time fighting him off. How could I know that would happen?"

"What did it feel like?" Emily whispered curiously.

"Not rubber." And both girls went into a laughing fit.

When they calmed down, Emily asked, "So, what's the moral to this story?"

"You have to give a man a decent feel, Em. You shouldn't slap them for making a move. If you liked that guy, you could have let him see your breast, even let him touch it like I did, but only give them as much as necessary," Coral smiled proudly. "Oh! And by all means, if you want to touch a man's groin to watch it grow, do it gently, not like I did. Or, hold on to your hat because you'll be fighting for your virginity tooth and nail."

"Well, thank you very much for the advice, Dr LeBlanc, but I don't want to see a man's thing that badly, especially after what you told me.

"You have to give a little, Em, and stop being so prudish. Otherwise, you're never going to get invited out," Coral smiled, winked at her friend, then stood straight and erect.

Emily pulled Coral back down by her blouse to the level where she sat and whispered back, "You're such a tramp," and both young women giggled together. "Who's this?" Emily nodded at the guy whose arm interlocked with Coral's.

"Oh," Coral giggled, "This is Herbert, an upperclassman." Smiling, she told Emily, "Herbert loves me. Don't you, Herbie?" Coral lowered her voice, and it became huskie, "Herbert wants to make love to me. Don't you, Herbie?" Still smiling, she massaged his arm erotically to arouse him, then asked Herbert, "You will marry me, won't you, Herbie? I mean, you'll still love me in the morning after we get naked and have wild sex, won't you, Herbie?" Coral giggled, "I'm going to make Herbie very happy. What do you want to do to me, Herbie? You can do whatever you like," Coral licked her lips seductively, lifting her skirt and exposing her thighs while slowly squirming her body lustfully.

"I think you've had too much to drink, honey. We need to head back home now. Other men will be waiting, and we have work to do." Emily then turned to Herbert and said, "You know we're prostitutes, right, Herbie?" Herbert's eyes widened as Emily turned to Coral and asked, "That infection you had, you know, down there, the test results came back okay, didn't they?" Herbert bid the ladies a good night, politely excused himself, and practically trotted away.

"C'mon, Coral; let's go. You know you can't hold your liquor."

"But Herbie wanted me to drink. He loves me," Coral smiled before she burped. "He made passionate love to me in the back closet. I'm surprised you couldn't hear me scream and his grunts. He drove me crazy; I was clawing the walls. I had three orgasms at least. Yes, I let him take me! I lost my virginity! It's gone. No man will ever want me. I'll live in cheap hotel rooms, servicing men, living on sex alone."

"Course you did, Coral, and Herbie will still love you in the morning, but I don't think you'll feel so good after you wake up," Emily laughed, "You can tell me more of your fake sex stories in the morning when you're sober, and can hear how stupid you sound for yourself. I'm sick to death hearing them–all the imaginary things you do with men. Yeah! You felt a man's penis and let men touch your nipple. I swear you get so ridiculous when you drink." Emily glanced at her best friend, who was already dozing off in a chair, "You would run away from a man's erection as fast as you could. You're a bigger prude than me!"

Though the two young women had fun and dated, laughed, danced, teased, and played tricks on men, as college women did, neither thoroughly appreciated the fullness and beauty of the youth they shared, taking for granted enjoyments reserved for the young as if they would pluck them from the tree of life forever. That treasure would occur when they reflected on them as older people usually do. The one truth was that they had a strong bond that would last their lifetime. They were '50-50 partners for life.'

One bright sunny day, Emily and Coral cheerfully walked together and mingled in the crowd of pedestrians in Youngstown. A young man let out a wolf whistle, and Coral humorously responded. She raised her skirt slightly, exposing her voluptuous legs, and bounced her hips as she walked erotically, smiling. She loved being a tease. Distracted by the streak of a speeding red car across the street, Coral stepped off the curb and into the forthcoming traffic. In that split second, she froze as a car raced toward her; Coral saw the coming vehicle but couldn't scream from fright. An arm from behind pulled her back instantly, and the car that just missed Coral screeched and fishtailed to a skidding halt. The person who saved her disappeared into the crowd.

"Coral!" Emily screamed. "Are you alright?"

Still dazed, Coral didn't answer. She stood there, her eyes widened in terror. Then, on the verge of tears, Coral forced her voice and said, "I almost got hit," her words were indistinct from fear. Coral's eyes now flowed with tears, and in shock, she asked, "Who was that guy who grabbed me? Where did he go?"

"I don't know. I only got a quick glimpse of him," Emily

put her arm around Coral, "Are you alright?"

"I'm a bit shaken," she mumbled. "Let's go sit on that park bench," almost pleading in a broken voice, realizing she nearly died. The two young women walked together toward a small corner park as people who witnessed the event watched.

While seated together and calming Coral, Emily began, "From what I saw, and that was really quick, he looked short, and his face was weird–it's the only way I can describe him in such a short amount of time I had." Emily recounted the experience, "He moved so quickly it was almost unnatural, and he seemed strong, though, by how he pulled you so quickly," Emily described what she saw. "You're lucky; that car could have killed you."

"You're right; I could tell it was a man by how hard he pulled me back on the curb," Coral said before she went back into a daze. Emily sat with Coral for a half hour, comforting her until she recovered.

When Coral fully recovered, Emily blasted her friend, "If you weren't flirting with that man, it never would have happened!"

In her second year of college, Emily met Christopher Martin, a senior at the school who wanted to go to law school as Emily did. That common interest bonded them, but it wasn't a serious relationship. After much coaxing from her friend, Emily, Coral began dating a young man named Peter Cummings, a senior seminary student from a rigorous God-fearing family. As college sophomores, they both had boyfriends, though Coral never referred to Peter as a boyfriend, only as a friend. She only went out with Peter because Emily wanted to double date Chris since she hardly knew him.

The girls now remained at the college three weeks out of the month and only returned home once a month. Coral was relieved when Peter explained that he firmly believed in avoiding all sexual contact before marriage because having any intimacy with him, even a handshake, was the last thing in the world she wanted. Peter was short and pudgy. Though she dated Peter to appease Emily, in an odd way, which she couldn't even put into words, she liked him despite his appearance. He seemed to have money and always picked up the tab when the four of them went on double dates–the only dates Coral agreed to. However, Coral never flirted with Peter; there was no physical contact or romance, and sometimes Peter seemed too weird.

Coral had ceased discussing her feelings for Robert with Emily before college, as it seemed like a childish notion. Once, Coral told Emily, "Other men find me irresistible. If Robert doesn't want to come back to see me, there are plenty of fish in the sea. Maybe after college, I'll hook one. Right now, I'm focused on school." Deep down, Emily questioned Coral's statement about Robert. She knew her best friend well and suspected Coral still harbored romantic feelings for her older brother. However, Emily presumed that dating Peter might be her friend's way of gradually moving on, and she never brought up that topic with Coral again.

As the years passed, Robert Bryant never returned to the little town of Rue. He always planned to make it home for Christmas but could never do so because of his conflicting schedules. No one back home knew or could even comprehend how much Robert had accomplished. Robert was making monumental strides in physics.

Knowing he was busy, his parents visited him there in Massachusetts often. Emily accompanied them as usual, from her senior year of high school to her second year of college. Her attachment to her older brother never diminished. She phoned her brother frequently, and they had lengthy conversations about various subjects. Robert always advised his sister when she asked for it but allowed her to spread her wings as every young woman must. Always wanting his sister to become an independent person, free from any other, including him, Robert guided Emily and coached her with the inherent anxiety that was life's most significant hold on his younger sister. Coral had given up on Robert or any interest he may have had for her. She was too busy studying and dating.

Since leaving for college, Robert had always maintained close contact with his best friend, Roger. They often spoke by phone and exchanged news about what was happening in their personal lives. The friends always talked about their time together in Rue and the surrounding towns.

"I remember those warm summer days when we all drove to Guilford Lake in groups," Robert reminisced to Roger.

"Yeah, we all spent our afternoons swimming in the bright sunlight," he chuckled, continuing, "and we fished and caught frogs at dusk." Robert could envision Roger's words, reminiscing about those simple times.

"Then everyone sat around an open fire, roasting our catches of catfish, bass, and frog legs and relishing those cool, soft breezes that floated down from the tree-covered hills around the water. They were great times, Roge."

"You still remember and talk about those times so well; maybe you should have been a poet," Roger chuckled.

"Same to you, buddy, but I really miss them," Robert said sincerely.

"So do I, Bob. So do I."

"I wish I could get back to see you and everyone else, but it's like I told you, something I can't let go of just now."

"You've explained it to me a thousand times, and if you tell me about it again, I'll understand even less. It's too advanced for me. By the way, I've got your car covered, so no worries there." Roger kept an eye on Robert's Corvette while he was away.

"Use it whenever you want, Roge."

"Yeah, I do. I take it out for a spin now and then; it reminds me of the old days and good times," Roger chuckled. I change the oil and put wax on it. It looks great."

"Thanks, Roge."

"Hey, Bob, stop sending me the money. I can cover the cost

of some oil and wax. You send far too much."

"Use it to impress a young lady so you can get married someday," Robert joked.

"Hey! What about you? You better take your nose out of the books and find someone, too!"

The two friends often updated each other about their latest girlfriends and new acquaintances as time passed. Robert frequently thought of that sleepy town, where memories became almost sacred to him. He missed everyone and wanted to go back, but every time he planned to, something important always came up.

In Roger's third year of college, he informed Robert of important news. "I met a young lady," he sounded sheepish. "We've begun dating." The tone of his voice aroused his friend's curiosity. He knew Roger so well that Robert assumed it was serious. "Her name is Mary Lou Bensen, and she's a freshman at my school. I like her, Bob, and she seems to like me."

"Well, good for you, ole man. About time."

"What about you, Bob?" Roger had an amusing ring to his question.

"No time."

"Ha! You have to make time, old friend."

Not long after his last conversation with Roger, Robert didn't hear from him for a while. Then Emily telephoned Robert with bad news about his best friend. Her tone sounded nervous, "Robert, Roger hurt his knee in a football game, and it's really bad. He's in a hospital here in Youngstown, recovering from surgery."

"What?" Robert almost screamed.

"It's worse, Robert. The surgery didn't go well, and the doctors say he won't ever be able to play football again," she paused, hating to be the bearer of such bad news, especially to her brother, whom she cherished. "They said it's permanent. From what I understand, he'll always be in terrible pain and walk with a severe limp for the rest of his life."

"Oh no."

"There's more, Robert. Please let me finish," Emily was crying but hiding her sobs from Robert to not upset him more. It was hard to hurt her brother by telling him so many bad things about his best friend. "That news devastated Roger. You know he always dreamed of playing football professionally. Now, the college forfeited his sports scholarship that paid his tuition. Aside from the pain, Roger is in a bad mental state. He's very depressed, and his family is worried about him. Robert?" Robert was so quiet that Emily thought the telephone disconnected until she heard the low sobbing sound. It hurt Emily to listen to her brother, who was so upset and wished she could do something.

"I'm coming. Don't tell anyone, Em. Okay?"

"I won't, Robert. I promise."

"Thanks. I can only make it a very short visit, but I have to see Roge."

Robert dropped his studies and took the next airplane flight to Youngstown to see his best friend. When Robert stepped into the hospital room, he was shocked. Since the accident, Roger had lost a lot of weight, his face was gaunt, and he appeared haggard overall. Roger seemed to be a very depressed young man, not the happy-go-lucky pal Robert remembered.

"Hey, Buddy!" Robert yelled out as he approached his friend. He kept a big smile and asked, "Sleeping in late?"

Roger appeared genuinely surprised to see Robert. He was sitting in the hospital bed with his right leg elevated by a rope and pulley contraption. Roger never expected Robert to come. Emily told Roger she explained everything to her brother about his injury against Roger's previous objections. Roger wondered how Robert got there so quickly. "Hey! Look what the cat dragged in," Roger joked back and tried to smile.

Robert pointed to the leg apparatus and asked, "Is this what you do for fun now?"

Roger did laugh at that one. His pal, Bob, was the only one

who could do that to him at a time like the present. Robert sat down in a chair, and the two friends spoke for a while before Roger explained the incident to Robert. "It was the quarterback," Roger blamed him for the accident. "That guy couldn't throw to save his life. I had to jump high and to my side, and that's how they caught me. If you were throwing, it never would have happened," Roger said as a joke, but Robert felt terrible.

Robert told Roger," I hired a specialist from Pittsburgh who is coming up to evaluate your medical situation." Robert knew that would agitate his friend.

"No!" Roger objected but sat there helpless. Robert ignored Roger's outburst.

"There's nothing you can do. It's already in the works." Then Robert said, "I'm also taking care of your remaining tuition." He knew Roger would object to that one, and he did.

"Like hell you are," he yelled out. "I don't want charity!"

"It's not charity," Robert paused. "It's called friendship. And besides, I'm on my way to settle that issue now." Robert rose from the chair and stretched from sitting for so long. He turned around and faced Roger. "I'm here to help, Roge." He looked directly into his friend's eyes and added, "You'd do the same for me."

The two friends remained staring at each other. Then Roger slowly bowed his head and said, "Thanks, Bob. It means a lot to me."

"Gotta go now, you stubborn bastard. I'll be back to see you soon." He walked over to the side of the bed and shook hands with Roger, and as he turned, a pretty young woman walked into the door. She was medium height for a woman with long brown hair, a stunning face, and a nice figure.

Roger introduced Robert to the young woman, "Bob, this is Mary Lou, my girlfriend. Mary Lou, this is the infamous Robert Bryant." Roger smiled at the introduction he gave.

"It's so nice to meet you, Mary Lou. Ignore Roger's comment about 'infamous.' I always disregard anything he says."

Mary Lou laughed, "Well, from what I hear, doesn't everyone want to meet the legendary Robert Bryant?" She laughed again. Mary Lou had a pretty smile, and the two immediately took to each other, which seemed to please Roger.

Seeing his friend perk up, Robert remained a little longer. The two friends explained their versions of everything they did together as pals, laughing, sometimes howling, and contradicting each other to Mary Lou's enjoyment, until Robert looked at his watch, "I'm afraid I have to leave. There's a return flight waiting for me." He eyeballed Roger as he continued, "And I have an Important errand to do first."

Robert left for Youngstown University to pay his friend's tuition before catching his return flight. Roger would stay in school to complete his education. His friend might require additional surgery, physical therapy, and other treatments, but Robert would cover those expenses as well. Roger would have the best doctors and top-notch treatment; he would make sure of that.

Coral LeBlanc arrived at the hospital later that afternoon to see her brother. She was upset that she missed Robert's surprise visit. Roger explained to her how busy Robert was and told Coral he had to rush back to college. Roger also told his sister about Robert's generosity.

"He's always been kind and considerate," Coral replied to her brother. Then she reflected on how that was just one of the reasons she had once loved him so much, but now, as an adult, she knew Robert didn't love her romantically.

Robert Bryant sat in a plush chair in his office. Now ready to receive his doctorate in physics, the young man sat observing the university grounds where he had spent so much time over the past years. He had achieved the almost impossible yet felt unfulfilled and lonely. "I feel as if I've accomplished nothing. There's so much more to do," whispering to himself as he sat in that comfortable chair, thinking something was missing in his life.

Robert's time at the university had been monumental. He

spent the summer after his second year working toward his Ph.D. in physics and resumed that work at the beginning of his third year at Harvard. Usually, a doctorate would take years of study and hands-on experience in physics. Then, it would require a challenging dissertation to achieve a Ph.D. But Robert was unlike average college students. Eerie, in a way, his intelligence was still expanding. Robert applied himself and worked feverishly throughout his third year of college, avoiding life and happiness. He taught classes, assisted professors with novel physics calculations, and ran study groups while working on his dissertation.

Midway through his fourth year at Harvard, Robert published a 350-page doctoral degree dissertation, and it was groundbreaking. In it, he created a new theory regarding time travel based on his superior knowledge of quantum mechanics, negative energy, quantum gravity, and the use of nuclear fission. It was a unique study of time loop logic using computer calculations for a computation box that could theoretically travel through time. Robert proved that time travel was bidirectional, meaning going backward and forward in time was possible within a concealed unit.

By the end of his fourth year of studies, when most students his age were completing their BA degrees, twenty-two-year-old Robert Bryant, dressed in a black graduation gown and wearing a tasseled cap, received his Doctorate Degree as his parents and Emily proudly sat in attendance. Naomi and William Bryant finally explained to Emily that her brother, Robert, had been born gifted. She was a young lady now and had the right to know. The audience applauded loudly for his unique achievement, but Emily cheered and clapped the loudest of all the people there.

Robert's thesis, now published into a book, aroused curiosity in the physics community worldwide within just a few months. The United States government was one among the impressed worldwide audience. It was a theory that could potentially be dangerous if proven and implemented. The Office of The Secretary of Defense caught wind of the subject. At first, they wanted to suppress Robert's work in the interest of national security. When they realized it was too late, they forwarded the issue to the intelligence sector for review by their best analysts.

In early 1960, twenty-three-year-old Doctor Robert Bryant was a teaching professor at Harvard. Professor Friedrich Kruger introduced Robert to a young woman who had also been a child prodigy, as was Robert. "It's an honor to meet you," nineteen-year-old Kathy Clarkson spoke boldly to Dr. Bryant. She was a stunning woman of above-average female height with an IQ equivalent almost to that of Robert. Already working on her doctorate, she anxiously awaited meeting someone on her intellectual level.

"The honor is mine, young lady. I've heard about your achievements."

As they were both Kruger's proteges at different times, Robert assumed they shared similar experiences and would hit it off together. Kathy sought Robert's guidance while preparing her thesis, and Robert obliged her and spent many hours helping her. Working with such a gifted young woman was refreshing until she expressed physical attraction toward him. But, as he was now a teaching professor, it was unethical to have a romantic or sexual relationship with a student. However, the more he resisted her, the more she asserted herself. Robert finally invited her to dinner to discuss the professional parameters of their working relationship.

While dining at a finer restaurant Robert had selected, he could better appreciate the woman facing him at the table. As he always saw her in a lab smock, he could never notice the voluptuousness of her body now displayed in the tight-fitting dress she wore. And with makeup, she appeared remarkably beautiful. She used her feminine allure to convince Robert that they would suit each other. Kathy had exhausted efforts of dating men who she considered below her mental capacity and referred to them as Neanderthals. Now that she found someone on her level, she resorted to subtle sexual body language and stroking Robert's forearm with her red-painted fingernails as the perfume she wore swirled around the air surrounding Robert, alluring him.

Robert's keen intuition made him suspect Professor Kruger had arranged this match. It might be some bizarre experiment, and he was possibly trying to mate his two former students. Kathy indeed aroused Robert, and he couldn't help envisioning making passionate love to her, but there was an aura about her. Robert's evolved intuition made him sense her as corrupted, maybe evil. Kathy reminded him of the same feelings he felt when he first met Sue Peters in high school. And he had worked too hard to get his early doctorate and didn't want to violate the college policy. He instinctively felt it would lead to a bad place. And by God and the saints in heaven, Robert used all his powers to resist her.

"We can't work together any longer." Robert realized he would eventually succumb to her if they continued working together; he knew he would never be able to resist her seductiveness. "I'm a professor, and you're my student," He finally let the words out even though he lusted her body and her touch and the stimulating sensual body aroma suffusing around her.

"What? How dare you reject me!" In anger, Kathy arose, her face contorting almost like a monster, and left the table hastily. Robert's evaluation of her was correct; she did come from an evil place. But he noticed how Kathy's high-heeled shoes accentuated the muscles behind the lower part of her legs and buttocks as her beautiful figure hastily but gracefully exited the restaurant. Robert forced himself to believe he had done the right thing.

7

Rue, Ohio 1961 Christmas Eve

By December 1961, many popular magazines aside from those that covered scientific news began writing articles about Doctor Robert Bryant's physics work. The young physicist was gradually becoming popular even outside the scientific community. The worldwide publication of his research book was generating fame for the youthful professor, a prospect Robert dreaded. The public finally knew his long-held secret: that Robert was born a super genius with the highest recorded IQ ever, and his intellect was still advancing. Eventually, that news would trickle down to his small hometown of Rue, Ohio. He feared they might consider him a freak. But, as of yet, no one in Rue knew about his work except his parents and his sister, Emily. Robert explained to everyone else that he was a post-graduate, not a professor, and that's what he would tell people when he visited Rue. Admitting he was already a professor would attract too much attention.

"It's been six years," Robert smiled as he answered the question from the clerk at the rent-a-car counter at the Cleveland Hopkins Airport. "No, five," he corrected himself. He hadn't seen Coral for six years, recalling that the LeBlanc family was on vacation the last time he visited Rue.

"Long time to be away from home," the young man smiled. "We have the beige 1961 two-door Cadillac Coupe DeVille waiting for you, sir. I just need you to give me your John Hancock right here," he pointed to an x on the paper document.

Robert couldn't believe it had been five years since he returned to Rue and looked forward to seeing everyone again. As a student, he was always busy studying or doing laboratory work. Yet after receiving his doctorate and becoming a professor, Robert found time. That's when he made a point of returning to Rue for the Holidays at the end of 1961. He sincerely missed the place and those happy times he had there. Robert drove the rented Cadillac, realizing it had been six years since seeing Coral but five since returning to the town. He had seen Roge at the hospital and another time. "What made me first think of the years I didn't see little Coral?" he mumbled before shrugging it off.

Robert arrived at his parent's home in the early afternoon. He would spend Christmas Day with his family and stay for a visit during his school's holiday break.

Emily heard a car pull up at the front of the house, peeked through a window, and saw Robert open the trunk to get his luggage. She excitedly ran down the stairs barefoot and threw herself into Robert's waiting arms after he saw Emily trotting toward him as he opened the door.

Emily's face lay buried in Robert's chest until her muffled voice finally released, "Welcome home, big brother!" Her arms remained around his waist, and she squeezed tightly. Now facing him and looking into his eyes, she almost screamed, "I missed you so much! I can't believe you're here!" But she wouldn't let go of her brother and kept holding him.

"Good to be here, Sis!" He held her shoulders and gently pushed her back slightly so that he could observe her closely. Emily now parted her darker blonde hair on the left side, and it curled to her mid-neck. She seemed to have more of a shapely figure and flowered even more to womanhood since last he saw her. Emily's unblemished skin pulled tightly around her large, blue-colored eyes and the delicate features that composed a flawless face, even without any makeup. Emily was now a beautiful young woman and looked so grown up standing before him.

Emily helped remove Robert's cashmere dress overcoat and admired the white knitted scarf he wore. She laid both on the arm of a chair. A smiling Isabella Russo, the housekeeper, gave Robert a warm embrace.

"Roberto! So long since I've seen you. Look at you; you're a grown man now!" Isabella's eyes teared, shaking her head as she proceeded to take Robert's jacket and scarf to the hall closet. There, she neatly hung them on a padded wooden hanger.

Naomi, who had been on the far side of the mansion, seemed to appear out of nowhere. When she heard her son's voice, she rushed to join her two children, sitting close together on a living room loveseat, talking and laughing. Robert rose to hug his mother, kissed her, and returned to sit with his sister. Naomi sat in a chair close to Robert and Emily. The three began talking about their family holidays while living together. William Bryant was still at the Christmas party he held at the plant and would be returning soon.

The Bryant family didn't celebrate Christmas Eve, so as soon as Louise LeBlanc learned that Robert was in town, she invited him to dinner that evening. Louise hadn't seen Robert in years. She was thrilled he was back in town and would see her son, Roger, and Coralie, her daughter. It would be a surprise as neither knew about Robert's arrival. No one truly believed that he would come as he had promised to do so often. Robert's sister, Emily, was already invited. Her boyfriend, Christopher Martin, who was now in his first year of law school, was also going.

Naomi noticed her daughter's nervousness when she brought up the subject of Christopher. As Emily sat on the loveseat with her brother, speaking to him and her mother, she looked at Robert, "You'll be meeting my boyfriend today," she said hesitantly. Emily blushed slightly and waited for a response from her big brother.

"Looking forward to meeting him," Robert replied sternly, then his face folded into a big smile. "I'm sure he's a nice guy if you picked him, Sis."

A seemingly relieved Emily had a big smile. "He is, Robert. He is. You'll see."

"I'm sure he'll fit right in," added Naomi. She realized how nervous Emily had been about Chris coming to meet the family.

Then, to change the subject, Naomi asked, "When will you find someone special, Robert?"

"Too busy right now, Mom. I will someday."

Emily was anxiously waiting for her boyfriend to arrive from Akron. Her relationship with Chris had gotten serious recently, and his visit was to meet Emily's parents before going to dinner with Emily at the LeBlanc home. Chris would stay overnight in a guest room, then leave after breakfast to visit his parents in Akron. However, Emily was more concerned about her brother Robert's approval of Chris than her parents. Emily had driven back from Youngstown alone the day before. Coral was coming with her unofficial boyfriend, Peter, who couldn't leave on Christmas Eve until late afternoon.

William Bryant arrived home just after 3 PM. He noticed the Cadillac out front and knew his son was home.

"Good to have you back, Son," he greeted, embracing Robert fondly after racing in to see him.

"Good to be back, Dad," Robert answered warmly. He was still reacquainting himself with the familiar surroundings after so long. Fond memories slowly flowed back from the deep corridors of his mind. His mother's loving attentiveness to her children and the long talks he always had with his father were at the forefront. After putting his coat away, William sat down and joined in the conversations with his wife and children. Eventually, Robert glanced at his watch and excused himself. He wanted to shower, and time was flying, and the evening was approaching.

Emily stood up, surprised by the time. It was 4 PM, and her boyfriend hadn't yet arrived. She announced that she had to get dressed and asked her mother to entertain him until she came down. "I won't be long," she promised. "I already took my bath. I can't imagine what's keeping him."

"It's probably holiday traffic," William said. "He'll be here," he assured his daughter.

"We'll entertain him. Don't worry, dear," Naomi humored

her daughter.

Robert came down first. He looked handsome in a stylish white, knitted, tight-fitting sweater shirt contrasting his tapered black dress pants and imported black Italian shoes. His clothes emphasized his muscular build, which he still maintained.

Emily trotted down the stairs in a fitted red plaid belted dress. Large red buttons fastened the front of the stylish garment, which reached just above her knees. She wore nylon sheers on her legs and held a pair of three-inch dark red pumps in her left hand while gripping the stair rail with her right. Now adorned with makeup, including eyeliner, mascara, and lipstick, she looked stunning.

"You look beautiful, dear, and Robert, you look so handsome. Let daddy take a picture of both of you together," said a proud, smiling Naomi.

After William took several photos, Robert decided to go to the LeBlanc home before his sister and her boyfriend. It was just after 5 PM, and he wanted to spend time with Roger before dinner. Robert put on his scarf and dress coat and headed for the door. He turned around and asked his parents again if they were sure they didn't want to come along as they also had been invited. But they preferred to remain home, sit by the fireplace, and watch the flicker of flames while listening to music as they always did on Christmas Eve. Robert opened the front door, and as he did, a young man of medium height almost fell into the foyer. Robert caught him by the arm just in time before he fell.

Emily rose, concealing her excitement, and walked gracefully to the door to introduce her boyfriend to her family. She took the young man by the arm. In her high heels, she was nearly as tall as her boyfriend. "Dad, Mom, and Robert, this is my boyfriend, Christopher Martin."

Chris first shook hands with Robert, since he was closest. The couple then walked over to Naomi and William. Chris greeted each of Emily's family members respectfully as he shook their hands. "I'm so sorry I'm late," he said to each of them. "Please call me Chris," he added.

Robert stayed home because he didn't want to seem rude to his sister's boyfriend. Sitting in a cushioned armchair, he helped Emily initiate a polite conversation among the group. Emily winked at her big brother, her lips silently forming the words, 'thank you,' as she recognized that Robert was helping her 'break the ice.' Chris was nervous, asking questions while also answering them, with Robert chiming in to ease the awkwardness and help Chris feel more comfortable. After about fifteen minutes, Chris was chatting easily with his girlfriend's parents. Robert placed his hand on Chris's shoulder, apologized for leaving, and said he would continue their conversation at dinner.

"See you in a bit," Robert shook hands again with his sister's boyfriend, bid his parents good evening, and left.

Robert opened the door of the LeBlanc home to let himself in as he always had done in the past. "Knock, Knock!" he said in the foyer to let them know he was there. Nobody seemed to hear him, so Robert walked toward the living room after throwing his coat over the arm of a chair.

Louise spotted him first. "Oh my!" she shouted as she rose from her chair and walked quickly to Robert. "It's Robert!" she cried as she opened her arms and embraced the young man she hadn't seen for so long. "How handsome you are, dear." She began to shed tears of happiness as she held him tightly. "You're a man, now!" Roger got up quickly, walked over to his best friend, and embraced him.

"How's the knee doing?" Robert asked.

Roger began doing an Irish jig. Then he hopped up and kicked his heels together to show how well his knee had healed. "All thanks to you, my friend."

"What did I do? I'm not a doctor," Robert smiled at Roger. He was humble and didn't seek acknowledgment for helping Roger financially, having all of Roger's medical bills forwarded to him and covering his friend's treatments, surgeries, and physical therapy. Robert had paid for everything and never expected a thank you in return. "It's great to see you looking as good as new."

Roger would not play football professionally, but he would walk perfectly and not be in any pain. He had a tremendous high-paying job at Bryant Aviation and a wonderful fiancée, Mary Lou Bensen. They had just purchased a beautiful house in Rue where the couple would live after their wedding. Roger was a happy man.

Mary Lou was already walking over to greet Robert. "Hi, Robert. It's great to see you again," she said as she hugged him and gently kissed his cheek. "I hope we can spend more time getting to know each other while you're here."

"Hi, Mary Lou," Robert smiled, "Keeping my friend out of trouble?" He held his smile.

She laughed and said, "I try to."

Roger LeBlanc Sr. was the last to get to Robert. "Good to see you again, young man. It's been much too long."

"Mr. LeBlanc. It's good to see you too. How have you been?" They shook hands, and then Roger Sr. placed his right arm over Robert's shoulder in a warm gesture.

"Oh, a few aches and pains. Not as young as I used to be."

"Mr. LeBlanc," Robert laughed, "that's nonsense. You've got a long, long way to go."

Standing beside Robert, Louise added, "You come back home more often, you hear? Everyone missed you!"

Robert became like a second son to Louise when he lived in Rue. She even did his dirty laundry when the boys came directly to Roger's home after some games. And Robert used to leave changes of clothes at the LeBlanc house, as Roger did at the Bryant home.

"You're right, ma'am. I'm sorry. I should have come back sooner." Robert looked sincerely apologetic. "But I will return more often in the future. I promise!"

"Enough of this negative talk," Mr. LeBlanc said as he poured Robert a glass of wine. "It's Christmas." Then he picked up his glass and proposed a toast. "To Robert! Welcome home, my son!"

The group began to chat. Robert mentioned that Emily and her boyfriend were coming over soon. He explained how holiday traffic held up Chris, who had arrived late.

"Oh," Louise said. "Coralie and her boyfriend will also be here shortly. They're driving down from Youngstown now. She had to wait for Peter." Louise frowned when she said the word, Peter.

By the look, Robert assumed that Louise wasn't too fond of Coral's boyfriend. "I didn't know she has a boyfriend now. She or Emily never mentioned it to me."

"Oh yes. Coralie is quite a young lady now, you know."

"He's pretty odd to me," Roger added.

"Now, Roger, you mustn't judge," Louise defended her daughter's choice. "He is different, I admit. It might just be a phase Coralie is going through."

"Okay, if you call dating oddballs a phase, Mom. Then so be it." Roger raised his glass of wine and toasted. "To oddballs everywhere," he joked. Louise LeBlanc didn't look amused.

"Be nice to him, Roger. He's not even staying long. He has to leave after dinner to go back to Youngstown." Then Louise frowned, "He doesn't think it's proper to sleep in the same house as his girlfriend while they're unwed." She shrugged her shoulders and drank some wine from her glass.

Thinking amusingly about how Coral's boyfriend sounded like a fun guy, Robert said, "I still think of Coral as a child. She must indeed be a remarkable young lady. Are they considering marriage?"

Louise shrieked, "God, no! I hope not!"

Roger laughed, "Wait until you meet him, Bob. Then you can help us pray that they don't."

Robert smiled at Roger, thinking about his little monkeyface dating. "Why don't we all sit at the dining room table?" suggested Louise. Just as she finished speaking, the door opened. It was Emily and her boyfriend, Chris.

"Hi, everyone! Sorry we're late," Emily said as she walked

into the living room. She moved around with Chris and made all the introductions.

"C'mon, let's all go sit in the dining room," Louise directed everyone. "Everything is prepared. We can start on some appetizers while we wait for Coral," she paused, "and her boyfriend," sounding somewhat reluctant.

They all sat around the dining room table, enjoying delicious appetizers. Louise prepared some, and the Italian store in town that sold all types of homemade delicacies made the others. Robert complimented his hostess twice as he enjoyed eating them. Suddenly, Robert's keen hearing picked up the seconds of a scratchy sound that all 45 record players made just before the music began. Then, the words and music of the Everly Brothers' 'All I Have To Do Is Dream' started to fill the air.

"It's Coralie," Louise declared, "and that song again."

Coral entered the large room accompanied by a short, stocky young man. As Coral bent over to kiss her father, she noticed Robert sitting at the table. "Oh, my God! Oh, my God, Robert!" She stopped speaking and appeared to be in shock. Her eyes stayed fixed on Robert. "I didn't know you would be here!" Coral tried to compose herself. She didn't want to ruin her makeup by crying in front of Robert.

"Coral? Is that You?" Robert stood up straight and began walking over to Coral. He appeared shocked, not recognizing Coral at all. "Hi!" he seemed dumbfounded.

"Robert, why didn't you let me know you were coming?" Coral slowly walked toward him. The chubby young man who was with her stayed where he was.

"It's a surprise!" yelled out her mother, Louise. "Robert's here!"

Coral's large, dark blue eyes remained fixed on Robert's as she stood on her tiptoes to embrace him. Resurrected feelings for Robert surged within her, and she nestled into his arms, turning her head to press it firmly against his chest as she said, "Oh, Robert, I missed you so much." His cologne, mingled with his natural scent, now excited her. She wanted to kiss him firmly on the lips but held back. Coral knew she had to resist the urge. Louise watched the reunion between her daughter and Robert closely, smiling as she did so.

Coral thought how handsome and irresistible Robert now was as a man. She finally composed herself and walked to the chair opposite Robert's. The music coming from the foyer stopped playing. "That's my favorite song," Coral said as she looked at Robert.

"I like it too," Robert said. "It reminds me of something good. A good feeling." Then, he thought how bittersweet his feelings really were. The thought of dreaming about someone was the good part. Never finding that special someone because of how I am is the flipside of that coin.

Coral pondered Robert's fondness for her favorite song while keeping her eyes on him, considering how strange that was and how her past love for him might have somehow reached him. Then she realized he never had the same feelings she once held for him. Or did he? Now she wondered.

Robert couldn't believe the young woman standing before him was Coral. He hadn't seen her in six years when she was still a skinny kid. Her large, deep blue eyes were the only part of her that hadn't changed. The woman he now saw was stunning. She had grown taller, and her body had filled out, becoming as curvaceous as an artist's sculpture. Coral embodied the essence of feminine beauty, wearing a tight-fitting dark green dress and black two-and-a-half-inch heels. The fabric of the dress was slit at the sides, revealing her well-defined legs, now even firmer from her heels. Cut lower at the front and back, the top of her dress showcased her bare shoulders down to the small of her back and the cleavage from her larger-than-average and well-shaped breasts. Her neck was long, and the curve added an elegant touch. With her big, wide eyes, enhanced by mascara and eyeliner accentuating their dark blue shade, Coral had truly bloomed into a beautiful woman.

"Aren't you forgetting something, Coralie?" asked Louise as she glanced at the young man who came in with her.

Coral looked back at her mother with a questioning look. Then she realized Peter was standing awkwardly by himself. "Oh! I'm sorry!" With the shock of seeing Robert, Coral had forgotten entirely about her pseudo-boyfriend. "Robert, this is Peter Cummings." She didn't use the word boyfriend. "Peter, this is Robert Bryant."

"Nice to meet you, Peter," said Robert while extending his arm for a handshake. He observed the young man closely. Peter was short and had a pot belly. His small stature accentuated the extra body weight he bore. He parted the prematurely balding black hair on his head in the middle. Robert wondered what Coral saw in this guy, thinking the saying, love is blind, is true. Peter didn't reply to Robert's friendly gesture of a handshake. He just stood there staring up at Robert. Peter smiled oddly as if his lips were artificial. It reminded Robert of a hand-drawn mouth seen in children's books or cartoons.

Nobody in the room spoke. They had all witnessed the emotional reunion of Coral and Robert. Now, her boyfriend was speechless. Finally, Mr. LeBlanc broke the icy aura that filled the room. "Coralie, would you and your boyfriend like some wine?"

"Peter doesn't drink alcohol, Dad, because it's against his religion, but I would like a glass."

Just then, Peter spoke. "So, you're the infamous Doctor Robert Bryant."

Robert quickly suspected the little guy knew about him and wanted to test Peter. "I hope to be a doctor someday. But famous? I'm not so sure."

"Oh, you'll be very famous," Peter corrected Robert. "A legend, in fact."

"What are you studying, Peter," Robert asked to get him off that topic.

"I'm a seminary student. I will become a minister of God just like my father and as his father before him." Peter spoke in a higher-pitched voice.

Emily was the only one in the room who knew what had

transpired between her best friend, Coral, and her brother, Robert. Coral still loved him; she knew for sure. However, by observing Robert and the way he kept staring at Coral, Emily wondered if he had developed an attraction to her friend. Peter was too strange for her, and he was becoming weirder by the day. "The appetizers are delicious, Mrs. LeBlanc, truly," Emily declared to steer the conversation in a different direction.

The flow of discussion changed, and throughout dinner, Coral and Robert kept glancing at one another when they thought the other wasn't looking. And when they spoke to each other, it was as if they were alone and having a private conversation. When conversing with Chris, Roger, or anyone else, Robert struggled to take his eyes off Coral. His being so infatuated with a young lady was out of character. Never before did he respond to a woman in such a way. Now, Coral aroused Robert in a way he had never before experienced.

While Coral was speaking to Emily, she noticed Robert watching her from the corner of her eye. Coral realized it was the first time that Robert looked at her in such a way as if he was seeing her for the first time. Keeping her direct eye contact on Emily, her attention remained on Robert until she almost lost her train of thought. Coral studied Robert in detail. He had become even more handsome than before. His body had matured, and now Robert had a perfect male physique. She could see the muscles of his arms and chest bulge through the tight-fitting sweater shirt he wore. Coral had watched his powerful thighs flex when he walked and how his perfect male buttocks responded harmoniously. To her, Robert appeared to be like a Greek god. Time had also matured the finely chiseled features of his face to perfection. His wavy, thick black hair complemented his dark blue eyes more than before. And when he looked into her eyes, she melted and felt a pleasurable quiver deep in her loins that utterly excited her. Coral had never been sexually aroused solely by speaking with or looking at a man. Coral viewed Robert as any mature, developed woman would do when seeing an extremely handsome man, and she now experienced many feminine passions for him for the first time.

Robert detected how much Coral's voice had changed while speaking to her in person and not through telephone lines. It was huskier, sometimes soft and soothing, and Robert found it appealing, even sexy. The way she moved was now also different. Her arms and hands flowed like a ballerina's movements. Her feline body swayed appealingly, forcing her tight, shapely buttocks to slowly and evenly respond one side at a time as if following a graceful, methodical beat when she walked. Coral even sat positioned on her chair majestically. Whenever Robert moved closer to speak to her, he could smell the enticing scent of her body, and he found it sexually stimulating. Robert finally saw Coral as the beautiful woman she had always wanted him to view her as.

After dinner, Louise moved her guests back to their large living room. Coral was sitting there speaking with Emily. Her right leg crossed over her left in a ladylike manner as it very slowly and gently swayed in erotic motion, causing her shoe to hang by her toes in a sexy way. From where he sat, Robert could see past where Coral's nylon sheers ended, exposing the soft white flesh of her well-formed upper thigh and a hint of her lower derriere cheek. He realized the fullness of the beautiful feminine being she was, remembering the tiny, skinny kid he used to love to talk to. Coral now appeared as an entirely different person. Her face and body had metamorphosized into a beautiful creature of perfection.

Coral caught Robert watching her out of the corner of her eye. She swayed her leg slower and more erotically, which purposely caused her dress to rise slightly higher, exposing a bit more of her naked flesh. Smiling, Coral watched as Robert sat uncomfortably, trying to hide the slight rise forming in his trousers. She recalled the fake sex stories she always joked about with Emily, but this was her Robert, and her feelings were real and sexually stimulating. Then Coral realized Robert was causing her involuntary reaction.

Peter Cummings left the dinner party early as he had planned. When the time came, he just got up and went to the closet in the foyer and took his coat. Peter slipped into it, returned to the living room, and gave a casual "Bye!" accompanied by a simple wave. Then he left. Everyone looked at each other in awe. Nobody said a word.

Coral felt guilty that she didn't give Peter more attention. But it had been impossible to do. Her bodily desires had taken over her entire thought process. Coral felt like a slave whose only purpose in life was to cohabitate with Robert, and from what she had seen, it seemed mutual. She sat in awe, wondering how easily the man she had loved ever since she was a little girl could now arouse her solely from a conversation or a touch. And now, as she stared directly into his eyes from across the room, he was doing it to her solely from how his eyes looked back at her.

Later that night, as Emily, Chris, and Robert prepared to leave, Robert nodded to his sister to come to where he stood by the closet. Privately, he whispered, "Why don't you invite Coral to our place tomorrow for Christmas Day dinner?" Robert paused, "Roger is going to Mary Lou's house, and I'm sure Coral would really want to come over."

That confirmed Emily's suspicions that her brother was attracted to her friend, Coral. And, knowing him so well, she sensed it was serious. Emily looked directly up and into Robert's eyes. "Are you sure that's a good idea?" her voice sounding concerned. She wanted to please her brother but worried about the consequences of his involvement with her best friend.

"Yeah, I am," Robert replied assuredly.

"Okay," Emily quickly conceded. The more she thought about it, the more she liked the idea of Robert with Coral, noticing what a lovely couple they were as adults.

Emily walked over to Coral and kissed her on the cheek. "Why don't you join us tomorrow for dinner? I don't know why I didn't ask before. You can spend the day with us instead of

Mary Lou's family. Please come?"

Coral looked at her friend Emily, then glanced over at where Robert was standing, sensing that Emily understood what was going on. "Are you sure? Is it okay with your mom?" Coral desperately wanted to see Robert again. She had never felt such a strong physical attraction to Robert, knowing she was too young when last she saw him. But she never had such a reaction to any other man as an adult.

"Of course, you're like one of the family."

"Okay, I'd love to come over. Thank you." Coral glanced back at Robert, who was standing and speaking with Chris. Her attraction to Robert was now evident to everyone, and she felt grateful they couldn't see the sexual intensity she felt.

"Good! It's settled! We'll see you at 2 PM!"

Emily kissed everyone goodbye and left with Chris. As Robert was preparing to leave, Louise LeBlanc called him. "Robert, may I see you in the kitchen? I want to send some of the appetizers to your mom for her to try."

"Of course," Robert politely answered. And he turned and walked to the kitchen just past the dining room. "It's very kind of you, Mrs. LeBlanc."

"I told her about them, and I know she'll like them." As Louise prepared a small container, she stopped what she was doing, turned, and faced Robert. "You know, Robert," she hesitated for a few seconds, then continued, "I always pictured that you and Coralie would..." she paused again, "you know... be together someday." She watched as Robert's expression changed, and he blushed slightly but said nothing.

Finally, Robert shrugged and said, "I never viewed her like that. I–I." Robert became tongue-tied.

"You never viewed her as a young woman, dear," Louise finished Robert's sentence. "She was always a child when you knew her."

"Right," Robert agreed.

"She's not a child anymore, Robert." Louise paused, then blushed a bit before continuing, "I couldn't help but notice how the two of you interacted tonight," she smiled.

"I'm so sorry if I was in any way disrespectful tonight–"

"No, dear, you weren't disrespectful at all." She didn't allow Robert to finish his sentence. "You were always the perfect gentleman, Robert," she smiled. "What I mean is you share a bond with my daughter. You both always did. You just never realized it. I hope you can spend some quality time together to get to know her as a young lady." Louise went back to finishing her package.

Robert mulled over what Coral's mother said, thinking she knew, and probably everyone, by how he acted. After a minute, he realized Coral's mother was right about how he needed to explore his new feelings for Coral. "I think you're right, Mrs. LeBlanc. And I will. Thank you."

"Here, Robert." Louise handed him a brown paper bag that held the filled containers.

"Thank you," Robert said as he took the bag.

"Oh, Robert?"

"Yes, Mrs. LeBlanc?"

"Please don't tell my daughter we had this conversation?" She gave Robert a big smile.

"No, ma'am, I won't." He smiled back at her. Louise and Robert walked together back to the foyer.

Robert walked over to his pal, Roger, shook his hand, kissed Mary Lou, and told them they would get together during the week. Robert shook hands with Mr. LeBlanc, kissed Mrs. LeBlanc, and thanked them for a wonderful evening. Then he turned to Coral, fearing any arousal might cause another uncontrollable embarrassment for him. Robert only briefly hugged Coral and then kissed her cheek. "Good night, Coral," he smiled. The mere touch of his hands on the exposed flesh of her naked back and the feel of its curve as her beautiful eyes gazed into his excited him beyond his comprehension. "Will I see you tomorrow?" Robert asked, straining to avoid more stimulation from the gaze of her stunning blue eyes and her soft touch.

Coral's eyes widened as she looked directly into Robert's,

her feminine spot tingling and trying to satisfy her body's lustful desire, which was now out of control. She answered calmly, "Yes, Robert, I'll see you at dinner," desperately wanting to feel his touch again, "Good night," she smiled. Then Coral noticed the slight expansion forming in his slacks again before seeing him quickly throw his coat over his arm to hide it. That brief sight was all Coral's libido needed to prompt her involuntary bodily reaction. Laboring to stop her legs from trembling, Coral stood motionless. Now in a daze, only a slight smile on her face, privately enjoying the satisfaction as her wetness released while secretly trying to regain control over herself. But at that moment, Coral didn't want to. She simply wanted to stand in total contentment, in her cozy stupor, apart from the outside world.

"Good night, Coral," Robert calmly said, fighting his reaction to her scent. He opened the door and entered the cold outside among the other wild animals.

8

Rue, Ohio 1961 Christmas Day

Isabella Russo and Naomi had prepared a hearty breakfast that Christmas morning. The Bryant family and their guest, Christopher Martin, feasted on eggs, home fries, bacon, pancakes, and various types of bread.

"I can't remember when I last had such a wonderful breakfast like this," Chris relayed his compliments with a smile and a nod to Isabella and Naomi. "Thank you all for having me over," Chris smiled in appreciation as a glowing Emily sat close to her boyfriend.

"We were so glad to meet you finally and have you over, Christopher," Naomi said first.

Knowing his daughter's boyfriend was at the University of Akron School of Law, William thought an excellent way to break the ice and form a good breakfast conversation was to discuss how Chris liked studying law. "So, Chris, how do you like law so far?" And to Naomi's dismay, law practice became the main topic of discussion at the table.

"Well, sir, so far, I love it, and as tough as it is, I'm doing rather well."

"He's being modest, Dad; Chris is at the top of his class," Emily added proudly.

Naomi wished to learn more of the personal side of the young man, and she interjected some appropriate questions to create a mix of discussions, which Chris politely answered. However, Chris took the conversation back to law when he told Robert, "I can't tell you how much I admire you for studying law and physics simultaneously." Chris was amazed when he learned that Robert had become a lawyer while studying physics; he didn't know what level of genius Robert was, as that was a family secret. "The law curriculum is intense by itself. Wow, that was quite an accomplishment, Robert."

"Please call me Bob, Chris, or I'll call you Christopher like my mother does," Robert joked to everyone's amusement.

"Will do, Bob," Chris offered a big smile.

That pleased Emily as she wanted both of them to get along well. Robert's approval of Chris meant everything to her.

After everyone finished the morning meal and enjoyed many conversations, Chris rose and thanked everyone for their polite hospitality. He told them how much he admired their beautiful home. Then, Chris shook hands with William Bryant, Robert, and Mr. Russo. He kissed Naomi and Isabella and walked to the foyer and the large front door at the end of it. Chris hugged Emily, kissed her lips, and told her he would call her. They wished each other a Merry Christmas, kissed again, and Chris left.

William announced shortly after Chris's departure, "I like him. He seems like a fine young man."

Naomi smiled, knowing how difficult it was for someone to get her husband's approval, especially about his daughter. "I like him too, particularly after you grilled him about law, and he held his own." her eyes looked directly at William.

After Chris's departure, Emily paced the floors of her bedroom, both concerned and joyed because she felt Coral and her brother would be compatible but didn't want them to get hurt because she loved them both. Emily would help each of them however she could, and she didn't want to entertain any negativity about the situation.

Emily was an open thinker and always enjoyed expressing herself. That was one of her qualities that Robert always admired. On the other hand, Robert was more of a 'complete person,' as she called it. He was a deep thinker and hid many of his emotions. Robert maintained a strong personality but accepted other opinions and would bend to the combination of logic and love for another. He often displayed that to friends, family, others, and especially Emily. That leadership quality made him excel in sports and school, and it was doing so in his chosen career. That was a big reason why people liked Robert. Worried she was, but decided to wait and see how things developed.

In the light of day, they both might feel differently. What she did know was there was chemistry between her best friend and her brother—and it was intense. Emily walked to her full-length bedroom mirror and began proposing the facts to an imaginary jury, acting like the lawyer she wanted someday to become. Then, she realized she had to stop hypothesizing, or she would put herself into a stupor. She adhered to a wait-and-see policy. Robert had taught her that. She put her ear against the wall, trying to hear Robert speaking. Emily giggled at the image of Coral raising her dress to lure her brother. Then she heard her mother call to tell her Coral was on the telephone.

Shortly after exchanging presents with her parents earlier that Christmas morning, Coral sat on the corner of her bed in her room, still in her pajamas and fluffy white socks. She had walked through both floors of her home in deep thought right after awakening, trying to process what had happened the night before. It was driving her crazy, and it had been all night while Coral tried to sleep. Having loved Robert since she was a child, now the confused young lady sat there and wondered about the new physical arousal she felt for him. Coral recalled that day at the lake with Robert, but she was an awkward child going into puberty then. Now, she was a fully developed woman with adult sexual desires. Before, it was solely in her mind, a mental thing Coral only shared with Emily in those magical childhood days. After seeing Robert, she realized she did love Robert and always had. But now, her relationship with him was an adult and physical one, which frightened her. Coral had never been with a man that way. Since the night before, she had felt an uncontrollable passion for Robert. "What is happening to me?" she annoyingly whispered, "I can't control myself."

"Did you want me, honey?" Louise heard her daughter speaking in the bedroom and thought Coral had called for her in the hallway.

"No, Mom, I'm just... I don't know what. I'm fine, Mom."

"Okay, dear; I'm here if you want me." Louise knew her daughter, and after seeing how she and Robert acted the night before, she understood Coral was now experiencing real love and no longer a childhood fascination. Louise wanted to help her but knew Coral also needed her privacy.

"Thanks, Mom, but I'm okay." She wasn't okay but didn't feel comfortable telling her mother. These new emotions were unique to her, traveled to the center of her soul, stirred bodily erotic sensations, and had an intense sexual chemistry, something she had never experienced before in her life. Coral had to fight from touching herself to satisfy those lustful sensations. "Snap out of It!" Coral whispered aloud once more. She needed to speak with Emily. Everything was too much for her to handle alone. Emily was the only person Coral could genuinely confide in this situation. She went to the phone in the hallway and dialed her best friend's number. "Em? It's me."

"I knew you would call. Now, calm down, and let's talk about it. Doctor Emily is ready," Emily giggled. She knew her best friend well.

Coral chuckled. She looked around and noticed that her mother had gone back downstairs. She dragged the phone by its long cord from the end of the hallway to her bedroom and continued, "It's real, Em," she whispered even though her mother was gone, "everything I've felt for your brother since we were kids is real."

"I know now," admitted Emily, "I was wrong. I see now that Robert feels the same way. He probably always has, but hid it well because you were too young. He always concealed himself in his loneliness after that Sue Peters thing happened."

"I remember. I wanted to kill her, and then the poor thing got hurt, and I felt so bad I had to go to confession."

"But you broke through his barrier, Coral. I'm his sister, and we have always been close. But do you realize you're the only other female he got close to?"

"Yeah, I've always been attracted to Robert since I first saw him, but I'll always remember when I fell in love with him."

"I know, and I never believed you that time when you said he loved you back."

"No, not that time. I must have been an annoying little kid, but Robert was always patient and kind to me," Coral sobbed softly.

"Are you crying, Coral?"

"Yes, and I want to. I fell in love with Robert the first time he gave me a ride in his Corvette. I played a trick on him, and he didn't even get mad at me. He was always so nice to–" Coral began crying uncontrollably.

"Oh, honey, don't cry."

"I can't help it because now I love that same nice guy in a completely different way," Coral sobbed. "God must be giving me what I deserve by making all those sexual jokes all the time. Now it's happening for real, Em."

"What do you mean?"

"We have a strong sexual chemistry, Em."

"Really? I mean, how do you know?"

"For heaven's sake, I had an orgasm from just touching and looking at him. How sick is that?" she whispered so nobody would hear her.

"Oh, my God! What about Robert?"

"He got a... you know... a bulge..."

"A boner?"

"Yes!"

"Are you sure?"

"I'm not blind, Em."

"Okay, okay. I just needed confirmation."

"Do you remember when we were kids and that guy exposed himself?" Coral asked out of the blue.

"How could I forget?"

"We became practically authorities on that male thing, remember?"

"Right." Emily was blushing even though Coral couldn't

see her.

Coral continued on that subject. "Em, did that ever bother you? I mean, what that guy did?"

"Well, we never really talked about it much as adults."

"So, it affected you too? I know you haven't done it with Chris yet, but did you ever see his?"

"No," Emily answered softly. "I'm afraid," Emily began to get upset.

"Okay, calm down, Em. Battle stations, we'll get through this together."

The two young women spoke for over an hour about the man who had exposed himself to them when they were innocent children. They candidly discussed this newly revealed admission, along with their other frustrations and worries about life, as they always did. Emily and Coral conversed like the true friends they were, having hidden their fear of sex for so long. They then agreed to continue their conversation later that day and hung up the phone.

After her call to Emily, Coral lay on her bed. To distract herself from the wicked impulses she felt for Robert, she pulled one of her dolls from a higher shelf in her bedroom, reminiscing about her childhood. She had saved her fine doll collection for a potential future daughter. As she held the doll, the thought of having children with Robert came alive. No longer a distant hope like when she was a child, he was the man she wanted to marry. The mere touch of his hand ignited every nerve in Coral's body, as if she had received an exhilarating shock that made her want to scream from desire. Coral longed for him to make love to her and fulfill the natural desires she now felt. "I love him, and I know he'll marry me. I'm going to let Robert take my virginity," Coral softly whispered.

Robert had been contemplating the events of the evening before. He dated many women since high school and was adept with female anatomy and psyche from knowledge and experience. Robert knew attraction and arousal well but only as spontaneous reactions between the sexes, as a scientist. All of his experiences could not account for what he now felt. It was different and as if a floodgate had opened. Did he harbor repressed feelings for Coral when she was younger? Was there always an attraction he suppressed toward her because of her age? These thoughts raced through his mind, and he knew he should speak to someone. He couldn't discuss this with his best friend, Roger, because the subject was about his younger sister, which would be awkward. His father, William, was someone he truly respected and the one person other than Roger whose advice he often sought.

When Robert approached him, William was reading a magazine, sitting on his favorite chair in the larger living room on the first floor. "Dad, sorry to interrupt, but can you spare a moment?"

"Of course, Son. What's up?"

"I need your advice, Dad."

William glanced up and observed his son's concerned expression, "Okay, Robert, shoot."

Robert knew his father's advice was always solid. He never held back his true feelings and was direct, which were only some qualities Robert admired in him. "I have a young woman-related problem," Robert blushed and instinctively smiled to hide his nervousness.

William was a high-ranking officer during the war and an excellent businessman, and he learned to observe things around him carefully. Even though he didn't show it, William listened to things most would ignore, watched facial expressions, and mastered a keen intuition. Smiling, he asked Robert, "Does this young woman-related problem have anything to do with a certain Coralie LeBlanc?"

"You always were perceptive, Dad," Robert smiled back nervously. "It does. I don't know how to explain it, Dad, but I now have completely different feelings about her than I did, and

I don't know why."

"Well, from what I remember, you always did. You just hid those feelings in a way suited to you at the time. Coralie was too young then. Your studies, sports, and friends exemplify how you suppressed those sentiments." William observed his son carefully. "You see, some of us hide our sincerest emotions out of fear. It's normal."

"Not you, Dad. You were a war hero."

"I'm a perfect example of what I'm saying. I was scared shit whenever I was under fire, just like every other combat soldier in that war whether they choose to admit it or not."

Robert smiled at his father, "Well, I always liked Coral. She was cute and bold, and I did enjoy speaking to her a lot. But that was because she managed to maintain mature conversations."

"Those are qualities that a person always possesses. You saw them in her when Coral was still a child, and you hid your affection for the same reason: she was in a child's body."

Robert realized those things he remembered were the soul of Coral. Now apparent to him, her physical development and those qualities formed the basis for his new feelings. Robert's speculations pushed on, and he answered, "But this is my little friend. It's monkeyface I'm talking about."

"Robert, you must stop being a scientist for a minute and realize what is happening with your newfound desire for Coral. You're human and a man. You didn't act on any love or admiration for her when you last saw her because she was a child. Now Coral is a woman; naturally, you're releasing any buried feelings."

Robert thought and finally admitted, "I always enjoyed being around her." He looked at his father and said, "I've never been in love before." Robert focused on the memory of being with Coral and her aura. He always avoided love somehow. His mission in life was his work, and he wouldn't let anything stand in his way—until now. Robert realized this passion, the first one of his life, was uncontrollable. These were all new feelings he harbored.

"Well, welcome to the club, Son."

"But, what if I'm overreacting to sentiments that I alone feel and probably not even shared by Coral?"

"These are things all couples go through. Trust your instincts, Robert; they'll never disappoint you. But I know that young lady is in love with you," William thought for a second, "and probably always has been.

Robert felt so much better. "You've helped me more than you might think, Dad. Thanks."

"Anytime, Son; I'm always here for you."

A curious day was at hand for the couple involved and those who knew what was happening.

Roger drove his sister, Coral, over to the Bryant home. Mr. and Mrs. LeBlanc didn't want Coral traveling back alone at night and assumed Robert would take her home. Oblivious of his sister's feelings toward Robert, Roger noticed and commented about how nervous she was acting in his car and how much perfume she was wearing.

When the doorbell rang, Robert quickly announced, "I'll get it." Impeccably dressed, he wore beige dress pants, a dark brown belt and matching-colored shoes, and a dark blue tapered-fitting dress shirt. As he walked to the foyer, Emily quickly followed and smelled the fragrance of his cologne that pervaded his trail.

Robert opened the front door to see Coral accompanied by her brother, Roger. They greeted Robert and Emily with a Merry Christmas as they entered the house.

Coral wore a full-length grey-white rabbit fur coat with cuffed sleeves. She wore her hair up, the front pulled back tight, emphasizing the aesthetic features of her flawless face even more.

"Merry Christmas," she repeated softly to Robert, stepping on her tiptoes to hug him warmly. She loved Robert and had already decided to let him take her virginity. She hid any remaining fears well, rubbing her body firmly against his.

Robert gently forced their embrace longer. The passion of it seemed like an eternity to him until he finally replied, "Merry Christmas, Coral. I'm glad you came." Coral was almost unable to withdraw from his grasp on her body.

Roger was going to his fianceé's house and could only come in for a minute. He kept his overcoat on and shook his friend Robert's hand. Then Roger walked toward the living room to where Robert's parents were sitting. He kissed Emily's cheek as he passed her.

Robert slowly helped Coral out of her coat and handed it to Emily, who was eagerly waiting. She could see that her brother and her friend were both nervous. Emily admired Coral's coat as they hugged, and then she hung it up in the foyer closet.

Coral looked ravishing in a dark red form-fitting dress with no shoulder straps that revealed even more cleavage of her well-defined breasts in the front than the dress she wore the night before. It again exposed her naked flesh from her shoulders to the small of her back. The designs of her matching dark red three-and-a-half-inch heeled shoes were cut and tapered at the fronts and along the inner sides, revealing just a hint of her upper toes and well-formed arches of her feet, which Robert thought was sensually appealing. Coral secretly referred to them as her man-killer stilettos because men couldn't resist the way they firmed up her thighs and calves and made them look even more voluptuous than her naturally appealing and shapely lower limbs. Her dress had a matching material bow attached at the front of a snuggly fitting belt around her thin waist, which added to her curvaceous figure.

Robert admired the elegant and seductive creature who stood before him. "You look beautiful, Coral," he complimented her.

"Thank you, Robert," Coral smiled. Her mouth was radiant when she did and revealed sparkling white teeth. The large silver-colored braces that she wore years ago were long gone. Deep red lipstick made Coral's shapely lips look seductive and sensual. It aroused Robert.

He took Coral's hand and escorted her over to his parents.

"Mom, Dad, doesn't Coral look lovely today?" He put his right arm over Coral's naked shoulders and could feel her warm, soft flesh. It excited him and made his manhood twitch.

Robert's touch on her naked shoulder exhilarated Coral. She felt a quiver in her loins and tried to ignore it. "Hi, Mr. and Mrs. Bryant. Merry Christmas to you both!" She gave them a big smile.

"You look beautiful! Merry Christmas," Naomi greeted Coral, recalling the broken-hearted little girl when her son left for college. Naomi embraced Coral. "We're so happy you came!"

"Merry Christmas, honey," said William, already on his feet. "We haven't seen you as often since you and Emily went to college." William smiled. "You look lovely, dear. You're a grown woman now," he said as he hugged her. "My God, where did the time go?" Then, he secretly winked at his son, recalling their conversation.

Coral sat down and chatted with Naomi and William. Roger bid everyone a 'Merry Christmas,' and Robert walked him to the door. Robert and Roger agreed to get together with the guys sometime that week and shook hands before Roger opened the door and left.

A few minutes later, Nicholas and May Stetson, Naomi's brother and sister-in-law, arrived with her mother, Eloise. Everyone sat in the living room. Robert re-acquainted Coral with the Stetsons. Everyone commented on how beautiful she had become. They hadn't seen her in a while. William served cocktails to his guests, who conversed until Naomi called everyone to the table.

Naomi had phoned Louise LeBlanc to thank her for the food she had sent. Louise told Naomi how Coral and Robert had interacted the night before. It was no surprise to Naomi; she had always observed how her son favored Coral.

"I hope they do become a couple." Naomi told Louise, "Robert needs a young woman like Coral."

"I do, too," said Louise. "They make such a lovely couple."

Therefore, Naomi sat Coral opposite Robert at the end of the table so they could speak and conveniently see each other. Emily sat next to Coral because she wanted to see her brother's expressions and be next to her friend in case Coral signaled her in any way. William sat at the opposite end of the table. The Stetsons sat close to him, as did Carlo and Isabella Russo, who usually joined the Bryants on holidays. Naomi had not said anything about Robert and Coral to William. He didn't mention to her he already knew.

With Isabella's help, Naomi prepared a beautifully decorated table and a delicious meal. Beautiful silverware, Christmas-decorated dishware, and gold-rimmed crystal glasses adorned the large dining room table. William held his glass of wine and made a toast to 'a Merry Christmas and a Happy New Year.' After acknowledgments to the toast, Robert looked directly at Coral, silently mouthed the words 'Merry Christmas,' and smiled at her. A chill ran up and down Coral's spine as she smiled back at him. Naomi grinned at her daughter, Emily, as a signal she picked up on it.

There were individual shrimp cocktails in festive-designed bowls given to each person. Then, Naomi passed portions of lasagne in matching holiday plates to everyone. After a pause, Naomi served a beautiful, sizeable prime rib roast, which William took charge of cutting at the table, a family tradition, while everyone passed their dishes. There were grilled potatoes and fresh green beans along with the meat. The green bean dish was Isabella's recipe and cooked al dente with sliced almonds mixed in, the way many Italians preferred. A beautiful mixed salad also accompanied the meal. Everybody ate while having polite conversations. Robert and Coral couldn't resist constant urges to glance at each other between answering and asking everyone questions. So as not to make both of them uncomfortable, Emily and Naomi only used their peripheral vision to avoid noticeable staring at the couple. However, the mother and daughter didn't miss anything that transpired between them, and they especially paid close attention to the sensual body language Coral and Robert used.

After dinner, William led his guests to a sitting room off the dining room. Robert immediately took Coral's hand and asked, "Would you like to stroll with me through the castle?"

Coral answered, "So you know my secret word for your home?" She smiled, "I've loved this house since I first saw it. It seems so long ago." Her smile widened, and Robert became excited by the sensual way her full lips parted. Emily had noticed Coral and Robert walking off together. Unsure whether or not to interfere, she decided to let them be alone.

Coral and Robert slowly walked through the large rooms, softly speaking while recalling old memories they shared in the house. Robert pointed to one of the elevators and asked Coral, "Would you like to ride up to the viewing lounge at the top of the world from the highest turret above the third floor?" Robert gave Coral a wide smile.

Coral whispered softly and soothingly in Robert's ear, "I would love to go to the top of the world with you." She took Robert's extended hand and smiled back at him as they entered the small elevator, standing close, each resisting touching as their bodily aromas exuded within the tiny space.

Still holding hands as they exited the lift, Robert asked, "Can you manage the wrought iron circular stairway with your heels?" Coral removed her hand from Robert's and put it on Robert's left breast as she stepped out of her heels alluringly. Robert could see that the toenails of her shapely feet were painted the same deep red color as her fingernails, which now gently touched his breast. He could feel the tips of her nails get slightly tighter as she moved them around the sensitive area that surrounded his nipple. Robert's manhood began to grow, so he took Coral's hand away from his breast and led her up the spiral stairway.

As they reached the top, Robert turned around, put his hands on Coral's waist, and lifted her past the last stair and onto the floor. Her deep blue eyes widened as she looked up and into his. Coral stood on her tiptoes and raised her arms to hold

Robert's back. Then she kissed Robert firmly on the mouth, his hands still on her waist, sliding them to feel the soft flesh of her lower back. Robert excitedly opened her lips with his and rolled his tongue with hers. Coral moaned as they passionately kissed. Her succulent lips moved, and she softly bit then licked his left ear like a lioness. The sensations between her legs were driving her emotions. Robert seductively kissed and then licked the precise part of Coral's neck that began to drive her wild. Coral screamed out, "Oh, Robert! I want you!" She couldn't help herself or hold back, "I want to feel you inside me! Please, Robert!"

Robert's mood tempted him to lift Coral in his arms, put her on the round sofa at the center of the viewing tower, and make passionate love to her, imagining the moisture of her inner softness. But as much as he lusted her shapely body, he knew he loved her. Unlike his experiences with other women, Coral had a special meaning to him, something that he had never ever felt before. Though Robert had never experienced it, he knew this had to be true love. So, instead, Robert moved his hands from her midsection and held her head between them, gently massaging her ears with his thumbs. "Not here. We can't!" It took every ounce of his will to seize his desire to take her on the plush round sofa. "Not like this. Not for the first time." Robert was breathing heavily, as was Coral.

Coral felt her wetness drip on her inner upper thighs and tried to control herself. She stood back and composed herself. "You're right. Not here." Coral looked up at Robert. Her lipstick, now smeared, made her look erotic and seductive. Robert strained to control himself; he wanted to consummate his love for her. "When? When can we?" Coral pleaded.

"Let's sit down and talk." Robert took her hand and sat her down on the round sofa. He sat next to her. "Coral, I think I love you." He paused. "I don't know, I've never been in love before. But–"

"I love you, Robert!" she cut him off. "I know I do. I feel it in every part of my mind and body. Take my virginity now, please! Make love to me now. I can't wait any longer."

"But are you sure you want to do this?" Robert gently rubbed the nape of her long, delicate neck. "Because I can't resist you. You are the only woman who ever made me feel this way," he softly told her.

"I'm certain!" Her big, wide eyes were begging him. "If not here, when and where?"

Coral and Robert sat close together, enjoying the view of the valley below from the six oversized windows at the peak of the house's highest and largest hexagon-shaped turret. Their strong efforts to contain themselves had defeated their lustful intentions. Holding hands, they reflected on the many happy times they shared when they were younger. Coral had fixed her makeup and lipstick with cosmetics she carried in her purse.

"Do you remember that time those kids were bullying me, and you came to my rescue?" Coral smiled fondly, recalling how gallant Robert appeared to her.

"Yeah, I do."

"You always protected me. I felt so secure whenever I was with you."

"I would never let anything bad happen to you, not then or now," Robert smiled as he remembered that incident. I love you, Coral, and I would never allow anyone to hurt you."

"I know, Robert; that's one of the reasons I love you so much."

"You're not a child anymore, Coral," Robert conceded, holding her fingers and kissing the back of her hand. Coral sat there, admiring the love of her life and imagining their future together.

The new couple had planned to start dating and fulfill their passions when they felt the time was right. Robert wanted Coral to be sure she wanted to be with him.

"I guess I can't use my pet name, monkeyface, for you anymore," Robert said, smiling.

"Oh? Why not?" Coral fondled Robert's hand, noticing he

was liking it.

Robert put his other hand on the side of Coral's face, his fingers gently sliding down, stroking it, and he spoke softly, "Because I told you a long time ago I would only use that term of endearment until you realized how beautiful you are. Do you remember?"

"Yes," Coral replied, still playing with Robert's hand, her fingers tenderly massaging Robert's palm. "I wanted to be beautiful for you."

"Now, you are the most beautiful woman I have ever seen." The feeling of her fingers stroking that sensitive part of his hand excited him.

"Thank you, Robert, but I've come to like that pet name," she smiled and chuckled softly, whispering, "When you first told me it was an endearing term, I thought you meant you cherished me."

"I do," Robert reached over and kissed Coral on her lips, careful not to smear her lipstick. "I do cherish you."

Coral cuddled in the arms of the man she had always loved. "I cherish you, too, Robert."

"I guess this is as good a time as any," Robert said as he handed a small Christmas-wrapped box to Coral. "Merry Christmas."

Coral took the box that Robert handed to her. She had a small gift for Robert downstairs and hadn't given it to him yet. Coral didn't know he was coming to town that year but bought a book for him the week before and thought he might like it. She planned to leave it with Emily to give to him. "Thank you, Robert." Coral had a surprised look on her face. "You thought to bring something for me," Coral softly said, "How sweet." Robert watched as Coral slowly removed the bow and then the paper wrap. Robert thought she did it sensually and envisioned her removing her clothes similarly. He suppressed the thought out of fear of them both getting aroused again. It was a flat jewelry box. She lifted the box lid, and her big eyes lit up. "Oh, Robert! It's beautiful!" She appeared shocked and carefully removed the piece of jewelry with her hand. It was a lovely, sizeable diamond-shaped heart in an 18-carat gold setting with smaller Amethyst stones surrounding the sparkling diamond rock at the center, attached to a petite 18-carat gold chain. "My birthstone," Coral whispered, "You remembered." Coral took Robert's hand. He was sitting close, and she kissed him gently on his lips.

"I'm glad you like it," Robert smiled. "I bought it for my little friend, not realizing she had become a beautiful woman."

"It's too much, though, Robert. It must have cost a fortune. Thank you!"

"We always had a special attachment, didn't we?"

"Yes, Robert. We always shared something special."

"I realize that now," Robert admitted.

"Please put it on for me. I want to show everyone–everyone in the world." Coral laughed at Robert. "I never had a diamond before." A tear rolled out of Coral's left eye.

Robert wiped it away with his finger. Smiling, he said, "Just like old times."

'You always wiped away my tears."

"C'mon, Let's rejoin the group." Robert finally said. "They'll be sending up a search party soon."

They descended the stairway, and Coral slipped back into her high-heeled shoes. She looked up at Robert. "Soon, Robert." Coral's beautiful dark blue eyes gazed deeply into his imploringly for what seemed like a lifetime to Robert. She whispered sensually in a soft and soothing voice, her lips close to his ears, "I want to make love to you soon. I'm a woman now and can't wait much longer to release this blazing passion for you. I want to feel your hard, naked body against mine and finally know the ecstasy of you deep inside me." She had never said anything like that to a man before, but Coral wasn't embarrassed. She was speaking to her Robert from the heart and had never been afraid to tell him anything.

Coral lay face down. Her head turned slightly left on the

king-size mattress in the hotel room in Youngstown, Ohio. Her voluptuous body was completely nude and wet from perspiration. Coral's shapely legs bent at the knees, and Robert held her feet in his hands as he kissed them at the back of her toes while sitting next to her on the large bed. Coral's vulva remained swollen and soaked as they had just finished making love for the third time. Coral let out little groans of fulfillment as she enjoyed the pleasure of after-sex. She giggled from the satisfying tickle as Robert's tongue began licking between her toes. Coral rolled over, sat up, cuddled with Robert, and whispered in a husky voice, "I never even thought it could be this good." Coral smiled at Robert, "You did things to me I never knew existed. You drove me crazy. It was beautiful."

"You're beautiful!" Robert smiled, "You drive me crazy."

"I love you, Robert!" Coral pushed Robert flat on the bed. She slid her legs around his lower body and sat as if she were riding a horse, rubbing against him, remembering that feeling in her loins from long ago. "You will marry me, won't you, Mr. Bryant?"

"I will because I love you right back. I know that now." Robert kissed her full lips, "I never knew I would be able to love a woman as much as I love you." Robert wanted to marry Coral as soon as possible, but first, he had to find a perfect ring suitable to how much love he felt for her.

Robert and Coral announced to everyone that they would be officially dating that Christmas Day before Robert drove Coral home. Everyone was amazed but joyed. Naomi had phoned Louise before Coral had arrived home. Both sets of parents were delighted with the news.

Robert and Coral let nature take its course during the week before going to the Youngstown hotel. They went out dancing and met friends for dinner. It was a wonderful time for the new couple. Coral proudly strolled about town holding Robert's hand. Robert had forgotten the gentle breezes that floated up from the river there in Rue. The memories of the countryside resurrected in his mind as the new couple enjoyed rides at a

Christmas carnival that came to town for the holidays. They walked together in wooded areas and talked the way they had before Robert left for college; only now, they held hands when they did. Coral introduced her new boyfriend to people who he had never met. But everyone knew of Robert Bryant.

"I wish it was summer so we could go to the lake," Coral laughed, thrilled to be with her Robert.

Robert envisioned Coral's voluptuous body in a bikini and said, "I'd have to fight off all the guys wanting to take you away from me." He laughed back at the young woman he would soon marry.

"Let's go to the Rue High School basketball game together," Coral asked with a smile that Robert cherished.

"Ah, they'll give me attention. You know I hate that."

"Oh, do it for me, for old time's sake," she said, holding her smile, which was irresistible to Robert. "Everyone here loves you."

"Okay," Robert said, giving Coral one of his broad smiles that drove her crazy. "For you," he kissed her lips gently.

At halftime, the school prepared a special tribute for Robert. Then, Coach Fred Wilson announced, "Let's hear it for a special alumnus, Robert Bryant, Rue's best athlete ever!" Robert rose with a bashful expression and waved to the roaring and cheering crowd that clapped furiously. Robert hated being in the limelight. But Coral was clapping, cheering, and laughing in her seat beside him.

Coral had phoned Peter Cummings to break off the relationship she felt never should have existed in the first place. Coral hated to do it over the telephone but knew she wouldn't see him again until after the Holiday break and didn't feel it was right to make him wait. Also, Coral didn't want him to travel from Youngstown to hear bad news. However, Peter didn't take it badly. He was calm and casual and only said something in Latin that she couldn't understand. Coral thought that Peter was just being his weird self. Then he added that he knew it was because of Doctor Robert Bryant. Coral assured him it was not because of Robert's arrival and that she had always loved him. But Peter interrupted her and quoted Shakespeare, "Cowards die many times before their deaths; the valiant never taste of death but once." Then Peter hung up the receiver of his phone.

"Wow! Peter's really gone," Coral told Robert about her bizarre phone conversation with Peter the next time they were together in his car.

"I never really saw you and him as a couple," Robert told her.

"That's because I was always in love with you," Coral smiled in a way that stimulated Robert, who had never been aroused solely by a conversation.

"I loved you always but never allowed myself to realize it." Robert's statement led to a simple kiss that slowly became sexually arousing for them both.

"Does little Robert feel like continuing this at a hotel?" Coral asked seductively.

"Little Robert is not so little right now." Robert revved up his Corvette's engine and told Coral, "Hold on, honey, we're on our way to ecstasy," as he floored the Vette to drive as fast as he could to make love with her for the first time. They both had decided they were ready. Robert finally understood that Coral loved him as a mature adult and no longer that of a childhood fantasy.

While driving to a luxurious hotel in Youngstown with Coral, Robert spotted a red four-door 1951 Oldsmobile 88 following him. He didn't think about it until he saw it again. He pointed it out to Coral, who agreed it was indeed following them.

"What type of a car does Peter use," Robert asked Coral.

"It might be his car, but we always use my car." Then, the red Oldsmobile streaked past them before it disappeared

"Weird, maybe it's a coincidence, or we're both seeing things," Robert said to ease Coral's fear.

"A UFO?" Coral giggled, "I don't know if it's him. He uses a different car sometimes."

*

One day merged into another within the dream-like world where Coral and Robert now lived. They dated and made plans for their future life together.

"I'll come back as often as I can while you finish college," Robert wanted Coral to finish getting her degree.

"Okay, but I want to set a date to marry before I finish," Coral insisted.

They would teach together wherever they settled. Rue, Ohio, was highest on their list of prospective places. Robert had changed. He had found love and given up his other ambitions. He wanted to raise a family with the woman he loved.

When Roger LeBlanc found out that Robert was dating his younger sister, he confronted Robert unexpectedly. "If you think a no-good louse like you is going to date my little sister, you have another thing coming, bozo!" He glared at Robert, who believed his best friend was being serious. Then Roger broke into a big smile and pulled Robert into a tight bear hug. "I think it's great! She couldn't have picked a better guy."

Robert left right after New Year's Day to return to teaching, and Coral returned a day later to Youngstown. Before they parted, Robert and Coral went to an exclusive restaurant for dinner on New Year's Eve. They enjoyed the festivities at midnight, kissing outdoors under a sky full of fireworks. Robert planned to return twice a month to be with Coral.

Once, after Coral returned to school, Robert surprised her with a late-night phone call. He said he was in Youngstown and told her to look out her dorm window. Robert was standing outside in the cold of late January, speaking from a phone booth. Coral sneaked out and left Emily a note while she lay asleep. They went to a hotel and spent a beautiful night together before Coral returned to class and Robert departed.

Robert saw Coral in January, February, and mid-March. He was loyal to his word, and she lived to see him just like when she was a child. But now, they had fulfilled their love.

Coral and Emily left Youngstown together for spring break on Tuesday, March 20, 1962. Robert was arriving on Thursday, and they both looked forward to seeing him. Coral couldn't wait to hold him in her arms.

Robert had a surprise for Coral. He had purchased a beautiful diamond engagement ring for Coral. Before Robert left Rue the last time he was there, He and Coral accompanied Roger and his fiancée to shop for an engagement ring, as Roger hadn't given her one yet. As the girls were looking, Robert overheard Coral excitedly tell Mary Lou, the one she adored. "It's the exact type I would love to have someday." That's how Robert knew the one to buy for Coral. Robert returned to the same store alone the next day. He asked the jeweler to make one styled precisely, only with a larger, better grade of diamond and a better quality of gold. Robert wanted it to be perfect for the woman he loved. The owner told Robert it would only take two days, and he picked it up before leaving town.

On Wednesday, March 21, at 4 PM, the two girlfriends were alone at Coral's home. Emily was helping her best friend, Coral, rearrange the furniture upstairs in her small bedroom. Now that Coral was coming home more often, she needed a desk for her college schoolwork. And the two young ladies were sliding things around to fit one next to the window.

"Really, Coral. I don't understand the urgency. You're getting married before you know it," Emily said, exhausted from moving the desk so many times, trying different places. "Why do you have to do this?"

"I'm giving you a chance to exercise, Em. You sit too often from studying," Coral chuckled. "And besides, I need your brute strength," Both girls laughed hysterically.

Suddenly, they both heard a loud knocking on the front door. Coral and Emily looked at each other.

"Expecting someone?" Emily asked.

"No," Coral answered, "Everybody's out. I'll go see who it is," she climbed over the desk to get to the door of her bedroom. "I hope we have a big bedroom after we marry. I've always had this small room."

"I'll come with you. Maybe Robert came back earlier than he planned," Emily said as she followed Coral.

The door came crashing inward as Emily and Coral neared the bottom of the stairway. The two wide-eyed girls noticed it was Peter Cummings, but he looked different, which scared them both.

Peter stood at the open entrance; the door leaned inward and on its side. He had a Bible under his left arm and began to quote scripture as he stared directly at Coral. Then, he started walking toward the stairs as the two frightened friends quickly turned in horror to go back upstairs.

Emily tripped on a stair and fell in her haste to escape, but Peter ignored her and continued after Coral. Peter cornered Coral before she could run away. One of his eyes rolled back, showing only the white of his eyeball; the other stared at Coral with a terrifying gaze.

"What do you want from me?" Coral screamed at him, frightened at his bizarre appearance.

Peter's one normal eye stared into Coral's deep blue eyes, but he said nothing. His thin lips fully opened, forcing his jaw to drop and remain open, making him appear like an evil machine. He raised his arm tightly and mechanically, then slapped Coral hard across her face. She fell to the floor and was in a stupor. Emily quickly ran up the flight of stairs to help her friend. She lifted a lamp from a table in the hallway. Emily swung it as hard as she could to hit Peter with it. But Peter's stiff arm blocked her swing, and his Bible fell to the floor. Peter's rigid arm rose from a lower position, hitting Emily directly in her forehead with his knuckles. The punch knocked Emily out while still on her feet, and she fell hard. Her head hit the solid oak wood of the side of a doorway, and she lay there unconscious.

Coral rose to her feet but was still groggy as she tried to fight Peter. He pulled Coral's hair tightly. She screamed, and her fingers clawed his separated and damaged face and tore a thin slice of flesh off, but it felt dry and rubbery, unlike skin. Horrified, she held it in her hand, but there was no blood. The hands of Peter's stiff arms grasped under Coral's swinging and fighting arms, lifting her off the floor with superhuman strength. His spine-chilling, one-eyed evil stare remained focused on her horror-stricken, dark blue eyes. Peter turned Coral sideways in his arms as she screamed, waving her arms to fight back, and threw her high in the air. Coral's terrified eyes remained wide open as she flew up and then floated midair for what seemed a lifetime. Her only thought was of Robert as her body descended, smashing onto the solid hardwood floor of the downstairs inner foyer near the open, damaged doorway. Coral appeared like a mangled toy doll. The fracture to her neck alone caused her instant death. Peter slowly walked down the stairway and sat on the floor next to Coral's still, dead body. He began to babble through his broken jaw and make hand gestures as if he were lecturing.

9

Rue, Ohio 1962

In June 1962, Robert Bryant sat on the summer lawn at Coral's grave. A hearty crop of fresh grass, planted in April, had filled in over her burial spot. It was as if God tried to hide the place where Robert's beloved lay buried to soothe the turmoil in his heart. Robert visited that site daily bundled up in a winter jacket, gloves, and a hat from the cold days of the remainder of March to mid-April. He still went every day in the early summer to that June day. In the snow and rain, Robert would sit there for hours each day and leave at dusk. Robert never spoke to anyone while he spent time at Coral's grave. He just sat there thinking. Robert quit teaching and doing research at his college to remain close to Coral. He lost weight in the past months since her death and appeared peaked from the constant exposure. His parents were extremely worried about him.

Emily had to be hospitalized for a severe concussion after hitting her head on the hardwood doorway the day Peter killed Coral. She didn't wake up for several days. When Emily finally did, she began to cry as she remembered Coral and asked about her. Emily had missed the funeral, which was probably for the best, as she became hysterical upon realizing Coral's death. She was deeply distraught over the loss of her best friend. Slowly, she recovered from her concussion and became well enough to confront the distressing experience. By the end of June, Emily started to sit with Robert, holding him and crying by his side.

The story of a deranged man murdering his ex-girlfriend made headlines throughout the river valley. The entire town of Rue mourned the tragedy. It was a sad time in the quiet community of Coralie LeBlanc, who dreamed of the day she would be Mrs. Robert Bryant. Authorities placed Peter Cummings in a psych ward at a hospital for the criminally insane in Youngstown, Ohio, while he awaited his trial. A state psychiatrist diagnosed Peter with paranoid schizophrenia, and a judge ruled that he was not criminally responsible for the murder due to insanity. This ruling meant that Peter Cummings would remain indefinitely at the hospital for the criminally insane in Youngstown, Ohio, receiving psychiatric care and treatment instead of a prison sentence. The LeBlanc family felt a deep sense of injustice about this. Roger vowed to confront Peter if the state ever granted him a release from the institution. Roger didn't believe Peter was human based on the appearance of his face and jaw, suspecting that they were secretly experimenting on him.

Roger had been the first to enter through the broken doorway. He was the one who found his sister's body on the floor in the foyer beneath the stairs. Mr. LeBlanc and Roger had been shopping for new tools earlier that day. Roger noticed the door hanging sideways while his dad put the car into the garage. When he entered the house, Roger couldn't believe what he saw. His first thought was that it was some sick joke or a rehearsal for a bizarre school play. Those were the split-second thoughts his mind manufactured before he perceived the actuality. Coral's eyes remained closed, and she looked at peace but lay in a pool of blood. Peter Cummings was sitting and speaking quietly through his broken jaw, saying gibberish while moving his hands. A piece of Peter's facial skin was missing, exposing what looked like a type of plastic but no blood. Then Roger heard moaning from the top of the stairs in the small hall foyer. It was Robert's sister, Emily. His first impulse was to beat Peter to death. Instead, he instinctively ran upstairs to attend to his best friend's sister as his father walked through the damaged front doorway to the horror.

Robert took all the blame, carrying the guilt for the death of the love of his life. Everyone told him he wasn't responsible, but he refused to listen; he believed he should have been there to protect Coral, especially after seeing the red Oldsmobile. Remembering his promise to Coral that he would never allow anything bad to happen to her only deepened his pain. Even Roger, his best friend, explained that a maniac had killed his sister and that there was nothing anyone could do to bring her back. Those words sparked the first glimmer of life in Robert's eyes since Coral's death. It ignited an idea. Robert wondered why he hadn't thought of it sooner. Since the tragedy, he realized his mind had been unfocused and that he was acting like a zombie. Now, he began calculating equations in his mind. Then, his sharp intellect snapped into focus. He knew what to do, and he was capable of doing it. By God, he would do it!

"I can bring Coral back," he softly said so Roger wouldn't hear, "I know how, and I will do it!" The new ideas filled him with hope. "No, Roge! You're wrong!" He looked directly at his friend. "I can do something!" Roger didn't understand what his friend was saying. He assumed it was just an emotional outburst from Robert. Roger couldn't grasp the complexity of Robert's mind or his plans.

Robert had to return to work. He visited Coral's grave one last time before leaving Rue. A thick, gloomy cloud rolled across the countryside, hovering over the cemetery in Rue where Robert stood. It felt eerie as if something was about to occur; only an omen could be that distinct.

Standing before Coral's resting place, Robert vowed, "Coral, my love, we'll be together again," his voice cracked, weak from exposure to the elements during the stressful months of sitting outside. But his enthusiastic words gave him vigor as he continued, "No matter the cost or time, I will return to you. I'll go to the ends of this earth and time if necessary, but I vow this: I will see you again!"

PART TWO

. . .to the ends

of this earth

and time . . .

10

1962-1982

Time travel studies had fascinated Robert Bryant ever since he was a child. He read books on the subject when he first began reading at an early age. The concept prompted him into the world of physics and formed the basis of his doctoral degree dissertation. Most of his colleagues had focused on the more acceptable idea of time travel: a unidirectional ability to travel to the future. However, Robert had theoretically shown that bidirectional time travel to the past and future was also possible. So now, the young physicist had to apply his innovative theory in practice.

Robert always surmised that knowing the future could change the present and thus the past, as time is ever-moving. And changing the past would, by all means, change the future. Could we change the past without affecting or hurting the future?

Such a novel idea and his pledge to his beloved drove Robert to develop a bidirectional method to travel to the past and future. To accomplish that, he knew he would have to pick up the broken pieces of his life to begin. The journey of a thousand miles always starts with the first step. And Robert made that first stride with his dedication to Coral. There was much work ahead of him, probably amounting to years. However, he was now mentally prepared because he had a purpose. He would someday go back in time to save Coral from the lunatic who killed her.

As he finished unpacking, Robert found the Christmas gift Coral had given him. He had never opened it, and a tear ran down his face as he thought of her. It was the book, 'The Last of the Just,' by Andre Schwarz-Bart. He planned to read it that evening.

In September of 1962, Harvard welcomed Doctor Bryant back wholeheartedly, especially when the board learned of the tragedy in his personal life. He resumed heading the teaching and research of advanced physics. However, the 25-year-old man was a changed person. He remained polite and kind but smiled rarely. That seriousness, with a slightly standoffish personality and good looks, made him even more attractive to some women. But Robert didn't have time for women anymore. He had already found the love of his life, and he would reunite with her–that became the sole reason for his existence.

Robert reviewed his work from his doctoral dissertation: his combined use of quantum physics and nuclear fission and his studies of time loop logic. But, to create a computation box that could travel through time bidirectionally, he had to discover and implement a calculation to travel at the speed of light. His large lab had several blackboards framed in wood with small metal wheels at the bottom of each. Robert used them to write his equations with chalk. As he finished one, he slid the large blackboard out of the way to use a different one. Going back and forth between the boards, resolving problems, and rewriting his equations while buried in other work, the days went by.

Robert had studied the recent theories of wormholes, which could have enough massive gravitational field to bend space-time. If so, there was the possibility of entering one side and traveling to the other side and vice versa between two distant points in time. These theories formed his doctoral degree dissertation and why it became so popular with his peers internationally. Bidirectional time travel was possible, and Doctor Bryant had proved it theoretically. But now he would prove it in actuality, having the emotional drive to do so.

Midway through one of his work days, Robert received an unexpected telephone call forwarded to him by one of his secretaries. A gentleman introduced himself as an agent of the United States National Security Council (NSC). His voice was urgent as he recommended the doctor allow him to travel to Harvard and meet for an appointment. Robert complied, and a team of three people arrived a day later to speak to him. The trio of feds dressed conservatively: the two men wore dark blue suits, and the woman wore a matching dark blue skirt and jacket suit. The older of the three was a man who Robert could tell was in charge, and he spoke first.

"I'm Agent Burton," he introduced himself. "This is Agent Tyrell," who appeared in her mid-forties and nodded to Robert. "And this is Agent Johnson," a younger man who seemed to be around 35 also nodded his introduction gesture. Robert remained quiet and allowed Agent Burton to establish why the three were there. He could see a bulge in his suit jacket, which was more than likely a handgun of larger than average size. Robert casually glanced at the same spot on the other agents. He saw that they also were concealing larger-sized weapons under their jackets, which caused him to consider why they armed themselves so heavily for an informal meeting at a college. That planted a seed for Robert to wonder who these people really were. Their credentials looked official and authentic, but Robert's keen intuition sensed something amiss.

"I'll get right to the point," Burton displayed no emotion, "we're here about your published dissertation, Doctor Bryant," he casually said while sizing Robert up. "I assume a man of your intellect not only knows why it caught the attention of the NSC but understands the implications it has to the security of the people of the United States."

Robert didn't reply, knowing Agent Burton wanted to continue. His only concern was how he fit in this puzzle and what they wanted him to do. He instinctively assumed an order, probably put into the form of a request, was forthcoming.

Agent Burton said, "If anyone can decipher your theory, there could be ramifications to detrimental proportions." Trusting Robert's quiet and calm demeanor, he divulged classified information to Robert, "Our government has been working on your theory since you published it. However, the assigned team of physicists is having great difficulty understanding how to break it down." Then Burton made an emotional statement,

"Doctor Bryant, the president himself has asked that you head the government project."

Robert nodded and spoke his first words, "I prefer to work alone, Agent Burton."

Agent Tyrell took over, "We understand you've suffered a tragedy in your personal life, Doctor Bryant. The NSC waited until you recovered enough to have this conversation," she paused for a few seconds, "but your country needs you, Doctor. We can't do this without you."

Then Agent Burton said, "We have been in touch with your university. They'll let us sponsor a larger laboratory with any equipment you desire." He watched Robert closely to see if he had yet aroused his interest. "You can have all the privacy you want and use the team however you choose."

It was difficult for most people to read Robert as he was a complex person or a 'complete person,' as his sister Emily always asserted. He realized all three agents were sizing him up, even the younger one, who didn't say much. As he quickly processed the idea, he concluded that this assistance would speed up his work and be a faster means to an end. "Let's talk about it some more."

Robert Bryant was a wealthy man at 25 years old, earning a good salary at the university. In addition to a hefty monthly allowance, his father had set aside a vast sum of money in a trust fund. That gave Robert additional monthly allowances if he desired, or he could roll them over into his investment portfolio within the trust, which Robert always did. The entire trust fund would be available to Robert when he turned 28, which would happen in 1965. An enormous sum of money would be accessible to him in less than three years. However, as opposed to spending his own money, the government had the means of providing him with everything he needed, even items considered challenging or impossible to acquire for a non-government employee. Even a small nuclear reactor would require uranium (U-235) or plutonium (Pu-239) to produce fission to power it. In addition, fuel, reactor coolant, control rods, shields, or a method of containment were just some of the things he required. As a private study group, he would eventually require government approval and interaction to implement his theoretical work. So, Robert felt he had opportunities by working directly in compliance with the US Government from the start. He would, of course, keep most of his discoveries a secret from the team. Robert had a mission: he had to be the one who first went back in time for personal reasons. Afterward, the US Government could have full knowledge of his work.

By the end of the four-way conversation, Robert had settled on a deal that satisfied everyone. Building the laboratory began immediately, and he would meet his team of subordinates as soon as the lab was ready. The three agents left to relay the news to their superiors.

A specialized workforce of laborers miraculously completed the new laboratory in one month. After which, Robert met his staff. Six of the twelve-person team consisted of lab assistants and clericals. The government took all precautions by conducting background and security checks, and each was insured and bonded. The rest of the team were his personal assistants. Four were junior assistants, and the remaining two were second and first senior assistants. A Professor named Gunther Schmidt would be Robert's first assistant. Robert was shocked when he learned that Kathy Clarkson was on the government team as his second assistant. Now a doctor, she looked forward to working with the now-famous Doctor Bryant. Of the junior assistants, there were two that stood out as third and fourth assistants. Darryl Thompson was a bright, young professor from Mississippi and was in the genius category. Doctor Thompson was the unofficial third assistant, and Leopold Hector was Robert's unofficial fourth assistant. The two remaining junior assistants had recently received their doctorates and had demonstrated exceptional skills as physicists. All of Robert's assistants were honored to be working with him.

Robert tapped his pencil against the wooden clip pad hold-er as he paused from writing blueprints of his plan. He now had a large private office laboratory to work out his equations privately, as he preferred. Odors of chemicals, solvents, and compounds permeated through the entire wing of the lab. The soft hum of ventilation piped constantly throughout each day. Soft music played to drown out the monotonous sound. Robert had already assigned his two highest assistants enough work to distribute to the others, and they became in charge of the overall progress. Most of that work was diversionary to keep his plan's blueprint as secret as possible. That blueprint, or outline of his actual work, was private. He trusted Gunther Schmidt, but Kathy Clarkson was a wild card, and Robert wondered how she rose to become his second assistant. From his past experiences with her, she acted erratic, as displayed by her reaction to Robert's decision against dating her.

After months of studies, Robert decided to simulate a wormhole. That is, determine by calculations two points in time and then create a device that could travel at the speed of light. Robert's plan was no longer to transport a box but instead enter the simulated wormhole, bringing him to the other side in a different time period. Robert gave an outline of it to his assistants to review. However, he didn't provide his hidden ideas on how he decided to develop a simulated wormhole. That project would take years. He divided that larger goal into smaller tasks. That way, each physicist wouldn't have the complete information, only divisions of it.

Robert only returned to Rue, Ohio, for special events. Each time was more difficult than the last, and the memories buried there ran deep in his heart. However, each time he was there, it was as if Coral was alive and still lived in that special place. This joy gave him the perseverance to continue his efforts to reunite with her once again.

Robert returned to Rue as the best man for his best friend, Roger LeBlanc, and everyone was thrilled to see him. Yet there was a shared sorrow as it brought back memories of Coralie

LeBlanc and the tragedy that had taken place there. It seemed that Robert carried her memory like a banner and had never buried those times now so dear to him.

In 1966, Robert attended the wedding of his sister Emily to Christopher Martin in Rue, Emily's hometown. Chris and Emily practiced law at the Bryant family firm in New York City. They had purchased a beautiful home in a lovely residential neighborhood of that city that reminded Emily of her first home there years earlier. It resembled the house where she had her farewell birthday party years prior. Robert believed it was an unintentional way for her to distance herself from the memory of Rue and her best friend who had lived there, Coralie LeBlanc.

One of Robert's few joys came while visiting Rue for Emily's wedding. He learned that his old coach, Fred Wilson, was in the city hospital, now renamed Rue General Hospital. Fred was receiving treatment there for a heart attack, and Robert decided to visit him. The hospital, completed years earlier, now looked entirely different from the dreary place it had been during Robert's last visit. While inquiring about Fred's room number at the hospital's main counter near the entrance, he thought he recognized someone from his past. Robert spared no expense to cover the medical rehabilitation of Sue Peters and ensured she received the best care. Now, he was shocked yet pleasantly surprised to see Sue sitting before him as a receptionist at the hospital. Plastic surgeons had done an incredible job of reconstructing the bone structure of her head and face. Rebuilt cheeks, eye sockets, and jaw gave her a normal appearance. Her artificial eye looked real, and her remaining eye appeared natural. The best orthopedic and neurosurgeons had operated on Sue's spine, repairing and reconstructing her damaged bones and vertebrae. The surgeons employed novel methods to implant various metals to replace or reinforce the injured areas of her body.

As Sue sat before the man who was responsible for her recovery, she softly said, "Robert? Oh, my God, Robert," as tears ran from both her eyes down her cheek.

"Sue? Is that you? My God, you look incredible!"

After a full minute of awkwardness, Sue spoke, "Robert, do you have a few minutes? Can we speak in the cafeteria?"

"Of course." Then Robert remembered why he was there. "Let me run up and see the coach, and I'll be back."

"Fourth floor, room 402," Sue smiled. Even her lips and grin were back to normal.

"I promised myself I wouldn't cry whenever I saw you, so I'll try my best." Sue sat across from Robert in the cafeteria. A salad and a soft drink rested on her side of the long folding table as she perched on a hard wooden chair, focusing more on speaking with the man who had changed her life than on her meal. Robert nursed a soft drink through a straw, listening intently. "Robert, I wrote so many letters to you but never mailed them," her gaze fell, "because I never knew what words to use to thank you." Sue began to cry, then wail. "You see, I already broke my promise. I'm crying already," she attempted to force a smile. "How can I thank someone who has given me back my life?" she sobbed.

"Ah, Sue. You don't need to worry about thanking me. I wanted to help," Robert replied, comforting her by placing his outstretched hand over hers.

"I do! Everything I have is because of you, Robert. I'm married to a wonderful man."

"Do I know him?" Robert smiled.

"Jim Walsh. Do you remember him from school?"

"Oh, yeah. Jim's the best."

"He thinks highly of you, too. Everyone does, though," Sue smiled. "We have a little girl. We named her Roberta after you. God, Robert, I don't know where to start. We go to church on Sundays. I pray for you every day. I thank God every day for what you did for me, especially after that horrible thing I did to you. I have a wonderful life." Sue stopped speaking and appeared sullen, "We were devastated about what happened to Coralie. I'm so sorry, Robert." Sue could see she had hit a nerve by watching Robert's expression and changed the subject.

Their conversation switched to old schoolmates, how the teams were doing, and other small talk. When they rose to part, they hugged. Sue whispered, "Thank you, Robert, for giving me back my life. You're a wonderful man."

"I'm so happy for you, Sue."

Robert returned to Rue a year after seeing Sue Peters for the Baptism of his sister's daughter, Coralie. They named her after Emily's deceased best friend. Emily did it to allow her dearest friend, her 50-50 partner for life, to live on through her daughter.

Constantly in touch with her brother, Robert, even as a married woman, Emily maintained a close relationship with him in her personal and professional decision-making. Emily and Robert shared a deep connection since Emily could remember, and she consistently worried about him. Emily knew he remained, and would probably always be, brokenhearted about Coral's death. As much as she had loved her friend, Coralie, she wished Robert would move on. Emily felt his pain because she was closest to him, and she hated seeing her beloved brother suffer as much as she knew he did.

Robert would never return to Rue for the Christmas Holiday. It was too hard to be in Coral's castle at that time. Instead, he would see his parents for the holidays at Emily's home or at his home, the one he purchased in Massachusetts, near the school. The memory of his last Christmas in Rue was too painful. Over the following years, Robert constantly adhered to his work. He was always in his lab after hours and on weekends. Robert's weekly progress updates to the government contained only some of his findings, scraps of his real plan.

Robert's research did, however, lead to a significant breakthrough in 1968. He had been working on submitting calculations to the human brain instead of a box. It showed credibility and promise of projecting a person's thought process into a future setting for observation only. It was a stepping stone. Robert put his cognitive mind into the future, where he was able to view ten years into the future. Then, he used reverse loop logic to do the same for the past, and he could see ten years into the past. The apparatus had a slight buzzing sound, and the visions were hazy but real. Robert had now factually proven his theory that time travel was possible. However, he needed to perfect a wormhole capable of transporting a physical being, and only he knew how to accomplish that goal.

Even though this research lab at his college was top secret, news of the breakthrough leaked to the press. Robert suspected that the government did it secretly to attain credibility over the Soviets, who probably had a similar team of scientists working on the same ultimate goal since he published his theories years before. However, the current breakthrough news made Doctor Bryant an international hero, requiring interviews by top radio and television correspondents for publicly. It also led the Swedish Royal Academy of Science to announce Doctor Robert Bryant as the Nobel Prize in Physics recipient in 1968. That made the young professor the most prominent figure in the physics world.

One weekend, while alone in his private lab, Robert activated his mind calculation box. "C'mon, kick in, damn it. Ah, there you go. Music to my ears." After adjusting the buzzing sound, he set the coordinates for his parents' home, Coral's castle, on December 25, 1961. For a few flickering minutes, he could see his love again, beautifully dressed for the holiday from when they were together, and he realized he loved her and always had. "I love you, Coral. I'm coming back to you," he sobbed softly. "I haven't forgotten you. I never will." It was frustrating to see her yet be unable to communicate with or touch her. Knowing it was futile, his emotions got the best of him, and he screamed, "Don't see Peter! He's crazy! It's dangerous!" Robert's head dropped to his lap as he cried. After calming down, Robert realized it was too painful to see his love so alive and beautiful again, but it renewed his hope. That bittersweet experience strengthened Robert's spirit and motivated him to persevere.

A year later, Robert concluded that if a human traveled to a time in the past where they had existed, they would assume the body and age of that era. A person could not inhabit two selves within the same time frame. He learned of a theoretical method to address this issue but had not yet developed it. Traveling to a past or future where they didn't exist would allow the time traveler to retain the same body and age they had before departing. However, Robert couldn't figure out how aging would impact either scenario. He also discovered that time would somewhat compensate for the paradox of time travel. He described it as 'time having a way of correcting, or healing itself to a point.'

Charles Bryant lay on his deathbed in the VIP wing of a hospital that the Bryant Law Firm had built and generously donated to since its founding. His son William sat close beside him in a cushioned chair. Naomi waited outside the room in a separate suite; Charles had asked her for a private moment with his son.

"I'll be just outside, Pap. Please have your nurse call me when you're finished," Naomi replied after Charles kindly asked. Pap was the affectionate name Naomi had given her father-in-law, and she had used it since the day she married William. Kissing his forehead as she left, she understood that there were personal matters he wanted to discuss with his son before departing from this world.

"Don't be sad, Son. I'm nearly 90 and have been fortunate to live a good life. Losing your mother was the worst thing that ever happened to me." Though Charles couldn't turn his head, his eyes met his son's. His voice was soft and frail as he continued, "I believe we accomplished a lot of good during my time as the head."

"You did, Dad, as an exceptional businessman and an incredibly generous person. You achieved remarkable things as the leader," William said, shedding a tear as he recalled his father's tenure as CEO of Bryant Law Firm, stretching back as far as he could remember. "Age is just a number, Dad. The longer we know someone, the more we come to cherish them." William bowed his head as more tears fell. "You've been an incredible father to me. You taught me everything I know. I love you, Dad."

Charles had tears in his eyes as he said, "I'm so sorry for what I did to your sister, Emily." Then he began to cry.

"Everyone makes mistakes, Dad," William said, recalling his sister and the events that transpired.

"But I killed my own daughter!"

"No, it was an emotional decision you made. You couldn't have predicted what would happen." William recalled and then whispered to his father. "I resented it at first, but I understand that now."

"So, the crown goes to you, Son. I wish you good luck; you were born for this role and will excel as its leader. Hell," Charles managed a faint smile, "you've been stepping up in leadership for several years now. I have complete confidence in you."

"Thank you, Father," William said respectfully, aware that Charles didn't have much time left. He watched as his father gradually faded away before his eyes.

Charles snapped back to attention and softly asked, "Do you know who will succeed you yet?"

"Emily has the aptitude but is plagued by–"

"I know," Charles whispered. "Robert lacks the desire, but the firm requires his genius."

"Emily always taps into that, and she always has; you know how attached they are."

Desperately straining his eyes to see his son, Charles gasped, "William, never tell your children the truth about themselves." He whispered so softly that William had to lean in and press his ear to his father's mouth to hear. "It will destroy them." Those were Charles's last words.

*

Years passed, and Robert remained buried in his labors. Robert's father, William, semi-retired in 1972 at age 65. He and his wife, Naomi, bought a home in Florida where they could enjoy warmer climates than those sometimes brutal winter winds of Rue, Ohio. They kept the mansion in Rue and left the Russo couple to care for it whenever they stayed in Florida.

Robert's devotion to Coral strengthened. He pledged never to give up his work as long as he lived and spent every available moment working toward bringing himself back to her.

Later that same year, Robert received some personal information from Doctor Friedrich Kruger. It became a life-changing event for Robert. Doctor Kruger had telephoned Robert at his home. He hadn't seen the old man in years.

"What a surprise, Doctor Kruger. We haven't spoken for so long." So consumed with his work, Robert felt guilty he hadn't connected with the one man who helped him the most ever since he was a young child.

"It is so good to hear your voice, Robert," the professor's voice was frail, "but I must see you at once. It is urgent."

"I'm so sorry to hear that, Doctor. I can find some time earlier next week if–"

"No, Robert," Kruger interrupted his former student. "It has to be now; it is a matter of life and death." The professor who had trained Robert was not well, and Robert could hear it in his feeble voice.

"Where are you living now?"

Doctor Kruger gave Robert an address in New York City and reiterated the urgency of seeing him as soon as possible. The following day, Robert dropped his work and took a flight to see his former mentor.

The address Dr. Kruger gave Robert took him to the Lower East Side of Manhattan. It wasn't a nice neighborhood, with gangs, unemployed mixed-ethnic people looking for work, and struggling actors trying to find any part in the theatre or film industry.

Robert found the address the doctor had given him. A cloud of dark fog hovered over the old building. It seemed evil and remained there and appeared as distressing as the discoveries Robert was about to make. Robert hesitatingly knocked on the door of what seemed to be a small apartment on the first floor of that old building. To Robert's surprise, Gunther Schmidt, the first assistant in his lab at the university, opened the door. Gunther didn't speak at first. He popped his head outside the door and looked down in every hallway direction.

"Doctor Bryant. I'm sorry for what must seem like an act of subterfuge to you." Gunther looked worried. "Please come in. I assure you we will answer and explain all of your suspicions."

As Robert passed through the doorway, he saw a propped-up hospital bed to the side of the main room. In it was a phantom of the former teacher he once knew. Robert was puzzled and appeared so. He slowly walked over to the old professor and greeted him. "Professor Kruger, it's so good to see you." Then Robert pointed to Gunther and asked the professor, "What's going on?"

"Sit down, my son. I have much to tell you, and I'm afraid I have little time left on this earth." Doctor Kruger spoke hoarsely and feebly. "It is so good to see you looking so well, Robert."

Gunther brought a plain wooden chair for Robert to sit on, then stood beside Doctor Kruger's bed. As Robert sat, he observed the surroundings. It appeared that his old mentor was staying in temporary quarters. A hideout was the first thought that went through Robert's mind. "Your First Assistant, who you know as Gunther Schmidt, is my son," said Doctor Kruger. "His real name is Gunther Schmidt Kruger." The doctor paused and swallowed. "Robert, what I have to tell you is going to be most distressing for you, I'm afraid. And by doing so, I am betraying a lifelong oath I made to your father many years ago." There were now tears forming in the eyes of the old man. "But it is necessary that I do because it has become much too dangerous for you and my son, Gunther."

"My father?" Robert was now even more perplexed. Then

he looked at Gunther. "What in hell is going on?" Doctor Kruger nodded to his son and asked him to explain everything to Robert.

Gunther got quickly to the point and asked Robert, "Do you know what the Lebensborn Program was?"

Robert quickly checked his memory and answered, "The Nazi ideology of breeding children?"

"Yes, precisely, Robert," replied Gunther. "The Fount of Life. The Nazi SS initiated it to increase the number of racially pure, healthy Aryans." Gunther explained that another secret program went far beyond eugenics. It was much more sophisticated and had remained hidden apart from Lebensborn. "The Nazis named it 'die unsterblichen,' or 'immortals' in English. That unique program went beyond eugenics to determine couples for mating. They matched only intellectual geniuses and those with superior strength and coordination to give birth." Gunther realized he was giving Robert such unsettling information too fast. "I'm sorry, Robert, these are a lot of facts to absorb, and I'm speaking too quickly." He continued his presentation much slower, "An elaborate facility existed to do much more extensive research into genealogy and manipulation of findings to create actual super people."

"Wait!" Robert exclaimed, his voice loud and agitated. "What does all of this have to do with me?"

"Please, Robert, I know this is surprising, but you will understand if you let me finish."

"Okay," Robert replied softly. He waved his hand as a sign for Gunther to continue, which he did.

"They experimented on humans to create flawless, physically superior, and intellectually advanced males and females. Revolutionary technology allowed them to increase the IQ levels of babies and enhance their physical stamina while still in their mother's wombs. It resulted in the most advanced, intelligent, physically, and sexually strong and appealing people. The Nazis designed these super people, or pioneers of a new breed, to procreate and bring forth others like them." Gunther stopped speaking and looked at his father, waiting for a sign of whether or not he should continue.

Doctor Kruger looked directly at Robert. There was sadness and regret in his old eyes. He told his son, Gunther, that he would explain the rest. "I worked as a doctor for them, Robert. I had to; the Nazis forced me into that malicious program. They threatened to hurt my nephew, Louis, who worked there, if I didn't." The older man paused. He appeared highly disturbed and hesitant, "You, Robert, were a child of this program." He bowed his head in disgrace.

Robert was shocked and speechless. He stared into thin air, and tears began streaming down his face as he sat, trying to absorb the intensity of what this meant. Slumped in the wooden chair, he finally asked, "How?" He paused briefly and then declared, "I'm a monster!"

"No, my son," said Doctor Kruger, "You are a perfect specimen of humanity. You must understand that your birth parents were very kind and caring people. Your natural mother was your father's younger sister, Emily." Robert recalled the old photo he found in the attic. The one with the name Emily scribbled on the back. He remembered his father's expression when he told him about it. The old professor became saddened and frustrated at his inability to relay the story. He thought it might be more comprehensible if he explained it chronologically. Robert remained in a zombie state as he sat and listened. "May I tell you the entire story, Robert? This way, you will understand everything."

A completely disillusioned Robert Bryant finally said, "Why not? I should know everything."

Doctor Kruger swallowed and then took a deep breath. In his heavy German accent, he began. "I met your father during some of my post-graduate studies at Harvard in the mid-1920s. I was older than him, but we became friends. That was long before Hitler took over. Your father's sister, Emily, fell in love with a friend of mine, Hans Keller. He was also doing post-graduate studies like me. Hans was brilliant, but your grandparents disapproved of Emily marrying him. Emily disobeyed them and eloped with Hans to Germany after he finished his studies at Harvard. Your father and I often corresponded when I returned to Germany, and William always kept in touch with his sister. Hans went to prison after Hitler came to power. They later executed Hans and put Emily into the 'die unsterblichen' program because her records showed she was born a high-level genius with an extremely high IQ. She was also beautiful," Doctor Kruger paused, reminiscing about Emily. "The Nazis forced her to mate with my nephew Louis, also a genius. They experimented on her, changing her biologically to produce an advanced breed of super-people. After William married in 1936, your mother, Naomi, could not have children. And they both desperately wanted to adopt. That's when I began working in the special lab at the Lebensborn facility I described. It was a place I planned to escape from at the first chance I found. I learned how to contact British intelligence, who arranged for my family's escape."

The doctor remained focused and determined, speaking as if reliving that terrible time. "Before we left, Emily gave birth to you. She faked a stillborn birth using another baby from a different woman who had died from reactions to an experiment to save you, Robert. She wanted you to live the life she never could. You remained hidden until I got word that arrangements to get my family out were ready. I took you with us, Robert. You traveled with my wife and my family. A little girl named Martha Weber acted as your sister and cared for you. I couldn't get my nephew, Louis, and Emily out. They knew they could never leave that retched place; it would have posed too many consequences to our plans. My son Gunther was a teenager and traveled with a different group, but the Gestapo captured them. British Intelligence rescued him, and eventually, he began working with them. Your father, William, financed the whole operation and worked directly with the American military to help the operation. William risked his life to succeed in rescuing children like you. He went through other great political maneuvers to assure our safety. Your adoptive parents are both wonderful people, Robert. They sacrificed everything to save us and bring you to them. They love you very much, my son. I call you that because I think of you as my second son. I have worked with you since you were an infant. Your father spared no cost to see you raised in a normal environment. William always planned to tell you, Robert. But as his and Naomi's attachment to you grew, it became too difficult under the circumstances. You must try to understand that. You are a fine young man, Robert, and a product of the love and care of good people." The old doctor's voice gave way to the strain of speaking so much.

"So, I was adopted," Robert said, still processing the shock of these revelations about himself. "My sister, Emily, isn't actually my real sister."

"No!" replied Dr. Kruger, his voice loud yet hoarse as he gathered the energy to continue. "Emily is your biological sister. Your birth parents, Louis and Emily, had prevented any further pregnancies after you, but they unexpectedly conceived another daughter, Emily. At that time, the Nazis were under bombardment from the Allies, and they couldn't manipulate her as they did with you." Dr. Kruger paused to swallow a sip of water. "Gunther had received word through secure channels that William's sister, Emily, had another child in 1941. William was already funding the rescue of numerous children during that time. So, your father arranged for Gunther to bring Emily to the United States to be with you. Unfortunately, your sister, Emily, suffered significant conscious and subconscious trauma as an infant throughout the entire ordeal. Imagine how roughly people handled such a young baby while bombs were exploding and she was being passed among so many different people while enduring so many other overwhelming stresses," Kruger explained. He hesitated momentarily; the memories reminded him of his years there before he managed to escape. Then he continued, "As a result, Emily developed a severe anxiety condition, which formed the strong bond you shared, and still have with your sister." Dr. Kruger smiled for the first time since he began speaking. "I vividly remember how your little sister, Emily, resembled a frightened little rabbit when I first saw her," he said, his smile fading as he expressed his feelings. "She was so adorable, but it was heartbreaking to see her so terrified." He then perked up and exclaimed, "But she found comfort in you, Robert. You helped her far more than you can imagine with your inherent goodness and kindness. You and Emily share a very unique bond. Tragically, your natural parents perished in a bombing raid shortly afterward." Dr. Kruger took another sip of water. "On that same mission to rescue Emily, Gunther also brought back a baby named Walter LeRoy and the young lady, Kathy Clarkson, whom I introduced to you. She was also a child of those experiments; your sister, Emily, was not. Kathy's birth name was Gisela Becker, which she changed later.

"Did you intend for Gisela and me to mate?" Robert asked sarcastically.

"I thought it might be a way to relieve your loneliness and avoid sexual frustrations for both of you. As with all things, you are more developed than an average man. Gisela, or Kathy as she renamed herself, is the female equivalent of you. Both your sexual development and capabilities are part of that advanced physical being, especially the strength of your sexual virility. I wasn't sure an average woman would be able to accommodate you. I only intended to help you, Robert. I see now that I was wrong. I am truly sorry about Gisela. Unlike the good and kind man you became, Gisela became bitter. You have super-human strength and intelligence but never used it for a bad purpose. Gisela has turned to evil and will use her advanced powers for wickedness. Beware of her, and remember what I tell you now." The frail old professor forced himself to sit erect in his hospital bed to show the importance of what he was about to say, "She will come after you!" He yelled hoarsely. "There is no sexual satisfaction for Gisela except you." The professor collapsed back to a lying position. "You and her are the only two survivors. She never learned to love as you did. Physical Sex became the sole reason for her existence. Gisela does not possess the ability to love. You are the only man who can completely satisfy her, and she hates you because you rejected her, Robert. Beware! She will try anything to become your sexual partner!"

"I'm sorry I snapped at you, professor. You were always kind to me and helped me in more ways than I ever realized." Robert paused and remembered how patient Doctor Kruger was to him in his early years. "You always looked out for my best interests. I owe you everything." Robert still adhered to some animosity toward the Professor regarding Gisela, now called Kathy Clarkson. But he resolved that it was a logical effort. And Robert didn't want the professor to go to his grave thinking anything other than the love he felt toward him.

As his father became too tired to continue, Gunther finished explanations of Robert's actual birthplace in detail and answered all of his questions. A bewildered Robert remained slumped in the wooden chair, thinking his entire life was a lie. "I was over four when my parents brought Emily from the hospital. I remember."

"You were experiencing many things as your brilliant mind was learning ahead of its time. We arrived at the airport where your parents met us," Gunther explained. "Your advanced intelligence must have sensed that Emily was a part of you, Robert—and that awful place. That's why you developed such a close attachment with Emily and always tried to protect and help her. She was only months old when you first saw her."

"Why are you divulging all of this to me now?" Robert challenged.

"It's dangerous!" the old professor intervened. Doctor Kruger used his hand to motion to his son, Gunther, to finish.

"They planted me as your first assistant on purpose, Doctor Bryant. I belong to, let's say, just for now, a different intelligence sector. I learned that the ultimate goal of this project is not for the betterment of the United States but for a more devious purpose."

Robert interrupted Gunther, "A devious purpose?"

"A secret international cabal consists entirely of the upper echelon of corporate magnates, along with their ties to their governments. They are determined to make this succeed and will do so if you help, Robert. Think about the potential profits they could gain." Robert quickly recalled the three agents who had first approached him at the college.

"But I already proved that time can heal," Robert replied. "Time would mend the damage they caused."

"Robert, the profit would still exist even if time could repair any damage. They would travel back and make investments they were certain would be profitable." Gunther paused, considered an example, and continued, "It's like betting on a horse in a rigged race; they couldn't possibly lose. Nothing would change that could harm time."

"The difference is that the combined cabal would attain everything, and everyone else would suffer. That would change the economics of the world," Robert replied.

"That's exactly what they want, and they're willing to take the chance either way. You can't finish your work, Doctor Bryant, and they can't do it without you."

"What am I supposed to do?"

"Resign from the government. Tell them we peaked and we can't go any further. We'll work out a believable explanation."

Robert focused on his ulterior purpose and personal mission, thinking of Coral. "Does anyone else know about my past?" Robert asked.

"No one knows, Robert. I assure you! I kept everything a secret for years. I saw to that," Doctor Kruger agreed. "Nobody ever found out; not even your adoptive parents know everything. They only know that you and your sister were Lebensborn orphans of William's sister and my nephew. Your parents know nothing about the experiments they did on your natural parents to conceive you. However, your father always suspected something amiss when you began exhibiting your gifts at an early age. I diverted such speculation as best I could."

"Okay. I'll resign but won't announce it for a month or so. I need time to prepare." Robert secretly needed time to move much of his equipment to another location to continue an alternative personal agenda. He was almost there and wouldn't give up on Coral now.

Robert bought the finest penthouse he could find in New York City. Columbia University graciously accepted him to their college to head their physics department. Robert hired a crew of armed doormen assigned to his separate, securely locked penthouse entrance. It led to a foyer where his private elevator was.

An architect redesigned Doctor Bryant's two-story home high on a skyscraper's top floors. The beautifully decorated finished work contained a laboratory with a locking mechanism. Then, the search for a home staff began. He needed a personal secretary and a housekeeping staff and preferred to keep a private chef on the premises. Robert maintained his health and build by exercise and proper nutrition. He bought an entire floor at the lower part of the building to house the people who worked for him. He had his architect divide it into separate apartments for those who wished to remain in the city and not commute.

Doctor Friedrich Kruger passed away just as Robert's apartment was ready. After the funeral service, Robert conversed with Gunther Schmidt Kruger. He gave Gunther his address and invited him over. Robert wished to discuss his departure from the government-controlled lab with him.

Robert had his new chef, Alfredo, prepare dinner for Gunther and himself. That way, they could relax and enjoy a good meal while they spoke.

"You remember my father told you about Martha Weber?"

"Yes, I met her several times, but I never put the dots together," Robert replied.

"When she was a child, Martha Weber not only escaped from Germany with you, but she also cared for you as your nanny when you first attended my father's school," Gunther smiled. "She remembers you well and developed an attachment with you in your early years."

"She always seemed like a good person."

"I recommend you use her to head housekeeping for you. You won't find anyone else as trustworthy."

"Yes, of course. I want to get to know Martha even better."

"Your chef is rather good. The food is delicious; I never tasted veal as good."

"Alfredo studied cuisine in Tuscany," Robert smiled, "He is excellent."

Robert selected Walter LeRoy as his personal assistant; he had secretly traveled to America alongside his sister, Emily, and Gunther recommended him. Walter gathered the names of everyone Robert and Martha chose to work under them, including himself and Alfredo, the chef. Although all had already been carefully screened and bonded, Robert asked Gunther to run all the names by his intelligence contact.

Robert trusted Gunther. Why wouldn't he? Gunther was the son of the man who trained him throughout his early years. And he was the person who brought his sister Emily home from Europe at his own significant risk. Robert also used his advanced intuition and instinctively knew Gunther was credible. So, Robert brought Gunther to see his private lab. He revealed to Gunther his true intentions: the plans of his mission to rescue Coral. Gunther was impressed with the laboratory and applauded Robert's planned noble attempt to bring back his lost love. However, he told Robert it was hazardous and that he had to do it carefully and without publicity.

The temptation of an actual time travel was too great for Gunther. He had to be part of this undertaking. "When do we start?" he asked Robert.

Robert needed an assistant, and he wanted it to be Gunther; he was intelligent and had experience with Robert's work. "When you say 'we,' do you mean you and me, or you, me, and your intelligence sector?"

"No, just me. Nobody else can know what we do, now or ever."

Gunther Schmidt phoned Robert the next day to inform him that the list of his entire staff passed a stringent security screening. Then, Robert telephoned his contact at the government and explained that he had reached a point that he couldn't surpass and believed it was futile to continue. Robert advised them that Doctor Kathy Clarkson should resume his work, reasoning it would be better to know where she was; Robert never trusted her. His intuition sensed an evil aura surrounding her. It reminded him of what he sensed in Sue Peters before she had her life-changing experience. However, he told the government Doctor Clarkson was most qualified because Robert knew she hadn't learned his authentic secret time travel methods or his full intentions. He also recommended that Doctor Daryll Thompson become Doctor Clarkson's first assistant and Doctor Leopold Hector become her second assistant. Neither were close to his time travel discoveries.

Robert sold his home near Harvard and moved permanently to New York. He gave Gunther the only other key to the lab. He also told him a five-digit code, which Robert changed daily, and showed Gunther how to operate it. Robert also explained the security of his entrance and the doormen. Now, Robert was ready to return to where he had left off with his work.

Robert already explored the simplicity of a cosmic string. He always approached subjects in their most basic form. A cosmic string's complexity was nothing more than a fold in the very fabric of spacetime. They were defective cracks and probably made when the Big Bang prompted the universe. Only during those seconds was energy forceful enough to twist and distort spacetime sufficient to leave such permanent wrinkles. Now, 40-year-old Robert Bryant had to replicate such a miracle of God in his lab.

All personal work done by Robert while in the government laboratory was awe-inspiring to Gunther when Robert first presented it. Robert had held back exceptional discoveries he made at that time. His assistants, including Gunther, didn't have a clue as to how close Robert already was to reaching his goal.

"How did you keep all of these things from us?" Gunther asked when he realized the complexity of what Robert had accomplished. "You have no written notes?"

"Very few." Robert pointed to his head. "It's all up here."

One day, when Robert was traveling to Columbia, he saw the same red four-door 1951 Oldsmobile 88 he had seen years ago when he was with Coral. At that time, Robert had suspected Peter Cummings was watching them but was never sure. Robert spotted the same red car again and was sure it was following him. He surmised the government was watching him.

Robert asked, "Gunther, have you noticed a red four-door 1951 Oldsmobile 88 following you at any time? Certainly, a vehicle that old would stand out."

"I have never noticed such an old car," Gunther said, "but I'll certainly keep my eyes open."

Robert and Gunther completed the project in 1981. The main component stood on the floor, touching the twelve-foot ceiling above it. It resembled a colossal CAT scan machine surrounded by an array of computers. When Robert first turned on the unit, it roared almost like a jet.

"We'll have to tone that down a bit," Robert sounded a little upset.

"I don't think it's necessary; it will only last a few seconds before it tones down. People will think it's a low-flying jet."

"Maybe you're right," agreed Robert. Then he chuckled, "One that disappears in a few seconds. They might think it's a UFO."

The unit had a circulating beam of light and a hole in the center large enough for a man Robert's size to walk through. It was ready for use. Robert and Gunther tested it by transporting a shoebox to the past and programming it to return. They experimented again, sending the same shoebox back and forth to the future.

"Everything looks good, but we have to experiment with living creatures of different sizes," Robert told Gunther.

"Absolutely!"

Robert estimated it would take at least a year to review and fine-tune everything to ensure it was in good working order for humans. While checking and making minor modifications, Robert decided it would be better to leave Gunther detailed notes about his time travel discoveries. He realized that if something went wrong, it would be better for his trusted friend to have them. Robert documented his complete studies for Gunther and hid them in the passcode-protected safe in a place Gunther would find.

After experimenting with various animals instead of inanimate objects, everything proved successful. They set a date for April 1982 for Robert to return to see Coral. Robert had already proved he would be the same younger age as when he last saw Coral alive. "It took 20 years, but I'm finally ready," he didn't know whether to laugh or cry. "I'm coming back to you, monkeyface."

11

New York City, Tuesday, April 12, 1982

In the early hours of Tuesday morning, April 12, 1982, Robert awoke to unfamiliar sounds. He glanced at the clock on the night table next to his bed. It was 3:16 AM. Robert rubbed his eyes as he gradually emerged from his deep sleep and heard what sounded like people whispering. Then, he recognized a distinctive voice, but the words were indistinguishable. He turned toward his bedroom doorway and saw Kathy Clarkson standing on the threshold.

"I said we need the entry code, Doctor Bryant," Kathy repeated. She looked determined.

In his early morning stupor, Robert's mind processed what was happening. Kathy Clarkson knew about his home laboratory. But how? And how did she get into my home? Those were his first drowsy thoughts.

Kathy Clarkson and Leopold Hector had attended Robert's lecture at Columbia the day before. They hid in the large, crowded hall and remained anonymous as Robert spoke to the cheering crowd. Kathy didn't believe Robert was retiring but thought it was a ruse to get the publicity off his back. She strongly felt that Robert would never give up his work. Kathy loathed Robert since he rejected her sexual advances years before when his ethics had prevented him from having a relationship with her at the same time she was a student of his. Robert had principles, and he drew the line. But Kathy didn't take kindly to Robert declining her intimate advances. No man ever resisted her before or after Robert Bryant.

The government had interviewed Kathy Clarkson for a position with a team of scientists based on her brilliance as a rising physicist. When she learned that the job involved working on the theories of time travel discovered by the internationally renowned physicist Doctor Robert Bryant, Kathy wanted assurance of being on the team and working directly with him, but only for vengeance. When she discovered they declined her on grounds of mental aggressiveness and belligerent behavior. Kathy secured her position as Robert's second assistant by performing oral sex with the government official heading team selection. After that, all unsatisfactory records of her disappeared. When younger, the female intellectual had studied men extensively and learned how to please them sexually, just as Robert had done with women when he was a young man. The difference was that Robert felt remorse for his sexual indiscretions. And he found true love in his life. Robert was the only man Kathy couldn't reach, and she hated him for that. But Robert had never spurned Kathy in any way. Her mind had manufactured these things over time. Robert only mentioned that they couldn't work together while she was his student based on how she felt about him. It was unethical and against the school's policy.

Born Gisela Becker in the Nazi 'die Unsterblichen' program, Kathy Clarkson's upbringing was very different than Robert Bryant's. She didn't have wealthy adoptive parents who cared for and supported her intellectual gifts. When Kathy came to the United States with Emily Bryant, the government put her in the foster care system. Her exceptional intellect alienated her from other children. Then, Doctor Kruger put her in his school because he knew she was gifted. She grew resentful of others, especially young boys who wanted nothing other than to have sex with her. Kathy decided to harness her attractiveness as her body prematurely blossomed into a marvel. Gisela Becker changed her name to Kathy Clarkson and learned to please men to get things she didn't inherit. She climbed the ladder of success by using the sexual skills she honed to perfection. Kathy's rewards were great. She received her higher education tuition from wealthy men; rich royals gave her priceless gifts; corporate executives took her on exotic vacations, and Kathy enjoyed a glamorous life with the rich and famous. However, none of these men could please her advanced libido until Kathy met her match with Robert Bryant. Kathy couldn't comprehend a man with kindness and principles, nor could Kathy seduce a person with an equal intellect as Robert. Ever since he decided he wouldn't please her sexually, it released an undying fury within her she had to satisfy. Only his commitment to becoming her sexual partner, or the total destruction of Robert Bryant, could placate Kathy's revenge, and she planned it carefully.

Kathy Clarkson always suspected that Robert continued his time travel work after he left the government-sponsored program. She had hired a private detective to follow him and study his movements. Reports showed Gunther Schmidt spending days at Robert's home in New York, making Kathy suspect Robert had a laboratory in his extensive home and was working with Gunther. Background information on Robert revealed that after Robert supposedly jilted Kathy, he met and fell in love with another woman from his hometown in Ohio. She learned about Robert's tragic loss in 1962, which sparked an idea of what Robert was planning. Kathy used her advanced mental capabilities and, putting two and two together, surmised that Robert was preparing a way to go back in time to rescue his lost love. But not if Kathy Clarkson could stop it in time.

On Monday, April 11, 1982, Kathy and Leopold Hector's plan was already in motion. The private detective she hired provided her with the name of someone from the underworld to assist her. This individual, known only as Knuckles, had a dark past and was a burly, crude man who would help Kathy and Leo break into Gunther Schmidt's apartment as well as Robert's. Gunther had a key to Robert's home and possibly his lab. Surveillance photos indicated it was an unusually colored blue key on his keychain. Numerous reports suggested that Gunther used this key whenever he entered or exited the premises without Robert being present.

Knuckles often used a pair of brass knuckles, which is how he acquired the nickname. When the huge thug got them inside Gunther's home, he would act as muscle support for Kathy and Leo. For inside jobs, he always brought a small Walther PPK. The caliber of the bullet was powerful and accurate enough, and it was a concealable handgun. Knuckles also carried a five-inch switchblade knife for close-quarter fighting. He planned to meet Kathy and Leo outside Gunther's building at 1:00 AM on Tuesday, April 12, 1982. Knuckles had told them both to wear gloves to hide their fingerprints.

After Knuckles swiftly opened the locked door to Gunther's apartment, he silently signaled for Kathy and Leo to follow him. They paused in the stillness, listening for any sounds. Knuckles assumed no one was home. Just then, all three intruders heard the front door handle turn. Knuckles motioned for Kathy and Leo to crouch down, then gradually positioned himself behind the door as it swung open. Gunther found himself in a choke-hold the moment he stepped into his apartment, with a switch-blade poised against his neck.

"What is this?" a surprised Gunther asked. Then he noticed Kathy Clarkson and Leo Hector standing as Kathy flipped on the light switch. "You two! What are you doing here?"

"We want the key to your friend Robert's home and lab, Gunther," asked Kathy in a sweet voice. "And you better give it to us, or the gentleman holding the knife to your neck will make you!"

"Do what they say, Gunther and no one will get hurt. Please, Gunther," Leo asked politely.

"Like you're not going to kill me anyway?" asked Gunther.

"I promise we won't hurt you, Gunther," said Kathy, "We want the key. Don't make me ask this big guy here to hurt you."

Knuckles pressed the knife a little deeper into Gunther's neck, just enough to draw a few drops of blood. That made Gunther think quickly. He could fight back and likely die, or he could comply. The trio had to get past the front doorman first. Moreover, they didn't know the secret passcode and couldn't access the lab without it. Gunther assumed they would tie him up to prevent him from warning Robert, but he had a small concealed knife in his sleeve. Having been in many tight spots before during his intelligence days, Gunther knew well how to escape from various gagged and bound positions and felt confident he could reach Robert before they harmed him. He chose to concede; it was the most sensible option he had.

"Okay! You win!" Gunther pulled all of his keys from his pocket. There was a blue key, as described in Kathy's surveillance report. Gunther held out the keys for Kathy to take. "The blue one opens the lab door. I swear it's real."

"Where's the key to the penthouse?" Kathy asked sharply.

"There isn't one," said Gunther.

"Liar!" Kathy screamed as Knuckles pressed his knife a bit deeper into Gunther's neck. "The doorman has it!"

"If you knew that, why did you ask me for a key I don't have?"

"I just wanted you to squirm a little more, you kraut bastard. I never liked you. Dr. Bryant always favored you, and now you're working on a plan together–that will never happen!"

"I ain't got time for this shit," shouted Knuckles.

Kathy told Knuckles, "Tie up Gunther and put a gag into his mouth."

Knuckles removed his Walther PPK and screwed a silencer onto the end of the front barrel.

"No!" replied Knuckles as he fired the pistol twice and hit Gunther Schmidt directly in the center of his chest with both bullets. Gunther grasped his chest with both his hands and fell face down on the hard floor, "I don't leave behind no witnesses." Kathy's involuntary response was to scream, and as she began to do so, Knuckles turned and pointed the gun at her, "Keep quiet unless ya want the same."

Leo Hector held his hands covering over his mouth so he wouldn't inadvertently scream at the horror of the shooting, a look of terror plastered on his face. His urethral sphincter had let loose, and he stood calm and motionless; then, he lifted his feet to move away from the puddle of his urine. Preoccupied with their emotions, neither Kathy nor Leo noticed Gunther's right arm twitch or see him struggling to raise his head before it fell back, and he remained still.

Leo's mess on the floor even diverted Knuckles, who looked at Kathy and said in his crude slang, "Clean up ya boy here, and den get over ta the otta place." Knuckles went to the door, and before he left, he said, "I'll meet yous dere."

They followed their established plan when the three reunited at Robert's building. Kathy would first distract the doorman. She did that when she stopped in front of him and lifted her skirt well past her upper thigh, exposing the lower part of her butt cheek. She then fixed her sexy laced sheers, reattaching them to her garter belt as she smiled at the doorman, whose eyes remained affixed to her shapely body. Knuckles passed by and stabbed the doorman deep in his neck. As blood spurted in a thin, straight line, he held the uniformed man and dragged him. An extremely nervous Leo took the key from the doorman's pocket. Then he opened the locked entrance as Knuckles dragged the body of the doorman further inside. He dropped him in a corner. Kathy followed behind.

"You're both on yer own now," whispered Knuckles, "Ya got da lab key, so ya ain't gonna see me no more." Then he walked out the door casually.

Kathy Clarkson and Leo Hector took the private elevator to the penthouse, searching with small flashlights. They were looking for the lab. When they finally found a suspiciously locked doorway, Kathy used Gunther's blue key. It turned and opened the door, but another locked door appeared. To Kathy's surprise, a small LCD screen lit up and displayed the words 'passcode required.' "Bastard!" she screamed. Furious, Kathy told Leo they had to find Robert before he awakened. They discovered a trail of Robert's clothes on the floor leading to the entrance of one of the rooms. They had him.

"I said we need the entry code, Doctor Bryant," Kathy demanded. Realizing that Robert was partially asleep, she repeated herself.

As Robert slowly awakened, he looked at the clock on his night table displaying the time. It was 3:16 AM. Leo turned on the light just outside Robert's bedroom. Leo yelled out, "It's her fault, Doctor Bryant. She made me do this! I didn't want any violence!"

Robert began to get out of his bed. As he did, Kathy pulled out a small Smith and Wesson snub-nosed 38 caliber revolver and threatened to shoot Robert if he so much as moved the wrong way. Robert moved slowly and rose from the bed. He only wore silk bikini briefs, and his arms and chest muscles glistened from the light of the other room. That excited Kathy and she purred like a cat from exhilaration, almost losing control of her actions.

"What violence?" asked Robert. "What do you want?"

"Gunther's dead," snarled Kathy. "And you will be if you don't give me the passcode to your lab."

"You killed Gunther? Why?"

"Because I didn't like him, and he lied to me! That's why!"

"What do you want from my laboratory? It's just a small home lab." Robert held his emotions about losing his friend, knowing he had to remain calm to deal with his adversary.

"Do you think I'm stupid?" screamed Kathy. "I know what you're doing! You dumped me for another woman! She died, and now you think you're going back in time to save her? No! I won't let you! Nobody jilts me!"

Leo ran into the bedroom. He looked at Kathy and pleaded, "Let's leave! None of this is important anymore!"

"Get out, you measly little ant! You disgust me, Leo! I only had sex with you to get your help! And what a disappointment both were!"

Robert realized Kathy was now delusional. She had killed Gunther, and he would ensure she paid for it. He watched the two interact and waited for the right time to grab Kathy and take her pistol. Robert would jump as soon as he distracted her.

He slowly began to lower his skimpy silk briefs, then reached into them and grabbed the bulge of his genitals, massaging but not yet revealing what Kathy wanted. Robert had noticed her erotic reaction when he arose from his bed. She had trembled as she watched his body, remembering his talk with Professor Kruger. The Professor was right: Kathy was a sex-starved nymphomaniac who needed him badly, and knowing that fact was now his only weapon until he could get her gun. His performance had to completely arouse Kathy's libido to divert her and accomplish that. Kathy's jaw dropped as Robert continued lowering his sexy silk briefs ever so slowly and seductively. Robert turned and pulled the back completely down, revealing his well-defined butt cheeks. Robert had difficulty suppressing an erection in the climate of the rampant and blazing sexuality radiating from Kathy. It was like an uncontrollable evil force he fought to resist. But as much as he tried, it slowly involuntarily hardened and grew substantially, forcing Robert to remove his scanty briefs.

He slowly turned to face Kathy, revealing himself. Kathy began moaning before the phallus, thick and long as if she were worshiping it, lowering her gun as her erotic secretion dripped to her sexy laced sheers. Robert could smell her feminine aroma. Kathy was out of control and knelt before him, sweating and making rapid cooing sounds, using one hand to massage Robert's muscular thigh upward. She held her gun loosely in her other hand. Kathy moistened her lips, as her mouth primed to take what she had lusted for years, now unveiled before her.

Robert licked Kathy's face to arouse the lioness even more. Saliva dribbled from her mouth as she breathed heavily. Kathy moaned while making animal sounds as she drooled, her mouth reaching as her body stretched forward, causing her pistol to fall. Robert quickly extended his arm to seize the gun. But Leo clumsily rushed toward Kathy one last time to beg her to leave, accidentally knocking her over. Robert promptly responded, but Kathy snapped out of her lewd trance and was agile and much too swift. She quickly grabbed the gun, reached her feet, and pointed the revolver directly at Robert's naked chest from just four feet away.

Kathy loathed the way Robert's body could spontaneously arouse her, and she screamed, "I hate You!" Kathy looked into Robert's eyes and fired the pistol. The gunshot echoed throughout the penthouse.

12

Robert felt around his chest for a wound. Indeed, at such a close distance, Kathy had to have hit him. Two male figures stood in the tight space between Robert and Kathy. They faced Robert and appeared to resemble perfect male mannequins of a short height. Both seemed to be similar, almost like twins. Each had dark, short, thinning hair parted in the center, and their expressions bore slight grins. Robert had a flashback to someone who looked like them. Then he remembered Peter Cummings, the deranged little guy who killed Coral. They could have been his brothers. One of them had stopped the bullet; it absorbed into his body. The other mannequin-like figure turned and removed the pistol from Kathy's hands at what seemed like supersonic speed. Leo got to his feet and ran out the door. Kathy instinctively followed Leo, running as fast as she could. "Don't let them get away," shouted Robert.

"It doesn't matter," one of the two men said calmly.

Robert looked at them closely and noticed their peculiarities. Their features were almost perfect, and their skin had the darker tone of a perfect tan. Both men wore casual 1950s-style button-down shirts with light-colored slacks. Each sported canvas slip-on sneakers on their feet. Their facial expressions were ever so slightly mechanical, with widened eyes when they spoke and mild grins when they were quiet. They spoke with deep but higher-pitched voices, similar to baritone singers. "Who are you?" Robert asked, "You're Feds, aren't you? I saw your car following me."

"It's an honor to meet you, Doctor Bryant," one said as the other looked at him with that grin. "Feds?" He looked at his partner. He didn't recognize the word.

The other man appeared to be thinking. "Oh, yes," he said, "Feds, short for Federals, as in police. Federal police is what I think you mean, Doctor Bryant. No, we are not Feds, Doctor Bryant. We are your friends." His widened eyes returned to normal, and he resumed that mock grin.

"Yes," said the other, "We are your friends, Doctor Bryant. We have watched you for a long time."

"Or for a short time," said the other. "It all depends on how you look at it."

The only discernible difference Robert could notice was that one's hair was slightly darker than the other. So, Robert considered their hair color to differentiate them until one introduced himself as Ricther, and the one with a little darker hair introduced himself as Wilthen.

Robert asked them, "Are you human?"

"Almost," replied Ricther, his eyes widened. "We are what you would call humanoids," his eyes retracted, and the fake smile reappeared.

Then Wilthen explained, "We are from your distant future."

"A terrible error has happened. We are here to correct it," Ricther finished Wilthen's sentence. The two seemed mentally connected and shared each other's thoughts.

"How do you know me?" Robert asked.

"We have been observing you since your birth in Lebensborn in 1937." Ricther went on to explain Robert's life history. They knew everything about him and explained it methodically.

Ricther continued, "Something has severely disrupted our timeline far into your future. We are here to correct it. The one you know as, or knew as, Peter Cummings was never supposed to exist in your space of time. He caused it."

Wilthen added, "He changed things as they were meant to be. The friend you refer to as Coralie wasn't supposed to die at the hands of Peter Cummings."

"Was Peter a humanoid?" asked Robert.

"Yes, but he was severely dysfunctional. It was an extremely rare occurrence. Peter Cummings invaded your timeline without our knowledge," answered Ricther.

"But that was 20 years ago. Why are you here now?" Robert questioned.

"It was 20 years, according to your time, Doctor Bryant. It is hard to explain to you. We just now discovered the problem caused by the ripple effect. Time is relative, Doctor. It all happens simultaneously. You already know that, but it is even more so than you might realize," Wilthen answered.

"Of course," Robert comprehended the advanced theory. "No, I do understand."

"Anyway, as I said, we must correct the wrong caused by Peter Cummings, Doctor Bryant. Time heals itself, as you know. Unfortunately, Peter Cummings posed a different scenario altogether. That is why we are here."

"How so?"

"We have already removed Peter Cummings. Now, you must return to the evening of December 24, 1961. That is where you must be to heal our future, Doctor."

The thought that Robert was going back to Coral resurfaced. He imagined falling on his knees to propose to her, and other romantic notions flew through his mind. Then he realized that if they removed Peter Cummings, that would have occurred before December 24, 1961, before Coral met Peter. That meant other things would have changed in Coral's life. Instead of Robert saving her from Peter, a beautiful young woman like Coral would undoubtedly be seeing a different man. Perhaps she was engaged or, worse, even married. Before he asked the time-travelers about those possible changes, Robert told them, "I've never tried my apparatus before," and watched the reactions of the two humanoids. "What if I fail?"

"You will not use your devices to go back," stated Ricther. Knowing that Robert would remember nothing about the conversations they were now having once he returned to his past, Ricther explained more facts to Robert. "We are taking you back, Doctor Bryant. Your method works as you thoroughly tested it. However, your generation is not yet ready to use time travel for many other reasons. The level of humanity in your time has not outgrown tempestuous urges. Your people would use your technology for the wrong reasons."

"When you arrive back at that period, everything will be as it was without the interference caused by Peter Cummings. Everything will be as it should have been," said Wilthen.

"I won't remember anything, will I?" Robert then thought about the amount of time and effort he had put into this project. 'Twenty years, and it would all be for naught.'

Wilthen was reading Robert's mind and said, "We cannot allow you to retain all your memories of this timeline. However, remember this, Doctor Bryant: everything you accomplished in this timeline remains retained in ours. In our history, you, Doctor Bryant, are the scientist who first broke the barrier of time and space. You are an essential person to us. You defined time travel in our timeline by your doctoral dissertation alone. And by your keenness, no one ever compromised it," he added. "You are to the people in our future what your people refer to as a hero, Doctor. We refer to you as one of the acknowledged few, quite a level of accomplishment in our world."

The other humanoid, Ricther, quickly added, "But it is too soon, Doctor Bryant. By killing the young woman Coralie, Peter Cummings created a situation that sparked your human emotions, which accelerated your studies. He gave you a valid reason and the motivation to put your theories to work. Without that, you would not have created your apparatus. Now you are at a point where you can go back in time, but it is too soon, and we cannot allow it to happen." Ricther, also reading Robert's thoughts, addressed Robert's fear about other changes because they had removed Peter before December 24, 1961. "Changes to that time and space after we removed Peter Cummings did affect Coralie's life because, as you know, she met him before December 24, 1961. You will discover changes in her life."

"There's no sense in asking about those differences since I won't remember anyway," Robert reasoned.

"Even though you will create a new timeline, this time and space will continue. You see, Doctor, as you have already discovered, time has a way of repairing itself," said Ricther. "Whatever you now do in your correct space of time will not change any of your future accomplishments in ours."

"I understand," said Robert. "You already indicated that, but will I have any recollections of my life from this timeline?"

"Yes," answered Ricther.

"Well, maybe," Wilthen quickly added as he turned and gave his simulated smile to Robert.

"Ripples might cause you to remember occasional things. However, many will be in a dream-like way. Most of your memories of this time will be as dreams, or what you call déjà vu."

Wilthen waved for Robert to follow them.

"Should I dress?" Robert was still naked from his altercation with Kathy.

"It won't matter," answered Ricther, and the two time travelers led Robert to his spacious living room, where a red four-door 1951 Oldsmobile 88 sat on the floor in the center of the large room.

"I always thought it was Peter Cummings watching us," Robert said as he pointed to the car.

"It was him years ago in your timeline," Wilthen replied, "using one of our transportation mechanisms."

"Would have been him." Ricther corrected. "As Peter Cummings no longer exists." Ricther opened the car's back door for Robert and gave him one of those mechanical smiles. "There was that time in that city of Youngstown when we were searching for Peter Cummings through time."

"Doctor Bryant was not there," corrected Wilthen. "The young lady, Coralie LeBlanc, spotted us, and that distraction led to an almost fatal occurrence. We had to reverse time so I could quickly pull her away from an approaching vehicle. If I had not, our fault would have caused terrible repercussions to our time structure," Wilthen explained.

"You are right. I must have thought of that time Dr. Bryant was a young man, driving with Coralie when she was a child," replied Ricther. "Or when He and Coralie were older and–"

"None of this is important right now," said Wilthen.

"Will not be important," corrected Ricther.

Such stories were of no interest to Robert as he entered the car and began to theorize what it would be like in 1961 without the Peter Cummings factor and what that would mean. Robert had already rationalized that he wouldn't have to save Coral because Peter Cummings wouldn't be there to hurt her. But what else will be different after he returned to that timeline?' Robert's mind raced with possibilities. Would Coral even be there? As a scientist, it was interesting. Though, as a human who had unleashed the passion of love for the first time, it was frightening. He had lived for 20 years past her death, struggling to return to save her. Now, he was returning to the same period, but before he and Coral fell in love. All his grief over the years that defined him and his work, experiments, and all the stress and energy expended would never have happened. Would he develop feelings for Coral as he had? Would she for him? Was Robert's and Coral's love based on that one spontaneous moment that had already passed through time? Then he wondered if they would fall in love again.

"Love?" Wilthen repeated the word from Robert's thoughts in question form. "Oh! Yes, love. I can't fully understand the concept. But, as I know it, true love is a human expression that is or is not meant to be. Nothing can change that."

Robert had a million questions but realized the implications of time travel. If not as thoroughly as the humanoids did, it was enough for him to accept what was happening. And he realized that time was the essence of a particular moment. Robert knew that he would remember nothing. Yet he still wondered if the essence of love was of one specific moment. And if so, did his and Coral's already pass in time?

The doors of the vehicle closed automatically. Wilthen sat on the driver's side, and Ricther was next to him in the front passenger seat. Wilthen immediately opened his door even though they hadn't driven anywhere. He walked around the car and opened Robert's door. Ricther turned and looked at Robert with widened eyes, "Everything will be fine, Doctor Bryant. Do not worry. Have faith, and know that you will always do the right things." he smiled with his mechanical grin. "Everything will be exactly as meant to be. You will remember as much as you need to. Always trust your instincts. Goodbye, Doctor Bryant. Again, it was an honor to meet you." Robert climbed out of the car and looked around in a daze; he couldn't remember where he was. He was standing outside the home of his best friend, Roger. Robert's mind was spinning, and he felt dizzy. Then he remembered the beige-colored Cadillac he had rented parked on the sidewalk. "I feel weird," Robert whispered. And again, Robert returned into a stupor and couldn't recollect anything for a few seconds. He had trouble focusing, and Robert felt he somehow didn't fit in his body. Then, his mind began clearing. He was there for Christmas Eve dinner and walked to the door to let himself in as he always did.

Before he opened the door, Robert's mind flooded with memories. He recalled being a famous physicist. Popular magazines wrote articles about his work, and his research book generated fame for him worldwide, which he dreaded. He always tried to hide his long-held secret that he had always been a genius. Now, that news would trickle down to his small hometown of Rue, Ohio. No one in Rue knew about his work yet except his parents and his sister, Emily. He wanted it that way and planned to tell everyone else that he was in graduate school and only that.

Robert recalled this trip as the first time he had returned to Rue in six years. No, it was six years since he had seen Coral, and most others five. Robert wondered why he made the mistake of thinking only of Coral. It gave him a warm feeling because he looked forward to seeing her and everyone again.

After receiving his doctorate and becoming a teaching professor, Robert found the time to return to Rue for the holidays at the end of 1961. His mind was still foggy, but he recalled flying in and renting a beige Cadillac, the one now parked behind him on the street. Robert recalled arriving at his parent's mansion late afternoon on Christmas Eve, where he would spend a traditional Christmas Day with his family and stay for a visit during his school's holiday break.

Robert smiled, remembering Emily throwing herself into his waiting arms after he saw her trotting barefoot toward him as he opened the door.

She yelled, "Welcome home, big brother!" Her arms remained around his waist, and she squeezed tightly, then almost screamed, "I missed you so much! I can't believe you're here!" Robert thought as his mind cleared. He had noticed Emily changed her hairstyle. Her figure was now that of a fully developed woman.

"I remember," Robert murmured, "I recall it all: seeing how beautiful Emily looked all dressed up, meeting her boyfriend and how he tripped coming through the door, reuniting with my mother and father, and Mrs. LeBlanc inviting me to her home for Christmas Eve dinner." Robert stood there wondering what had happened to him that made him forget. "I shook hands again with Emily's boyfriend, Chris, bid my parents good evening and left for the LeBlanc's home. And, here I am."

13

Christmas Eve, Rue, Ohio 1961

As Robert prepared to open the door of the LeBlanc home, as he always did, he heard that scratchy sound that all 45 record players made just before the music started. Then, the words and melody of the Everly Brothers song, 'All I Have To Do Is Dream,' began to fill the foyer of the house. He decided to knock instead of letting himself in. Seconds later, the front door swung open, revealing Coral LeBlanc standing in the doorway.

"Coral? Is that you?" Robert didn't recognize his little friend. "My God, you look incredible! Hi. Merry Christmas." Robert was shocked at Coral's appearance. She was no longer a skinny little kid; she had a voluptuous figure and was beautiful.

"Oh, my God! Robert! I didn't know you were coming!" Coral almost screamed. She practically jumped into Robert's open arms. As Coral buried herself in his arms, her head turned and firmly pressed against Robert's chest. She smelled Robert's natural body aroma combined with the same cologne he had used years before. The memory of it stirred something within her that gave her pleasure. Thinking how wonderful it was that Robert was back, Coral instinctively said, "Oh, Robert, I missed you so much."

"I've missed you too. You're so..." Robert was tongue-tied and couldn't find the right words to describe the ravishing creature Coral had become. You're so beautiful, Coral." "I can't believe it. You're a woman now!" he gasped, smiling but amazed. Coral tightened her arms around Robert's waist, her eyes fixed on Robert's. She now wore perfume, and it blended well with her natural scent. Robert found it appealing, even stimulating, sensually. "Step back so I can see you better!" Robert removed his overcoat and temporarily folded it over an armchair. As Coral stepped back, Robert saw that the woman standing before him was stunning. Coral had grown taller, and her body had filled out. It was now well-proportioned and beamed with sensuality.

Coral wore a tight-fitting dark green dress and black two-and-a-half-inch spiked pumps. The dress fabric, slit at the sides, displayed her well-formed legs, now firmed up from her heels. Cut lower in its front and back, the top of Coral's dress revealed her nakedness from her shoulders to the small of her back and the full cleavage of her ample and well-formed breasts. Her neck was long, and its bend made it look elegant. Her eyes were big and wide. The mascara and eyeliner she wore enhanced the beauty of their dark blue color. Her face was magnificent, and her features were like an artist had painted them. Coral was now a beautiful, alluring woman, and Robert found her irresistible. Robert's keen eyesight noticed slightly more makeup above her right eye as he scrutinized her features closely. There was a slight discoloration.

Robert gently touched it and asked, "Did you hurt yourself?"

"Oh, clumsy me, you know. I banged it on my drawer."

"Oh," he smiled, but his senses made him wonder.

"Robert, I'm so happy; I think I might cry." A tear began to form in Coral's left eye, and Robert quickly and gently wiped it away. "Just like old times," Coral giggled, "You always wiped away my tears." The thought that Robert found her beautiful filled her with delight. Robert looked handsome in his stylish white knitted sweater, contrasting his tapered black dress pants and imported black shoes. She noticed how his clothes showcased the muscular build he still maintained. Coral reached up and kissed Robert directly on the lips. "Oh!" she exclaimed, "I got some lipstick on you." Coral laughed and wiped it away with her right thumb. The music from the foyer stopped playing. "That's my favorite song," Coral said as she gazed at Robert.

"I like it too," Robert said. "It reminds me of something

I can't quite place right now. A good feeling, though." Then, Robert had déjà vu, and for a split-second, he remembered something about Coral and her song, but how?

Coral wondered why he enjoyed her favorite song, which she always played while thinking of him. He said it gave him a good feeling. She kept her eyes on Robert, contemplating how strange that was and considering whether her love had somehow reached him since the last time she saw him.

A delighted Coral took Robert by the hand and led him to the dining room, where he could hear people talking. "No one told me Robert was coming!" Coral exclaimed.

"It's a surprise!" yelled out her mother, Louise. "Robert's here!" As they walked into the room, everyone got up to greet Robert. Louise LeBlanc opened her arms and embraced the young man she hadn't seen for years. "How handsome you are, my dear Robert." She began to shed tears of happiness as she held him tightly. "You're a man, now!"

Roger got up quickly, jogged over to his best friend, and embraced him.

"How's your knee?" Robert asked. "Looks good, the way you're running." He chuckled.

Roger began doing an Irish jig. Then he hopped up and kicked his heels together to show how well his knee had healed. "All thanks to you, my friend."

Robert had déjà vu again. He remembered that exact moment when Roger danced and then thanked him. 'All thanks to you, my friend,' Robert recalled that Roger had said that already. He smiled at Roger. Robert also recalled telling Roger that he didn't do anything because he wasn't a doctor. 'What did I do? I'm not a doctor,' he somehow remembered. Robert did help Roger financially. He had all of Roger's medical bills forwarded to him and paid for everything. But Robert felt as if that whole conversation had already happened. "It's great to see you looking as good as new." Those were the only words Robert could say in such an awkward state of mind. But he recalled saying that also.

Roger said, "I won't play football professionally, but honestly, I never really expected to with all the prospects out there that year." He smiled sheepishly and added, "What I appreciate is that I will walk perfectly and won't have any pain from this. Plus, I have a fantastic job at Bryant Aviation thanks to you and your dad." Turning to face Mary Lou Bensen, he continued, "The most important thing is that I have the most wonderful fiancée in the world, and we just bought a beautiful house here in Rue where we're going to live after our wedding. I'm a happy man," Roger said, smiling.

"I'm glad," Robert replied, "But to tell you the truth, you accomplished all those things by using your natural charm," Robert said as Roger roared with laughter.

Mary Lou was already walking over to greet Robert. "Hi, Robert. It's good to see you again," she said while smiling. She hugged him and gently kissed him. I hope we can get to know each other better while you're here."

"We will," Robert smiled.

Standing beside Robert, Louise added, "You come back home more often, you hear? Everyone missed you!"

Roger LeBlanc Sr. got to Robert last. "Good to see you again, young man. It's been much too long." He shook hands with Robert and then placed his right arm over his shoulder in a warm gesture. Robert quickly chatted with Mr. LeBlanc, asking how he had been.

Finally, Coral introduced Robert to a young man standing at his place at the dining room table. "Robert, this is my boyfriend, Benjamin Joyce," Coral hesitated and blushed slightly, and her voice indicated she was somewhat uncomfortable.

The young man was around Robert's age. He walked toward Robert and extended his arm for a handshake. He was a good-looking, dark-haired young man of good height with a good build. "Everyone's heard of Bob Bryant, who brought his teams to the state championships. Nice to finally meet you, Bob."

"Likewise," said Robert as the two men exchanged a handshake. Robert smiled, thinking about his little monkeyface having a boyfriend. It was no surprise to him, seeing how beautiful she had become. But Robert sensed an intense fear radiating from Coral. Then he thought it might just be his complex mind until thoughts of jealousy arose, making Robert contemplate his feelings.

Benjamin Joyce and Coral had been dating for four months. A 1960 business major graduate of Youngstown College, he worked in his hometown of Youngstown as manager of a family-owned retail store. He wanted to marry Coral the following year. Coral met Ben in a bar. She was there with Emily and Chris, jokingly having fun flirting with young men and then brushing them off. When Coral amusingly lifted her shirt slightly to entice a young and bashful freshman student in jest, her voluptuously shaped lower limb in sheers with spiked heels attracted the attention of Ben Joyce. That made the mature young man approach Coral in a cavalier manner that she couldn't resist. She had long ago given up any hope of Robert returning and wanting her, and she succumbed to Ben's magnetic charm.

When Coral met Ben, she was impressed with his sincerity, character, and intelligence–or the pretense of it, as she found out soon after. At first, Ben reminded her of Robert in a way. But that changed quickly. Any feelings for Ben ended that past October. A horrible experience completely changed her sentiments, and her body still trembled while recalling it. This evening was only the second time she saw Ben since that happened. Another troubling incident occurred two weeks prior. Now that Robert had noticed her, Coral focused all her attention on that, putting those bad memories with Ben out of her mind.

Ben planned to have Christmas Eve dinner with Coral's family before traveling alone to visit his parents in Youngstown, Ohio, for Christmas Day. He said he felt guilty about leaving the family store on Christmas Eve and wanted to return that evening. Ben told Coral the store would remain open until midnight on Christmas Eve, and he expected to make it back to Youngstown well before it closed to help tally the day's receipts. The truth was he had other girlfriends and had made plans to be with one that night, unbeknownst to Coral.

Coral sat Robert across from her. She wanted him in a spot where she could see him. Just then, the doorbell rang again. Coral rushed to the door, her heart still pounding about seeing Robert after so long. Robert listened to the slight taps of her heels while inconspicuously watching her legs flex and expand, looking even more physically gratifying as she trotted, and a beautiful sight to him. Coral escorted Robert's sister, Emily, and her boyfriend, Christopher Martin, to the dining room. After Emily made all the introductions, Coral sat the couple across from her next to Robert.

Throughout dinner, Coral and Robert kept glancing sensually at one another when they thought the other wasn't looking. They seemed mesmerized when they spoke to each other as if they were alone and having a private conversation like lovers do.

Robert found it hard to take his eyes off Coral while talking with the others. Being so infatuated with a young woman was unusual for him. He had never reacted to a woman like this before. Robert realized that Coral stirred feelings in him he had never encountered, and it was exhilarating.

As Coral and Emily talked, Coral caught sight of Robert watching her out of the corner of her eye. While maintaining her primary eye contact with Emily, she found her attention drawn to Robert until she lost her train of thought. Coral recognized that it was the first time Robert had looked at her in such a way that suggested he was seeing her as a woman for the very first time.

Coral studied Robert in detail. He had become even more handsome than before. His body had matured, and now Robert had a perfect male physique. She could see the muscles of his arms and chest bulge through the tight-fitting sweater shirt he wore. Coral had watched his powerful thighs flex when he walked and how his perfect male buttocks responded harmoniously. To her, Robert appeared to be the epitome of handsomeness. It excited her in a way that never happened to her before. It was as if her body now controlled her.

Emily knew she was the only one at the table who could tell with certainty what happened between her best friend, Coral, and her brother, Robert. She could easily see that Coral still loved him even though she was dating Ben. But by watching Robert and the way he kept staring at Coral, Emily was sure her brother had now developed an attraction to her best friend. It was that obvious. "The appetizers are scrumptious, Mrs. LeBlanc," Emily blurted out to not draw attention to her puzzlement. Emily couldn't know that almost everyone had similar suspicions seeing her brother's and Coral's interchange.

Time had also matured the manly features of Robert's chiseled face to perfection. His thick, black, wavy hair complemented his dark blue eyes more than before. And when he looked into Coral's eyes, she melted and felt a pleasurable quiver deep within her loins, those womanly throbs stimulating her tremendously. Coral had never experienced sexual arousal merely by speaking with or looking at a man. She was experiencing many feminine passions for the first time.

Robert noticed how much Coral's voice had changed when he spoke to her in person rather than over the phone. It was eloquent, huskier yet soft and soothing at times, which Robert found appealing and enjoyably sexy. This sharply contrasted with how her voice sounded as a child. Now, he enjoyed talking to her even more than he had during their long conversations years ago. Her movements were also different now. Her arms and hands flowed gracefully, and her feline form swayed enticingly; her tight, shapely buttocks moved fluidly, one side at a time, as if following a rhythmic tempo when she walked. Coral even sat regally in her chair. Whenever Robert moved closer to Coral to say something, the scent of her body excited him. He pushed his chair closer to the table to hide the slight bulge forming in his trousers. Only Coral's keen eyes noticed it, and the sight excited her.

Louise arose and said, "Come, everyone. Let's go into the

living room. We'll be more comfortable there."

"Good idea, hun," Roger Sr. agreed. "We'll have drinks and dessert there."

Mary Lou and Roger walked off together in their private lover's world, holding hands and laughing. Coral sat speaking with Emily. Her right leg crossed over her left in a ladylike manner as it gently swayed in erotic motion, causing her shoe to hang by her toes in a sexy way. Ben sat on a separate armchair, noticing the sensual way Coral was sitting. Chris rested on one side of a couch, his head leaning back, relaxing from his long day. Robert selected a plush chair across from Coral so he could pay attention to her. He hadn't seen her for so long and couldn't believe what a marvel she had become. Robert wanted to examine everything about the child he once knew, now a woman. Roger Sr. walked around and saw that everyone had drinks filled while Louise prepared a special after-dinner treat in the kitchen. From where he sat, Robert could see well past where Coral's nylon sheers ended, exposing the soft flesh of her well-formed upper thigh and lower derriere cheek. He envisioned touching and caressing the creamy white flesh of that forbidden realm and stimulating her womanhood to erotic orgasm. Robert imagined the feel of her. He fought the lure of nature, realizing the battle that now lay before him in resisting the fullness of the beautiful feminine being that Coral was, unable to remove his eyes from that sight. Remaining frozen in such a private passion never before felt, Robert crossed his legs in a struggle to hide the slight bulge now forming in his trousers from his wicked thoughts. Coral spotted it with her peripheral vision and continued speaking to Emily. Coral became a temptress and slowly moved, deliberately causing her dress to rise even devilishly higher, exposing much more of her naked flesh. Turning slightly, Coral glanced directly into Robert's eyes and smiled erotically, licking her lips and pretending not to notice her seductive performance.

Benjamin Joyce left the dinner party earlier than he had

planned. He had noticed what was taking place between his girl-friend and Robert, annoyed by how Robert lusted his girlfriend and how Coral accepted it and openly responded sensually, exhibiting her body for Robert's pleasure. It was embarrassing for him as everyone could see it.

Ben abruptly rose from his seat and said a cold goodbye to everybody. Then he asked to speak to Coral privately, and she accompanied him to the foyer. Coral went to the closet and took out Ben's coat. As he slipped into it, Ben removed a small box from one pocket and gave it to Coral. "Open it," said Ben, but in a tone that sounded more like a demand.

Coral was aghast. She had planned a few private minutes to confirm her split with Ben quietly, knowing Ben wouldn't get agitated when her family and friends were around. Now, she had to wait because she feared how Ben acted. Coral had already told Ben it was over weeks before, but he entirely disregarded that conversation. Therefore, she hadn't announced their breakup to her family or Emily, allowing Ben over that evening only to confirm the end of their relationship. Exhibiting her fear, she complied and opened the small packaged gift. "Is this an engage—"

Ben cut off her words. "It is an engagement ring. I know you weren't expecting this, Coral, but you belong to me, and we should marry now." Ben looked directly into her eyes, "There's no reason for us to wait any longer."

Ben tried to kiss Coral, but she turned, and a terrible fright filled her body. "I can't take this," Coral said, "you know that. I already told you it's over." Coral looked around, not wanting to make a scene, feverishly trying to return the ring.

Ben looked annoyed and wouldn't let her give him the ring. Coral appeared to be in shock. "I'll call you," Ben blurted out, frightening Coral even more. Then Ben turned toward the door.

Coral was as white as a ghost; her eyes stared blankly, as if into space, while she watched an angry Ben open the door and slam it shut behind him as he left. Coral now realized that Ben was mentally unstable. However, she didn't believe Christmas was the appropriate time to inform anyone about what had just happened. She placed the ring into one of her coat pockets in the closet. After everything that had occurred in late October, Coral refused to let Ben back into her life. Now, with Robert back, things might be different. She glanced over and observed him. Robert had always made her feel safe as a child, recalling how he rescued her from bullies years ago and always looked after her. But now, the way Robert spoke and moved excited her, awakening her femininity with sexual desire. Coral contemplated this newfound longing for him, so different from how it had been years ago.

Later that night, as Emily, Chris, and Robert prepared to leave, Robert nodded to his sister, Emily, to come to where he was standing by the closet. Privately, he whispered, "Why don't you invite Coral to our place tomorrow for Christmas Day dinner?" Robert paused, "Roger and his parents are going to Mary Lou's house, and Coral won't want to go there out of boredom. You know that."

That confirmed the suspicions that her brother was attracted to her friend, Coral. She looked directly up and into Robert's eyes. "Are you sure that's a good idea?" she asked, her voice having a concerned ring to it. Emily wanted to please her brother but was also worried about the potential consequences of him with her best friend. Coral was in a relationship with Ben for four months, and Emily didn't want Coral to make any hasty decisions.

"Yeah, I am," Robert replied assuredly.

"But she's dating Ben now, Robert." Then Emily thought she shouldn't have said that. Robert might want to spend more time with an old friend, and only that.

"Is she serious about Ben?" Robert didn't want to cause a breakup if that was the case.

"I really can't say for sure." Now Emily wondered. She had sensed a problem between Ben and Coral earlier in the evening. Lately, Coral had avoided conversations about her boyfriend.

Then Emily realized Coral hadn't seen Ben recently. As far as she knew, they hadn't been together for a while. With Emily's preoccupation with Chris, it hadn't registered before.

"I'd like to see her again while I'm here." Robert mentally debated, wanting to know why he had these feelings.

"Okay, Robert."

Emily walked over to Coral and kissed her on the cheek. "Why don't you join us tomorrow for dinner? I don't know why I didn't ask before. You can spend the day with us. Please come?"

Coral looked at her friend and then glanced over to where Robert was standing, thinking Emily knew how she felt about Robert. "Are you sure? Is it okay with your mom?"

"Of course, it is. Mom would love to have you over; you're family."

"Sure, I'd love to come. Thanks." Coral looked back at Robert, who was talking with Chris. She felt it must be obvious to everyone how attracted she was to Robert. However, she was thankful they couldn't see the intense sexual energy behind her feelings.

"Great! It's settled," Emily smiled with joy. "We'll see you at 2 PM." Emily kissed everyone goodbye and left with Chris.

As Robert was getting ready to leave, Louise LeBlanc called out to him. "Robert, can I see you in the kitchen? I want to send some appetizers to your mom for her to try."

"Of course," Robert replied politely as he turned and walked to the kitchen beyond the dining room. "It's very kind of you, Mrs. LeBlanc."

"I told her about them, and I think she'll like them." As Louise prepared a small container, she paused from her task and turned to face Robert. "You know, Robert," she hesitated for a moment, then continued, "I always imagined that you and Coralie would," she paused again, "you know... be together someday." She observed Robert's changing expression as he slightly blushed but remained silent. Louise added, "But Coralie is seeing someone now, dear." She continued watching Robert's reaction and added, "She's not a child anymore, Robert." Louise paused once more and said with a smile, "I couldn't help but notice how the two of you interacted tonight."

"I'm so sorry if I was in any way impolite tonight–"

"No, dear," she interrupted Robert. "On the contrary. You were always respectful, always the perfect gentleman," she added with another smile. "What I mean is that you share a special attachment with Coralie. You always have. I would love for you to see my daughter. Just make sure you understand your feelings first. Coralie would probably break up with Ben in an instant if you asked her. Spend some time together to get to know Coralie as a young lady." Louise returned to making her package. She paused again, "You never saw Coralie as a woman, dear. You did tonight. She was always a child when you knew her. Tonight, you recognized her as a woman for the first time."

Robert thought that Mrs. LeBlanc and everyone else probably noticed how he acted. After a minute, he realized Coral's mother was right, and he should explore his new feelings for Coral. "I think you're right, Mrs. LeBlanc. And I will. Thank you." Robert shrugged and added, "Mrs. LeBlanc, I will never hurt Coral. That I promise you."

"Oh, Robert, I know that. You're a fine young man–my God, Robert, I feel like you're a second son to me. Here, dear." Louise handed him a brown paper bag containing the filled container. "Oh, Robert?"

"Yes, Mrs. LeBlanc?"

"Did you know Sue Peters recently started working at the new general hospital?"

"No, I didn't," Robert said, appearing surprised.

"They did remarkable work on the poor thing; she looks wonderful now. I saw her there the other day."

"I'm so glad to hear that," Robert replied, genuinely pleased.

Louise looked fondly at Robert and said, "I know you helped her, honey. Word gets around in a small town. I think it's wonderful that you did that." Louise's eyes were filling with tears. "You're a kind and wonderful young man, Robert. I know that's why my daughter loves you as much as she does." Louise wiped her tears. "I'd be honored to be your mother-in-law someday," she smiled through her tears. "I just wanted you to know that, honey. Just make sure of your feelings."

"Thank you," Robert said warmly. "Thank you very much, Mrs. LeBlanc."

"Please don't tell my daughter we had this conversation?" She forced a big smile as she wiped her tears.

"No, ma'am. I won't." He smiled back at her. "It'll be our secret."

Louise LeBlanc and Robert walked together back to the foyer. Robert walked over to his pal, Roger, shook his hand, kissed Mary Lou, and told them they would get together during the week. He shook hands with Mr. LeBlanc, kissed Mrs. LeBlanc, and thanked them for a wonderful evening. Then Robert turned to Coral, desperately trying to keep himself under control. As Coral escorted Robert to the door to say goodbye, he spontaneously held her shoulder, unconsciously sliding it downward. Robert became stimulated by the soft skin of her fully naked shoulders and back to the small of it, and the swelling in his slacks reignited. His hand on her flesh and seeing the protrusion before he could hide it under his coat instinctively aroused Coral instantly.

"Good night, Coral," he said, watching her eyes widen as she looked directly into his; the beauty of their dark blue color electrified him again. Robert smiled, his coat folded over his arm, blocking his groin. "Will I see you tomorrow?" He opened his arms and leaned in to hug Coral and kiss her cheek gently. He did so clumsily, fearful of Coral seeing his arousal, and lost his balance from nervousness and tripped. Robert felt a spark of bliss as he inadvertently impacted Coral, his torso pressing firmly against hers as he held her from falling.

Coral stood speechless for a few seconds after briefly relishing the feel of his protrusion during their collision. She stood dreamy-eyed, her legs weakened and wobbled a little, secretly enjoying the eruption of her pleasurable feminine tears oozing in her loins and the ecstasy it gave her. Coral's eyes went into a daze as she said, "Yes, Robert, I'll see you for dinner at 2 PM. Good night." Her reaction caused her tongue to involuntarily lick her full, shapely lips seductively. Everything was happening too fast. Their sudden attraction caused their bodies to rule them, and they labored to suppress that natural urge. Robert savored the scent of her feminine bouquet, sweet and rich, pervading around her and rushed out the door. Coral needed a cold shower quickly.

14

Rue, Ohio Christmas Day 1961

Christopher Martin sat next to Emily in the living room of the Bryant mansion. He was saying his final farewells to the Bryant family before departing for Akron to spend Christmas Day with his family. "I can't remember when I ever had such a sumptuous breakfast like that before," Chris relayed his compliments with a smile and a nod to Mrs. Russo after feasting on pancakes, eggs, home fries, bacon, bread, and muffins. As he forwarded his attention back to the Bryants,' Chris said, "Thank you all for having me over," as a proud Emily smiled and sat closer to her boyfriend.

"We were so glad to meet you finally and have you over, Christopher," Naomi said first.

Knowing that his daughter's boyfriend was attending the University of Akron School of Law, William thought a great way to break the ice and spark a good breakfast conversation would have been to ask Chris how he liked studying law. However, he hadn't had the chance to discuss law during breakfast. Naomi had bombarded the young man with questions, eager to learn more about his personal life. Now, he had his opportunity: "So, Chris, how do you like law so far?" To Naomi's dismay, she lost the spotlight to her husband, and law practice became the main topic of discussion in the living room.

"Well, sir, so far, I love it, and as tough as it is, I'm doing rather well."

"He's being modest, Dad; Chris is at the top of his class," Emily added proudly.

Naomi tried to interject some appropriate questions to create a mix of discussions, which Chris politely answered. However, Chris took the conversation back to law when he told Robert,

"I commend you for studying law and physics simultaneously." Chris was amazed when he learned that Robert had become a lawyer while studying physics. He didn't know what level of genius Robert was, as that was a family secret. "The law curriculum is intense by itself. Wow! I respect such an accomplishment, Robert."

"Please call me Bob, Chris, or I'll call you Christopher as my mother does," Robert joked to everyone's amusement.

"Will do, Bob," Chris chuckled, smiling. That pleased Emily as she wanted both of them to get along well. Robert's approval of Chris meant everything to her.

After everyone finished the morning meal and enjoyed many conversations, Chris rose and thanked everyone for their polite hospitality. He complimented their beautiful home. Then, Chris shook hands with Mr. Bryant, Robert, and Mr. Russo. He kissed Naomi and Isabella and walked to the large front door at the end of the foyer. Chris hugged Emily, kissed her lips, and told her he would call her. They wished each other a Merry Christmas, kissed again, and Chris left.

After exchanging presents with her family earlier that Christmas morning, Coral sat in a stupor with her mother at the kitchen table, sipping coffee from a mug. She was still in her pajamas and white fluffy socks.

"Are you all right, dear," Louise fondly asked, noticing Coral's bleak expression and knowing that her daughter and Robert now realized their love for each other in an adult way.

Coral glanced at her mother, "What do you mean?"

"I couldn't help but notice how you and Robert," Louise hesitated for a few seconds trying to find the right words, "acted together last night."

"Was it that obvious, Mom?" Coral asked. Louise simply smiled in response. "Did Dad notice it?"

"Oh, no. Most men become oblivious to body language after a while," Louise smiled again. Of course, unless they're the ones using it."

"Thank God," Coral sighed.

"Though it wasn't too subtle at times there, dear."

"I couldn't help it, Mom. Honestly, I don't know what came over me."

"You're in love, Coralie," Louise smiled at her little girl, now a woman. "Simple as that."

"But Mom, I couldn't control myself with a man for the first time in my life. It was like getting shocked by electricity." Coral's eyes widened. "I was always attracted to Robert when I was little. I know that; everyone knows that, but last night was different," Coral raised her arms in frustration, then took another sip of her hot, steaming coffee.

"Coral, honey, that's because you and Robert were reacting to suppressed feelings. Like spontaneous combustion," Louise giggled. "You see, you and Robert always loved each other, but differently," Louise smiled at the surprised expression on her daughter's face. Coral's jaw dropped slightly, and she gazed at her mother as she placed her coffee cup on the table.

"You think Robert always loved me?" Coral asked, dumbfounded.

"Robert always loved everything about you, sweetheart, but it was your soul that he truly saw. My God, you could talk for hours and go for car rides together. You were such a cute little thing sitting in his car; you looked like his little princess." Louise pondered, her eyes lifted as she reminisced, smiling. Finally, she continued, "And you both shared common interests in books, places to explore, even philosophy. I remember listening to you both discuss so many topics," Louise shook her head, recalling the memories. "Your mind was mature for your age, dear. You challenged Robert, probably the only one who ever did, and that drew him to you. But he couldn't let himself express affection in the way you wanted at that time. You were just a little girl. And a little girl's body doesn't attract a young man, either, dear," Louise chuckled. "Everything came to a head last night. I thought it might when you both saw each other as adults."

Coral smiled at her mother while sipping her coffee, "So

you think he loves me?”

“I know he does, dear. The question is, what are you going to do about Ben? You know you don't love him.”

“Mom, I was going to break off with Ben last night over something else, even before Robert was in the picture.” Coral didn't feel like telling her mother the whole story about Ben; she didn't want to ruin the moment, only savor it. Robert had always loved her, and she smiled at the thought.

“Good idea. I never wanted to tell you before, but I don't like that Ben, even from the few times I met him.” Louise also noticed the bruise on her daughter's eye and others before and had her suspicions.

Emily was pacing the floor of her bedroom, rethinking what had transpired the night before with her best friend and brother. She knew what had happened with Coral and Robert the night before, suspecting Coral still maintained something special for Robert, even with Ben in the picture. That opened her eyes to Coral's relationship with Ben. Something was going on between them, a problem of some type. Emily had noticed the signs. Now, finally realizing that Coral's attraction to Robert in their younger years wasn't a silly schoolgirl crush, it was apparent that her love for Robert resurrected. She couldn't possibly love Ben. Something had happened between them that Coral hadn't yet told her.

Now that Coral was a young woman, Robert realized his emotions differently. Emily was both concerned and joyful because she felt they would most likely be compatible. But Emily didn't want either of them to get hurt because she loved both of them.

On the other hand, Robert was more of a 'complete person,' as Emily called it. He was a deep thinker who hid many of his emotions. Robert maintained a strong personality but accepted differing opinions and would adapt to a blend of logic and love for others. He often expressed this to friends, family, and especially her. Robert possessed leadership qualities that enabled him to excel in sports, school, and his chosen career. This is a big reason why so many people liked him. As worried as Emily was, she decided to wait and see how things developed. Perhaps in the light of day, they both might feel differently. She had to stop hypothesizing, or she would put herself into a stupor. She followed a wait-and-see policy. Robert had taught her that. Just then, Robert stepped into the open doorway of her bedroom.

"Can I speak with you, Em?" Robert asked, appearing concerned and serious.

"Of course, Robert," Emily worried. She and her brother had never asked to speak to each other; they just began conversations impulsively. Something was wrong.

Robert walked into the room and sat on the edge of Emily's bed, meeting her gaze. With his blue eyes locked onto hers, he asked, "Did that guy, Ben, hit Coral?"

Emily blushed. How could he know? Then she recalled Coral didn't cover her eye bruise as well as she should have, and her excuse for it sounded silly and unable to fool her brother. Emily could never lie to Robert. "Yes," she admitted.

Robert remained calm and hid his anger well, but his sister knew it was brewing. "Did he do it before?"

"Oh, Robert, I," Emily was getting nervous. She knew her dear friend was having problems with Ben—she could feel it. Emily never liked the idea of Benjamin Joyce dating Coral; even the way they met bothered her. Holding her emotions in for so long was making Emily a wreck. Now, confronted by Robert about the very same thing that had been bothering her, Emily felt like she would break down.

Robert could see it. She began trembling, and Robert's long arms pulled her close to him. As he embraced his sister, he whispered, "Shh, it's okay," just like he did when she was a baby to calm her down whenever she shivered from fright. "I'm not going to make a scene, sweetheart, okay? I just want to know," Robert continued, holding Emily, swaying her gently in his arms. "How about we talk about this later?" he said calmly.

"No," Emily said, feeling secure in her brother's arms. "You should know," she stepped back but still held Robert's wrists,

"Ben does. He hits her. I know of at least a couple of times because I saw the bruises on her body," Emily sighed, "Coral is terrified of him, Robert. Something else is going on; I can feel it." Tears rolled down Emily's cheeks, and she pulled her brother toward her, pressing her head against his chest like she always did.

Robert's keen intellect and his concerns about Ben hitting Coral pushed him into scientific mode. He said, "This could be part of a larger issue Ben has; I hope it's not. But it could relate to what psychology describes as sadomasochism." Robert frowned, deep in thought. "Has Ben shown any satisfaction with Coral when he hits her, do you know?" The professor within Robert emerged.

"I think so, but I don't know for sure."

"Is it sexual arousal?"

"Oh, Robert, I wouldn't know," Emily's head remained pressing against Robert's chest and answered in a muffled voice.

"Okay, okay, honey; we'll figure something out. Ben could be a sadist, maybe even engaged in sexual sadism. Some men want to leave bruises on women. It's a form of branding in their twisted minds, just like cowboys brand cattle. Possession. But we'll definitely take care of Ben." Emily couldn't see how Robert's face grimaced in anger or sense his inner fear for Coral.

"Okay," Emily replied in a muted voice.

"Coral has to break off with him, but we'll devise a special way to do that together, all three of us," Robert whispered.

That reminded Emily of their adventure together when she was younger, planning to relocate to Rue from New York years before. The memory pulled her out of the uneasiness caused by her anxiety. She raised her head and faced her brother, "I know now that you love Coral, Robert. I saw it last night. I think you always did in a way."

Now Robert blushed. "Yeah, I guess I do." He was embarrassed that his kid sister saw him like that, but Emily was no longer a kid. "But that's in no way the reason I want her to break off with Ben. You know that."

"Oh, Robert, Of course I do."

Coral stood naked before her full-length bedroom mirror, wondering if Robert would find her body beautiful. She had walked along both floors of her home in deep thought right after awakening, trying to understand what had happened the night before. The discovery of her sexual attraction to Robert was driving her crazy, and it had been all night while trying to sleep. The conversation with her mother helped, but she still had to process everything. Coral put back on her pajamas, sat barefoot on the edge of her bed, took an older photo of Robert and her from a shelf, and chuckled. Robert appeared to be an extremely handsome teenage young man whose body and face had prematurely developed. She looked like a late developer, tiny and skinny for a kid her age with big braces on her teeth. "Why would Robert even want to be seen with me?" she laughed heartily. Now, the confused young lady sat there and wondered about the new physical arousal she felt for Robert. Before, it was solely in her mind, a mental thing she only shared with Emily in those past days, or so she thought, knowing now so many others knew how she felt as a child. But now, after seeing Robert, it was also physical, which frightened her. Since the night before, Coral had felt a wild and unruly love for Robert. "What is happening to me," she whispered loudly, "I can't control myself."

Coral agreed with her mother's words and understood she was now experiencing real love, not a childhood fascination for Robert. But she never knew she could feel like she did for a man, especially acting the lewd way she did the night before, for real, and not joking as she did in her earlier years of college.

Even after she chatted with her mother, Coral needed to talk to Emily. "Everything is too much for me to handle alone, and Emily is the only one I can genuinely confide with in something like this. I have to telephone Emily and explain everything, especially Ben and the engagement ring he gave me last night," she whispered, but softly this time. As Coral walked to the telephone in the hallway, it rang.

"I've got it, Mom," she heard Louise's voice speaking to Emily.

"Okay, dear, I'll hang up."

Coral waited for the click that her mother disconnected and said, "Hi, Em." She didn't give Emily a chance to finish saying hello and continued, "I was waiting for your call, Dr. Emily Bryant; I knew you would after last night," she joked.

Emily and Coral knew each other well; they had discussed everything since they were kids. "I know this is awkward for you, Em, because it's about your brother, but–"

"Since when did that ever stop you before?" Emily interrupted, exhibiting her close bond in friendship. "Start spilling, kiddo. I saw how you and my brother connected last night, especially when you lifted your dress," Emily giggled, "you little whore," now openly laughing.

Coral chuckled as she dragged the phone by its long cord from the hallway to a private spot in her bedroom and continued, "It's real, Em; everything I've felt for your brother since we were kids is real."

"I know now," admitted Emily, "I was wrong. I see now that he feels the same way. He probably always has, but hid it well because you were too young."

"Everything's different after last night. The mere touch of his hand now ignites every nerve in my body. It's like sparks are flying out of me that make me want to scream out from desire. I have compulsions I never before knew existed." Coral didn't know how Emily would handle these new revelations she felt for her brother. "I can't help but follow this instinct because it controls me now, and I can't resist it. I had an orgasm from just touching and speaking to him. How sick is that?" Coral blushed out of embarrassment even though Emily couldn't see her. Coral whispered lowly, "I saw Robert with a ... you know ... he was hard," she blushed again, "more than once."

"Wow! Okay, calm down, Coral. Alert! Alert! Battle stations! I'll help you get through this."

"I can't; it's different now. I feel a strong sexual chemistry radiating from my body, unlike anything I've ever felt before. I think Robert feels it, too. I told you about his, you know."

"I know; he got a boner. I heard it the first time."

Coral calmed down a little and, out of the blue, asked, "Em, do you remember that guy who exposed himself years ago?"

"How could I forget something like that?" Emily groaned. "Why do you ask?"

"Because we never talked about it much as adults. I mean, we were specialists on those things men have after it happened. Remember? Going to the library. And all the illustrations."

"I remember." Emily found some humor in that memory, but she said nothing amusing. Other, deeper emotions stopped her.

"But we stopped talking about it, Em. As we got older, we never mentioned it. Did it affect you, Em? Did you ever see Chris's? You never said."

Emily sighed. "Well, we didn't really know what they were back then, Coral." Emily had been taken off guard and dwelled for a few seconds. "Come to think of it, the shock of that made me fear them in a way. It was a horrible way to learn." Emily paused and thought back to that time, her emotions rising. "As much as I love Chris, I've never touched his until recently. Well, I didn't touch his penis; I only felt the bulge of his pants and rubbed it, and it did make me very emotional," Emily's eyes were in a daze. "It caused me to explain that story to Chris; I felt I owed him that," Emily paused again, thinking. She said, "He was sweet about it; he tried to understand, even though I know he couldn't. He said we'll wait, but that made me love him more and feel like wanting to try to, you know, do it with him."

"You mean go all the way?"

"Yes. I love Chris and plan to marry him, so I'm going to." Emily told Coral, "You're right; we never discussed that incident as adults. It's the one secret we kept from each other. I wonder why? Did it affect you, Coral?"

"I thought about it a lot over the years. I was afraid of them, too," Coral's eyes looked up and appeared dreamy as she thought. "I mean, that disgusting guy did that to us. We were kids, and I became afraid of a man's thing."

"You still can't say the word penis."

Coral thought deeply, ignoring Emily's statement. "I think I hid my fears by being forward with men, flirting with them. And by doing all those stupid sexual skits in our early years of college," Coral pondered, "I realized it more after last night when I saw Robert's bulge and–"

"Hard on. Say it, Coral," Emily interrupted her. "It might help."

"That sounds so slutty. Anyway, I liked seeing it and realizing Robert's attraction to me did that to him. I excited him so much he couldn't control himself either. I wanted to touch it because it was Robert's. And I'm going to let him take me, Em, because I know he loves me. I feel it, Em, and I only wish I was a virgin," Coral began sobbing.

A shocked Emily asked, "You're not? You never told me. With Ben?"

"I was ashamed to," Coral wept louder. "I feel so cheap."

"Oh, Coral, dear, don't cry," Emily comforted Coral as the two friends had done for each other since they were kids.

"Brace yourself, Em. Okay, Robert never returned, and I felt like he never would. Ben was good to me and kind at first," Coral paused to gather her thoughts. "Ben took me to nice places, and I genuinely enjoyed his company. I liked Ben, but I never loved him, and I definitely never felt any sexual attraction toward him at all. I realized early on that he didn't love me, only my body; that's all he ever cared about–putting his hands all over me," Coral sobbed too softly for Emily to hear. "I lost my virginity to Ben on a sunny day in late October while we were having a picnic in a secluded spot with no other people around. Ben arranged it that way. How foolish of me; he set me up. We lay together on a blanket covering the grass, and then Ben started kissing me." Coral sobbed again but put the telephone receiver aside so Emily couldn't hear.

"Do you want to talk about this later, honey, when we're together?" Emily felt helpless, unable to comfort her friend in person over such a serious thing.

"No, Em, let me do it now. It's my fault; I allowed it. I felt obligated to kiss Ben." Coral took another deep breath, released it, and continued, "Ben smacked me lightly on my cheek and asked me if I liked it. When he saw my shock, he told me a lot of girls find it stimulating. When I told him I didn't like it, He asked if he could gently hit me on my body to see if I liked that. Emily, I don't know what others do when they make out. I know I'm naïve with men, so I let him. I thought he was only going to tap me lightly, but Ben hit me hard and roughly, frighteningly. It hurt badly and left a mark, so I told him to stop. Did Chris ever want to hit you?"

"No! Hitting is not normal–to me, anyway!" Emily was annoyed, and she sounded so. "People who do–" Emily stopped explaining; she always knew Coral was a little ditsy when it came to men, "I remember when you met Ben. You were flirting with some guy, exposing your leg and thigh, seductively. I always warned you that kind of joking would get you into trouble and could attract the wrong element of men. I'm sorry for getting mad at you, honey," Emily knew Coral was gullible at times with men and never should have gotten angry with her best friend. "Go ahead, Coral, and tell me the rest."

"I told him to stop hitting me, but that only made him more excited, you know, like wanting to feel me up more. His hands were all over me. I was so afraid he was going to hit me, so I let him touch me down there, you know, my vagina," Coral sobbed again. "Before I knew it, Ben quickly drew up my pleated skirt and pulled off my panties frantically." Emily immediately recalled her conversation with her brother about hitting and sexual arousal, making the connection that when Ben hit Coral, he became sexually exhilarated. She dared not tell Coral what she was thinking.

"Why did you let him?" Emily blurted out in shock.

"Because I was afraid. It happened so fast," Coral was now crying. "Seeing his thing scared me; it was so ugly, and I froze, not able to pull away or kick him. I hated myself for just lying there naked from the waist down, paralyzed from fright and letting him take my virginity, Em," her tears flowing, "I didn't even fight him," Coral whispered loudly, but not loud enough for anyone nearby her bedroom to hear her conversation. "I let Ben put that horrible thing into me," Coral sobbed. "Penis!" she screamed. "Okay, I said it! Happy?"

"Please calm down, Coral. Someone might hear you in your house. I'm so sorry I called you out on that word. I was only trying to help you. I know this goes deep. I'm so sorry, honey," Emily now recognized how disturbed Coral was from talking about this incident.

"It's okay. I overreacted. I'm a bundle of nerves." Coral continued, "It hurt me, Em. He was rough, grunting like an animal, drooling." Coral calmed herself to recollect her thoughts, "I had no arousal whatsoever and wasn't wet at all. That constant thrusting motion irritated me so badly that I screamed from the pain. Ben yelled, 'That's right, baby, let out all that sexual tension you got bottled up inside you!' He thought I was enjoying it. I couldn't speak like when you're in a bad nightmare; I couldn't even tell him to stop. The whole experience was so quick. Ben finished in less than a minute; thank God it wasn't any longer," Coral sighed from the agony of reliving that time. "But right before he finished, he punched my thigh really hard, screaming out, 'Yes!' Ben sounded like a wild animal. Then, he quickly lifted himself off of me and fixed himself. I was in shock, crying there on the blanket, alone, my upper leg reddened where he hit me."

Emily was horrified and had been in a state of shock while listening to Coral's account. Now, it all sank in, and she fell apart. Emily began crying frantically, "Oh, Coral, why didn't you tell me these things before," she sobbed. "You didn't have to go through this alone; I could have been there for you like you are for me so many times." Her dear trustful but gullible friend had been raped, and she might not even understand that in her current mental state. "He took advantage of your innocence," Sobbing, Emily didn't want to tell Coral Ben raped her. If her trauma didn't allow her to comprehend that, it would be better to discuss it another time.

Coral, almost as if reading Emily's mind, said softly, "I think Ben raped me, Em. Wouldn't that be what it really was?"

"Yes, Coral, but I'll help you. Do you feel like telling me more about what he did to you, or maybe that's enough for today."

Coral wanted to continue; she wanted her dearest friend to know everything, "I lay there recovering from the throbbing pain in my vagina. The place where he hit me on my thigh was already bruising and hurt so much. It was so horrible being there. I felt like I was going to smother. After Ben caught his breath, he asked me how I liked it. Did he actually think my screaming was a sign I enjoyed such a dreadful experience? I shouted I hated him. He looked so angry, like crazy. He hit me on my upper arm hard. He's strong, and it hurt me and left another big bruise. I limped when I finally got up, holding my arm. I was in so much pain."

Emily understood more than Coral thought, realizing Robert was right and Ben was a sexual sadist. But she couldn't tell Coral that her brother had said that or even that he suspected it. Emily had hoped Robert was wrong but knew he was a genius and absorbed countless books on all subjects; he had to be correct. Robert had a keen intuition on top of that. "I remember seeing some of the bruises on you. Your excuses never convinced me. Why are you still seeing Ben after he did that to you?"

"I only saw him once since that time in late October. It was a couple of weeks ago. He must have been following me because I bumped into him in Youngstown, and he asked to speak to me. I was afraid, so I insisted we go to a small park crowded with people to talk on a bench. I made it clear I didn't want to see him anymore. Ben got annoyed and smacked me right there in front of people. Everyone ignored it. They simply looked away; nobody wanted to get involved."

"Your eye?"

"Yeah, but I haven't seen Ben since that time in the park. I avoided him and kept making excuses. Oh, Emily, I've been so afraid of him since that happened. He likes to hit women; it excites him, I think."

"He's a sicko!" Emily yelled.

"I only agreed for him to come over last night because I planned to tell him to stay away from me, where there were people who always loved and supported me and could protect me from him. But Ben got up quickly. I think he saw the way Robert looked at me and got mad. Em, Ben proposed to me last night before you left. I didn't even have a chance to repeat what I said in the park. How crazy is that? It's as if he never heard a word I said."

"He did?" Emily was astonished. Then, she recalled hearing the door slam after Ben rudely said goodbye to everyone. "Come to think of it, I remember how he acted, and I heard the door slam."

"He didn't really propose. I don't remember his exact words, but he pretty much told me that I belonged to him and we should marry. I don't even want to see Ben anymore. I know now he's delusional if he thinks I would want to even be around him, let alone marry him,"

"We should tell Robert or Roger about some of–"

"Oh, no, no!" Coral screamed, "What would Robert think of me? We can't tell Robert."

"Coral. Robert knows Ben hits you."

"Oh, Em, why did you tell him? Robert will kill him. He'll probably tell Roger, and they'll tear Ben apart, not that he doesn't deserve it. But they'll go to jail."

"Coral, dear, relax. Robert already knew. He probably saw your eye. Your makeup didn't fully cover it."

"That's right. He asked, and I made up an excuse."

"He just needed confirmation, and you have no idea how terrible I felt being the one to substantiate such a hideous thing–

to use a legal term because of my fascination with law and becoming a lawyer," Emily made the casual joke to ease Coral's tension and her own recalling how upset she got having to tell her brother. "And nobody's getting killed."

"I'm sorry, Em. How did Robert take it?"

"I know Robert, and on the inside, he fumed and probably killed Ben over and over, but Robert kept his calm because it was upsetting me, and he knew. We're going to plan a way with you to get rid of Ben where no one gets killed or hurt. I won't tell Robert anything about what Ben did to you sexually. That's between you and Robert."

"Thank you, Em."

"We'll fix Ben. You and I will talk about this later when we're alone."

"Okay, Em. Thanks for listening. I'm going to get ready. I feel a little better now. We'll talk later."

"Don't worry, Coral, we'll think of something. Okay, bye for now. I'll call you later if I think of anything. Bye."

After hanging up with Emily, Coral lay on her bed, thinking about Robert and fighting the urge to touch herself. Coral knew Robert was gentle. She was sure from knowing him for so long and observing how gentle Robert was whenever he touched her in the past, deeply sensing how different making love with Robert would be. He would never hurt her like Benjamin did. She knew it. However, Coral wondered if Robert would still want her, knowing she had sex with Ben, even though it was only one time. Coral recalled when she had a schoolgirl crush on Robert and waited for him to come over to see her brother, remembering those wonderful days–and now reliving them. But did Robert feel the same way toward her as she did for him? Coral saw him watching her, but perhaps he only admired her as a friend who had changed since the last time he saw her. Then she remembered the rise in his pants, the aroma of his excitement, and his eyes watching her lovingly, which put her at some ease. "But these sensations might blow over naturally, and I don't want them to leave," Coral whispered.

Coral knew she had to get rid of Ben immediately, especially now that he had proposed. Her mind retained that awful experience of that past October, and she had nightmares often. "But now, Robert is here, my knight in shining armor," Coral smiled at that long-ago childhood fantasy. She rose from her bed and pulled one of her dolls down from a shelf in her bedroom, thinking of her childhood. Coral had saved her fine doll collection for a possible daughter someday. Now, the thought of having children with Robert came alive. No longer the fantasy of a child, he was the man she wanted to marry. Unashamedly, Coral enjoyed how Robert made her body feel. She went back to her bed and began touching herself, imagining making love to Robert.

Robert was pacing the floors in his parent's house. He had been doing it since after breakfast that morning, finally realizing his emotions for Coral. Their ages separated them when they were young, but not now. Robert had been contemplating the events of the evening before. He dated many women since high school and was adept with female anatomy and psyche from knowledge and experience. Robert knew attraction and arousal well but only as spontaneous reactions between the sexes, as a scientist. All of his experiences could not account for what he now felt. It was different and as if a floodgate had opened. Did he harbor repressed feelings for Coral when she was younger? Was there always an attraction he suppressed toward her because of her age? These thoughts raced through his mind, and he knew he should speak to someone. He couldn't discuss this with his best friend, Roger, because the subject was about his younger sister, which would be awkward. His father, William, was someone he truly respected and the one person other than Roger whose advice he often sought.

When Robert approached him, William was reading a magazine, and he didn't want to interrupt him, seeing how relaxed and comfortable his father looked. However, from the corner of his eye, he spotted his mother sitting, relaxing, her arms folded. Robert knew his mother's expression well. Naomi appeared to be waiting for a conversation with someone, even if it meant making a phone call.

"Mom, sorry to interrupt, but can you spare a moment?"

"Why, of course, Robert," her immediate reaction was that her son couldn't find something or perhaps wanted a snack and began to rise from her comfortable loveseat.

"I'd like to talk to you about something." Naomi appeared surprised her son wanted to speak to her.

"Why sure, Robert; is something wrong, honey?" her motherly instincts resurfaced, and she suspected Robert might not be feeling well or coming down with something. "Are you alright, dear?"

"I'm fine, Mom." Robert smiled. "I need your advice, Mom." This stunned his mother even more, and she sat back in her seat. Robert had sought guidance from his father since he was in his teens.

Naomi glanced up and observed her son's worried expression, "Okay, Robert, sit next to me," she patted the bottom pillow of the loveseat. "Make yourself comfortable, honey."

Robert sat beside his mother, recalling how long it had been since he and his mother had had a nice chat. It felt comfortable, like when he was younger. "I have a young woman-related problem, Mom." Robert blushed and forced a smile to hide his nervousness. He sensed he had made the right decision to discuss such a delicate matter concerning Coral with another woman. Naomi always kept her affairs confidential. She was intelligent and well-briefed on social issues and those of the heart. Most of all, Robert loved and admired his mother.

"Alright, Robert," Naomi smiled lovingly. "May I ask if this has anything to do with the young lady, Coralie LeBlanc?" now she smiled widely.

Robert fondly smiled back at his mother and said, "You know me better than anyone in my life."

"Shouldn't I, dear? After all, I raised you."

"It is about Coral. I don't know how to explain it, Mom, but I now have completely different feelings about her than I did, and I don't know why." Robert knew his mother never held back her true feelings when asked and was direct, which were only some additional qualities Robert admired in her. He also knew his mother's advice was always stable and wholesome.

"Well, dear, from what I remember, You always had feelings for Coralie but hid them in a way suited to you then. Coralie was too young then for you both to share that love maturely. Naomi observed her son carefully. "You see, Robert, we all hide some of our sincerest emotions for different reasons. It's normal."

"Well, I always liked Coral. She was cute and bold, and I did enjoy speaking to her. But that was because she managed to maintain mature conversations, but I did enjoy her company. I recognize that now. There was always something about her I liked, but couldn't put my finger on it," Robert now began remembering.

"Those are qualities that a person always possesses. You saw them in her when she was still a child, and you probably hid your affection for the same reason: she was in a child's body."

Robert realized those things he remembered were the soul of Coral. Her physical development and those qualities formed the basis for what he now felt. His speculations pushed on, and he answered, "But this is my little friend. It's monkeyface I'm talking about."

"Robert, you must stop being a physicist for just a minute to realize what is happening with your newfound desire for Coral. You're human and a man. You couldn't act on your emotions for her when you last saw her, but now Coral is a woman, and it's natural for you to release any buried feelings."

Robert focused on the memory of being with Coral and her aura. He always avoided love somehow. His mission in life was his work, and he wouldn't let anything stand in his way–until now. Robert thought it might have been a distraction all along to keep his mind off Coral. But now Robert realized this passion, the first one of his life, was uncontrollable. These were all new feelings he harbored. "I've never been in love before."

"Well, welcome to the club, dear."

"But, what if I'm overreacting to these sentiments I alone feel and probably not even shared by Coral?"

"These are things all couples go through. Trust your instincts, Robert; they'll never disappoint you. But I have a funny feeling that young woman loves you an awful lot." Naomi smiled at her little boy, now a man.

"Thank you, Mom. You've helped me more than you might think." Robert smiled back at his mother.

"I'm always here for you, Robert." Naomi was pleased she was able to help her son. "Oh, Robert. One other thing," she said to her son as he began to rise from the loveseat. "I just heard that Sue Peters is completely rehabilitated and working at the hospital. I'm on the board there; that's how I found out. Did you Know?"

"I just found out last night at Roger's house. Mrs. LeBlanc told me."

Naomi looked at her son lovingly and said, "Your father and I are so proud of what you did for her, dear. It's an example of a fine Christian thing to do for someone who faulted you. You've become a wonderful young man, Robert. We're overjoyed with the way you turned out. A mother couldn't be more pleased."

"Thank you, Mom," Robert smiled at Naomi. "I had good parents to teach me."

Even after his conversation with his mother, the anticipation of seeing Coral again weighed heavily on Robert. Coral had grown into a beautiful young woman, and Robert couldn't shake the yearning he felt deep in his soul. But who am I? he thought. Even if Coral broke up with Ben, she could have her pick of any man she wanted. He would have to wrestle with his feelings privately and see how Coral reacted to him at dinner. Perhaps everything would be different today. Then, he recalled what Coral's mother had said, along with his mother's words.

For both of them to mention these things made him think Coral might indeed love him. Yet, he also remembered Mrs. LeBlanc's advice to ensure he understood his feelings for Coral before acting on them.

Roger drove his sister, Coral, to the Bryant home. Their parents didn't want Coral traveling home alone at night and assumed Robert would take her home. Along the ride, Roger told his sister, "Hey, Sis, couldn't help but notice you watching Bob last night. Feeling something for my best friend?" Roger smiled, watching Coral with his peripheral vision but keeping his eyes on the road.

Coral was shocked that even Roger noticed. Her brother had been in a dream world since he met Mary Lou and never noticed anything else, especially about her. "I do, Roge; I think I always have." Still shocked that her older brother noticed anything about her, she asked, "Did anyone say anything to you?"

"No, but I know my pal well, and Bob's a really good man." Roger smiled again, then turned to Coral and said, "You look really nice today, Sis. All dressed up like you are makes me wonder what happened to the time. You're a beautiful young woman now, Coral." Roger was sincere, and his voice and mannerism showed it.

"Thank you, Roge. Thank you very much," Coral also spoke honestly and from her heart. What's happening? Coral thought, Is the world coming to an end? Roge never said anything as lovely to me before, fighting a tear from it because she didn't want to ruin her makeup.

"I hope it works out for you, Sis. I really do. Bob's the only man good enough for you in my book."

As they pulled past the wrought-iron gates and into the cobblestone driveway of the Bryant home, Coral said, "Thanks, Roge. It means a lot coming from my big brother."

As they walked to the front door, Roger coached his younger sister. "Now, stay calm and don't be nervous. Everything will work out fine," Roger said as he put his finger on the doorbell, smiling at his sister again.

"Thanks, Roge."

When the doorbell rang, Robert announced that he would get it. Impeccably dressed, he wore beige dress pants, a dark brown belt, matching shoes, and a dark blue tapered-fitting dress shirt. As he walked to the foyer, Emily quickly followed and smelled the fragrance of his cologne that pervaded his trail. Robert opened the front door to see Coral accompanied by her brother, Roger. They greeted Robert with a 'Merry Christmas' as they entered the house.

Coral wore a full-length grey-white rabbit fur jacket with cuffed sleeves. Her hair, now worn up and pulled back tightly, emphasized the delicate features of her beautiful face even more. "Merry Christmas," she repeated softly to Robert, stepping on her tiptoes to embrace him.

They hugged for a few seconds, and then Robert replied, "Merry Christmas, Coral. I'm so glad to see you again." The feeling of her embrace aroused Robert even more than the night before. He had anticipated the feel of her all night and that morning.

Coral smiled back at Robert, concealing the sexual thoughts she nurtured from his embrace.

Roger was on his way to his fianceé's house and could only come in for a quick visit. He kept his overcoat on and shook hands with his best friend. Then he walked toward the living room to where Robert's parents were sitting, kissing Emily's cheek as he passed her and wished her a Merry Christmas.

Robert helped Coral out of her coat and handed it to a waiting Emily, who could sense that her brother and Coral were both nervous. Emily admired her friend's coat as they hugged, then hung it in the foyer closet.

Coral looked ravishing, dressed in a dark red form-fitting dress that revealed more cleavage in the front than the dress she had worn the night before. It was strapless and exposed her entire back and shoulders. The designs of her matching dark red three-and-a-half-inch heeled stilettos were styled cut and tapered at the fronts and along the inner sides, revealing just a hint of her upper toes and the well-formed arches of her feet, which Robert found sexually appealing. The higher spike heels also firmed the muscles of Coral's voluptuous legs even more, making them appear alluring and enticing. She privately referred to them as her man-killer spiked heels and wore them purposely for that reason. Coral's dress had a small matching material bow attached at the front of a snuggly fitting belt around her thin waist, which added to her shapely figure.

Robert admired the elegant and seductive creature who stood before him. "You look beautiful, Coral," he complimented her. "I guess I can't call you monkeyface anymore."

"Oh, why not?"

"Because you're beautiful, and I told you I would only call you that endearing term until you realized how beautiful you are. You would have to be blind not to see it now," Robert smiled at Coral lovingly.

"Thank you, Robert," Coral beamed. Her radiant smile revealed sparkling white teeth. The large silver-colored braces she wore years ago were long gone. Deep red lipstick made Coral's full lips look even more shapely and sensual, stimulating Robert. "But I grew fond of that term over the years." Chuckling softly and sensually, Coral told Robert, "I actually believed an endearing term meant you cherished me."

"I do cherish you, Coral," Robert was shocked that he verbalized his thoughts.

"I cherish you too, Robert," Coral felt no reservations saying her true feelings.

Robert took Coral by the hand and escorted her over to his parents. He put his right arm over Coral's naked shoulders and could feel her warm, soft flesh, and it excited him. "Mom, Dad, doesn't Coral look lovely today?"

Robert's touch on Coral's naked shoulder exhilarated her. She felt a quiver in her loins and tried to ignore it. "Hi, Mr. and Mrs. Bryant. Merry Christmas to both of you!" She gave them a big smile that revealed her beautiful teeth.

"You look breathtaking, my dear. Merry Christmas to you also," Naomi greeted Coral while she rose from the armchair where she sat and embraced her. "We're so happy you came!" Then, Naomi secretly winked at her son.

"Merry Christmas, my dear," said William. "You look very nice." He was already on his feet and hugged Coral. William smiled, "You're a beautiful woman now. Where did the time go? We haven't seen you as often as we'd like to." Coral sat down and chatted with Naomi and William. Roger bid everyone a 'Merry Christmas,' and Robert walked him to the door. Robert and Roger agreed to get together with the guys sometime during the coming week, and they shook hands before Roger opened the door and left.

A few minutes later, Nick and May Stetson, Naomi's brother and sister-in-law, arrived with her mother, Eloise. Everyone sat in the living room and commented on how beautiful Coral had become. They hadn't seen her in a while. William Bryant served cocktails to his guests, who conversed until Naomi called everyone to the table.

Naomi phoned Louise LeBlanc earlier to thank her for the food she had sent over. Louise updated Naomi about how Coralie and Robert had been interacting the night before. Naomi wasn't surprised; she had always observed her son's attraction to Coral. "I hope they do become a couple," Naomi told Louise, "Robert needs a young woman like Coralie. But I'll throw cold water on them if they get out of control," she laughed. "Oh! What about the young man Coralie is dating?"

"I don't know. I never really saw my Coralie with him," replied Louise. "I don't like him," she whispered, "there's something about him I can't explain." Louise didn't feel Christmas was the appropriate time to discuss her suspicions of Ben hitting her daughter. "Anyway, I always imagined Coralie with Robert. Let me know what happens, Naomi."

"Oh, you bet I will," Naomi giggled.

Naomi sat Coral opposite Robert at the end of the table near her place setting so they could speak with each other and she could conveniently see them. Emily sat next to Coral because she wanted to see her brother's expressions and be next to her friend in case Coral signaled her in any way. Earlier in the day, Emily had two telephone conversations with Coral, which, among other things, resulted in Coral's commitment to take things slowly with Robert.

William sat at the opposite end of the table. The Stetsons sat close to William, Carlo, and Isabella Russo, who usually joined the Bryant family on holidays. Naomi hadn't mentioned anything about Robert and Coral to William.

Festive decorations adorned the large dining room table for Naomi and Isabella's holiday meal. They had both worked feverishly on them since the day before. Christmas-decorated dishware, with beautiful goldware and gold-rimmed crystal glasses, was set to the side of them. Everyone seated complimented the decor. William took his wine-filled glass and gave an eloquent toast to Christmas. Robert looked directly into Coral's eyes, smiled, and mouthed the words 'Merry Christmas' as everyone exchanged accolades to the toast. Coral smiled back before seductively putting her lips to her glass. Naomi and Emily smiled at each other as they both noticed the exchange.

Isabella passed festive-designed bowls bearing chunk lobster meat cocktails to each person first.

"The fish store in town buys everything fresh from Pittsburgh," Naomi announced. "For some reason, there's a shortage of shrimp this season, so we substituted the lobster for the cocktails."

"Nothing wrong with that," her brother, Nick, answered, "Fresh lobster meat is a real treat."

"I know," Naomi chuckled, "but Isabella and I were going to use them to make Lobster Newburg. So now, Isabella made her famous Fettuccine Alfredo instead," she said while readying to serve steeping dishes of the rich Italian cheese pasta recipe on matching decorative plates to everyone.

Afterward, William took charge of cutting a giant roast turkey at his end of the table. It was a tradition for him to cut the main meat dish on that holiday every year.

"Wow! That's a monster of a bird," May Stetson complimented.

"Almost 40 pounds," William proudly answered, sliding his lengthy carving knife against a long sharpening stone. "Got it from a local farm just outside of town."

"Russo's?" asked Nick.

"Yep!"

"I thought so. They raise good birds."

William asked his guests whether they preferred white or dark meat while he carved. Afterward, he placed each person's choice of sliced turkey on clean dishes and passed them to everyone seated. Isabella walked around the table, serving a portion of her specially prepared Swiss chard with onions, black olives, and homemade sun-dried tomatoes. It was another of her Italian recipes that everyone enjoyed. Isabella also made her unique and delicious stuffed mushrooms, which prompted all seated at the table to compliment the remarkable spread of cuisines. Naomi served everyone grilled potatoes and set a large bowl of beautiful garden salad on the table for them to share.

Robert and Coral couldn't resist the constant urge to look at each other between conversations. Naomi and Emily noticed the sensuous body language and enticing facial exchanges when they did.

After dinner, William led his guests to the large sitting room off the dining room. A smiling Robert asked Coral, "Would you like to stroll with me through the house, your castle?"

Coral's eyes squinted like a cat. "So, someone let my secret desire out of the bag." She smiled widely and seductively at Robert as he enjoyed the seconds of that pleasure.

"Actually, I overheard you say that long ago," Robert confessed. Coral smiled and happily agreed. She always adored the large home she once secretly dreamed of as a castle, which she shared with Robert, her knight in shining armor. Robert put his arm around Coral's naked shoulder, escorting her, his hand feeling the nakedness of her exposed flesh there and that of her back. Coral spontaneously twitched from the arousal she felt in the center of her womanhood. They slowly walked through the large rooms and spoke softly to each other while recalling old memories they shared in the house. As they approached an elevator, Robert tenderly asked Coral, "Like to ride up to the viewing lounge above the third floor?"

She whispered her answer sensually, in a soft, husky voice, "I would love to go up there with you." The soothing way she said it aroused Robert, causing a slight rise in the crotch of his trousers. Coral took Robert's hand and smiled at him, noticing the bulge in his pants as they entered the tiny elevator, fighting herself from touching it. The ride seemed like it lasted for years of pleasure as one admired the other, each fighting natural desires in an atmosphere of sensuality.

Still holding hands as they exited the lift, Robert asked Coral, "Can you manage the circular stairway with your heels?" Coral removed her hand from Robert's and put it on his left breast as she stepped out of her heels alluringly, exposing her beautiful feet. Robert had déjà vu again as he remembered how Coral stepped out of her heels, and that simple action aroused him. Coral could feel the hardness of Robert's chest muscles, and it inflamed her with desire. Robert could see that the toenails of Coral's shapely feet painted the same deep red color as her fingernails, now gently touching his breast. He could feel the tips of her nails get slightly tighter as she moved them around, deliberately massaging the sensitive area surrounding his nipple. Robert's manhood began to grow more. Coral continued the battle within her and strained herself from touching it. Robert took Coral's hand from his breast and led her up the circular stairway. As they reached the top, Robert turned around, put his hands on Coral's waist, and lifted her past the last stair and onto the floor; the bulge in his slacks accidentally rubbed against her body as he did, inflaming Coral with lust as her loins wettened. Her deep blue eyes widened as she looked up and into his.

Coral stood on her tiptoes and raised her arms to embrace

Robert. He could feel her soft touch on the back of his neck, gently massaging his skin. Then she kissed him with an open mouth as his hands remained on her waist. Robert excitedly rolled his tongue with hers. Coral moaned as they passionately kissed. Her succulent lips moved, softly kissing before her tongue licked inside Robert's left ear. The sensations between her legs were driving her passionately. Robert slowly kissed and then licked the precise part of Coral's neck that began to drive her completely wild, his hardness now pressing firmly against Coral's body. She reached to feel it and screamed out, "Oh, Robert! I want you!" She couldn't help herself or hold back as she tried to grasp his manhood, "I want to feel you inside me! Please!" Coral vaguely thought of her conversation with Emily about taking things slowly as a nervous, reflective action. But she couldn't help it. Coral was utterly out of control.

Robert moved his hands from her midsection and held her hands tightly, preventing her from touching him, knowing if she did, he wouldn't be able to stop himself from what he imagined doing to her. Instead, he held her head between his hands, gently massaging her ears with his thumbs. Panting softly, he said, "Not here. We can't!" It took every ounce of his will to seize his desire to make love to her at that moment. "Not like this. Not for the first time." Robert was breathing heavily, as was Coral.

Coral felt wetness drip on her upper thighs and tried to control herself. She had never felt anything like this passion before with any other man. Coral stood back and composed herself. "You're right. We should wait." She looked up at Robert; the smear of her lipstick made her look erotic and seductive. "When? When can we?"

Robert said, "Coral, I think I love you." He paused. "I don't know, I've never been in love before. But–"

"Oh, Robert, do you?" she cut him off, "because I feel it in every part of my body and mind. I want you to love me, but it couldn't equal how much I love you."

"But are you sure you're ready to make love with me?" Robert gently rubbed the nape of her long, delicate neck. "Because I can't resist you. You are the only woman who ever made me feel this way," he spoke honestly. "And what about Ben?"

"I never loved Ben. I'm certain I want to be with you!" Her big, wide eyes were pleading with Robert. "When? When will you make love to me?" Then Coral realized she had to tell Robert the truth about her and Ben. "Robert, I have to tell you something."

"Oh?" Robert quickly feared what Coral wanted to tell him.

Coral also began to worry about Robert's reaction, and her eyes watered. Robert's hand reached to wipe her tears away. "No, Robert." Coral stopped his hand and removed a tissue from her purse. She gently patted her eyes and her nose. "Please let me continue, or I might not be able to," Coral explained to Robert what happened between her and Ben. She told him how Ben got off on hitting her and told Robert about the engagement ring he had given her. Coral explained how she tried to break off with him, and he hit her eye. Coral opened up to Robert about everything, even the dreadful and frightful way Ben had sex with her while smacking her.

Robert leaned down and kissed the bruise over her eye covered with makeup, just like he did when Coral scrapped or bumped herself as a child. Coral relished the fond flashback to her childhood, but the feeling of his lips on her wound now made her feel sexual passion, entirely different than the happiness of getting Robert's attention when she was a skinny kid. "What a bastard. Emily never told me. I already knew he hit you; I saw your eye. But I never knew the rest, and I feel like killing him for everything he did to you."

"Emily didn't know the whole story when she spoke to you. I talked to her earlier and told her everything about Ben and me. I was so ashamed to tell her before. I can't get rid of him. I don't know what to do," Coral sobbed.

Robert calmed down, holding his rage about Ben within him, and held Coral tightly in his arms, gently holding her face between his hands, massaging the sides of it the way Coral had loved since she was a child and had his attention. He softly whispered, "We'll plan a way to get rid of Ben once and for all. You, Emily, and me. And without me going to jail," he smiled at Coral." Then Robert reflected on Ben's horrible things done to Coral in a calmer, more rational way, finally saying, "Oh, my dear Coral, I'm so sorry about what Ben did to you. If there were any way I could make your pain go away, I would." Robert held her close to him, appearing upset, and a tear formed in each of his eyes. "I think under the circumstances, you should fully recover from that trauma from Ben before we make love."

"No, Robert! I want to now. I can't wait."

"Ben molested you, sweetheart. You have to heal."

"Oh, Robert. I love you! I'm certain of it." Coral looked into Robert's eyes passionately. "I always have." She looked deeper into Robert's eyes. "I feel something for you that I can never give to another man." Coral lowered her eyes, raised them again, and said, "I want you, Robert. I want to make love to you now," her lovely eyes rolling downward like a disobedient child. But Robert remained quiet and in deep thought. He had déjà vu and remembered being here with Coral before but in a different way.

Robert now knew he loved Coral and always had, but differently, knowing now it was a true mature love that he felt for her. However, aside from the despicable things Ben did to Coral, Robert remembered her mother's advice about getting to know her better as a grown woman. Robert leaned over and kissed Coral on her lips. He whispered to her, "Let's sit down and talk." Robert took Coral by her hand and sat beside her on the circular sofa in the center of the turret room. His arm around her bare shoulder aroused him. Robert resisted the temptations and said, "You don't have to be afraid of anything anymore. I promise you I'll never allow Ben to hurt you in any way ever again–I swear it!" Coral glanced up, saying nothing; her eyes said it all. There was a security in those deep blue spherical droplets from heaven that spoke of the security she felt with Robert, his arm holding her and knowing he would protect her.

Robert softly told Coral, "Ben is a very sick man. Based on

what you told me, he's delusional. He has other issues," Robert didn't feel it was the right time to discuss sexual sadomasochism or psychology at all. "Ben's the kind of man who gets joy from hurting and intimidating people. Aside from everything else, he's a bully, sweetheart, and only forcibly hurts those he knows can't hurt him back." Robert looked lovingly at Coral, "I'll always be here for you, Coral, in all ways, no matter your decision. There can be no other woman for me than you. But I want you to take your time and decide about us before we make love, and take time to heal also."

"No, Robert! Please don't! I'm not a child anymore. I know what I want."

"Coral, I love you and want to marry you. I want us to be like one. I never before understood the intensity or the deep meaning those words have. But I also want you to think carefully and be sure. Let's go out together and get to know each other again." Robert smiled at Coral. "You give me your answer when you're ready." Robert was sure he wanted to be with Coral but didn't want to influence her in any way. Robert knew it had to be entirely and independently her decision. He wanted her to recover from the ordeal with Ben, which would give her time to do so.

"You can have my answer now."

"How could I justify our love if I agreed? Give yourself time, and then let me know."

Coral's lovely eyes rolled downward again like a disobedient child.

Coral and Robert sat together cuddling, enjoying the view of the valley below from the six huge windows at the peak of the house's most prominent and highest hexagon-shaped turret after their strong efforts to contain themselves had defeated their lustful intentions. Holding hands, they laughed and talked about the many happy times they shared when they were younger. Coral had fixed her makeup and lipstick with cosmetics she carried in her purse. "I guess this is as good a time as any," Robert said as he handed a small Christmas-wrapped box to Coral. "Merry Christmas."

Coral took Robert's box. "I bought a small gift for you," she said. The week before, she had bought a book she thought he might like. "I mailed it to you, not knowing you were coming."

'The Last of The Just by Andre Schwarz-Bart,' Robert remembered, wondering how he knew; It didn't make sense.

"Thank you, Robert." Coral looked surprised. "You thought to bring something for me," she said. "How sweet! It's nice to know you were thinking of me. "She smiled, licking her lips seductively.

Robert watched as Coral slowly and gracefully removed the bow from the gift box, fighting the arousal her seductive mannerism gave him. He thought, then said, "Not now. I don't want to sway your decision with a gift. You keep it and open it on a special occasion when we're together."

"You'll never be able to sway me, Robert," Coral smiled.

"I bought it for my little friend, not realizing she had become a beautiful woman," he smiled at Coral. "We always had a special attachment, didn't we?" Robert admitted. "I know that now."

"Yes, Robert, we always shared something special."

"C'mon, Let's rejoin the group." Robert finally said. "They'll be sending up a search party soon."

They descended the stairway, and Coral slipped back into her man-killer stilettos. She looked up at Robert. "Soon, Robert." Coral gazed into his eyes, "I want to make love to you soon. I'll never change my mind." She had never expressed anything like that to a man before. But Coral wasn't embarrassed; she was speaking to her Robert and had never been afraid to say anything to him.

"First, you have to decide. That's the deal." And they both shook hands on it just like they used to do years before.

15

Rue-Youngstown, Ohio 1961-1962

Coral's body lay face down. Her head turned slightly left on a large mattress in a beautiful, luxurious Youngstown hotel room. Her magnificent and appealing body was completely nude and still wet from perspiration. Coral's feminine fragrance filled the area where she lay, smiling in total contentment. Her body still trembled as she savored every remaining tingle of her most electrifying emotional and bodily pleasure ever. Never before could Coral even comprehend such a feeling from the most titillating experience she had ever known. Her shapely legs bent at the knees as Robert held her feet with his hands and kissed them at the back of her toes while sitting behind her on the large bed. Coral's vulva remained swollen and soaked as she recovered from making love with Robert for the third time. Coral let out little groans of fulfillment as she still enjoyed the pleasure radiating throughout her in that secure area near Robert where the aroma of sex permeated. As Robert's tongue gently licked between her toes, Coral giggled from the satisfying tickle. Rolling over and now sitting facing Robert, her ample shapely breasts hung alluringly, mesmerizing him. Coral moved closer and cuddled with Robert, her voluptuous legs wrapped around Robert's waist as her lower abdomen pressed firmly against his. Her toes grasped the hardened, muscled skin of his back as she whispered in a husky voice, "I never even thought it could be this good." She smiled, "You did things to me I never even knew existed. You drove me crazy. It was beautiful." Coral smiled from complete fulfillment, her deep blue eyes wide and looking into those of her lover, "You're so gentle but very effective," she giggled, then kissed Robert softly.

"Wow, that was a gentler kiss than from the wild woman I

was with for the last three hours," Robert chuckled.

"That's because you turned me into an animal," a smiling and contented Coral giggled in a husky seductive manner.

"You're the most beautiful woman I've ever seen!" Robert smiled, "And you drive me crazy."

"I love you, Robert!"

"I love you too, Coral. I know that now." Robert kissed her lips, "I wish there were words to express how much I love and need you. I never knew I would be able to love a woman as much as I love you."

"Are you ready to go again?" Coral's beautiful eyes widened as she enticingly asked. "I mean, if you can?" Coral smiled, challenging him. Then Coral jokingly turned and began crawling away from Robert after she insulted him.

"Here I come, tiger woman." Robert grabbed her ankles, sliding her back toward him, then feeling the softness of her flesh at her calves as his hands slowly moved higher as if he were playing the fingerboard of a violin, ready for the main concerto. Coral moaned from the pleasure, and then she screamed as Robert began again.

Robert and Coral decided to let nature take its course during that time before going to the Youngstown hotel. They went out dancing and met friends for dinner. It was wonderful for both of them as they reminisced about old times while now enjoying an adult romance. Coral and Robert held hands and strolled through town together, just as Coral had dreamed of as a child. Now, as an adult, she could introduce her new boyfriend to people he had never met. But everyone knew of Robert Bryant; he remained a sports legend in the area surrounding the town of Rue. Coral and Robert were truly happy together.

When Roger LeBlanc discovered that Robert was dating his little sister, he jokingly came at Robert unexpectedly. "If you think a no-good louse like you is going to date my kid sister, you have another thought coming, bozo!" He glared at Robert. But Robert knew Roger was kidding. He somehow lived this moment already but wondered how. Then Roger broke out in a big smile and grabbed his friend in a tight embrace. "I think it's great! She couldn't have picked a better guy." But Robert also remembered his best friend saying that.

Roger and Mary Lou double-dated with Robert and Coral at times. They all went to a Rue High School basketball game together.

"I'll be right back," Coral yelled to Robert over the noise in the crowded gymnasium as they stood by the doorway, "I just want to say hello to someone real quick." Roger and Mary Lou were talking to Stan Swarovski. Robert couldn't help but notice a woman standing by the main door. It was Denise Beck.

"Hi, Robert!" Denise had to raise her voice over the noise, and her smile was the same as when Robert first met her years ago after his first football practice. "It's good to see you after so long."

"Hi, Denise. How have you been?" Robert felt a little awkward. After that incident at the homecoming dance, Denise never spoke to him again.

"Oh, I'm married with a daughter." Denise looked around before saying, "Robert, I always felt terrible that I ignored you after that thing with Sue Peters, especially after discovering the truth. It was immature of me."

"Congratulations, I hope you're happy. Ah, don't worry about spilled milk. Everything worked out for you, and I'm happy about that."

"You always were a nice guy, Robert. I miss you and still do at times." She smiled again. "Maybe things would have turned out differently with us–" Just then, Coral returned, bubbly and with a big smile plastered on her face.

"Hi, Denise!" Coral happily greeted her. Then she turned to Robert and said, "I just saw Rosetta. She my Italian friend who came to Rue when Emily and I first started high school," Coral smiled, and her eyes widened. "She speaks perfect English now."

"Hello, Coralie. It's nice to see you again. I better go. Oh, I heard you guys were dating. Congratulations, you make a beautiful couple."

"Thanks, Denise. Good luck to you and your family," Robert bid her goodbye. Coral remained silent but smiled, nodding goodbye to Denise.

"Cheating on me already, honey?" Coral giggled, her face beaming.

"Not in a million years, sweetheart."

"You better not," Coral held Robert's arm tightly as they entered the gymnasium.

At halftime, the school prepared a special tribute for Robert. Then, Coach Fred Wilson announced, "Let's hear it for a special alumnus, Robert Bryant, Rue's best athlete ever!" Robert rose with a bashful expression and waved to the roaring and cheering crowd that clapped furiously. Robert hated being in the limelight. But Coral was clapping, cheering, and laughing in her seat beside him. She felt like a child again.

"Let's not forget Roger LeBlanc and the rest of the team," the ever-humble Robert shouted back at the crowd. "I was the captain of Rue's best teams ever, but I couldn't have done it without them," he made Roger, along with Stan, Jasper, Bill, and the rest of his team, who were all there, stand. Coach Fred Wilson proudly introduced them, and the crowd roared again.

Coral loved and admired her Robert for gestures like that, and by midweek, she gave Robert her decision. As they passionately kissed after an evening of dining and seeing a drive-in movie, Coral told Robert, "I've decided about what I've known all along, and I commit myself to you body and soul," she smiled before resuming making out with the man of her dreams, seeming wholly recovered from what Ben did to her. The love of Robert and Emily had helped her with that. Coral came up for air and said, "I had to make a quick decision after I saw you with Denise."

"Thank God Denise was there that night. You've made me the happiest man in the world," Robert whispered in her ear.

"Can we begin looking for a room in a hotel now," the ever-bold Coral whispered back seductively.

Coral dealt with her problems regarding Benjamin Joyce right after Christmas week. She phoned Ben and asked to meet him in Youngstown at a luncheonette to talk. Ben could tell by her voice that it wasn't good, and Coral sensed his anger, making her a little nervous. Coral wanted to rid herself of Ben before returning to school, where she would be vulnerable in Youngstown. She and Emily conspired a secret plan: Emily would wait outside and position her car where she could sit with a view of where Coral sat in the diner. Emily didn't trust Ben or anything he might do and wanted to be there for Coral if Ben became angry. At first, she toyed with the idea of bringing her father's pistol but decided against it. Then Emily thought of taking her mother's large cast iron frying pan but didn't. Instead, Emily would scream as loud as she could. That would get everyone's attention if Ben tried to hurt Coral in any way. When they ran their plan by Robert, he insisted on one change, disregarding his sister's foolish idea of bringing a weapon.

Robert took Coral aside and privately told her, "Sweetheart, I spent my whole life looking for someone like you, and I had you all along. I never realized it, but I admit it now," he bowed his head, his words bringing a tear to Coral's eyes. "I guess I'm not as wise as everyone thinks, but I don't want to lose you now. I won't take any chances; I'm coming inside the diner with you."

Coral sniffled and went to wipe her eyes from Robert's emotional comment. Robert quickly wiped the tear away from her eye before she had a chance. Coral smiled at the man she loved and softly said, "Okay, Robert."

"Thanks, monkeyface," he smiled back.

When they returned to Emily, Coral told her, "Em, Robert's going to come inside the restaurant with me."

"I think that's a good idea," Emily agreed.

As much as the bold Coral wanted to assert her independence, she now knew Ben was delusional and dangerous and realized Robert was right.

Emily waited in Robert's car. She wanted to be there to support her best friend, and in case anything went wrong, she could alert people or get a policeman. Emily sat in the driver's seat of the Cadillac, watching as Coral and her brother entered the diner. They planned to be there well in advance of Ben's arrival.

Chills ran up and down Emily's spine when she spotted Ben arrive, and the hair on the back of her neck rose as she watched Ben enter the luncheonette where Robert and Coral had already seated themselves at a table and chairs.

Ben appeared stunned when he saw Robert sitting next to Coral. "I see you brought your muscle with you. I knew you two were an item," Ben's eyes bulged from anger, but he didn't dare toy with the husky and able-bodied Robert. Coral's body tingled even though Robert was beside her. Being in the same room with Ben reminded her of that dreadful experience. All of it came flooding back, and she shivered.

Robert felt her quiver and put his arm around Coral, encouraging her and showing his support. He kept his composure, calmly saying, "That's none of your business anymore, Ben." Robert's coolness and words rattled Ben even more, and his reddened face showed his disdain. "Coral has something to say to you," Robert said placidly, sensing he was agitating Ben and enjoyed doing it.

Recalling all that Ben did to her, Coral became enraged. She pulled herself back together and focused. First, Coral's dark blue eyes stared fearlessly and angrily into Ben's. When she was ready, she sternly said, "We're not here for lunch. I'm returning your engagement ring whether you like it or not!" She looked at Ben boldly, knowing Robert was beside her. "I'm a person and don't belong to anyone," she said while flinging the engagement ring to Ben from across the table. "I make my own decisions–and I definitely don't think we should marry." Robert was shocked but elated with Coral's display of courage, remembering the tiny but spirited kid she used to be.

Ben listened in awe or shock, and Coral couldn't tell which.

He remained quiet and listened to her, and Coral enjoyed the self-esteem it brought.

However, Ben didn't take it well. After his private moments of silence, the veins in his face and neck expanded, reddening even more and bulging his facial features. "You made this decision because of him!" He yelled, his thumb indicating Robert.

"No! You and I never had a relationship. I told you that already. And I told you that whatever you call what we had in your sick mind was over. You are the biggest mistake I ever made in my whole life," Coral paused, her face now flushed and angry. She screamed, "You beat me and scared me out of my wits. You forced yourself on me. That's rape, for God's sake!" Everyone seated in the luncheonette turned, hearing Coral's horrifying accusations.

"Liar!" Ben angrily shouted at the top of his breath, knowing people were now staring and judging him. He had to defend himself, his warped mind not realizing Coral's claims were true. "You liked it!" as people in the diner continued looking at Ben pathetically–the paranoia within him, changing Ben into a wild beast inside, his troubled mind taunting him.

"You know something, Ben, I was so afraid of you, but I'm not anymore. You're nothing more than an animal!" Some by-standers clapped, and others cheered encouragement to Coral for her bravery.

Ben erupted, his demented mind plaguing him. He jumped off his heavy wooden chair, picked it up, and repeatedly smashed it onto the table. Robert covered Coral with his body to protect her. Then Ben quickly took the empty chair beside him and threw it at the doublewide window of the diner. It crashed through, broken glass flying inside and out as people scattered from the large pieces of flying projectiles. Ben screamed at the top of his voice like a raging lunatic, "You'll see! You'll miss my hands on your body, you slut!" sneering at Coral before he stormed outside.

Robert considered going after Ben, but his instincts made him comfort the woman he loved and ensure she was safe and unharmed.

Emily cried out from behind the wheel of the parked car, "Oh, my God!" as she saw the chair come through the window and the glass shattered and flew. Then, she shivered at the sight of Ben charging out of the diner like an angry, raging bull. As soon as Ben left the immediate area, she opened the car door and ran inside the restaurant, worrying about her brother and best friend the whole time.

When they finished that horrible encounter with Ben in Youngstown, Robert drove Coral and Emily back to Rue. Everyone remained quiet and in a daze during the first fifteen minutes of the ride. It was Emily who spoke first, timidly and quietly, "Well, it was nice of you to pay for all the damages, Robert," she paused and looked at her brother to see his reaction, "I mean, being it wasn't your fault and everything."

Emily's words broke the icy aura, prompting Coral to say, "I can't believe I got so crazy with Ben."

"It wasn't your fault, Coral, you're the victim here." Emily's words were now louder and bolder. "You're the one with the trauma. Ben's a psycho, like that Hitchcock movie. Today, everyone saw what he is–a stark, raving lunatic."

"Are you mad at me, Robert?" Coral asked cautiously. "I mean, do you think I was wrong?" She glanced at him while he drove and uneasily asked, "Is that why you offered to pay for everything?"

Robert quietly entertained himself with memories of Coral as a spunky kid, now a stunning woman sitting beside him, yet still as bold as ever. He observed Coral with his peripheral vision and said, "Actually, sweetheart, I'm proud of you." Keeping his eyes on the road, he added, "It took a lot of... courage and fearlessness." He paused momentarily to find the right word to honor the bravery of his girlfriend fully. Robert then leaned over and gave Coral a quick peck on the cheek, smiling as he did so.

"But it's going to cost you a lot of money, honey," Coral

said, still unsure.

"Sweetheart, it was definitely worth seeing your performance," Robert chuckled.

"Amen to that!" cried Emily from the back seat. "Amen to that!" She started laughing. After her laughter subsided, she added, "The scary thing is, he's out there running free somewhere. You guys should have seen him charge out of the diner. He looked like a bull in an arena; his eyes were terrifying."

"The police said they would eventually find him," Robert interjected after noticing Coral's terrified reaction to what Emily had said.

When they arrived in Rue, Emily felt stressed and exhausted from the tension, and she now had a terrible headache. Robert dropped her off before taking Coral home.

Coral almost jumped into Robert's arms as soon as they entered her home. She needed to feel his body hold hers after that horrifying experience at the restaurant. Then she remembered her Christmas gift. "Can I open my present?"

Robert looked at her, puzzled, then remembered, "Oh, your Christmas present. Got it!" He smiled at Coral, her face now displaying that same mischievous expression she sometimes had as a child. "I'm sorry I made you wait. I've been acting like a zombie since we... I just forgot. I wanted you to open it in a romantic setting."

"You've been acting like a zombie since we made love? That's what you were going to say!" Coral kissed Robert, opening his lips with hers, and their tongues rolled together. It was an erotic kiss Coral gave him, sloppy and wet as she licked around his mouth. She was turned on by how he felt about her. Mighty Robert acting like a zombie because of the incredible way they made love together affected him. "I like that. Now I don't feel alone acting like a zombie," Coral said with a captivating smile, her deep blue eyes widening. "This just became a romantic setting. Let me go and get the gift; I'll be a second. Please don't run off with Denise Beck," she joked.

"You're never going to forget that, are you?"

"Never!" Her voice was faint, as she was already at the top of the stairs, running to her bedroom. "I'll always use it as ammunition whenever I need to," she laughed as soon as she returned next to Robert. "Let's sit down," Coral gestured toward a cushioned loveseat, looking eager to open her gift.

Robert watched Coral slowly and meticulously remove the bow and then the paper wrap. She did it erotically, her sexuality oozing out of her, almost like a burlesque queen, to arouse Robert in her mood of being turned on so much. It was a flat jewelry box. Coral lifted the lid and melted, her big eyes lighting up. "Oh, Robert! It's beautiful!" She carefully removed the piece of jewelry with her hand. It was a lovely, sizeable diamond-shaped heart in an 18-carat gold setting with smaller Amethyst stones surrounding the sparkling diamond rock at the center, the jewelry piece attached to a petite 18-carat gold chain. "My birthstone," Coral whispered, "You remembered!" Coral took Robert's hand. He was sitting close. "I love it!" Coral smiled. "You bought it for your little friend, not realizing she had become a beautiful woman." Coral looked at Robert, "It's too much, though, Robert," she said as her first tear fell from one of her beautiful eyes. "It must have cost a fortune! Thank you so much! I love it! I never had a diamond before," whispering again as her eyes teared more. "Please put it on for me. I want the whole world to see how much you love me!" she shouted.

"This doesn't even come close to how much I love you, sweetheart. Nothing can."

"Thank you," she said again, admiring the jewelry piece in the mirror, now crying. Robert needed two fingers to manage the tears.

In the dream-like world where Coral and Robert now lived, one day led to another. They dated and made plans for their future lives together. "I'll come back as often as I can while you finish college."

"Let's marry first," Coral said.

"Do you mean elope?"

"No, we can't do that to our parents, but I can't wait."

"Sweetheart, you have such little time left at school; by the time we finish making arrangements, you'll have graduated," he smiled. "We'll set the date for as soon as possible."

"I don't want to lose you," Coral said meekly.

"You know you'll never lose me. How could you even think that?"

"I believe you, but I feel worried about something," Coral glanced up at Robert wide-eyed. "I don't know what it is, but I sense something. I don't want anything to happen in the meantime."

"Nothing is going to happen, Coralie. I'm returning to marry you, and nothing in this world will stop me." Robert never addressed Coral by her full name, making her think he might be getting angry.

Coral thought and then told Robert, "Forget what I said. We'll make the date for as soon as possible. We can arrange everything in the meantime," Coral answered as if it were her idea.

"I'm giving my notice to Harvard. It will give them time to replace me," Robert appeared to be thinking.

"Is that what you really want, honey? I mean, you're not doing it for me, are you? I don't want you to have any regrets, Robert." Coral looked at him with sincerity in her heart. "You've worked awfully hard there, and I'm so proud of you. I can teach near your college. I don't mind moving."

"I'm sure. We already talked about this far too much, and I agree that Rue is where we should be. We can both teach and eventually raise a family–just like we discussed." Robert had changed. He had found love and given up his other ambitions. Robert wanted to have children with the woman he loved and adored. Rue, Ohio, was high on their list of prospective places to settle down.

"It is romantic," Coral's voice became husky, "We'll live

where we first met."

"Careful, tiger-woman; you know what happens when you speak like that."

Robert prepared to leave for Harvard a few days after the New Year's Day holiday. Roger reminded his pal, "Just make sure you're here for my wedding in the spring, buddy. You are the best man you know." He and Mary Lou had set a date to marry long before Coral and Robert began their preparations.

"Too bad we couldn't have a double wedding."

"I know, but we made our plans a while ago."

Coral and Robert enjoyed an exotic dinner on New Year's Eve, still part of the festive season. At midnight, they celebrated the fireworks, embracing each other closely on the balcony of the upscale hotel where they secretly stayed. They made passionate love, creatively exploring imaginative ideas and positions under the colorful lights of the rockets still firing, discovering each other's bodies in new ways.

After their first climax, Robert whispered into Coral's ear, "I never thought in a million years I would ever actually see fireworks while making love."

"I hate this to be over," Coral told Robert before they parted ways. She was returning to Youngstown, and Robert was going back to Massachusetts a few days after the new year. Before they parted ways, Robert planned to return twice a month to be with Coral.

Once, after they had parted, Robert surprised Coral with a late-night phone call and said he was in Youngstown. Robert told Coral, "Look out the window, monkeyface."

Coral looked out her dorm window. Robert was standing outside in the cold of late January, speaking from a phone booth. Coral held her hands to her mouth to prevent herself from becoming hysterical, "I'll be right down," she whispered. Emily was fast asleep, so Coral scribbled a quick note so Emily wouldn't worry if she awoke and didn't see her. They went to a hotel where they spent a beautiful night together before Coral returned to class and Robert departed.

Robert saw Coral in January, February, and mid-March. He was loyal to his word, and Coral lived to see him, just like when she was a child. The difference was that Coral and Robert had now fulfilled their love for each other as adults.

16

Rue, Ohio 1962

Coral and Emily left college together for spring break on Tuesday, March 20, 1962. Robert was arriving on Saturday, and they both looked forward to seeing him. Coral's anticipation about seeing Robert again was driving Emily crazy. Coral couldn't wait to hold him in her arms.

Unbeknownst to Coral, Robert was bringing a surprise for her. He had purchased a beautiful diamond engagement ring. That past Christmas week, after Robert returned to Rue and fell in love with Coral, he and Coral accompanied Roger and his fiancée to shop for an engagement ring, as Roger hadn't given her one yet. Robert and Roger waited as the girls looked at different styles of rings.

"A little boring, isn't it?" Roger whispered. He was getting impatient while the girls spent so much time as Mary Lou decided.

"Patience, my friend. It's a virtue."

"Ha!" Roger whispered back loudly, "so is hope, as in, I hope she decides soon."

"It's an important thing to a woman."

"I went over to see Sue Peters at the hospital. She works there," Robert said.

"That was a nice thing to do, buddy," Roger sincerely said as he looked at his best friend, "You always were a good guy, Bob," remembering what Robert did for him.

"She's doing well; looks good." Just then, Robert heard Coral tell Mary Lou something, and his ears tuned in.

Coral excitedly told Mary Lou, "Oh, I adore this one." She pointed to a ring and said, "It's the exact type I would love to have someday." Coral looked so happy, glancing down at the diamond ring. It reminded Robert how much he wanted to marry her. He stretched his neck to see which one it was so he would remember that ring specifically. That's how Robert knew the design style to buy for Coral.

The next day, Robert returned to the same store alone. He showed the jeweler the ring he wanted. "Yes, that's the one." He said as the salesman reached into the glass counter, finally taking out the one Robert had pointed at.

"A beautiful ring, sir. Weren't you here yesterday? Yes, I remember. Your friend seemed very anxious," the jeweler chuckled.

"Yes, he's getting married," Robert smiled.

Now holding the ring Coral secretly wanted in his hand, Robert asked, "Can you make an engagement ring styled precisely like this one, but with a better grade of gold and a larger diamond?"

"Yes, I can, sir, but I must warn you that the cost of the diamond goes up with the stone's quality as well as the size." The man peered at Robert, his Ben Franklin eyeglasses positioned low on his nose.

"I want it to be perfect," Robert said calmly but firmly. He wanted it to be as flawless as his love for Coral.

The salesman's eyes widened so much that his glasses almost slid off his nose, "Yes, sir!"

"How long will it take?" Robert asked pleasantly.

"Well, if you can come back tomorrow," he whispered, "after you make your selection, it would only take a day or two. I prefer the security guard to be here when I take the better diamonds out of the safe."

"No problem. I'll come back tomorrow right after you open, and I'll make my choice then."

Robert picked up the elegant diamond engagement ring before leaving town, intending to give it to Coral when he returned to Rue. Knowing how much it would delight the woman he loved, he felt a surge of joy.

On Wednesday, March 21, at 4 PM, the two girlfriends were

alone in Coral's bedroom at her parent's home. Emily was helping her best friend, Coral, rearrange the furniture in her small upstairs bedroom. Now that Coral was coming home more often, she needed a desk for her college schoolwork. And the two young ladies were sliding things around to fit one next to the window. "We tried it like that already, Em," Coral said, "it's not close enough to the window." Coral was getting stressed.

"You'll be getting married in no time anyway, Coral," seeing her friend's frustration.

"I hope we have a bigger bedroom when we do," Coral laughed. "I've always had this small bedroom. I want a really huge one someday."

"Stand back!" commanded Emily, and Coral stepped away just before Emily used all her strength and pushed the desk butted thoroughly against the window frame with not a centimeter to spare. "How's that?" she asked sarcastically.

"It's looks good, Em!" Coral was amazed. "How did you do that?"

"Brute strength," and both girls laughed themselves almost to a frenzy.

Suddenly, Coral and Emily heard a thunderous knock on the front door. They could feel the vibration. Looking at each other, they decided to go together to see who it was. As the two young ladies neared the bottom of the stairway, the door came crashing inward. The two wide-eyed girls noticed it was Benjamin Joyce.

"The police are supposed to be looking for him after what he did in that diner," Coral murmured in fright.

"Never mind that now. Let's go back upstairs and lock ourselves in your bedroom," Emily was horrified.

"I should take the phone from the hallway with us," Coral said but stopped less than midway up the stairs.

"Good idea." Then Emily shouted, "Why did you stop? Why are you staring at him?"

"I remember something really dreadful happening here."

"C'mon Coral. Let's go!"

Ben stood at the open doorway. The door wobbled as only the top remaining hinge kept it from falling sideways. Ben stared directly at Coral. She sensed something terrible and couldn't draw her eyes away from his. Coral went into shock. Ben's eyes had an evil glare; they looked terrifying. Emily slapped her friend across her face to get her out of her daze. Then, Ben strolled toward the stairs where the two girls stood in fright, appearing unnatural as he stepped abnormally slowly. Coral snapped out of her trance from Emily's smack, and the two frightened friends turned in horror to go back upstairs quickly. Emily tripped on a stair and fell in haste to escape back to the second floor, but Ben ignored her and continued after Coral. Benjamin cornered Coral in the upstairs hallway before she could run away.

"What do you want from me?" Coral screamed at him.

Ben screamed back, his eyes glaring as red as a devil's. "I told you, you're mine! You made me fall in love with you!" He panted. "Did you think you could humiliate me and then dump me, you tramp?" Ben stared into Coral's wide eyes with his demonic glare. He began acting even crazier. "I told you, bitch," he said, his eyes widening and head twisting as if he were looking around. He spun his body entirely around on one foot to face Coral again before telling her, "See, you didn't go anywhere; you can't get away from me." He smiled a maniacal grin. "I told you," twisting his head again. "but you wouldn't listen." Ben pointed his forefinger at Coral, swaying it as if reprimanding her. "I said you would miss my hands on your body. You probably didn't expect it to be like this." Ben's laugh was ghoulish and monstrous; his veins bulged, and his face contorted with reddened eyes. Benjamin Joyce appeared insane.

"You raped me, you bastard!" Coral shouted as her eyes began to tear. "You won't get away with this. Everyone knows."

That angered Ben, and he made a fist and pulled his muscular arm far back. By the length of his stretch, Ben's poised fist was ready to punch her hard in her face. Coral watched in horror; her eyes instinctively closed as she waited for the crippling punch, knowing it would hurt her severely. In that split second of fear, her thoughts were of Robert, wishing he was there and agonizing over the prospect that she would never see him again.

Emily began to lift herself on the stairs where she had fallen; she wanted to help her friend. Then, suddenly and out of the blue, Robert Bryant crashed through the broken door. His muscular thighs catapulted him high and over Emily as he leaped to the top of the stairs in one stride and into the small hall foyer. Robert's jump looked supernatural, and he quickly blocked Ben's raised fist and kicked him hard in his groin with one swing of his muscular leg. As Ben folded over, Robert grabbed Ben's hair and smashed his face hard into the solid plastered wall three times, the tendons of Robert's arm bulging. Ben rolled around still on his feet, his face battered, and he spit blood and teeth out of his mouth. Then, in his fury, Robert punched him with his large, tight left fist and then again with his right solidly on Ben's nose, using all his superhuman strength. Robert struck him so hard with that left-right combo that he knocked Ben out cold on his feet. Ben's body flew far back, appearing as if he was being dragged high and through the air. Ben's head hit the upper solid oak trim of the doorway as his body broke through a closed door. Then Robert quickly reached for Coral and held her in his arms. "Are you okay, honey?" He brushed back her long blonde hair in a loving manner and dried her tears with his index finger. "It's going to be okay, sweetheart," he said, comforting her.

Trembling from shock and unable to speak, Coral recalled when she was a little girl and Robert had used the exact words after some bullies harassed her. She remembered how Robert always looked out for her, but in her stupor, she wondered where he had come from. Robert was supposed to be at his school back in Massachusetts.

Emily then asked while running up the stairs, "Robert, how are you here? Where did you come from?" But Robert didn't answer; he was busy kissing Coral.

*

Roger returned from shopping with his dad, both worried when they saw the flashing lights of police cars and an ambulance. They didn't notice the old red Oldsmobile 88 slowly driving by them in their haste to get inside their home. "What the hell happened?" Mr. LeBlanc shouted as he nervously swerved his car to a skidding stop at the curb, and he and his son raced toward the house. They saw police officers upstairs, so they hurried up the stairs. On the floor lay what appeared to be Benjamin Joyce in a pool of blood. The ambulance attendants were feverishly trying to revive him.

Police Chief Robertson calmed Roger and his father, saying, "Everything's okay. The guy lying knocked out on the floor attacked the girls, but Robert Bryant stopped it." Roger and his father froze in the foyer, puzzled, knowing Robert was away at school. The chief added, "Emily and Coral are fine and downstairs with Robert."

"When did Robert get here," Roger asked the chief. "He called me from Massachusetts earlier and never said he was coming. We just had a regular bullshit conversation."

"I don't know. I thought Robert was supposed to be here."

"No, he's away or supposed to be. I don't..." Roger slowly became speechless.

Mr. LeBlanc remained upstairs and explained the mystery to the chief as Roger proceeded downstairs to find out what happened.

"Robert saved us," Coral yelled to her brother. "You should have seen him! He was amazing! He was wonderful, wasn't he, Em?" Coral still held on to Robert.

Emily asked Robert, "But how did you know? How did you get here? You never said." Still confused, Roger was ready to ask Robert the same question.

"I can't explain it," Robert said, looking disturbed. "I had a really terrible feeling. It came on quickly, right after I talked to Roge. I couldn't shake it off. It felt like a premonition, I guess. The feelings were so intense that I called Roge again after that first time, but there was no answer, so I trusted my instincts and took the first flight I could find, and here I am."

"Wow! It's a good thing you did, Bob. That's all I have to say," replied a bewildered Roger. "Thank God you used your instinct."

Robert kept holding Coral. He had a déjà vu so strong he couldn't explain. The feeling slowly subsided as he held Coral tightly, but Robert's arms wouldn't let go of her.

Once all the commotion had settled, Roger and Robert assisted the girls with fitting Coral's desk. Emily's brute strength seemed too much for the desk, so the guys pulled the piece of furniture back a bit from the slightly cracked windowsill.

Later that evening, after Coral's fears and anxieties had subsided, she was alone with Robert. They sat together, cuddling on the round sofa, enjoying the view of the valley below from their favorite window at the peak of the highest hexagon-shaped turret of the Bryant Mansion.

Everyone was still in awe about Robert's arrival. Coral had learned long ago about Robert's secret of being a genius. Emily had spilled it to her during one of their discussions. But Coral never thought much about it. She loved Robert, and that was all. But that fact made her better understand him.

Coral decided to tease Robert. "Maybe somebody was lonely," Coral whispered in Robert's ear. "Maybe that's why you rushed back to see me so quickly."

But Robert didn't laugh or even chuckle at Coral's witty remark; he remained serious. It had been too close for him. A feeling deep within his soul forced him to go to Coral earlier that day. He knew with certainty that she was in trouble, a feeling he had already experienced. Robert couldn't risk ignoring that ominous prophecy, knowing he could never live without this newfound love of his life. Then Robert looked straight at her, his lips close to hers, and softly said, "I love you, Coral." He gazed deeply into her beautiful, wide, dark blue eyes and held her tightly. "I love everything about you," he paused, staring into her eyes as if seeing their beauty for the first time. "I love making love to you." He closed his eyes and held Coral even tighter, she relinquishing her body entirely to Robert's arms. Opening his eyes and continuing, "And when we do make love, I feel like we become one. Yet, I love merely holding you like I am now and feeling your heartbeat against mine." Coral's eyes remained locked onto Robert's as if she were communicating with him emotionally, succumbing to his words silently. Robert slowly continued, "I love waking up, seeing you lying beside me, and knowing you're near. I love you, Coral. I always have.

Coral's eyes began to tear while starting to say, "Oh, Robert, I–"

Robert didn't allow her to finish, nor did he wipe her tears. He pushed himself off the round white sofa and kneeled before Coral, where she sat regally like a queen on a cushioned throne. Robert presented her with a small black jewelry box. Slowly, he opened it to display the engagement ring, the exact one she dreamed about.

"Oh, my God!" Coral put her hands to the sides of her face; her eyes flooded with tears as she realized what was happening.

"Coral, sweetheart, I love you and always have. Will you marry me?"

Coral couldn't answer at first; she was in shock, her wide eyes looking into his. Finally, through her tears, she forced the words, "Oh, Robert, how did you know this was the ring I always–"

"You haven't answered my question, my lady."

Coral leaped from her seat, wrapping her arms and legs around Robert with such force that she knocked him over. "Yes!" she screamed, "Yes!" They lay together on the carpet as Coral kissed Robert uncontrollably.

"May I place the ring on your finger?"

"Oh, yes, please do." Coral was panting from excitement.

Robert had to search for it between piles of the floor's carpeting. The jewelry box and the ring flew from his hand when Coral attacked him. "Ah, here it is," Robert said, smiling.

As they remained on the floor, Robert reached for Coral's left ring finger, but she quickly stopped him. "Oh, Robert, please ask me again. I went into shock, and I don't remember everything."

Robert smiled; her expression was so beautiful that he couldn't resist her. He rose again from the carpeted floor to his knees and said, "Coral, my love will–"

"No, just like you did the first time; I mean the exact same words."

Robert thought, recalling the exact words he had used, and again asked, "Coral, sweetheart, I love you and always have. Will you marry me?"

"Yes, Robert, I will marry you." She had dreamed of saying those words to him since she first fell in love with him when he took her for her first ride in his sports car. After Robert placed the ring on her finger, he needed tissues to wipe her tears away as they rolled around on the carpet, kissing.

"I'll wipe away every tear you ever shed," Robert told a speechless Coral.

17

Tuesday, April 12, 1982

On Tuesday, April 12, 1982, 45-year-old Doctor Robert Bryant awakened to a familiar sound. It was those scratchy seconds that all 45 record players made just before the music started to play. Then, the words and music of the Everly Brothers' song, 'All I Have To Do Is Dream' filled the foyer downstairs. The bedroom door partially opened, and Coral Bryant slid through. Coral climbed into the bed and whispered in Robert's ear, "Happy anniversary, honey," as she cuddled beside him.

"You're still the most beautiful woman in the world," a groggy Robert whispered back, "Happy anniversary, sweetheart." He turned and looked deep into Coral's gorgeous dark blue eyes, appreciating how much he loved her. "I've always thought of you whenever I heard that song since long ago."

"It's been our favorite song for years," Coral giggled, "but there was a time when we didn't know we secretly shared it and thought about each other whenever it played." Coral smiled and shed a tear recalling those long-ago days. "I hope our next 20 years will be as good, Robert."

Robert wiped her tear with his forefinger, "I told you I'd wipe away every tear you ever shed." Looking deeper into Coral's captivating wide eyes and pondering for a few seconds, he added, "I thank God I came back to Rue that Christmas Eve," he smiled in a way that caused a chill to run up and down Coral's spine. "You would have gotten away from me if I hadn't." His thick, wavy black hair was slightly greying at the sides above his ears.

"No, Robert. We were meant to be together," Coral smiled assuredly, "I told you that long ago."

Robert smiled, remembering a tiny and boney-legged Coral

telling him those exact words, and replied, "I guess we were. I can't imagine a life without you." He put his hand on Coral's thigh, still enjoying the feel of her lovely flesh as he always had since years before.

"Can't get fresh now." Coral smiled again. "Tiger woman can't play now, honey. The kids are waiting downstairs for their daddy. Hurry up, honey—get dressed." Coral rose from the bed, pulled back the curtain, and peered out one of the gigantic windows in the enormous-sized bedroom. Bright white puff clouds floated slowly in the clear blue sky as far as she could see. It was a beautiful feeling and a happy sign. "It's another beautiful day, honey."

Coral and Robert wanted to marry immediately after Ben's terrifying and life-threatening deed. They could wait no longer and had a church wedding ceremony in Rue, Ohio, on March 31, 1962. It was a Saturday, and even with such short notice, Robert was able to make reservations at St. Michael's, the church his family had always generously supported. Roger LeBlanc stood as the best man for his best friend Robert, and Emily served as maid of honor for her best friend. Coral looked stunning in her mother's wedding gown. The beautiful veiled bride shed tears while walking down the aisle to the soft music of Pachelbel's Canon in D, her arm in that of her father's. Robert wiped her tears at the altar before taking her hand. Coral, Emily, and their mothers had made thorough arrangements for an extraordinary reception in the spacious ballroom of the Bryant mansion in the short time they had. Decorative wedding ornaments adorned the large home, and caterers brought in scrumptious appetizers and plenty of delicious food. Isabella had worked hard in the kitchen, preparing many of her special exotic recipes, a labor of love she wanted to offer the newlyweds. An elegant wooden table accommodated the impressive five-tier wedding cake. With no time to hire a substantial number of helpers, Robert, Chris, Roger, his father, and William, along with Robert's old football buddies, pitched in to move things and tackle other heavy tasks before the big day. There was no time for a honeymoon since Coral had to return to her classes. Coral and Robert spent their wedding night at their favorite upscale Youngstown hotel, this time in the honeymoon suite. They planned to have their official honeymoon at a later date.

Shortly after, Roger and Mary Lou had their wedding. That sparked an idea for Emily and Chris to marry. All the newlyweds chose to wait until Coral's graduation and Emily's summer break to take their honeymoons together to Europe. It was Robert's gift to them all. Once there, the newlyweds saw sites they had only romanticized about before. That was only the beginning of beautiful places, things, and times the happy couples shared and enjoyed together. Emily and Coral still shared Robert's winning football from his first game in Rue. They remained lifelong friends and '50-50 partners for life' with that precious game ball that had made them local celebrities as children.

For his lovely bride, Robert purchased the house of Coral's dreams, the Bryant Mansion, her castle. The newlyweds settled in right after they returned from their honeymoon. Coral had the most enormous bedroom she had ever imagined. Naomi forced her husband to retire early to live in Florida, feeling William, who had worked too hard his whole life, should finally rest his mental and physical war wounds, and she wanted to travel and see the world with him. The only place William didn't want to visit was Normandy, France.

Robert retired from Harvard over a year before winning the Nobel Prize for Physics in 1963 for his work on time travel, which he presented in his 1961 350-page doctoral dissertation and published in a book. That led to many job opportunities for Doctor Bryant. Everyone seemed to want a piece of the famous scientist, from top corporations to the United States government. A steady stream of the top journalists worldwide wished to interview him.

Robert always shied away from social attention and did the

same when international notoriety came his way. The infamous Doctor took a job teaching physics at Rue High School alongside his wife, Coralie, who taught business and finance.

Robert was now the football, baseball, basketball, and track coach for Rue High School and was proud of it. His best friend, Roger LeBlanc, was his assistant. All four teams were winners in the rural Ohio River Valley. Coach Fred Wilson had retired. Robert and Roger always called for applause for their old coach at any games he attended.

Emily earned her law degree three years after she married. She and Ben bought a beautiful home in Rue to raise their family. They worked as corporate lawyers for Bryant Aviation in Midland, PA. Charles and William's plan had worked well, and Emily and Chris took over management after William retired.

Robert and Emily had never learned about their biological parents or the ordeal of escaping Lebensborn, where they were born. Doctor Kruger had passed away, and although William had strong suspicions, Kruger never disclosed any details about the experiments performed on Robert at 'die unsterblichen.' William risked his life by financing many covert American military operations that intercepted and supported the British commandos who rescued his children and other victimized infants. William remembered his father's dying words, and he and Naomi agreed that learning the truth about their natural birthplace and the sins tied to that place could emotionally devastate Robert and Emily. They raised William's beloved sister's children in the warmth of their loving family since they were little babies in diapers, always embracing them as their own. William and Naomi felt it was best to keep things that way.

Robert couldn't remember anything that occurred or the many people he interacted with in his 20-year-labor to bring Coral back to him in that different dimension of time. Nor did he know his life had renewed on Christmas Eve, 1961. For him, that date marked the most important point in his life when he fell in love with Coralie Leblanc.

Benjamin Joyce went to prison for multiple charges. After

a psychiatric evaluation, a judge assigned Ben to a state mental facility. Even though they felt Ben should be doing a hard-time prison sentence, the LeBlancs and the Bryants were grateful that Coral and Emily escaped harm, thanks to Robert.

Emily better managed her anxiety issues, unbeknownst to her, inflicted upon her by trauma from horrible ordeals in infancy from traveling with a commando rescue team while escaping the Nazi stronghold at Lebensborn. Her improvement was due to the love of her family, her husband, Coral, and most of all, her big brother, whom she still called regularly as she always had. She appreciated everything Robert had done for her throughout her childhood and early adulthood. Robert was enormously proud of Emily's achievements, which made her happy. Emily and Robert still took time out of their busy schedules to spend quality time together as brother and sister and to do things like stop off at Chuckwagon Burgers and enjoy burgers and fries together, sometimes even splitting an ice cream sundae.

"Did you have one of those silly dreams again, honey?" Coral asked. "You haven't had one in a while. The last two were about robots and Nazi experiments. They were fascinating and so exciting, too," she giggled.

"Humanoids, sweetheart. They were humanoids, not robots," Robert smiled back at the woman he loved more and more each day. "Last night, there was more time travel, Nazis, and–oh! a wicked woman who wanted my body."

"Should I be jealous of her?" Coral beamed, eyes widened, pretending to be envious.

"Absolutely not. She was an evil and... oh, forget it! I need a kiss from you really badly!"

After making out like teenagers for a few minutes, Coral forced Robert to throw on some clothes. "You know we always get carried away once we begin," Coral smiled at the man she had loved since she was a little girl. "I have something special planned for our anniversary," she said seductively. "Tiger woman will be there." Then, Coral took Robert's hand and led him to the bedroom doorway. "C'mon, let's join the group. They'll be sending up a search party soon," Coral said.

"Okay, monkeyface."

–The End

Coming in 2025 My Dream Lover: The Sequel

Also Coming Soon
Informative about books, articles of interest
to writers and readers, publishing,
and other information, contact:

DavidNavarria.com